Weekends with You

A Novel

ALEXANDRA PAIGE

AVON

An Imprint of HarperCollins*Publishers*

HarperCollins books may be purchased for educational, business, or sales promotional use. For information, please email the Special Markets Department at SPsales@harpercollins.com.

FIRST EDITION

Designed by Diahann Sturge

Flower illustrations © krupenikova.olga/Shutterstock

Library of Congress Cataloging-in-Publication Data

Names: Paige, Alexandra (Writer of fiction) author.
Title: Weekends with you : a novel / Alexandra Paige.
Description: First edition. | New York : Avon, 2024. | Summary: "For fans of Beth O'Leary and Josie Silver, a heartwarming and romantic debut told over the course of one year in monthly weekend installments, about found family, new love, and the magic of London"—Provided by publisher.
Identifiers: LCCN 2023016387 | ISBN 9780063316522 (hardcover) | ISBN 9780063316539 (ebook)
Subjects: LCGFT: Novels. | Romance fiction.
Classification: LCC PR6116.A384 W44 2024 | DDC 823/.92—dc23
/eng/20230719
LC record available at https://lccn.loc.gov/2023016387

ISBN 978-0-06-331652-2

24 25 26 27 28 LBC 5 4 3 2 1

To London, to the magic and chaos of your twenties,
and to the "family" you find along the way

Weekends with You

August

Flowers have always been the best communicators. They've mastered falling over one another in the perfect way to announce exactly what they need: sunlight, water, space, time. They let us use them again and again to say *congratulations* or *I'm thinking of you* or *I'm sorry*. They do not rush. They do not bloom before their time. They do not take without giving in return. They are nothing like the rest of London.

I knew I shouldn't have been at work, seeing as I was supposed to be packing the last of my things in my old apartment to move that afternoon, but I couldn't resist finishing this project in the clarity of the morning light. All weekend I'd been putting together an arrangement for a proposal, and the remainder of the cosmos had been delivered to the shop before sunrise this morning. It would only take a minute.

I twisted the firm stems of the cosmos around one another so the pale pink petals faced outward, then filled in the spaces with delicate white sweet peas. The combination of colors was meant to mimic the blush of promised love, but I was sure that would be lost on both parties. Most people came in requesting something "beautiful" or "extravagant" with little regard for the actual arrangement, but that didn't bother me. It meant I was able to take creative liberties and share in my customers' celebrations or sorrows, which was the whole reason I had found myself in this business in the first place.

This particular customer told me he was proposing with his grandmother's ring to a woman he'd been with since school, so I opted for something traditional.

"Lucy, is that you?" Renee's voice startled me from my reverie, and I spun on my stool to see her poking her head into the office.

"In here," I said from the studio.

Renee had secured this space before I was even born at a fraction of the price I imagined it would be now, and I was lucky to reap the benefits. The studio had a mix of tables, some pale wood and others shiny metal, but the tops were always hidden by masses of flowers, stems, shears, ribbons, and whatever else we could get our hands on. Bolts of canvas paper bookended our workspace, and old photos framed in antique bronze crowded the walls. It was the kind of clutter that made me feel nostalgic instead of claustrophobic, which made this place feel even more like home.

"I could hardly see you," she said, turning on the rest of the lights as she came in. They flickered to life, bulbs asking to be replaced, bathing us in a dull fluorescent glow. "How can you work with such little light?"

"Well, I'm younger than eighty, so that might have something to do with it." I looked up from the last of my ribbon curls to check if she was smiling. I could tell she was fighting it.

"I'm only seventy-four. And careful with that sharp tongue, pet," she scolded. "You're going to end up cutting yourself."

"Spoken like a woman with years and years and years of wisdom."

A dry laugh slipped from her coral lips, followed by a quick pinch of my earlobe. I swatted her hand away, relishing the sound of her clinking bracelets in the silence.

"What are you doing here so early?" she asked.

"I could ask you the same," I said, eyes narrowed. We had both, admittedly, been spending way too much time in the shop lately. Some days, it didn't feel like we had much of a choice, if we wanted to keep the lights on.

She sighed and lowered herself onto a stool beside me, hands braced on the worktop. "I was planning on finishing this arrangement once the dahlias were finally delivered, since you're supposed to be moving today . . ." She trailed off, prompting me to fill in the blanks.

"Which I will be, just as soon as I finish this," I said, picking at a singular dry leaf and keeping my eyes locked on my work.

I was only moving across the city, so I wasn't sure what the big deal was. I'd moved before. More than once. Across the Atlantic, in fact. But always on my own and never into a warehouse conversion with seven other roommates.

Renee took her turn swatting my hand from the flowers. "It's finished, Luce." Her tone was firm but not unkind, and I knew it was her way of shooing me out the door.

"But the delivery," I tried.

"Will be handled by Carla when she arrives later this morning." Carla was our new part-time hire, and I hadn't yet gotten used to having the extra weekend help. "It's taken care of. Go. Those last bits aren't going to pack themselves." She nodded in the direction of the door, and I had no choice but to obey. As much as I hated to admit it, Renee did usually know best.

"Call me if there are any issues," I said from the doorway.

"I can assure you the only issue is how late you're going to be if you don't get moving."

I rolled my eyes and let the door close behind me, the familiar chimes announcing my departure.

The "last bits" Renee was referring to were basically the entire contents of my apartment. When I got home, I stood barefoot on the kitchen tile and looked at the piles in the living room still waiting to be boxed: records, books, mugs, more throw blankets than I could count. Does everyone amass this much shit when they're living alone? In truth, I loved all my shit. In my tiny studio, there was a place for everything, and it all seemed to serve a purpose. So what if I was one person with eighteen mugs? Maybe I was prone to eighteen different moods, each of which required a specific mug.

It had been less than four weeks since my landlord announced he was selling the building to a major conglomerate and the rent was set to double. I was almost certain it wasn't legal, but then again, I'm almost certain nothing about being a landlord in London is legal, so I wasn't prepared to take him to court. I already knew there was no money in the North London Lotus for a raise. I had no choice but to move out.

In the week following the letter from my landlord, I did a lot of crying. Giving up my freedom to wander around in my underwear all day or put leftovers in the refrigerator with the confidence that they'd still be there in the morning felt like a tragedy. When I signed the lease, I had bragged to my friends that it was too good to be true, and after two years this city had, once again, proven me right.

Once I had gotten my act together and resumed behaving like an adult, I called Raja for advice. We had been roommates in college, and she was practically the Patron Saint of Inexpensive Housing. She was pursuing an MBA and living on a student's budget in Seven Sisters, so I figured she'd have some advice. What I did not figure was that she'd offer me a room in her warehouse apartment.

"You have to come live with us, Lu," she'd said over drinks in a local pub one night soon after I got the letter. "Alice just moved out to live with her horrible boyfriend, remember them? So her room is free. We haven't even listed it yet. And there's a studio space if you ever pry yourself from the shop and want to do some floristry at home. It's perfect, really."

There was little chance of convincing Raja otherwise when she thought she had a brilliant idea. But when she saw me waffling, staring into my gin and tonic and contemplating going from a studio to an apartment with seven roommates, she delivered her final argument. "Besides," she said, "you have nowhere else to go."

Silence settled around us, satisfied on Raja's end and uncomfortable on mine. She was right. I'd been on my own since I moved here from Long Island for undergrad, and I had little going on outside the shop. Plus, I was becoming more insecure about my paycheck by the day, so my back was against the wall. And with this arrangement, I wouldn't have to stretch that paycheck to make rent anymore. I might even have some spending money for the first time in years, so I really was left without any semblance of a counterargument. For now, anyway.

"Fine," I conceded after prolonged tense eye contact and an unreasonably large swig of gin. "Let's do it. But only until I'm back on my feet. Once I find another affordable flat, I'm out. This is just temporary."

"Deal," she said, though I wasn't entirely sure she'd registered anything after "fine." "Toast to it so I know you mean it?" Her hopeful eyes glistened in the dim lights of the bar.

"Toast to it."

We signaled the bartender for another round and held our breath while we waited. Ever since college, a toast had been Raja's and my version of a pinkie swear. Over the years, we'd toasted to travel plans, passing exams, secret sexual partners, stolen cigarettes, long, aimless nights out, and, most often, our friendship.

Raja had moved to the UK from Dubai for college, desperate to put some distance between herself and her parents. She was one of those career students, but as long as she kept her grades up, her family didn't seem to mind. She sent home photos of her travels and her studies and omitted those of her secret piercings and late nights at clubs. She never said so, but I imagined she loved warehouse living because she missed her big family at home.

The bartender returned with a second cocktail for each of us, and we raised them to each other in unison.

"Cheers to you . . ."

"Cheers to me . . ."

"Cheers to the drinks we get for free!" we finished together. It was a silly toast from when we were too poor to buy our own drinks in college, but it had stuck.

We drank, and there was no looking back.

So a few weeks later, I was shoving the last of my belongings into bags and wondering how on earth I was to fit everything in Alice's old room. I used to think my studio was small, but the bedrooms in the warehouse made my last apartment seem like a villa.

I'd only been to the warehouse a handful of times since Raja had moved in, and never for any significant amount of time. I remembered some of her roommates (who were now my roommates) by name, and I knew Alice's room was the last one on the end of the mezzanine. There were a few living spaces and maybe some workspaces downstairs, and I remembered running into neighbors outside the building, so there were definitely some other units in the warehouse, but beyond that, I was in the dark.

I pulled out my phone to text Raja before I left my apartment for the last time.

Ready for me?

She replied before I could even get my phone back into my pocket.

I was born ready for this moment. Also, I don't do anything on Sundays ever, so.

Oh, how nice to be Raja. I laughed to myself and headed out, but not without a dramatic look back at my apartment from the doorway. It was silly to think I could stay in an apartment in North London alone on a florist's salary. With my keys under the mat, per the landlord's request, and the rental truck loaded on the street, I was warehouse-bound.

"She's here!" I heard Raja announce through the intercom seconds after I buzzed the doorbell. The "2B" on the buzzer was faded, well-worn from constant visitors and tons of Deliveroo. "It's open, Luce."

I looked from the open bay of the truck to the doorway and back again. "Mind coming down and giving me a hand?"

"We'll be right down!"

I was unloading luggage onto the sidewalk when Raja bounded out the door with two men in tow. "Welcome home," she said, wrapping her arms around me and squeezing tight.

"Flatmates again at last," I said. I could at least indulge her, despite my rising anxiety.

"This is Jan," she said, indicating the edgy guy on the left with a pale pink buzz cut and a pair of black shiny earrings. He saluted me and said nothing, but his lopsided smile was kind.

"And Henry," she said, gesturing to the man on the right. About a head taller and significantly more muscular than Jan, Henry looked like he'd be of more assistance in this task.

"Pleasure," he said, extending a large hand, his voice low. He wore a boyish grin and a battered Henley unbuttoned at the top, both of which made my cheeks warm.

"This is, like, the only time you'll see Henry before he's off again to another country for work or whatever, but Jan is quite the opposite," Raja said. "You'll be sick of him before you know it."

"Piss off, Raj," Jan laughed.

"Leave the flat once in a while, then," she said. Henry rolled his eyes at their banter. I found myself wishing she had them mixed up, and it was Henry who was always home.

Then I found myself mortified that I was behaving like a teenager. I was an adult woman, despite how it felt to be moving into the warehouse, so I couldn't afford to turn to jelly just because my roommate was hot. Even if his cheeks were dotted with freckles that spread across his nose and his voice rumbled like he'd just woken up. I had to get a grip.

"This is it, then?" He gestured to the open bay, pushing his sleeves to his elbows and exposing tan forearms.

"Yeah, just that, but Raja and I can take care of it. You really don't need to, I mean, thank you for coming down, but you didn't—"

"Lucy is terrible at accepting help," Raja said, interrupting my rambling, though I'm not sure this overshare was any better. My blush deepened, and I shoved an elbow in her ribs. "But I'm not keen on carrying anything heavy," she continued, "so we do need you lot after all." Her smile was saccharine, but we all fell for it anyway.

"Lucy," Jan said, lugging the last of the boxes from the truck, "are you anything as annoying as Raja? Because if so, I might just leave everything here on the pavement."

"How dare you?" she said, swatting his arm. "Lucy is an angel, most of the time. You'll love her. Probably."

"I'm standing right here, you idiot," I said.

"Aye, someone who snaps back at Raja. It's a shame I'm not around more," Henry said. "We'd really get along." The sun turned his eyes from sage green to a shimmery jade, and I opened and closed my mouth without thinking of a reply. Thankfully, Raja spoke again before I had time to say something embarrassing. I blamed my dry mouth on the stress of the move.

"All right, enough," Raja said. "Get this shit inside so we can have a drink to celebrate." Henry and Jan shook their heads and muttered to one another, and we followed them inside.

The elevator slowly rattled up two stories before opening its rusted doors and spitting us out directly into the apartment. A sliver of late-afternoon sun bathed the concrete in a buttery hue, reminding me of marigolds wrapped in silver paper.

The warehouse was a lot to process as a visitor, and even more overwhelming as a new resident. Raja must have sensed my unease, because she looped her arm through mine and dragged me into the kitchen. "The boys can drop your luggage, and we can get started on a cocktail."

"When am I meant to unpack?" I laughed, trying to sound like I didn't care, but I did. Very much. If I was to get an ounce of sleep tonight, I needed to be fully unpacked and settled in my new space.

"After the cocktail, duh." She grabbed two glasses, and I felt a pang of disappointment that it wasn't four. "Sit," she said, and I obeyed.

I hopped onto the counter, careful not to hit my head on the shelves of fermenting jars or tattered flags from various European countries hanging from those shelves. The cherry-red appliances needed a cleaning, but the mismatched pots and unruly ferns hanging from the rafters gave the place a boho lived-in look that people paid decorators to achieve.

After pouring unidentifiable clear liquids into a jar with the juice from a few limes and some vigorous shaking, Raja handed me a cocktail, and we toasted to my new home. I tried to forget the long night of unpacking ahead of me and focus on how good it felt to be Raja's roommate again. Silver linings weren't really my thing—I preferred to just feel how I felt—but this one was undeniable.

"So," I said after a sip, "is it usually this quiet?" I peered out from the kitchen to see if anyone else was home, but it was hard to tell.

"God, no," Raja said, nearly spitting her drink onto the floor. "It's a madhouse. Proper carnival. But on Sunday nights, especially after Warehouse Weekends, you can hear a pin drop. Everyone's recovering, pretending to prepare for the workweek, bingeing trash TV, or sleeping."

"Warehouse Weekends?"

"Yeah," she said, as if it were obvious. "Haven't I told you about those?" I shook my head, hoping she really hadn't and it wasn't that I'd just forgotten. "We do them once a month, usually when Henry is home, so we have a full house. Even though we all live together, we hardly see each other, like, in a social way, so we pick one weekend a month to spend together as a flat."

"That is . . . surprisingly really cute."

"I thought so too! Not everyone was on board when I first proposed the idea, because Cal and Margot pretty much hate fun, but now it's a hit."

"How do you decide what to do?"

"Each month, someone else picks the plans. We have a rotation. Alphabetical, per Liv's request."

I nodded for long enough to make it seem like I was processing, when in reality I was killing time before asking what I really wanted to know. "And why is Henry only home once a month?" I hoped I sounded casual.

"He's a music photographer, which I've definitely told you, because he goes to the best gigs and I'm jealous even though I would never want that job, and he's been doing this thing where he spends every month in a different venue. Keeps the room in the flat, though, because it's cheap and he comes home for one weekend every month. Doing a weird soul-searching thing, trying to decide where he wants to live, I don't know. It's all very *Eat Pray Love*," Raja explained, without taking a breath.

I nodded along again, actually processing this time. "So since he's home this weekend, that means he's gone again for the month?"

"That's usually how it goes!" Raja swallowed the remainder of her drink and shot me a quizzical eye. "Any other pressing questions about Henry's job?"

Yes, a million, actually, I refrained from saying aloud. "No, uh, sorry. Just strange, is all." I looked around the kitchen instead of meeting her eyes so as not to give myself away. "All right, then," I said, rinsing my glass in the sink. "Off to unpack."

"Find me when you're done and I'll give you the lowdown on everyone else. It's a lot to remember, so be prepared." Raja planted a kiss on my cheek and sauntered off in the direction of her room, and I slipped into mine, undetected by Henry and Jan. I was anything but prepared to process more roommates tonight, so I intended to make the unpacking last until Raja went to sleep.

As soon as I laid eyes on the heap of luggage in my doorway, I was sure that wouldn't be a problem—I'd be unpacking until the next Warehouse Weekend.

My room was at the end of the mezzanine, between the bathroom and Liv's room. I hadn't yet met her, but the fairy lights around her doorway told me we'd get along just fine. I separated my clothes from the boxes filled with my other belongings and got to work.

By the time I was ready to call it a night, I was proud of my progress. My clothes hung from a rack, organized by season; stacks of old books were piled up on floating shelves, candles huddled together at the base of a full-length mirror, and pothos leaves tumbled from the windowsill, just inches below the ceiling. It was a start.

I flopped on my bed in all my clothes and texted Raja.

Nearly finished, but totally exhausted. Catch up tomorrow?

Deal. We can do that easily now because we're flatmates ☺
Buckle up. It's going to be a ride.

With that, I let my eyes flutter closed. She was right. It was definitely going to be a ride.

September

If you lot don't get your arses down here, we're going to be late!" Finn was shaking the loose banister on the staircase and yelling to the slower roommates upstairs.

"Since when do you care about being late?" Margot asked on her way down the stairs, not looking up from her cuticles.

"Come on, Mar," Jan said, hopping down the stairs two at a time behind her. "You know how much Finny cares about pub quiz."

It was Finn's month, which meant we were doing a pub quiz tonight and a horror movie in the flat tomorrow. As a delivery driver/bike repairman, Finn was tight on cash and liked to keep his weekends budget-friendly, according to Raja. It was surprising he was willing to give up deliveries on Friday and Saturday nights once a month, since surely drunk North Londoners were willing to pay unreasonable amounts to have a grilled cheese or kebab hand-delivered, but I gathered Warehouse Weekend was serious business.

"Aye, we all care about pub quiz," Finn corrected. "2B or Not 2B has a legacy to uphold at the Bag, Lucy, so we play to win."

"As opposed to . . . ?" I teased.

"Told you she was cheeky," Henry said, joining us in the

space between one of the lounges and the studios, which seemed to serve as a general meeting spot.

I knew Henry would be coming home this weekend, but with all the settling in, I hadn't given it much thought. This was the first time I'd seen him since last month, and the immediate banter made the hair on my arms stand on end.

"Welcome back," I said, trying to offer a casual smile.

"Good to be home." He returned my smile, and for a fraction of a second, the rest of the flat dropped away. But when it came back, I realized all eyes were on us.

Margot had looked up from her cuticles to size us up, and I felt my blush deepen under her scrutiny. "Now that we've gotten the pleasantries out of the way, are we ready to crack on?"

"Er, let's see," Finn said, counting our heads. "Six, seven, eight. That's a full house! Let's get to it, then."

The Bag was a local watering hole less than two minutes on foot from the flat, and it was becoming increasingly clear that no one in the flat was interested in finding another pub in the area. Though with its proximity, the cheap pints, and the monthly pub quiz, I couldn't blame them.

As we set out on the walk, Liv slipped her arm through mine, as she was prone to doing now. If Liv liked you, it didn't matter whether you'd known each other for ten years or ten seconds, you were instantly as familiar to her as family. That level of vulnerability was kind of inspiring, if I allowed myself to think about it; foreign to me, but inspiring nonetheless.

"Are you any good at a pub quiz?" she asked.

"Uh, average, I suppose."

"She's lying," Raja added from a few paces ahead without turning around. "She's brilliant at a pub quiz."

"Thank god," Cal said from the back of the pack. "We need

someone to replace Alice. And since Liv is rubbish, maybe you're brilliant enough to replace her, too."

Liv gasped. "Cal, you like, never speak. And then when you do, it's just to wind us up. But then you never laugh. I don't understand you."

"I don't understand you, either, Liv," he replied. "But don't you think we're better off that way?"

"I think you're a grumpy old man, that's what I think. Especially in that corduroy jacket."

"Thank you."

"That wasn't a compliment."

"You'll get used to it," Henry said, leaning surprisingly close to my ear. His breath was warm, and he smelled like citrus. For less than a second, I wondered if he tasted the same.

"Used to what?" I asked, as soon as I remembered we were having a conversation.

"The constant bickering. Living in this flat is like living with a bunch of siblings no one asked for, but eventually, you're able to tune it out."

"Is that what you do, Hen? Just tune us out?" Raja pretended to be hurt, and I couldn't help but laugh. "Do we even mean anything to you at all?"

"See what I mean?" he whispered, and it felt a bit like we were already sharing a secret. "Raj, I couldn't tune you out if I wanted to," he said, louder this time, returning to their conversation and slinging a long arm around her shoulders as they pulled ahead.

The Bag was a humble classic British pub. Pennants lined the walls under exposed beams, cozy high-tops nestled along the windows, and a dark, glossy bar stood proudly at the back. The bartender was someone Cal knew from his years in the restaurant industry. As a bartender himself, he was usually in charge of getting drinks, with Finn helping on the carry.

We pulled a few high-tops together to make a table as long as ours at home, sliding onto stools and giving our drink orders to the boys. They set off toward the bar, and we cleared the table of all menus and condiments, leaving only coasters and plenty of room for focus.

"All right, then," Finn said, doling out drinks when they returned. "Four Stellas, a whiskey for Cal, a vodka tonic for Liv and Raja, and a cider for Lucy. Everyone set?"

We responded with nods and grunts as we sipped our drinks, made sweeter after a long week and by the fact that we were all together. At first thought, the past four weeks had seemed to pass in a heartbeat, but looking around at the faces of my roommates, who had mostly been strangers a month ago, it seemed much longer.

"So, give me the update," Henry said, leaning his elbows on the table. "What've I missed?"

"Every month we have to do this, since Hen is shit at keeping in touch," Raja said to me. Her tone was warm, so I guessed they didn't really mind.

Everyone took turns giving a two-sentence update. This month, it seemed, there was little to report. Margot was working on the costumes for another show none of us had heard of, Cal was still the manager of the cocktail bar where he'd been working for years, Finn was still slinging takeaway curries and leaving bike parts all over the flat, Raja was still in school, Liv had started a new year as an elementary school teacher, and Jan was still tattooing full-time in Camden.

It was a lot to keep track of, so I was thankful we did the recap for Henry. I would remember everything eventually, but not today. As an only child with just a few close friends, I wasn't used to keeping track of so many people. My parents called every so often, but it was normally on a Sunday night after they'd eaten dinner, with the two of them on speakerphone.

When I left the States after high school, I'd long since outgrown my hometown friends, so my parents were basically the only people I had left behind. I'd made a few close friends in London in the six years I'd been living here, but we all required little more than the occasional happy hour to stay connected. As far as managing relationships went, that was about all I had to do. Until I moved into this flat, that is.

"And tell me again, Lucy, what is it that you do?" Henry asked when it was my turn to give an update.

"I'm a florist at a small shop in Islington. Been there since I graduated uni." Talking about my job usually felt like drinking something warm on a cool day, but lately, that cool day felt more like an impending storm.

"Are you doing big events? Weddings and the like?"

"I'd like to be," I said, then immediately felt like I was betraying Renee somehow. "I mean, someday. The owner of the shop is a bit old and not ready to tap into that market. It requires a lot of energy to keep up, so I think she'd rather stick to what we know. We've always done smaller projects, like arrangements for garden parties and engagements and shivas, but we won't be able to stay open much longer just doing that, if I'm honest. So lately I've been imagining what it'd be like to expand our business and take on more clients, bigger projects, that sort of thing."

"Luce!" Raja said. "You didn't tell me that."

I felt a wave of embarrassment that I hadn't even told my best friend what I'd managed to spill to a near stranger. And a very handsome one at that, who was probably just asking to be polite.

"Sorry, that was kind of a lot." I forced a laugh. "Much more than the allotted two-sentences."

"You're new, so it's allowed." A gentle smile spread across his face and a dimple formed in his right cheek beneath its constellation of freckles. If he hadn't been a roommate, I'd have already told Raja I thought he was hot, but it felt off-limits.

"Do you give us an update, too?" I asked, trying to redirect the attention from my overshare.

"Ah, yes, he regales us with stories from faraway lands that we're too poor to visit," Finn answered, and Henry laughed.

"Finn forgets I get paid to travel, so I'm not just on holiday all the time. But yes, I give an update, too. This time I've been away in Mallorca, soaking up the last bits of summer and shooting for an outdoor venue near the water."

"Henry's job is really hard," Liv added. "We all feel really sorry for him because he works a lot."

"Everyone's just taking the piss, aren't we?" he said, taking a large swig of his beer.

"It's all love, darling," Liv said. "Remind us where to next?"

"Reykjavík. Kind of the opposite of sunny Spanish beaches, but I'm looking forward to it. But enough about me," he said, shaking his head. "We need to get in the zone."

Disappointment crept up my throat at the thought of him leaving again so soon. I needed to squash that, and fast, so I decided to focus on the quiz. The pub. Getting to know my new roommates. Anything other than his dark eyelashes and the way he kept glancing in my direction.

We might have seemed like a bit of a mess, but we actually made a decent pub quiz team. Henry and Jan covered all questions about music, Cal covered business and politics (he'd gotten a political science degree before becoming a career mixologist), Finn covered sports, Raja and Liv had pop culture, I had literature from all my hours spent reading in the shop when it was slow, and Margot covered the arts. 2B or Not 2B was a force, if we could stop yelling over each other long enough for Finn to write down an answer.

As we neared the end, a score update from the host told us we were only one point behind the leading team, and all we had left was a two-point question they had already missed. If we answered correctly, we'd win.

"Your final question," the host began, "is as follows: What type of flowers symbolize romantic longing?" Seven pairs of eyes shot in my direction, and my breath caught in my throat.

"Oh my god." Liv looked at me with hopeful, tipsy eyes. "Lucy, this is all you. It's literally your job. You know this, right?"

My stomach dropped to my feet. *They're all looking at you because you're a florist, not because they know about your own romantic longing, you idiot.*

"Pink camellias!" I shouted at the host, despite the silence in the pub as everyone waited for our response. "Oh god," I said as soon as I realized I hadn't consulted the group. "I'm so sorry, I didn't even check with you guys. I am the worst pub quiz teammate."

The host, having written something on a piece of paper out of our line of vision, interrupted my apology. "All right, the final scores are in, and congratulations are in order for this week's pub quiz champions, 2B or Not 2B!"

We erupted in cheers before he even got the sentence out, high-fiving one another and clinking glasses.

"You are far from the worst pub quiz teammate," Henry said over the commotion.

"I told you guys she was brilliant," Raja said, beaming at me like a proud mom. I tried—and failed—to focus on her face instead of Henry's.

We finished the last of our drinks and stumbled home, everyone hanging somewhere in the delicate balance between tipsy and battered. The cool night air felt fresh on my skin, giving me a bit of a second wind.

As soon as we walked into the flat, Cal retreated to his room, presumably to call his long-distance girlfriend, who was still living in Scotland. Liv headed to bed on account of an early-morning workout class and Margot went to her studio, claiming she worked best late at night. Jan made for the couch in the second living room, the one that was covered in tapestries and floor cushions and burning incense from his own soul-searching trip to Mumbai.

This left Henry, Finn, Raja, and me to our own devices.

"Fancy another drink on the roof?" Finn looked from face to face with raised eyebrows, and I wanted to hug him for the excuse to extend the night. We confirmed by nodding and following him to the kitchen.

"You do it, Hen," he said, handing Henry a bottle of gin. "You're better at it."

"You're just a lazy sod, I think," Henry laughed, accepting the bottle. "Luce, grab those limes and give me a hand, will ya?"

Surely, I could do this like a normal person. Grab the limes, give my roommate a hand, behave like an adult.

Everywhere I stood, I seemed to be in his way, but he didn't say a word. Instead, he pressed dangerously close to my body to reach glasses, cocktail shakers, ice trays. I cut limes at a glacial pace, savoring his closeness. Raja and Finn were engaged in an argument about whether *Die Hard* was a Christmas movie, so I was sure they didn't notice whatever was going on over here. If anything *was* going on.

This was not the first time I had romanticized a crush. I was prone to convincing myself there was sexual tension where there wasn't, which generally ended in disappointment. In an effort to keep myself in check, I had to remember we were merely making cocktails in a crowded kitchen, 25 feet from two of our roommates.

But the way Henry gently rested his fingertips on my back to squeeze past me to the sink crushed the heap of rational thoughts I'd been struggling to build.

"Let me get out of your way," I mumbled, trying to mitigate the dance we'd been doing before I got too clumsy.

"I like you in my way."

I snapped my head in his direction, equally surprised and flustered by his comment but trying not to show either. The corner of mouth curled up softly on the left side, and I had to look away before the right side caught up and I was left with the full force of his smile.

"To the roof," he said, breaking the spell and handing us each a cocktail. We climbed the metal staircase single file, bracing against the cold wind as soon as we opened the door.

"Getting a bit cold already, innit?" Henry exhaled hard, presumably to test if he could see his breath.

"And it's only September. Maybe I shouldn't have ended things with Maria just because the summer was over," Finn said. "I could use her for these cold nights, don't ya think?"

"That's really nice, Finn," said Raja. "Using women in place of a space heater. Maria's a lucky girl."

"I'm sorry, Raj, when was the last time you had someone to keep your bed warm, hm?"

"I don't kiss and tell." We all tried to suppress a cackle, which told me the boys knew Raja's habits as well as I did. Raja loved kissing and telling. In fact, I had a feeling she liked the telling more than the kissing.

"What about you, Lucy?" Finn asked. "Are you one to bring a bloke home from the pub once in a while for a little shag?"

"Finn!" Raja scolded. "You can't just ask people that."

"Just did," he said, flashing us a cheeky grin.

"Lucy, you do not have to answer that," she said.

"No, you don't, but then we'd be even more suspicious," he said.

"Well, I hate to disappoint, but no," I said. "Not often impressed by a man at the pub, to be honest. And I like to have my bed to myself."

"Smart woman," Henry said, tipping his drink in my direction. "Finn and Jan are the only ones still shagging a rando from the pub. Finn's newly out of uni, though, so we can allow it for another year or so. Not sure Jan's excuse."

"Jan's excuse is that he somehow always bags the hottest guy in the place," Raja said. "Makes the rest of us look like peasants."

"You would look like a peasant either way," Finn added, only to be flicked in the ear by Raja's perfectly manicured fingers. "And Hen's only saying that because he also hasn't brought anyone home in ages."

Jackpot. I didn't want to risk being too forward by asking, but I had been holding my breath waiting for this information.

"That's because I'm hardly ever home, you tosser. Besides, you have no idea what I do when I'm on the road." The way Finn and Raja both cracked up made me think Henry was terrible at being coy.

"Sure we do," said Raja. "You take photos, you take long contemplative walks, you eat alone in bars, scribble in your journal, sleep late, and try to imagine living wherever you are. Definitely no women involved."

Henry rolled his eyes in defeat. "Only because I've no time for women," he explained. "Not because I couldn't chat them up if I wanted to."

"Yeah, yeah." Raja shoved him lightly and we settled into a comfortable silence, staring out at the city lights. I didn't think we were supposed to have access to the roof, but I was glad we did. There was a small garden of chipped ceramic pots and dying plants up here, which I was determined to tend when I had the time, and a handful of mismatched chairs, not unlike the ones around the kitchen table.

Sleep nudged my eyelids and I had reached the end of my drink, hardly able to concentrate on small talk any longer. Raja's obnoxious yawning told me I wasn't alone.

"Time for me to head in," I said, stretching slightly. "Need to get some sleep if I'm to stay awake for movie night tomorrow."

"Good call," Finn agreed. "Maybe for once you won't be the first to pass out as soon as we turn the telly on."

"I'm not always the first!" I said, though we all knew it was true. Embarrassing as it was, something in my chest warmed at hearing I had any kind of role in the flat. There were definitely worse things than becoming predictable to new friends.

"Lucy, please," Finn said, scoffing so loud the neighbors could have heard. "Don't kid yourself. Besides, I have a good film on deck, so you should all prepare yourselves." He waggled his fair eyebrows, and we chuckled in return.

"Looking forward to it," Henry said to Finn, though I could feel his gaze on me. My crush increased with each stolen glance, and I was sure I was setting myself up for disappointment. But nothing a good night's sleep couldn't fix.

"LUCE, ARE YOU WITH ME?" Renee stood over me with a bundle of roses in her hand, and the look on her face told me she'd been standing there far longer than I'd noticed.

"Yes, sorry, the roses." I reached for them, and she was slow in her release.

"You look like you've not slept a wink. Why don't you go down the block and get a coffee? I can manage here while you're gone." She gestured to the empty shop. And she was right, mostly. I had slept, but not well. Or for long. I had tossed and turned in a daydream like a teenager for the better part of a few hours before my body finally settled into sleep, which didn't bode well for movie night later.

"I'm fine, really," I assured her, discreetly pinching my cheeks as soon as she turned away to give them a bit of color. "Besides, we have work to do."

"Listen, pet." She sat on a stool and swiveled it to face me head-on. "I can manage here on my own. You know that, right? Just because I'm getting old doesn't mean I've lost the plot. You don't need to be here every hour of every day, weekends included, to check on things. You should make time for yourself and your life while you're young! Otherwise, you'll end up like me: a batty old bird with dirt permanently caked under her nails and thorns stuck in her hair."

Where is this coming from?

"Renee, I love working here. I don't come in on weekends because I think you can't handle it. I come in on weekends because I want to. Because I love our work and our flowers and our clients more than anything." *Also, because I'm worried if we turn down a single client, we'll have to close our doors.* I didn't quite think I needed to add that part.

She studied me under furrowed brow, taking an uncomfortably long time to respond. She did this sometimes, waiting so long to respond, knowing I had more to say. I fell for it every time.

"And I just think we could do big things here. Not that we aren't already. But did you know the Jacobs bridal shower said we were in contention for hire for the wedding? Not that we do weddings, but if we're both here all the time anyway, couldn't we?" It slipped out rushed and insecure, but I was glad I'd said it. Until she sighed that familiar sigh and pushed her glasses up onto her head.

"Lucy, darling, you know the answer to that. I love that you have such big ambitions, I do. You remind me of myself at your age. But the Lotus just isn't prepared for that kind of project. We're a boutique shop, and you know we do only smaller arrangements because—"

"They're artisanal and intimate, I know, I know," I finished for her, the same familiar sense of defeat pricking my palms like thorns.

"Don't sound so gutted, pet. We're doing the best we can. Besides, I don't want you to feel like you have to work here if you don't want to."

I bristled. "I hate that you always say that. You know I'd never leave." It was something I'd been saying for what felt like ages, but every so often I had to reconsider its truth. "Will you at least think about it?" I pressed. "It's been so long since I've asked you in earnest. The least you can do is humor me." I put my hands together, all but begging on my knees.

"Only if you promise not to look so disappointed if the

answer doesn't change," she said, her soft smile nearly reaching her eyes.

"Deal."

She was tough, but she was a woman of her word. Consideration was better than nothing. And since she didn't seem to be worried about the business, maybe *I* didn't need to worry so much about the business. Or maybe that was exactly why I needed to worry about the business.

"And Lucy," she said, halfway out of the studio and into the office, "make sure you make room for loves that aren't work. I'm proper chuffed you love it here as much as I do, but make sure it doesn't become your only love, will you?"

I contemplated protesting, but what was there to say? I hadn't been on a proper date in what felt like years, but surely that wasn't because of work. Everyone spent a lot of time at work now, didn't they? Wasn't that how we all afforded to live in London?

"Consider it sorted," I said, matching her soft smile. She tutted, suggesting she didn't believe me, and I didn't blame her. I wasn't exactly convincing.

"Come over for Yom Kippur this week," she said, changing the subject. She sipped her tea and studied me from head to toe, and I already knew I had no choice but to say yes. Not that I had other plans for the holiday, what with my parents being back in the States. "You could use a good meal and some time with family. You're looking a little gaunt."

"I'm fine," I laughed. This was not the first time she had declared I looked unwell, when I was, in fact, just vaguely sleep deprived or hungover or not wearing any makeup.

"Humor me, then."

"Deal." I knew I might face more grandmotherly ridicule over a meal, but Renee was practically family, so I was looking forward to the holiday regardless. It would be nice to get out of the house and to eat a home-cooked meal for once.

I returned to my work and busied myself with an apology bouquet. I pulled together rich purple bundles of verbena, imagining how they'd look lining a walkway in someone's expansive home garden. I could pair them with periwinkle sea holly and turn the whole garden into a watercolor, cool colors dripping into one another under a gray September sky.

Instead, I wrapped them in cellophane, wedging a note inside that read, per the client's instructions: *Babe, sorry I was a right wanker. I'm done being shit. Please forgive me. Xx*

Not every story was inspiring.

By the time I managed to pull myself from the shop and return to the flat, movie night preparations were in full swing. The projector in the living room was up, a case of beer sat in the middle of the coffee table, and every throw blanket in the flat was strewn across the couches and the floor.

"Lucy, perfect timing," Raja said as soon as I walked in the door. "Go put on some sweats and meet me in the kitchen. It's our turn to do the takeaway order."

"I thought it was Finn's turn?"

"Well, technically it is, but he's rubbish at it, so we're taking over. It's bad enough he gets to pick the film, so it's the least we can do. For everyone's sake."

There was hardly a moment to breathe in this flat, but living with Raja in college hadn't been much different. And the pace did distract me from work-related stress, so I couldn't complain. Maybe this was why she was so happy all the time.

I inspected a pair of joggers I'd worn around my room for the past two nights for any evidence they weren't fresh, but they passed the test. Paired with a knotted white tank and an open corduroy shirt, I hoped I looked sort of cozy-chic. I let my hair loose from the claw clip that kept it out of my eyes while I worked, stared at the frizzy mess around my shoulders, then wrestled it right back into the clip. That would have to do.

"Margot, Cal, Jan, and Finn managed to actually respond to the group text, so we have their orders," Raja said as I padded into the kitchen. "That just leaves you, me, Jan, and Henry," She handed me a crinkled, stained menu for a local Thai spot, making me laugh. It was so old school. Who still looked at a paper menu instead of a digital copy? And who actually needed a menu for Thai? Didn't we all get attached to something like pad see ew in uni and order only that for the rest of our lives?

"Wanna run upstairs and get orders from the boys? They aren't answering my texts," Raja said.

"Are your legs broken?" I teased, before clocking that Henry was part of "the boys." When she looked at me with raised brows, I snapped my mouth shut. "Okay, I'm on it," I said, already on my way out of the kitchen.

Henry's door wasn't closed all the way, so when I knocked it swung open.

"Oh god, sorry," I said. "I meant to just knock. I didn't mean to barge in here like that."

He laughed and turned his desk chair to face me, long legs stretched in front of him. "Good thing you barged in now while I was just editing some photos. If you'd come in a few minutes ago, I'd have had some explaining to do."

My shock must have been palpable because he put his hands up in surrender. "I'm kidding, Lucy."

"Right, of course," I said, trying to shake it off. To be cool. "I was just coming for your takeaway order. Raja and I are about to call that Thai place, and we're just missing yours and Jan's."

"Ah, shit. Right. Forgot to answer the text. Let me come look at the menu." I tried to suppress a laugh but couldn't contain it for the life of me. "Something funny?" he asked, clearly bemused.

"Who looks at the menu for a Thai place? Isn't that like looking at the menu before you order a sandwich? Like, you know what the options are."

"Spoken like someone who orders the same thing every time," he said, pushing his chair in and stepping closer to me in the doorway. "Don't you want to branch out a little? Try something new?"

"Not if I know what I like."

"How do you know you won't prefer something else if you never try anything else?" He lowered his voice and eyes just enough for me to notice, and my hands went clammy. Were we still talking about Thai food?

I fumbled for a response and came up empty. It was a really good point.

"All right, then," I said, squaring up to him, feeling bold for a moment. "Order for me."

"What?"

"If you're so sure I need to try something new, order for me." Thankfully, my voice sounded more confident than I felt.

"Aye, someone who takes a risk around here. I like it. Anything I need to know?"

"I'm a vegetarian."

"No meat, got it."

"Please don't make me regret this."

He laughed, a hoarse, warm laugh. "Quite the opposite. I'm about to change your life."

I rolled my eyes, trying to be playful, but the fluttering in my stomach could have started a tsunami.

"Jan," he called down the hallway, over my head. "Get your arse into the kitchen so we can put in our takeaway orders."

"Khao pad," Jan shouted back from his room.

"Told you no one else looks at the menu," I said.

"Maybe I'm not like everyone else."

That's for sure. His smile was blinding, and the heat from his body as it slipped past mine and out of the doorway matched the heat of my face.

As Raja called in our orders, I covered my ears, per Henry's instructions, so my order would be a surprise. While we waited, Finn rallied the gang and we made our way to the living room for the night.

The tapestries draped over the walls and hung from the ceiling blocked out any light and made the living room the perfect place to watch films. That, and the projector, which, I'd been informed, Cal had nicked from a band who'd left it at his bar last year. There were two sagging couches and a smattering of cushions spread on the floor around the coffee table, and we all settled into our usual places. Mine, which had previously been Alice's, was a cushion on the floor beneath Liv's seat on the couch.

We passed around beers and blankets, listening to Finn's introduction of the impending low-budget horror movie until we heard the promising buzz of the Deliveroo driver at the door.

"On it," said Henry, the only one still standing.

When he came back with the food, we cheered like he'd just returned from the war. Everyone took turns raising their hands as he called their orders, and I sat anxiously awaiting the reveal. It was only takeaway, but it was something between us. For the second time that weekend, I felt like we were sharing a secret.

Then he flopped into his spot, which was just inches from mine. "I already like you better than Alice in this spot," he said. "I can tell you're not going to criticize every film at top volume while it's still playing."

"Aye, man, don't speak ill of the dead." Jan nudged him from where he sat on Henry's other side. "Even if you *are* trying to chat up the new kid."

"She isn't dead, idiot. Just living with that bloke," Henry said.

"Which pretty much equals death, if you ask me."

"No one asked you."

I held my breath, waiting for Henry to address the other half of Jan's comment, but the moment never came. Was the thought of chatting me up so ridiculous that he didn't even need to dispute it, or was he ignoring it because it was true?

He interrupted my speculation by passing me a greasy cardboard takeaway container, for which I was grateful.

"Well?" I said.

"Massaman curry. Taste it and tell me what you think."

I put a small forkful in my mouth, tentatively letting the flavors melt on my tongue. Warm spices mingled with subtle chiles, and the vegetables were perfectly tender. The saturated rice tasted of fresh coconut, and the entire mouthful had all the comfort of a family recipe. He was dead-on.

I had to all but force my eyes not to roll back into my head while I was eating it, but I couldn't resist the opportunity to wind him up. "It's okay."

"You're a liar," he said, a victorious smile plastered across his face. "Say you love it."

"Everyone ready?" Finn interrupted, and we grunted in confirmation. Jan killed the lights, and we settled into silence as the opening credits rolled.

"I love it," I whispered in Henry's direction in the darkness, only partially talking about the curry.

"Me too." He leaned over and stuck his fork into the container, putting a huge bite of my food into his mouth.

"Hey!" I protested.

"Hey, both of you," Jan said in a mock whisper. "Shut up, would ya?"

We stifled giggles and hung our heads like children, trying to focus on the screen.

By the time the end credits rolled, I was confident I'd focused on no more than 20 percent of the movie. Even that might be generous. It was something about a woman alone in a house, somewhere near the woods, I didn't know.

What I did know was that about halfway through the movie, Henry had relaxed into his spot on the floor, and we sat with our shoulders leaned against each other until the end. My entire butt had fallen asleep, but the pins and needles were a small price to pay. Surely Liv had noticed, as she was sitting right behind us on the couch, but she was kind enough to let us have the moment. The really, really small moment that was making me behave like a fifteen-year-old.

All eight of us collectively reviewed the film as we tidied the graveyard of empty beer cans and takeaway containers, and I was thankful there was finally conversation again. I wasn't sure how much longer I could have lasted sitting in the same position, holding my breath, trying not to move a muscle.

"Whose turn is it to take the rubbish down?" Margot asked, sweeping the last of it into the trash bin.

"That would be Lucy," Jan said, shooting me with finger guns.

"How come everyone seems to forget their own chores but somehow you all remember mine this week?" I asked.

"Because you have the worst one," Jan laughed, taking the bag from the trash bin and handing it to me. "We always know the Rubbish Runner."

I groaned, accepting the bag and heading for the elevator.

The dumpster was in a creepy spot behind the flat, and while it was tempting to just drop the bags from the window, one of us was always assigned to drag them into the elevator and out to the trash.

"I'll give you a hand," Henry said, and before I could even process thought of the two of us out back in the dark together, Jan shot him down.

"That's cheating," he said. "The Rubbish Runner goes alone. Lucy knows the rules."

"That might be the dumbest rule of them all," I said, and not just because of what was at stake. "Why do we make this more miserable for ourselves?"

"We're masochists, that's why," Jan said.

"Didn't Finn help Liv last week?" I said.

"Liv's a waif," Finn said. "Can't do anything on her own, that one."

"I'm right here," Liv said, swatting his arm. He made a kissy-face in her direction, and she waved him off.

"I'll do it in her place," Henry said. "There's no rule against Rubbish Runner substitutions, is there?" He grabbed the bag from my hands, and I savored the brief touch of our fingers.

"Only because no one else has ever volunteered," Raja said, looking Henry up and down.

"There's a first for everything," he said. "Back in a min." And with that, he disappeared into the elevator, rubbish in hand, before anyone could argue.

"Oh, Lucy," Jan said as the elevator groaned to the ground floor.

"What?" I said, trying to pretend I didn't know exactly what he was implying. And trying harder to pretend I wasn't hoping it was true.

"You're just shaking things up in here, that's all. First with the weird shower playlist, now Henry's volunteering to be the Runner. What have you done to us?"

"My shower playlist is not weird," I said, trying to avoid the second half of his comment. I was still mostly convinced my chemistry with Henry was a figment of my imagination.

"I like your shower playlist," Finn said, coming to my rescue.

"Thank you, Finn. Someone here has taste," I said.

"Terrible taste, maybe," Margot said, but I detected a smile on her lips.

"A bold comment from someone with a septum piercing," Finn said. Margot threw a rogue empty can in his direction, and he let out a shriek like a small child.

"Crazy. All of ya," Henry said, returning to the living room.

"Says the person who volunteered to do the rubbish," Raja said.

"Some of us like to do something nice around here once in a while," he said, shooting a smile in my direction. "I know you're all strangers to the concept."

"Don't you have a flight to catch or something?" Jan said, waving him off, because no one was immune to the incessant ribbing around here.

"Ah, shit," Henry laughed, looking at his watch. "For the first time ever, you're right, Jan. It's late, and I've gotta be up before the sun, so I should head in."

Just like that? He's here for a movie and then we don't see him again for a month? I wanted to blame the knot in the back of my throat on the curry, but even I knew that would be a lie. And disappointment didn't suit me, so I found myself suddenly looking for my own excuse to go to bed early.

"Ugh, Hen," Raja groaned. "Already?"

It was nice to know I wasn't the only one frustrated by his departure.

"You know how it goes, Raj. Gotta stay on schedule if I want to make this work. When I convinced the agency to let me do this, that was part of the contract."

"Do you think Reykjavík will be the place you find yourself?" Liv asked from the couch, and Henry laughed.

"I don't think it's that easy, but it's worth a try. I'll get incredible photos, if nothing else, which you all seem to forget is what I do while I'm away."

"Not as interesting as the soul-searching." Liv yawned.

What was "soul-searching," anyway? We all claimed to do it, but did any of us have a clue what we were actually doing? I made a mental note to ask Henry what it meant to him, if I had the chance someday.

"October will be here before you know it," he said. "And it *is* my month, in case you've all forgotten."

"Oh please, not another museum," Liv groaned. "We love you, but the National Gallery is bloody dry."

"Okay, first of all, I'm going to pretend you didn't just say that, because the National Gallery is one of England's proudest achievements and no one in this house knows how to appreciate a good old painting. Second, it's not another museum. I have something good planned, don't you worry."

"Good by whose standards?" Margot narrowed her eyes.

"Margot, honestly, stop pretending to hate us," Jan said. "We know you're obsessed. Get over yourself." Margot opened and closed her mouth, but said nothing, and the rest of us laughed, despite her expression.

"Trust me," Henry said.

"Well, we'll be counting the minutes, then." Liv smiled, and the rest of us added our agreement. If only she knew how true that statement was for me.

October

*O*ctober as a florist meant two things: finally saying good-bye to summer colors, and stocking up for the holiday season. We did most of our buying around this time in preparation for the holidays, which meant we spent many early mornings scouring local shows and wholesalers for the best deals.

We combed the entire city on a hunt for the most promising winter honeysuckle, delicate magnolias, and fragrant rosemary. The most magical part of this work was the moment just before the sun rose into the sky, casting itself through slanted warehouse windows and across waxy green leaves like a spotlight, gently announcing the day into the silence.

Renee broke the silence from a sale counter, rubbing the budding petals of an orange dahlia between her bony fingers. "These will be perfect for the Fall Fest on Sunday, don't you think? And I think we can afford them," she said, releasing the petals to search for a price tag.

"They're on sale," I said. "How much can they be?" We almost never checked prices at the sale counter.

"I just want to be sure," she said, lowering her thin eyebrows. "We have most of what we need for Sunday, so we don't want to be spending money we don't have."

The phrase "money we don't have" was a thorn in the back

of my throat, and I had to make a concerted effort to swallow it away.

"Ah, it's our lucky day," she said, confirming the low price with the seller. "They're a proper steal." Her smile was back, and I forced mine to match it. "They'll be perfect, if we can keep them alive until the festival."

With only two weeks' notice and a decent amount of convincing, she had agreed to let me do the arrangements for the Temple Tefilo Israel Fall Fest. It wasn't quite the big break I'd been hoping for, seeing as she was a member of the temple and it was a friend of hers who'd asked for our help, but it was good practice. A chance to prove myself. And, at times, a distraction.

Henry was due home late that afternoon, and Warehouse Weekend was to commence immediately upon his arrival. The plans were still a secret, so I couldn't prepare myself. I had taken to raiding Liv's wardrobe lately, though, so at least I knew I had options for what to wear. Part of sharing her clothes meant letting her pick them out and dote on me when we found something we liked, but I could live with that for closet privileges. My own tattered denim and earth-tone crew-neck sweaters were starting to get old.

Renee and I placed an order for Christmas roses and cleared the wholesaler out of the orange dahlias, then headed back to the Lotus in the delivery van. It was early enough that I could finish the arrangements for the Fall Fest and get home with enough time to pull myself together, if Renee was willing to work quickly.

Spoiler: She wasn't. When we got inside, she pored over every petal of every flower, trying to determine the perfect way to include them in the arrangements we'd put together so far.

"Why don't we just do the dahlias the way we did them last

time?" She sighed, both of us thinking back to an arrangement we'd done last month. We rarely repeated arrangements, because we were both usually determined to come up with something new and creative, so I was surprised that she'd suggested the callback.

"Oh, uh, I suppose we could," I said, mostly eager to complete the pieces and be done.

"I just want it to be perfect," she said. "I want it to be worth their money, you know?"

"I thought you were giving them a discount?" Didn't she tell me that when she accepted the job?

"I meant to," she said, "but we couldn't afford it." Her voice was measured and quiet, and I wasn't sure exactly how to respond.

"Well, maybe if we're lucky, they'll spread the word, and then we can do some more of these for some extra cash." I knew I was pushing my luck, but I couldn't resist. This had the potential to be the first of many bigger opportunities, and I didn't want to waste it.

"Oh, I don't know, pet. Let's not get ahead of ourselves." There she went again. "This is already a lot." She was fussing over a centerpiece we'd done and redone the same way a hundred times. I sighed but had little else to offer by way of response. *Baby steps, I guess.*

As morning crept into afternoon, I snuck another peek at my watch. I wasn't one to wish my life away, but I was about ready for the workday to end.

"Hot date?" Renee asked.

"I'm sorry?" *What does she know?*

"You've been checking your watch every few minutes for the past hour. Is there somewhere you need to be?"

"Oh, uh, just the flat. Henry, one of our roommates, the

one who's away all the time, is coming home for the weekend, so we're all set to do something together. Not sure what it is yet, but I'm supposed to be ready around five thirty. It's not a big deal, though. I'll just head home whenever we're done. No rush," I lied.

She stopped fussing and looked me right in the eyes. "And do we fancy this Henry?"

"What?"

"You just talk about him an awful lot for a flatmate who's never home, that's all."

"I do not."

"You sound like my granddaughter."

"Does your granddaughter appreciate it when you butt into her love life?"

"So you do fancy him?"

I threw my hands up in surrender. "I don't know. I hardly know him. But he *is* gorgeous, and I think he was flirting with me last time he was home. But it's impossible to tell. He's practically gone again before he's even home."

"Ah, he sounds like quite the mystery. You better get home and get yourself ready so you can try to figure it out." Her eyes softened, as did the teasing, for both of which I was grateful.

"Not until we're done here."

"We are," she said, admiring our work. "And I think we have been." We both laughed. "Besides, I'm exhausted. I'm getting too old to be lugging these heavy arrangements around and bustling about on my feet all day. Let's call it." With that, I headed home to get October's Warehouse Weekend underway.

RAJA AND I were flopped on her bed staring at our phones when Henry's voice filled the flat, both announcing his arrival and requesting our presence downstairs. "Let's get this show on the road," he was yelling as we made our way downstairs.

"Miss me?" He beamed.

"Terribly," Raja and I said in unison. Only one of us was exaggerating. It had only been a month, but his hair looked longer. It curled behind his ears in a way that made me wish I could run my fingers through it.

"All right, Hen," Finn said, joining us. "What's the craic this weekend, then?"

We all piled in around each other, perching on the edges of thrifted armchairs and leaning on the pillars.

"Everyone ready?" Henry spread his arms for the grand reveal. "Dim sum. Football. Jack the Ripper."

"I'm having trouble connecting the dots," Liv said. "Anyone else?"

Jan raised his hand. "We live in London, mate, isn't Jack the Ripper like a tourist thing?"

"But isn't the point of Warehouse Weekend to be 'tourists in our own city' or whatever?" Margot said.

"It's about bloody time someone listened to me!" Raja said, but Margot hardly batted an eyelash.

"Margot's right," Henry said. "And Halloween is right around the corner, and it's the perfect opportunity to take pictures of something other than musicians for once."

"Aye, there it is," Finn said.

"So it's that new dim sum place in Stokey tonight, then, since tomorrow is supposed to be great weather, we're off to Finsbury Park for a bit of football, then a Jack the Ripper tour at night."

"Do we have to actually play football, or can we just have a kip in the grass?" Jan asked.

"Well, Jan, when we went to karaoke a few months ago on your weekend, was I allowed to simply sit in the booth?"

"Well played, you wanker. Football it is."

"You know I love a seasonal Warehouse Weekend," Raja said. "Well done, Hen. Sensible and fun. Let's do it."

"Atta girl, Raj. Thanks for the enthusiasm."

"Focus, people," Jan said. "Are we ready to roll? I'm starving."

"You're always starving."

"And you're always whining, Liv, but you don't hear me moaning about it."

Henry rallied the troops and shoved us out the door before Liv and Jan could really get into it. It was a quick tube ride to Stoke Newington, and we made it in time for a seven thirty reservation.

The restaurant was a trendy spot with only the letters *MW* in a sleek black font above the doorway. Henry held the door while we filed in, so I slipped to the back of the line.

Inside, the lights were low and a running fountain welcomed us from beside the host stand.

"Good find," I whispered.

"I know how to pick 'em," he whispered back.

We followed the host to our table in the same order in which we'd arrived, leaving Henry and me sitting beside each other. I gave myself a silent round of applause for my tiny victory before diving into the menu.

"Isn't dim sum really supposed to be breakfast or lunch food?" Liv asked, turning the menu over in her hands.

"Can't just let people enjoy things, can ya?" Finn teased.

"She's right," Margot said, eyebrows raised, as if this were the first time Liv had ever been right about anything. Poor Liv. "But dim sum is so good that I can overlook the sacrilege. No one tell my mum, though. If she even knew I was eating Chinese that wasn't hers, she might drop dead on the spot."

"No one is telling your mum anything," Jan said. "She is the scariest woman alive."

"Makes a lot of sense how Margot got to be this way, then," Henry added.

"Do you lot write your own material?" she asked, which shut them up.

At most of the dim sum places we frequented, we simply filled out a card with our order, but here the service was apparently more attentive. We had to tell the server we needed "just another minute" three times before we stopped arguing long enough to settle on an order.

Henry ordered for the table, and his confidence was astonishing compared to the men in my life prior to now. After years of sitting across the table from men who ordered without looking the server in the eyes or mispronounced even the most basic items on the menu, it was strangely attractive to see Henry rattling off dish after dish to our waiter. Either that, or my standards were at an all-time low. Hard to tell.

When the server returned with our food, we were just getting into our two-sentence updates. We paused to pass around plates piled high with dumplings, shumai, rolls, buns, and some other round foods I couldn't identify, knocking elbows and slinging chopsticks as we made our picks.

"Mar, show me again how to use these, would ya?" Jan was tapping his chopsticks on the table like he was playing the drums.

"If you would just listen, we wouldn't have to do this every time," she said, grabbing them from his hands.

"We can't all have Chinese parents, you know."

"No one else at this table has Chinese parents, and they're all doing just fine."

"So, the update from Jan and Margot is that they're still mortal enemies, is it?" Henry laughed.

"No, the update is actually that I got a spot in the East London tattoo convention this summer." Jan looked at our astonished faces, and I think I heard a pair of chopsticks clatter to the floor.

"Are you having a laugh, mate?" Henry asked, holding a dumpling inches from his mouth.

"Nope. Quite lucky, aren't I?"

"Jan, I don't think you're lucky, I think you're talented," Raja said.

"Agreed," I said. "Isn't that, like, impossible to get into?"

"Apparently not, if Jan can do it," Margot said.

"Bugger off, Margot," Jan shot back.

"Sorry, I couldn't resist. Congrats, mate." She raised a glass, a genuine smile on her face.

"To Jan," Liv said, raising her glass and motioning for us to do the same.

"You know this means one of you is going to have to let me put some art on ya," he said as we clinked.

"Give it up, man," Cal said. "Never gonna happen."

"Famous last words, Callum."

"Not sure how anyone is going to top that," Henry said, getting us back on track. "But who's next?"

The rest of us took turns with our updates, mostly mundane, as usual. I was also congratulated when I shared that Renee and I had undertaken a bigger project, but I was too ashamed to admit that it was not only the first but probably the last, too. Raja shared that she was on track to graduate with first-class honors, which came as a surprise to no one, and Finn hit a new record on miles ridden in one night of bike deliveries.

"How was Iceland?" Cal asked once we had finished.

"Beautiful, cold, expensive," Henry said.

"So is it ruled out of places to live, then?" he asked.

"Sadly, I think so. Bit too remote for full-time, and I'm not sure I would do well with all that darkness. The search continues. Next month I'm off to Berlin, so wish me luck."

"Has the constant traveling been hard at all?" Liv asked, wide-eyed.

Henry laughed, swirling cheap wine around in his glass and following it with his eyes. "Sometimes," he said. "If I stay focused, it isn't difficult, but that's been a bit tougher in the past few weeks, if I'm honest." He raised his eyes from his glass, letting them float in my direction.

I tried to clear the lump from my throat, but really all I did was draw more attention to myself.

"Is that so?" Raja asked, running her tongue over her teeth and glancing in my direction herself. "And why might that be?"

"Just some new perspective in my life, that's all." He brought the wine to his lips, staring Raja down with some sort of mutual understanding. My skin all but caught on fire, so I kept my gaze locked on a plate of soup dumplings to avoid having to face either of them.

We had hardly known each other more than a few days, really, so I would be getting ahead of myself if I thought I might have been the "new perspective." After so much time working at the Lotus and making endless bouquets that had probably ended up in the trash, I knew what it looked like when someone was getting their hopes up. I vowed a long time ago not to be that person. That only ended in disappointment.

But every time he relaxed back in his seat and slung his arm on the booth behind me, I slipped dangerously close to hopeless-romantic territory. My body betrayed my brain, inching ever so slightly into the space between us, wondering how I would fit into the crook of his arm.

I let a cool sip of wine settle on my tongue, hoping the acid might burn away the desire. This was a recipe for disaster, and I needed to make sure I wasn't distracted by any "new perspectives," either. I ran my fingers down the length of my chopsticks, over the hairlike splinters, trying to bring myself back to the present.

The remainder of the meal was not unlike the ones we usually had in the flat, although the food was in another league. We ate off each other's plates and argued over which dumplings were better, Finn charmed the server into a few free samples, Jan drank one too many, and we laughed so hard we cried.

"Bloody nice when Henry comes home, isn't it?" Finn asked with his mouth full as Henry handled the tab. I watched as Henry made small talk with the server, his single dimple appearing in his flushed cheek, his body dangerously close to mine.

Bloody nice was an understatement.

THE SUN BLASTED into the flat long before any of us were ready to be awake. I shuffled into the kitchen for a cup of tea, having to actually shield my eyes from the reflection off the chrome giraffe head perched high above the door. Thank god the disco ball wasn't in the line of the sunlight.

While I stood by the stove waiting for the decrepit old kettle to boil, my thoughts floated to work. As always. I had promised Renee I wouldn't come in today so I could be fully present for Warehouse Weekend, but the Fall Fest was the next day, and I hated not being there to finalize things. Even though we'd both sworn up and down that we'd finalized them yesterday.

I grabbed the kettle the second it began its gentle whistle, trying to keep it from waking anyone else. We had more tea in the flat than in all of London, but none of it was kept in the same place. Some was in jars beside the jars of fermenting vegetables, some above the bread bin, some in the makeshift plywood pantry. I had thought the bathroom would be the most hectic part of having seven roommates, but the kitchen proved me wrong time and time again.

By the time I settled on a breakfast tea and a few cookies, the sun had floated higher than the giraffe head and I was able to curl up in the living room, glare-free. We had an eclectic collection of throw blankets from everyone's previous apartments, all of which smelled like acrylic paint and burnt sage.

"Early riser, then?" Margot's voice was even drier in the silence of the morning.

"Oh, uh, sometimes," I said. "Couldn't fall back to sleep with the sun in my eyes."

"At least your room has a window." She had a point.

"What are you doing up so early on a Saturday?"

"Had to finish something for work." If there was anything I knew to be true of Margot, she was a woman of few words. "You can see it if you like," she said, her tone noticeably softer. She must have seen me glance toward the studios and knew I was curious.

"Are you sure? I don't want to intrude, I—"

"Come on," she said, motioning for me to follow her. Was it that simple? Cracking Margot was just taking an interest in her work?

She pulled back the curtain of her studio space to reveal what looked like backstage at a West End show. Luxurious fabric clung to mannequins, metallic pins littered the countertops, and blinding painters' lights illuminated a small platform in front of angled mirrors. For two months, I'd been curious about this studio, as it was the only one shielded by a curtain, and it did not disappoint.

There was a mannequin on the platform, clad in oxblood velvet and deep emerald costume jewelry, standing in a pool of pins and measuring tapes.

"It's for a period piece," she said, watching me admire her work. I knew she was talented, but I hadn't expected this.

"Margot, this is—"

"Isn't it?" She cocked her head to the side as if she was seeing it for the first time.

"Thank you for letting me in. To see it, I mean." The studio alone revealed more to me than Margot had herself in the months I'd been living here. It had a certain chaos I didn't expect of her, and frankly, it was humanizing.

"Yeah, yeah. It helps sometimes to look at it from someone else's perspective, that's all."

We stood in silence, staring at the mannequin. "Be careful getting involved with Henry," she said eventually.

"Me? Oh no, we aren't—"

"I know you aren't. But I do think he fancies you, and it isn't easy trying to be with someone you hardly ever see. Trust me."

I wanted nothing more than to ask what had given her the idea he liked me, but I figured it was best to keep my mouth shut on that front. Figured I'd sound a bit desperate. And I wasn't sure I had any real reason to trust her, but she did seem convincing.

"I don't think he fancies me," I said, hoping that might prompt her. It didn't. "But duly noted. Thanks for the tip."

She offered her version of a smile, and I searched for an excuse to leave the studio. *Is that why she brought me in here?* Since this was more than I'd ever gotten from Margot, I decided to save my questions for another early morning run-in. Best not to scare her off, I supposed.

I spent the rest of the morning journaling, pretending to clean, practicing a bit of yoga, convincing myself I didn't need to go out for a takeaway coffee, and waiting for the others to get the day started. It was slow. Eventually, a group text from Henry got the ball rolling.

> **Be ready to go in 30 mins. In trainers!**

Athletic-chic it is, then. I rummaged through my wardrobe, trying on my clothes as if I didn't know what they looked like. After deciding a cropped workout top was a bit much, I settled on a perfectly vintage oversize tee from college and a pair of black athletic shorts. I was shit at soccer, but I'd be damned if I didn't look good.

Fancy helping me put together a picnic? There's no way we can all spend the day at the park without something to eat, Raja texted me outside the group chat.

> **HA. You're right. I'll meet you in the kitchen.**

"Lu, I should warn you, this flat is very competitive," Raja said as soon as I walked in.

"I don't think that's a secret," I laughed. "Not after last month's pub quiz, anyway."

"Henry, Margot, and Finn played in school, so they're quite good, but the rest of us just mess about."

"It's a good thing I won't be alone, then. Less embarrassing that way."

"Nothing to be embarrassed about," she said, then dropped

the knife she was holding and turned to face me. "Unless there's someone you're trying to impress?"

"Raja, please." I tried to laugh, but it was forced.

"I knew it!" She stepped closer to me and put her hands on my shoulders. "It's Hen, isn't it? I saw you guys last night. I knew something was up. It was written all over your faces."

"Nothing is 'up,'" I said, swatting her hands away. "And you didn't see anything last night, because there was nothing to see." I wasn't sure I meant that, but I hoped I sounded convincing anyway.

"I don't know, Lu. I haven't seen you flirt in public like that since that flatmate of yours right after uni." She snapped her fingers, trying to jog her memory. "What was her name? Emily?"

"First of all, it was Amelia, and second of all, I thought we agreed to never talk about that again." It was the worst case of an unrequited crush I'd ever had, and I had no intentions of reliving it.

"We could go back to talking about Henry instead," she said.

"Or not, because there's nothing to talk about. Let's just focus on today, shall we?"

"If you say so," she said, disbelief crowding the air between us.

On cue, Henry appeared at the entrance to the kitchen with a soccer ball under his arm. His shorts bared most of his still-tan legs, and his long-sleeve shirt was just old enough to be a bit snug. This was going to be a long day.

"Ready?" he asked.

"As we'll ever be," Jan said.

"That's the spirit. Come on, then."

We walked the short distance to the park in a pack, and

I tried to stay in front of Henry so I wouldn't be tempted to study the way his hands gripped the ball or how his shoulders rippled under his shirt.

"All right, usual teams, then?" he said as we came into a clearing. Everyone immediately pulled to opposite sides, leaving me standing in the middle. "Lucy, you take Alice's spot on our team." Aside from Henry, Liv and Finn were the other two members of our team.

"Reckon you can kick a ball, Luce?" Finn asked, and I tried not to be offended.

"Yes," I laughed. "I think I can manage that much."

"Brilliant! You're already better than Alice, then."

"Knew you were a good replacement," Henry said. The compliment and the callback to our conversation last month made my knees weak. At this rate, maybe I couldn't kick a ball after all.

Halfway through the game, we were up by one and playing pretty well. Until the sun caught the beads of sweat along Henry's jaw, that is, and Cal booted the ball past me and into the makeshift goal while I wasn't looking. *Damn it.*

Henry ran a frustrated hand through his hair, then bent over, hands on his knees, to catch his breath. I had to catch mine, too.

"Shit, sorry, guys," I said. "That's on me."

"Nah, that's all of us," Finn said. "But now it's tied at four, and we're only playing first to five, so we need a plan."

Henry called a time-out and pulled the four of us into a huddle, holding us by the shoulders. His hand was warm and strong, and I could have stayed under its grip for the rest of the day.

"Right, then. Pass to Bernstein."

"What? That's the plan? That's a terrible plan," I protested. Was he insane?

"Lucy's right," Finn said. "Sorry, Luce, but, you know."

I nodded.

"Why Lucy, exactly?" Liv asked.

"They'll never see it coming," he explained. "And she's not half bad. Definitely not as bad as she thinks she is." He shot me a quick smile before he put his game face back on, and I was giddy. And also extremely nervous.

"And you want me to just shoot it?"

"Quite simple, isn't it?" His smile returned. "You can do it. Hands in."

"Pressure's on, Lucy," Finn said.

"No shit," I laughed.

"All right," Henry said, giving my shoulder a squeeze. "Let's do this."

It really wasn't a high-pressure situation, but I felt like I might as well have been on a World Cup team. My palms were slick from a combination of nerves and sun, but the play was practically over before it started. Henry to Finn, Finn to me, me to the goal.

Pass, pass, shoot, score.

"Bloody hell!" Henry cried, arms in the air. "You've done it!" Before I had a chance to react, he scooped me up effortlessly into his arms in a celebratory hug and spun me around. When my feet were back on solid ground, we took a beat to straighten ourselves, both dizzy from the spinning. Or at least I told myself it was from the spinning.

"Jammy bastards," Jan complained. He had hardly touched the ball, but he was notorious for being a sore loser.

"Not quite sure it was luck, mate," Henry said. "This one

here might be a proper big-game player after all." Holding the ball in the crook of one arm, he slung the other over my shoulders and tousled my hair, and I could no longer blame my flush on the exercise.

"Does this mean we can eat now?" Jan asked, already digging through the cooler. Raja threw a ratty old blanket onto the grass beside him, and we all flopped down at once.

"Do you want to change your answer?" Raja whispered to me, and I rolled my eyes.

"Not yet," I whispered back. "But ask me again tomorrow."

"IF WE LEAVE in the next ten minutes, we'll make it to Aldgate East in time to catch the start of the tour. All we need are a couple flasks for the road, huh?" Henry was standing in the foyer looking at his watch.

"One step ahead of you," Finn called from the kitchen. After the soccer game, we'd spent a few hours napping or reading or sitting around doing nothing at all until it was time to leave for the Jack the Ripper walking tour. It was good I'd had time to clear my head, but I had a feeling I would be dizzy again soon enough.

The biting chill in the late-October air crept through my leather jacket and into my bones, adding to the already ominous night. Was London always this windy? Or this dark? We huddled together for warmth and comfort, but mostly to discreetly pass the flask between us.

Starting the tour was like stepping into a time machine. We were only 30 minutes from the flat, but we might as well have traveled back over a hundred years. Our guide was also leading several other groups of mostly older tourists, and we fell into pairs at the back as we squeezed down tight alleys. I had to force myself to focus on the tour instead of where

Henry was standing, but it was proving more difficult than I had hoped.

Cool, damp air clung to the sides of historic buildings and dripped from stone overhangs. Under the soft light of the streetlamps, the dripping gave the illusion that something was moving just out of view. I linked my arm through Liv's and nicked the flask from Jan's back pocket.

"I need a little liquid courage," I whispered when Jan shot me a look.

"Scared, are ya?" he taunted me, wearing that crooked smile.

"Duh," Liv answered for me. "This is so creepy. I mean, the man who might have been Jack the Ripper literally cut hair in the basement of this building." She took the flask from me and took a swig herself.

Jan shook his head at the pair of us. "At this rate, you two are going to be smashed by the time we even get to the end of the tour."

"That's the plan," Liv said.

The shutter of Henry's camera was the only sound breaking the silence as we peered into the windows of the building. It looked like a film set, but I couldn't decide if that made it more or less horrifying.

Just as I was certain I'd seen a shadow move inside, someone shook my shoulders hard from behind. I let out an embarrassing, high-pitched scream, startling the rest of the group for less than a second before they dissolved into hysterical laughter.

I turned around so hard I nearly gave myself whiplash, only to see Henry starting a slow clap, trying his best not to laugh as hard as the rest of them.

"What the hell is the matter with you?" I swatted his arm, trying to play into the flirting despite my heart making a home in my throat.

"I didn't think you were going to get that scared," he said, giving in to the laughter. "Really, I didn't. I'm sorry." He bit his lip to gain his composure, and my heart rate rose again. I grabbed the flask back from Liv, hoping to steady my nerves.

"You know, when I asked about my new flatmates, no one told me you were an asshole," I teased.

"What *did* they tell you?" We might have still been joking, but his question was charged.

I thought for a minute but came up empty. "They didn't tell me much, if I'm honest. So you're kind of a mystery."

"Good," he said. "They would probably make me look bad, anyway."

"Is there something you want me to know that would make you look good?"

"What fun would it be if I just told you?" he said. I rolled my eyes, and he snatched the flask from my hand and brought it to his lips, drawing my attention there for the second time tonight.

He disappeared into a conversation with Cal, and Raja materialized by my side at the back of the group as we meandered to our next destination. The tour guide was saying something about a former convent, but I was too distracted to care.

"Well?" she asked, glancing in Henry's direction. She was relentless, and I was a terrible liar.

"You already know the answer," I whispered. "Besides, I thought we decided we'd table this until tomorrow?"

"I'm impatient. And it's not a secret. Like, there's definitely something going on." I shoved her and she nearly crashed into a tourist, sending us both into a fit of distracted laughter.

We continued winding around the city in the dark, dutifully following the guide, and *ooh*ing and *ahh*ing when we were supposed to. We were also getting pretty drunk in the process, but I think we were alone on that front.

"Jack the Ripper was a real wanker, wasn't he?" Jan slurred, gesturing to a doorway where the only clue to the Ripper's identity was said to have been discovered.

"I don't even think 'wanker' begins to cover it," Henry said.

"Why couldn't the police just catch this arsehole?" Margot said, running her thin fingers over the doorframe.

"Have you been listening at all? I'd like to see you find an elusive serial killer without forensic science equipment or technology," Jan said.

"Piss off, Jan."

"Ladies first."

We shushed each other as we crammed into another alleyway, so narrow we could barely stretch our arms out at our sides. The cobblestones were the same as everywhere else in London, but I could nearly hear horses trotting over these. It reminded me of the scene in *A Christmas Carol* when the Ghost of Christmas Yet to Come chases Scrooge through the city on a carriage drawn by black horses. It was only a cartoon, but even that was creepy to think about right now.

Henry's big hands cradled his camera just in front of his face, capturing the fog drifting across the cobblestones. There was something gentle about the way he took photos, the way he held the camera just so, the way his eyelashes fluttered closed over his left eye. The way he breathed with every shutter of the lens.

"Do you think he was a dish?" Liv whispered over my shoulder.

"Who?" Had she seen me watching Henry?

"Jack the Ripper, duh. Kind of a hot nickname, don't you think? Maybe it was a Ted Bundy situation."

"Liv!" I scolded, though I was relieved. "Are you insane?"

"Just smashed, I think," she laughed. I could accept that. "Henry, is it almost done? I'm not complaining, I swear. It's just someone is going to have to carry me home pretty soon." She touched his arm lightly with her fingertips, and I felt a flare of jealousy creep into my chest.

Right on cue, the guide offered some closing remarks. The tourists huddled together in small, shivering crowds, already asking where they could buy Jack the Ripper tour merch. I admired their willingness to shamelessly embrace everything corny.

We said goodbye to our companions as we headed in the direction of the Tube, stumbling into one another with arms linked. I wasn't sure whether it was the cold or the lingering feeling of the tour that sent shivers up my spine, but I visibly shuddered all the same.

"All right?" Henry asked, eyeing me.

"Just cold," I said, wrapping my arms around myself for reinforcement.

"Aye. So, should I not ask if you wanted to reprise drinks on the roof when we get home, or might you just need another layer?"

I was stunned into silence for a second. "Uh, no, definitely ask. I mean, you don't have to actually ask, because you kind of just did, so yes. Yes to the drink, I mean. And the layer."

His laugh was a warm, inviting sound that came from somewhere low in his throat. "Good."

Okay, so we were doing this. Which was fine. I was prepared for that. Everyone was always prepared for a handsome roommate to ask them for a drink on the roof late at night, weren't they?

By the time we got home, half the group was ready for bed. Liv and Jan had nodded off on each other's shoulders on the Tube, and Margot claimed to have had enough socializing for one night.

"Anyone fancy a cheese toastie?" Cal was banging around the kitchen with little regard for the roommates who planned on sleeping.

"Callum, that idea makes me want to kiss you on the mouth," Finn said, dropping into a yellow metal chair at the giant kitchen table and checking his phone with one eye closed.

"Please don't."

"Make them for the whole lot, please, darling," Raja said, joining Finn at the table.

Henry grabbed two beers from the fridge and nodded at the staircase up to the roof. I snagged a jacket from a rack near the doorway, unsure who it belonged to. "Just gonna get a bit of fresh air," he said to the others. "Be down in a bit."

"We won't wait up," Raja said, throwing me a look.

Shut up, I mouthed.

"It's freezing out there. And haven't we been getting fresh air all night?" Finn said, raising an eyebrow.

"Sorry, Finn, didn't realize you were the gatekeeper of fresh air," I shot in his direction. "Should we have checked with you first?"

He held up both middle fingers, and Henry and I laughed lightly before disappearing up the stairs.

"Have I mentioned I'm pleased you moved in here?" Henry said when we reached the roof. "We needed someone to keep everyone's attitudes in check, so you fit right in. And you're way nicer about it than Alice was."

"Thank you?"

"It's a compliment," he said, leaning against the half wall at the edge of the roof and turning to face me. We smiled at each other before we dropped our eyes back to our shoes.

"I'm also pleased I moved in here," I said eventually.

"Are ya?" He sipped his beer slowly, not breaking eye contact this time. When he was finished, he ran his tongue lightly over his lips.

"I am," I confirmed. "Moving in with seven flatmates after having lived alone for years was definitely an adjustment, but I think I'm getting the hang of it."

"Was it lonely? Living alone, I mean?"

I wasn't sure anyone had ever asked me that before, which might have answered the question. "Sometimes," I said, recognizing the truth as I revealed it to Henry. "Which I might not have realized until I moved in here. I thought that was what I wanted, and it was what I wanted when I graduated, anyway, but you know. Things change."

"What kind of things?"

Normally I'd think this many personal questions was an invasion of my privacy, but something in Henry's voice coaxed me into answering them. The depth, maybe. The softness that didn't match the way he looked.

"Well, the money, for one," I said.

"Aye, I know that well," he said. "Not always a lot of money when we follow our passion, is there?"

My brain knew he was talking about work, but my body warmed at the mention of passion.

"I'll drink to that," I said, and we clinked. "What about you?" I continued, before I could stop myself. "Do you get lonely on the road?"

His short laugh and the way he cast his gaze toward the

sky told me this was a question he'd thought about before, so I waited patiently for the answer.

"Of course I do," he said eventually. "Not always, but I would be lying if I said I didn't miss it here while I was gone."

"But you still do it? The traveling thing?" If he was going to probe, so was I.

"I was like you, at a bit of a crossroads, when I moved in here. I wasn't feeling satisfied by London anymore, which is why my boss and I set up this program. I'm kind of piloting it, and we plan to open it up to other photographers once we iron out the kinks, but it makes the most sense for me right now."

"What's the plan, then? To leave London?" I tried to hide the worry in my voice at the thought of him disappearing before I knew him at all.

"Ah, it is. By July, in fact. That'll mark a year of this traveling gig, which will be the end of the agreement with my boss, and I keep thinking I'm going to find somewhere I love by then. But then I come home to London for a few days and it suddenly seems difficult to leave. I don't know. I'm trying to find my place, which I guess we're all kind of doing in our late twenties."

He took a long swig and I did the same, sensing we were drinking in agreement. The stars blinked brighter in the sky as we shared anecdotes about what had led us here, where we hoped to go, what it was like to work for emotional satisfaction instead of money. We asked about each other's family vacations, favorite foods, habits on airplanes. We made judgments based on each other's coffee orders and preferred tube lines.

He put a hand on my knee when he laughed. I touched my fingertips to his forearm when I was surprised. We pulled in and out of each other's orbits like the tides. I drank slowly as he spun stories from his time on the road, neither of us noticing the increasing chill in the air or the quiet that fell on the city or the passing of time.

"Sorry if that was a lot," he said eventually, rubbing his eyes with the heels of his hands. "I don't usually talk that much at once. Especially about work. Perhaps I should have put 'existential crisis on the roof' on the agenda for Warehouse Weekend."

I laughed, and I was relieved to see he returned my smile. "It wasn't a lot at all," I said, hoping to reassure him. The last thing I wanted was for him to stop talking because he thought he'd shared too much. I wanted the opposite, really. "London's pretty much the only place I've ever been that isn't New York," I continued, "and I've never taken a single decent photo, so your work is fascinating to me. Any time you want to talk about it, I'd love to listen."

"Then you'll have to allow me to return the favor. I'm not sure I could identify even a single flower, so it seems like we both have something to learn from each other."

"I'd like that."

"Maybe we could start with tulips . . . ," he said, leaning a bit closer to me, hardly able to control his own laughter.

"That might have been the worst line I've ever heard. And I've been a florist since university," I laughed. Thank god I was laughing, because he was suddenly so close, I wasn't sure I'd be breathing otherwise.

"I couldn't even get that one out with a straight face. I'm so sorry." He put his head in his hands like a child, and we both fought to compose ourselves. "I don't know what came over me."

"Well, the overwhelming urge to kiss me, apparently," I said, complete with a dramatic hair toss.

It must have been the drinking that emboldened me, because without it I'm not sure I would've had an excuse for my behavior. I wasn't usually driven by lust, if that's what this was. But the way he was looking at me, the silence of the roof, the intimacy that came with sharing something personal—it was almost too much to bear.

He stopped laughing and held my gaze, inches from my face. "Lucy, I've had the urge to kiss you since I met you."

"And you've resisted flower puns until now? Very impressive, Henry." I suddenly wished I didn't make jokes when I was nervous.

"I'm all out of resistance, if I'm honest." He tucked a curl behind my ear, seemingly searching my face for consent.

"Then there's only one thing left to do," I said. It came out as more of a whisper. He cupped my face with his lingering hand and brought his lips to mine.

It was a gentle kiss at first, the kind that starts out like a question mark. It asks, *Are you into this?* or *Is this all right?* Half-closed eye contact answered both questions with a resounding *yes*, and the kiss melted into an ellipsis.

His hands on the sides of my face were almost damp from the heavy London air, but I reveled in their warmth. Eventually, they worked their way into my hair, grip tightening just enough for me to notice. The traffic had slowed at this hour and the only sounds wafting through the night were our occasional sharp inhales or deep, satisfying exhales.

I rested my hands on his forearms and felt his exposed wrists, the result of a hoodie that had been shrunk in the wash one too many times. His pulse matched mine and that of the dark city below us. A steady, coursing drumbeat.

The kiss was as delicious as it was confusing. This couldn't go anywhere, so it'd have to be over before it even started. Which was sad, really, because it was off to a brilliant start.

By the time we disentangled ourselves from each other, he must have sensed I was lost in thought. Absolute class of me to always ruin a nice moment.

"Sorry if that was, or if I—" he started.

"It was perfect," I said, and I meant it. It was just also the end. He furrowed his brows, sensing I had more to say, and I knew I wasn't getting away with stopping there. "It's just that you leave tomorrow, and then—"

"I keep leaving," he finished for me.

"Yeah."

"But," he said, touching his fingertips to my jaw, "I also keep coming back."

He did have a point. But with those mossy eyes and the way his jaw cast a shadow in this light, he could have said Earth was flat and I would've thought he had a point.

"Then I guess we'll just have to see what happens when you do," I said, trying to save the moment.

"I like the sound of that," he agreed. "And I'm very much looking forward to it." He pressed his lips to mine once more, then stood and held out his hand. "Shall we? If we head in now, we'll have at least a few minutes before we're blinded by the sunrise."

November

I'll be home in about an hour. Don't start without me. X

That was the text from Henry I'd been waiting for. We'd taken to texting almost daily outside the group chat since The Kiss, but none mattered so much as the one announcing his homecoming.

It was Jan's month, but he had it easy. The city had planned things for him: Bonfire Night. He made some mention of perhaps having plans tomorrow, too, but we all knew he'd be too hungover to go through with them. We'd spend the day recovering in our rooms, only crawling out to eat dry toast or use the toilet, and then we'd come together for a greasy dinner or something.

"Renee," I called from the studio to the office, "What time did you say you were going to meet your grandchildren?"

"Why do you ask? Trying to sneak out early because Henry's coming home tonight?" I couldn't get anything past her. Ever.

"Wouldn't you just lose your mind already? Become a little senile so I can live my life?" I groaned like a child. She came into the studio laughing, pulling her frizzy gray curls into a ponytail.

"Me? Never," she said. "Besides, who would run this place if I did?"

"I don't know . . ." I trailed off, looking around. "If only there was someone capable and willing . . ."

"Lucy Bernstein, I know you are not trying to get rid of me, are ya?"

"Me? Never." We smiled at each other, and I felt a familiar pang of warmth in my chest. Admittedly, things around the shop had been a little off since Fall Fest. It had been a massive success, but the one thing that had been missing was Renee's usual enthusiasm. She had seemed pleased with the work I did, so I knew it wasn't that, but a successful event didn't seem to inspire her the way it used to. I chalked it up to general shop-owning stress or whatever else might have been going on behind the scenes, and tried to put it out of my mind, knowing I'd spiral if I didn't.

"Would you look at that," she said, untying her apron and gesturing to the clock. "I'm due to meet my grandchildren right now."

"So you *are* a senile old lady after all," I said, smiling like a maniac.

"When I want to be. Now go, before I change my mind. And don't forget we're coming in tomorrow for that thing for Hattie's niece!" she called after me, but I was already almost out the door.

I returned Hen's text with the giddiness of an elementary schooler as I boarded the Tube.

Leaving work now. Excited to see you. Xx

Tonight was going to be brilliant.

"RAJ, ARE YOU HOME?" I called as soon as I got off the elevator.

"Lu? I just got out of class. Come in here!" she answered from her room.

When I walked in, she was on the floor surrounded by piles of books. "Thank god you're here," she said. "I can't study for another minute."

"Finals are going well, I take it?"

"They're going. And going. And going. This econ class is killing me."

"You're great at math, though. How hard can it be?"

"Oh, love, I'm absolutely killing it. I'm just dying of boredom in the process. I need a break."

"Well then close the books and let's start getting ready," I said, pulling her to her feet. "Bonfire Night waits for no one."

"Unlike you," she mused.

"What is that supposed to mean?"

"Don't tell me you haven't been pining over Henry since he left and counting the minutes until his return."

I moaned, collapsing onto her bed. "I'm nervous to see him, Raj. Is that dumb?"

"First of all, no feelings are dumb. Second of all, have you been talking since he left?"

"Here and there. We've been texting on and off about our jobs, what we've been up to, that kind of thing. A rogue call once or twice." I watched her eyes light up and tried to play it off just in case mine were doing the same. "But this really makes no sense," I continued, "so I'm not sure what he's getting at."

"Don't be daft, Lucy, really. It's not cute." I shoved her, and she grabbed my hands. "He's obviously into you. What's the harm in having a little fun each time he's home?"

"The harm is that he leaves," I moaned. "And I want to have a little fun all the time."

"Well, he isn't the only bloke in London, you know."

"I'm serious, Raj!"

"So am I! What's stopping you from seeing other people?" It was a great question.

"I guess that I don't want to?"

"You're in deep, babe," she said. "And from the looks of you two last month, so is he."

"This is going to end in disaster."

"With that attitude, you're absolutely right. Now quit whining. We have getting ready to do. Bonfire Night waits for no one, remember?"

We tore through her wardrobe, then mine, then Liv's when she got home, trying to decide what to wear. Eventually, I decided on a pair of light-wash straight-leg jeans, a bulky gray sweater, my leather jacket, and a pair of Dr. Martens.

. "You always end up in the same thing," Liv said, pulling a floor-length cardigan over a silk top.

"Because I know what I like," I said. We were looking at ourselves in the same mirror, and I had to admit, I looked good. Casual. As if I had no idea Henry would be home in exactly twenty-two minutes.

"Ugh," she groaned, throwing the cardigan to the floor. "Must be nice."

"What do we think of this?" Raja turned to face us, spreading her arms and showing off her outfit. Her height made everything look good on her. She was wearing a pair of high-waisted pants and a cropped sweater vest, and holding a longline coat in one hand. It was all very vintage. She looked incredible.

"I might even flirt with you tonight if you're going out looking like that," I said.

"Lucy, please don't joke. You know that would be my dream."

"Ladies, focus," Liv said. "Should I do the distressed flannel or that long Free People shirt with the collar?"

"Free People," I confirmed. "Distressed flannel isn't you."

"You're just saying that because you want to steal it."

"Maybe."

"Fine, take it," she said, rolling her eyes and tossing it in my direction. "It does look better on you anyway."

"So, are we settled, then?" Raja asked after Liv was dressed, giving us all a once-over. "Henry should be home any minute, and I think Cal just walked in, so we can finally get this thing started."

Henry would be home in exactly three minutes, according to his text.

"Let's make drinks."

Like moths to a flame, everyone made their way to the kitchen as soon as we turned on music and took out cocktail glasses.

"Finally," Jan said, cracking the tab on a beer. "Been waiting all day for this."

Me too, Jan. Me too.

"Finn, get your skinny arse down here, we're starting!" Liv shouted up the stairs in the direction of his room.

"What happened to not starting without me?"

I spun around to see Henry standing behind me, luggage at his feet, smile creeping into his eyes.

"You're home!" *Duh, Lucy.*

"I am."

"Welcome back," I said, actively resisting the urge to throw my arms around him.

"Good to be home. So good, in fact, that I'll forgive you for starting without me. Let me drop my stuff and shake off the flight, then I'll be ready for ya."

He was definitely addressing the entire group, but it didn't feel like that when he was only looking at me. Conversation swirled around me as he took the stairs up to his room two at a time, but my roommates sounded like they were underwater. I only resurfaced when his voice drifted into the kitchen again, loud and confident and irresistibly deep.

"Cal, deal me in," he said, gesturing to Cal's lineup of cocktails on the counter. "Right, then, what's the move, Jan?"

"Well, 2C is having that bonfire in the garden, so I figured we'd start there, then make our way to the Bag for Race Against Time and fireworks later. All in favor?"

The seven of us responded with an excited chorus of "ayes," coupled with the clinking of glasses. The "garden" was really just a dirt patch with a few broken planters and a smattering of plastic chairs behind the warehouses, but it did have a great firepit and a lot of room.

"Jan, even though you didn't grow up here, you're turning into a proper Londoner," Henry said. "I'm proud."

"Not that I had much of a choice, living with you idiots. England is still shit compared to the Netherlands, though."

"Which explains why you left the Netherlands, I'm sure," Margot said.

"Jan came here for uni and just ended up staying for good," Henry whispered to me over Margot and Jan's bickering. "Like you."

"Isn't that what you plan on doing when you find somewhere you like?" I didn't mean to sound so accusatory, but it just slipped out.

"Do we have to worry about that now?" He sounded just on the wrong side of tired.

"Who's worried?" I smiled, but he was slow to return it. "Let's enjoy this weekend, yeah?"

"I like that idea."

Note to self: Say nothing to Henry about his impending move.

Outside, 2C already had a roaring fire going, complete with cases of beer, sausages on sticks, and a Bluetooth speaker. I'd met these neighbors once or twice since I moved in, and while they were a decent bit older than we were, they were still a good time.

After some pleasantries and the distribution of warm beers, we settled in and turned our collective gaze toward the fire. There was a certain magic in the air on Guy Fawkes Night, and I wasn't sure it was because we were actually celebrating that some dudes stopped some other dudes from blowing up Parliament four hundred years ago.

The fire popped and crackled, demanding our attention and warming our cold fingers. The rose reds turned to dandelion yellows as the flames climbed higher into the dark, and I imagined what it'd be like to stack those colors in a centerpiece. Above the fire the night was clear, the moon a bent sliver carving through the blackened sky.

"Jan used to shag that guy," Liv said, sitting beside me on a bench I thought had been stolen from a local park and interrupting my musing at the cosmos.

"And he's gonna do it again tonight if he's lucky," Jan whispered, clearly not out of earshot. The guy in question was covered in tattoos, and I wondered if Jan had done any of them.

"Any other pressing gossip I need to know?" I asked Liv.

She chewed her manicured thumbnail while she considered my question. "Okay, don't tell her I told you this," she said, leaning in, "but Margot was dumped pretty bad last year by some girl she had back home in Leeds. None of us think she's really recovered."

That explained her comments to me in the studio about my situation with Hen. If she had firsthand experience with long-distance relationships, maybe it was worth heeding her warning after all.

"Ooh, and that guy punched Finn in the face over the summer," she continued, gesturing to a guy who looked like he was trying way too hard to look young. "Stupid pub fight. Some misunderstanding or something. But they're mates again, so we can keep hanging out with them when they have parties out here."

"I can't imagine Finn in a pub fight. His poor little face," I said, and we both laughed. Finn wasn't all that much younger than we were, but he felt like the resident little brother.

I pretended to survey the rest of the crowd, but really I was scanning for Henry. A head taller than almost everyone except for Cal, he was an easy find. He looked impossibly relaxed, with one hand curled around a beer and the other in his pocket. I allowed myself a minute to study him from the back: shirt stretched gently over his broad shoulders, hair curling up at the nape of his neck, jeans perfectly cut above his boots.

"Sausage?" Raja interrupted my daydreams, standing over me with a skewer. Good timing.

"Please. I'm starving." We both put our skewers directly into the fire, snuggling together on the bench for warmth. "How's this for a break?" I gestured to the party, which was beginning to fill up with friends who didn't live here.

"Exactly what I needed," she groaned. "You must have needed one, too. I feel like I've hardly seen you these last few weeks."

She was right. I had been working excessive hours, partially to keep the Lotus afloat and partially to keep my mind occupied.

"Yeah, we've been swamped lately. What with cuffing season and all, people are getting engaged left and right. Or dying. People seem to die a lot when the holidays are approaching."

"That's really positive, Lu. I'm so glad you shared that with me." I looked at her and we both burst into laughter.

"I have no idea why I said that," I said, catching my breath. "But that's kind of how it's been feeling in there lately. One minute, everything is fine and we're working on celebrations, and the next, Renee is morbid and stressed. I think something's going on that she isn't telling me." I took a long swig of my beer, hoping to clear my mouth of the bitter taste left by those words.

"Like what?"

"I'm worried the Lotus is going under. I mean, I doubt it is, because I think Renee would have said something, but she's been crunching a lot of numbers lately. Spending a ton of time on the books. That kind of stuff. I'm trying not to dwell on it, but it's hard."

"Didn't you just do that big Octoberfest thing? Why don't you do more stuff like that if you need more money?"

"I'm trying, but Renee doesn't seem so excited about the idea. She was kind of hands-off with the Fall Fest stuff, which is unusual."

"Maybe she has something personal going on and she's burying it in her work."

"Yeah," I agreed. "Maybe you're right. Either way, I don't want to think about it tonight. We're supposed to be taking a break."

"You're right, you're right. Let's get back to drinking a lot of beer and flirting with our roommates, yeah?"

"Yes, please."

We pulled the sausages from the fire and blew out the remaining flames, breathing in the scent. My hair and clothes would smell like a bonfire for days, but at least I'd be reminded of tonight. In which case, I needed it to be a night worth remembering.

"Are we about ready to head to the pub, then?" Jan asked, glancing around at each of us.

"Race Against Time's about to start, so now's as good a time as any." Finn chugged the rest of his beer and spun a finger in the air, signaling to the group that it was time to go. "Let's crack on."

We followed suit, downing our drinks and signaling to the neighbors that we were headed out in case a few wanted to tag along. I snagged Henry by the arm as we left the garden, and we fell to the back of the pack.

"Race Against Time?" I asked.

"Oi, I forgot you've not done a Race Against Time at the Bag yet," he laughed. "You're in for quite a ride. Basically, draft beers start at twenty-five p, and every hour they go up until they reach a pound. By which point we're all expected to be proper smashed."

"Bloody hell," I said. "And we're expected to make it to midnight like that?"

"Well, we're not expected to make it to midnight sober, so it's not so bad." He smiled, and I realized how much I'd missed that smile in the past month. "Besides, the fireworks are worth the wait."

I tried to ignore any intrusive thoughts, as I had another Race Against Time to focus on.

The Bag was more crowded than I'd ever seen it, clad in cheap decorations and armed with two additional bartenders. "Why don't you lot go see if you can find us a table?" Henry said, gesturing toward the back of the pub. "Cal, fancy coming to the bar to grab drinks?" Cal nodded, and the boys disappeared into the crowd.

By the time they returned, we had crammed ourselves into a booth between a coatrack and an exceptionally loud live band.

"Let the games begin," Cal said, handing us all cheap ale in plastic cups. We toasted, and from then on everything turned into a blur of sloshing drinks, uncontrollable laughter, loud, aggressive banter, and unbearable heat between me and Henry.

We were sitting far closer than we needed to be in the booth, and I could feel his eyes boring holes in my head every time I spoke. It was almost too much to turn and meet his gaze. When I did steal a glance at him, his lips were parted in a way that made me imagine what they'd feel like on my body, and I had to drown my thoughts with another cheap beer for fear of what might happen if I didn't.

"Who's going for a midnight snog tonight?" Jan slurred, checking his watch.

"It's not New Year's, you git," Raja said. "I don't think that's how it works."

"No one gave me the memo that New Year's was the only time you can kiss at midnight," Finn said. "Sorry then, Liv. Not gonna be able to snog ya after all."

"Gross," Liv said. "What about you two?"

"Us?" Henry asked, gesturing at the two of us while I turned to stone beside him.

"No, Jan and Margot," she said, rolling her eyes. "Yes, you two. We all know something's going on. So will it be a midnight kiss or what?" She leaned back and twirled a piece of her hair.

"Didn't we just establish that Guy Fawkes isn't a midnight-kissing occasion?" Henry said, coupled with what sounded like a forced laugh. I'm not sure what I was expecting, but it wasn't this much resistance.

"But didn't we also just establish it totally could be?" I could tell Jan was only asking because he was eyeing that guy in 2C who had convinced his friends to come with us to The Bag, but I was glad it helped my case.

"I mean, I suppose any night could be," Henry said. "Did you guys get nosier since I was last home?"

"Darling, we've always been this way," Raja said. "You know that. It's what you signed up for when you moved into the warehouse."

"I'll have to revisit my contract," he said, his laugh a bit more natural this time. I forced an exhale, trying to recover my resolve.

The rest of our roommates booed him and moved on to the next topic of interest, but I wasn't yet ready to do the same. Had I read this totally wrong?

Maybe he was just one of those private guys who kept his mouth closed about his personal life. Though he did tell me quite a bit about his job and his life that night on the roof, so I wasn't sure the theory held up. The lingering bonfire smell was becoming more threatening by the minute.

Liv gasped, then immediately hiccupped. "We never did the two-sentence update! Are we too drunk to do it now?"

"Depends," Henry said. "Does anyone have anything major to share?"

We looked around at each other, mostly in silence.

"Nothing at all?" Henry prompted.

"It's been slow," Cal said. "Anyone else feel like these past few weeks have been a blur?" We all agreed, murmuring about *same shit, different day* before returning to our drinks.

"What about you, Hen?" Raja asked. "How was Berlin?"

"Full of history. And the venue I was shooting was an old church, so I got some brilliant material."

"But not the future home, right?" I had gotten a sense of this from our texts, but suddenly felt the need to confirm.

"Sadly, no. Still at odds on that." He leaned his knee against mine under the table, and I couldn't resist sneaking a glance at him to see if that was an accident. He cut his eyes back down to me, his smirk confirming that no, it was not an accident at all.

"And where to next?" Margot asked.

"Copenhagen. Here's hoping I don't freeze to death." He raised his glass and we did the same, but I dreaded another month of him leaving.

I thought back to Margot's words, and I wondered if I would even get far enough to have to worry about a proper relationship. How was I even supposed to get to know someone who was always away, let alone consider trying to date them?

"It's almost midnight, isn't it?" Henry said, looking for a wall clock and bringing us all back to the moment.

"Finish those pints, then. I have a perfect spot for watching the fireworks," Jan said, swallowing half a beer in one gulp.

"Better than the shit part of the park we watched from last year?" Liv asked.

"Or that shit pub with all the tourists the year before?" Margot and Liv giggled together, which was how I knew we were all hammered.

"Bugger off, the both of you. Just trust me on this one," Jan said.

"After you," Henry said, exiting the booth.

Jan led us to a multilevel parking lot, which couldn't have been less appealing.

"A car park?" Liv said. "You're taking us to a car park?"

Jan said nothing, but motioned for us to follow him up the stairs.

"Leave it to Jan to take us to a creepy garage for his month," Liv whispered to me, looking for someone who would entertain her complaining.

"We couldn't have just used the roof at home?" Margot asked as we climbed higher.

"Didn't I say to just trust me?" With that, Jan pushed open a lopsided metal door and we stumbled out onto the roof.

And then it became clear that no, we could not use the roof at home. From this roof, it felt like we could see almost all of Seven Sisters. Fireworks were already beginning across the city, and we had a breathtaking view. There was a handful of folding chairs facing the side of the roof with the lowest wall, opening up to the city.

"How'd you find out about this place?" Finn asked, wandering to the edge.

"One of my mates from the tattoo shop," Jan said. "He's been coming here for ages, and we came up one night after work for a smoke. Not bad, right?"

"Not bad at all," Cal said, clapping him on the shoulder. "Well done, mate."

"So if you look over to the right behind that grayish building, you can see the flags outside of the Bag." We craned our necks to where he was pointing, and sure enough, he was right. "So when the park fireworks go off right behind it, we'll see them over there."

We made ourselves comfortable in the chairs and on the cold concrete, turning our gazes toward the sky. I was sitting on the ground, with Henry in the chair behind me; if I wanted to, I could just lean back into his knees.

At the very moment I was talking myself out of it, an explosion of color and light spread across the sky exactly where Jan had told us it would. And if gunpowder could be so bold, certainly I could, too.

While we were all distracted by the display, I leaned back into the space between Henry's legs, feigning calm and comfortable. It felt like an eternity before he reached down and ruffled my hair, and I could relax. There was hope for the night after all.

All eight of us sat quietly, in awe. Or just in a drunken stupor. It was hard to tell. The fireworks continued to rip through the sky, splashing neon across the darkness, and we took turns passing around a small bottle of gin Margot had produced from her bag.

"Let's play a game," Jan slurred into the bottle.

"Like what?"

"Truth or dare?" he suggested.

"That's a child's game," Finn said, eyes half closed.

"Then it's perfect for you, Finny," Jan said, handing him the bottle.

"Piss off. You first, then. Truth or dare?"

"Dare, obviously."

"Text that bloke you've been staring at all night," Liv said. "You've been doing a lot of talking but not a lot of doing."

"Hardly a dare, because he obviously fancies me, but as you wish." He had to squint his right eye to look at his phone, which was never a good sign. We laughed, the endearing, headshaking kind of laugh. Jan might have been a bit abrasive at times, but I had to admire his bravado.

"All right, Hen. You're next," Jan said, sliding his phone back into his pocket and wearing a satisfied smile.

"Why me?"

"Because we're going clockwise."

"Says who?"

"God, Hen, could you be more difficult?" Raja asked. I was still on the ground, back to him, so I couldn't read his facial expression.

"I probably could if I tried," he teased. "Right, then. Go on."

"Truth or dare?"

"Truth."

"Boo."

"Shut up, Finn."

"What's the real reason you're so keen to leave London?" Margot asked before any of us had a chance to think of a question. "I mean, there has to be more than this soul-searching rubbish." My breath lodged in my throat while I waited for the answer.

Henry shifted in his seat, rubbing his hands on his thighs and forcing me to sit upright. I was almost too distracted waiting for his response to be disappointed we weren't touching anymore.

"Right, er, not quite sure trying to find my place in the world counts as rubbish, does it?" he said.

"But what makes you so sure you couldn't find yourself in London?" Liv asked, her voice noticeably kinder than Margot's.

He exhaled long and slow, like he was in a losing fight against a dramatic sigh.

"There's nothing for me in London," he said eventually. Factually. Like there was no disputing this, no changing his mind.

"How do you know?" Liv asked, taking the words out of my mouth.

"Lived here all my life. Just worry it hasn't much left to offer, I guess. But it's hard to say, isn't it? Doesn't everyone feel that way about where they grew up?" We sat in silence, collectively unsure how to respond. "I mean, look at you lot. Half of you left home in search of something different, didn't you?"

"The man has a point," Cal said.

"So it might be my time to do the same. Or at least to think about it."

"Well then, that's one way to kill the mood," Jan said, stumbling to his feet.

"You asked," Henry protested. "If you play stupid games, you win stupid prizes." We all rolled our eyes, most of us lovingly, and got ready to head home.

I knew it hadn't been more than a kiss. In my brain, I knew that. But in my chest, hearing him say there was nothing for him in London made me realize I hadn't accepted that it was just a kiss at all.

Despite the dropping early November temperatures, the heat under my skin was rising by the minute. I gathered my hair in a sloppy bun at the nape of my neck in an attempt to cool myself down, breathing intentionally and hoping I looked more relaxed than I felt.

I failed.

Henry grabbed my elbow as we were heading down the stairs, letting go the second I turned to face him. "Walk home with me," he said.

"We're all walking home together, aren't we?"

"Let them go ahead." I obliged, but didn't look him in the eye right away. I was more embarrassed than I should have been, given that I was certain he hadn't even been thinking of me when he said that, but embarrassment isn't one of those emotions you can talk yourself out of.

Cal looked back and stopped walking, realizing we weren't all together.

"We'll catch up with you guys," Henry called down the stairs.

Raja and Liv made kissing noises, and the heat climbed higher up the back of my neck. I tried to laugh it off, but instead just blew hot air into the night.

"So," I said as we finally started walking. I wasn't sure where to go from there, but someone had to say something.

"Lucy, I hope you're not upset about what I said." He was a man who got right to the point. Normally, I'd like that, if it was about something pleasant. Like how much he wanted to kiss me last time.

"Oh, that? Of course not," I lied. "I get it. Your time in London has run its course. When a place has nothing to offer, you leave. I understand that."

"I didn't mean it had nothing to offer."

"Well, that's what you said, isn't it?" I wasn't trying to be argumentative. I just didn't want him going back on something he meant because he thought it might have hurt my feelings.

"Yes, and I did mean it in some ways. Like, career ways. I didn't mean it in terms of people."

"But you're leaving London regardless, right? Even if people here have something to offer?"

He rubbed the back of his neck, watching his feet as we walked. I felt bad for doing this tonight because I knew we were supposed to be enjoying the weekend, but in a way, he had started it. Or Margot had started it. Either way, it wasn't me.

"I guess so. I mean, that was the plan. Is the plan. It's just, I don't—"

"Hen, it's fine," I said, desperate to stop his rambling. "You don't have to explain it to me. Go do your soul-searching. Find wherever home is." I wished he would find home in London, but what else was there to say? It would be selfish to be anything but supportive.

He stopped walking and once again touched his fingers to my elbow.

"I really liked kissing you, Lucy. And I've liked getting to know you even more. I don't want a comment I made after a few drinks to make you think otherwise." God, could this man be any more direct? The last guy I kissed had left me on Read when I texted to ask if I'd left my earrings at his place.

"Thank you," I said. "And me too." More fireworks exploded somewhere in the distance, and we both jumped at the sound.

"Is there a chance I might get to continue doing both of those things?" he asked, running his fingers from my elbow to my hand. Everything in me wanted to say yes, except my brain. My body certainly wanted to say yes to his exposed collarbone under his sweater, the warmth of his calloused hand in mine, the gentle way he held my gaze. But my brain wanted to run for the hills, knowing Margot was right and this was a recipe for disaster.

I had to protect myself. As much as I wished I was the kind of woman who didn't mind her relationships having an expiration date, who would throw herself into something she knew was going to crash and burn just to enjoy the heat of the flames, I wasn't. Not even close.

"Henry, I want to say yes, I just—"

"Can't, because I'm always leaving. I know. And even though I keep coming back, it isn't enough."

"You read my mind," I said. "I don't know what's more difficult—only getting two days a month, or being left to wait for the rest of it. But I'm not sure I'm okay with either. I'm sorry."

"Don't be." He shook his head and dropped my hand, which immediately turned cold. "It's an unreasonable ask. I get it." We smiled sorry smiles at each other and returned to the walk.

"But," he said, without looking at me, "if you change your mind . . ."

"I know where you live."

"LUCE," RENEE SAID as soon as I walked into the Lotus. It was first thing in the morning, but she looked like she'd already been working for hours. "You have ideas for these arrangements for Hattie's party today, don't you?"

Hattie's niece was turning six, and because Hattie was the sort of peculiar woman who thought every occasion required high tea, we were preparing flower arrangements for the birthday party of an elementary schooler.

"Yeah," I said, trying to make sense of the tone in her voice. "I have some sketches. Do you want to see them?"

"Do you mind getting them started? My work in here is taking longer than I thought, and I'm afraid I haven't left the office to get into the studio yet."

"How long have you been here?"

"Oh, I don't know, some time," she said, waving the question into the air, her eyes still trained on the papers in her hands.

"Is this something I can help with?" I asked, nodding toward the papers. They looked like invoices, or bills, perhaps. I couldn't see exactly what, but I recognized the pale yellow carbon-copy paper on which we handled most of our finances. Only these were more crumpled than usual, like she'd been holding on to them all morning with a vise grip.

"Yes," she said, distracted. "The arrangements, pet, will you?" Not quite what I meant, but I headed into the studio to do as I was told. If she didn't want my help, I wasn't going to press it. No matter how concerned I might have been.

I grabbed my sketches and got to work, trying to push any concerns from my mind and focus on enjoying the morning.

We had to keep the studio cool for the flowers, which meant we had to stay bundled up all year long, but between the layered sweaters, the soft classical playlist humming from the speakers, and the bottomless cups of tea, the cold months really were quite cozy at the Lotus.

Pink geraniums littered the worktops, and when Renee finally joined me in the studio, we took turns winding them around delicate white cosmos and into centerpieces. The rhythm of the clippers and shuffling of stems lulled me into a meditative state, and everything from the night before melted away.

Until Henry wandered into the shop.

"Good morning, sir," Renee said, stopping her work to greet him like any old customer. "How can we help you?" She wiped her hands on her apron, and he flashed her an award-winning smile.

"Good morning," he said. "I'm looking for some sort of olive branch. Something that says, 'Can we start over and try just being friends?'"

I swallowed a sound before it could escape my lips, as I was still trying to pretend he was a stranger.

"Oh my," Renee started, gazing around the studio. "Let me think of just the thing. Clever boy, coming in here for that."

"I appreciate that. Perhaps your colleague could lend a hand?"

Renee looked back and forth from Henry to me and back to Henry, before clocking what was happening. "Lucy, do you know this man?" Her eyes told me she knew exactly who he was, and I made a mental note to thank her later for pretending she didn't.

"Hi, Hen," I said, without looking up from the centerpiece I was working on.

"Hi, Luce." I could feel him staring at me, and I could hear him smiling. He wasn't going to make this easy.

"I'll leave you to it," Renee said, ducking into the office and forcing me to turn my attention to Henry.

"Well then," I said. "Tell me a little bit about the person this olive branch is for. If I have a better sense of who she is, I can better make a selection for you."

"Right," he began. "She's quite beautiful, really." A warm blush spread over my cheeks, but I kept quiet, hoping he would continue. "And she's kind, and terribly clever. And she's just a friend, so don't get any ideas."

Our light laughter melted the tension, and it became fun to play into his game. I reminded myself not to make a habit of it, but I could indulge just this once.

"She sounds lovely."

"That's because she is."

"Then I know just the thing." I disappeared into the back of the studio and returned with a small bundle of lilyturf. He watched while I wrapped the lilac-topped stems in canvas paper, tying the bundle with a single piece of twine.

"These were just delivered this morning," I said, inhaling their scent. "Your friend is very lucky."

"I hope she likes them," he said, stepping closer to me.

"I have a feeling she will."

We stared at each other, and I tried to focus on the gentle sound of the music instead of the curve of his lips. Not quite sure Beethoven would be proud his music was being used for this purpose, but I had no choice.

"I'd better get going, then," he said, trading me the bundle for a few pounds.

"Good luck."

"Thanks. I think I'm going to need it."

Renee reappeared in the studio before the bell above the door was finished announcing his departure. I was still standing at the cash register, watching him walk away.

"Oh, pet, you didn't tell me he looked like *that*." She pulled her glasses down and peered at me over them.

"Well, it doesn't matter either way, because we're just friends, as you heard when he walked in and as you were eavesdropping from the office."

She tutted, waving off my attempts to wind her up. "And why on earth would you have made that decision? Surely you're both mad."

"We are not," I said, returning to the centerpieces. "The only thing that was mad was to think this ever might have worked in the first place. It doesn't make any sense, and I'd rather have that sorted now than later, when it would hurt a whole lot more."

"Being so protective of the heart is no way to live, you know."

"I'm not so protective of my heart." I could hear myself getting defensive, but with Renee, I wasn't sure I cared. "I put it into my work every day, don't I? Don't I give a little piece of it to every customer, every celebration, everyone in mourning?"

"There's no denying that," she said, reaching out to rest a wrinkled hand on mine. Hers felt like ice, but the sentiment was warm. "Just make sure you're as generous outside of work. Would hate to see that heart of yours confined to the walls of this shop."

"Spoken like a true grandmother."

"Just because I'm not your biological grandmother doesn't mean my grandmotherly obligations don't extend to you."

"Are we ready to get back to work? These pieces aren't going to finish themselves, and we're running out of time. I want to use all of these geraniums, because if Hattie's niece is forced into a stuffy high-tea birthday do, she should at least have fun arrangements to look at."

Renee glared for a moment but kept her mouth shut and returned to work. We settled back into our rhythm, and the arrangements were looking even more beautiful than before. This was a perfect place to share my heart, as far as I was concerned.

When I got home, the bundle of lilyturf was sitting on the small desk in my bedroom, with a note bearing my name. I unfolded the small cardboard flap and read:

> *Lucy,*
>
> *I'm sorry for last night. I was a bit of a drunken sod and didn't mean to offend, though I realize I have. I hope you can accept these as a peace offering (you should know a lovely local florist picked them out). Friends?*
>
> *Hen x*

When I proposed friendship, I'd thought it would be a whole lot easier than this. I didn't expect visits at work, sweet gestures, the impossible challenge of resisting the urge to make it something more.

She has great taste. Consider your offer accepted, mate, I wrote back and slipped the note under his door—there wasn't much else I could do. We were going to have to commit to something one way or another, and this felt like a much safer bet.

December

The lights on Oxford Street were nearly blinding. Twinkling angels stretched their wings from one side to the other, floating watchfully over the throngs of shoppers. Hundreds of thousands of sparkling lights rained from the storefronts, bathing the street in a warm glow. We could moan about the monotony of London's day-to-day all we wanted, but we would be lying if we said it wasn't enchanting during the holidays.

Liv, like Jan, had her weekend planning made easy: We were all to attend the Warehouse Holiday Party. According to Raja, this had been tradition since even before she lived in the flat, and it was one of the best nights of the year. Everyone seemed to agree it was best to do it at the start of the month in the hopes that everyone could come before plans really ramped up as the holidays got closer, and it seemed to work out well. The party was held in the garage/storage space/makeshift gym on the first floor of our building, and each flat was responsible for contributing something to the party. This year, we were in charge of decorations, which meant I was responsible for flowers (which they'd never had at this function before but were apparently essential this year).

The holidays were such a busy time for everyone, so tonight was the only time all eight of us could save for Warehouse

Weekend. We all had to squeeze in a bit of family time, especially Hen, since he only had off on Christmas Day, so December's Warehouse Weekend was a One Night Only sort of job. (Well, One Night Only plus a quick breakfast the morning after. Liv insisted on a brunch before we all went our separate ways.) Meaning, we had to make the most of it.

Since Liv didn't have a whole lot of planning to do for the weekend, she wanted to surprise each of the roommates with a little something for the holidays, which had brought us to Oxford Street. Typically bothered by the bumbling tourists, we were too spellbound by our own city to care.

Rather than focus on the task at hand, we were easily distracted by the magic of the holiday and spent most of the morning drinking coffee and wandering aimlessly down the busy streets. Overlapping Christmas songs spilled from invisible speakers outside every storefront, and we sang along, off-key and maybe a bit too loud.

"What about books?" Liv asked, refocusing, peering into the windows of a bookshop.

"Depends," I said. "Have you ever seen Jan or Finn open a book?"

"Ugh, you're right," she groaned. "How is anyone supposed to find one gift for the whole lot?"

"I don't know," I laughed. "It was your idea. What about candles? Everyone loves candles."

"I'm sorry, Lucy, are you suggesting even *more* candles in the flat? If so, we're going to have to start selling the furniture to make room."

She was right. We were both shit at this.

"What about socks?" she asked. "Everyone loves a good pair of cozy winter socks."

It was funny that socks might have been the only thing all eight of us had in common, but it was an excellent idea.

"Socks it is," I agreed. "Maybe scarves to match?"

"If I had money to buy all eight of us matching socks *and* scarves, I wouldn't have to be living with seven flatmates in a converted warehouse flat in the first place, would I?"

I laughed. "Socks it is," I repeated. We linked arms and ducked into Selfridges, dodging workers dressed as elves and well-dressed women pushing men's cologne as one of Michael Bublé's holiday albums blared from the speakers. Since my family didn't celebrate Christmas, I hadn't grown up thinking much of the North Pole, but I imagined that if it existed, it would look just like this.

We were out nearly as quickly as we went in. Selfridges was intense on its best day, but during the holidays, it was a different beast. We piled onto the Tube with throngs of holiday shoppers, eight pairs of fuzzy socks in hand (Liv had made me close my eyes while she chose mine so it would still be a surprise), as well as a heap of individually wrapped cookies, each the size of my head.

"This is really generous, Liv," I said. "We're lucky to have you."

"You're going to make me cry on the Tube," she said, bringing her hand to her chest. "Love ya, Luce."

"Love ya back." I leaned into her for a quick side hug, careful not to squish the bags between us. I'm not sure what it was about Liv, but she made me mushy.

Renee thought she knew me so well, but she was wrong. I could easily share my heart outside of work. Here I was, hugging a roommate on the Tube. If she could only see me now.

"Liv, do you feel like making another stop on the way

home?" I asked, already prepared to change lines. "I was going to pop into the studio in a bit to do the arrangements for later, but I think I'll grab the flowers instead and use the empty studio space at home. If you don't mind, of course."

"I've always wanted to see the Lotus," she said, gathering her bags.

"If we pop off at the next stop we can transfer and head straight there."

Renee wasn't in when we arrived, so I used my spare key to let us in.

"Is it just you two in this whole place?" Liv asked, looking around.

"More or less. We have some part-time help, Carla, but she really only manages the till and handles the occasional delivery. Renee and I are the only ones doing the arrangements." I fumbled around in the back, looking through recent deliveries for the perfect pieces for the party.

"That must be a ton of work," Liv continued. "Do you ever dream of having your own shop?"

I stopped fumbling to carefully consider her question. Of course I'd imagined what it would be like to have my own shop. Doesn't everyone who works for someone else imagine what it would be like to work for themselves? But it seemed like nothing more than a pipe dream most of the time. I couldn't imagine leaving Renee, or leaving the place I'd been working since college, but I would be lying if I said I hadn't dreamed of it.

"Do I dream of it? Sometimes. Do I have any plans to pursue it? Not quite," I said, hoping she wouldn't press it. "Maybe someday. Ready to go?" I left the back with bags full of crimson winterberry and leafy viburnum, imagining lush, Christmas-colored centerpieces.

Henry had arrived late last night, and we'd since exchanged

a few pleasantries around the flat. We'd texted only once or twice this time in the weeks he'd been gone, making it easier to come to grips with a platonic friendship. He was in his studio editing photos when Liv and I got back to the flat, and I tried to slip into the empty studio beside his as quietly as possible.

I unloaded the flowers and the extra tools I knew it was safe to nick for this project, and prepared to get to work. Just before I put my headphones in, I heard Henry's voice.

"Hey," he said, leaning against the makeshift doorway that separated the studios.

"Hey."

"Does being just friends mean we can no longer learn things from each other? Because now that you're here, and I have the opportunity to see you in action, I'd like to learn something, if you'll let me."

"Are you just saying that so you have an excuse to hang out in here?"

He gasped, feigning offense. "Are you calling me a liar? I might be a lot of things, Lucy, but a liar isn't one of them."

"Come in, then," I said, gesturing to a stool beside me. "Have a seat. Learn something."

By the time he sat down, it would have been awkward to inch my stool in the other direction, but he was dangerously close.

No one had ever really watched me work before, save for Renee and the occasional customer, of course, but it didn't make me as nervous as I thought it might. I was at peace when I was working, and I would be damned if Henry Baker was going to disturb that.

I talked him through the motions as I worked, explaining what flowers I was using and why, what techniques would make the best arrangements for this function, and what effect I hoped to create.

"They all look like mistletoe," he said. "Was that the effect?" He wasn't teasing, he was genuinely asking, which made me all the more tempted to say yes.

"That's the beauty of floral arrangements," I explained. "You can interpret them however you please. So, if you choose to see mistletoe and the rest of us choose to see holly and mulled wine and white winter snow, then who am I to stop you?"

He laughed softly at the irony of my question, and I knew we were both thinking about Bonfire Night, when he'd tried to pick up where we left off and I was exactly the one to stop him.

"This is really something, Luce," he said, admiring the pieces. "I mean, you came in here with bags of plants, and now you're leaving here with something that makes people think of kissing or singing Christmas carols by the fire. I didn't realize there was so much to it."

"Most people don't. But that doesn't bother me. I realize how much there is to it, and everyone benefits whether or not they realize it, so it's okay with me."

"You are impressively humble. If I had a talent like this, I'd be demanding everyone in the city admire my flowers."

"Well, I'm sure you're equally talented in your own right. But I'd have to see you in action to find out."

"Ah, is that how this works?"

"We made a deal, didn't we?"

"Sealed it with a kiss." He flashed a cheeky grin, and I swatted him on the arm.

"Henry! Friends don't talk about the times they've kissed. Especially when they've agreed to never do it again."

"You're right. I'm sorry," he said, but I couldn't tell if that was the truth. "And we did make a deal. Why don't you let me shoot you?"

"What?"

"Be my subject. Let me take photos of you, and I'll teach you everything you need to know."

"You can't be serious."

"Of course I am. Photography really is quite easy when you have the right subject, so it'll be the perfect first lesson."

"How am I supposed to learn if I'm in front of the camera, hm?"

"Do you trust me?" It was a loaded question. One I wasn't quite sure how to answer.

"I suppose I don't yet have reason not to," I said. It was the best I could come up with.

"That's the spirit. Liv asked if I'd bring my camera to the party tonight anyway, so we can get started right away."

This was already more than I'd signed up for, but I couldn't back out now.

I popped downstairs to deliver the arrangements, and the transformation of the space took my breath away. Silver tinsel and LED lights lined the windows, and along the opposite wall stood a plastic table prepared to hold classic holiday nosh and another doubling as a bar. A few high-tops dotted the space, surrounding what would be a dance floor in the middle. We were going to have a proper party in the garage/storage space/makeshift gym, and I needed to get ready.

Just over an hour later, I stood staring at myself in the full-length mirror, preparing to join the rest of the flat downstairs. I was wearing leather pants and a velvet bodysuit with a deep V, where a thin gold pendant hung against my sternum. I had blown my hair straight just to curl it properly, then pushed one side behind my ear and secured it with a pin. Raja had told me twice that people went all out for this, so I had to make sure I did the same.

"Lu, we're going to leave without you!" Raja shouted up the stairs, and I realized I was the only one still missing. *Shit.*

"Coming!" I slipped my feet into a pair of black pumps, then jogged down the stairs and dashed into the foyer to join my roommates, apologizing for holding anyone up. Finn started a slow clap upon my arrival, and Raja wasted no time jumping right in.

"Damn, Lucy," Raja said, running her tongue over her teeth. "I don't even know the last time I've seen you in anything other than sneakers and oversize T-shirts, but this look is really working for you."

"I second that," Finn agreed. "Yer a babe when you put the work in."

"Finn, why are you the way you are?" I asked, trying not to laugh. I'd been living here long enough that comments like this from Finn no longer surprised me, but it was best not to laugh and encourage him.

Besides, the way Henry was looking at me was more than enough attention for the moment. The slow, appreciative drag of his eyes up and down my body was anything but platonic, and the night was getting longer by the minute.

"How else would you like me to be?" Finn waggled his eyebrows, redirecting my attention.

"God, Finn," Liv said, repulsed. "You look great, Luce."

"Okay, enough talking about how I look, please. And thank you, Liv. So do you. Are we ready to go?"

"Been ready," Jan said from the couch, two empty beer cans on the table beside him.

"Bugger off, Jan," I said. "Let's do it."

As we made our way downstairs, Henry and I slipped to the back of the pack, as was becoming routine. I tried to pretend I didn't feel the heat of his gaze, that I hadn't been feeling it since the moment I walked down the stairs, but we were too close now to pretend anymore. Just out of earshot of the others, he leaned into me and whispered so close to my ear I could feel his breath.

"'Babe' doesn't even begin to cover it," he said "I'm serious, Lucy. I'm not sure how I'm going to focus on a single other person at this party tonight with you looking like that."

"So don't," I teased, feeling emboldened by all the praise. He inhaled sharply with a slow shake of his head, and neither of us said another word. The glance we exchanged was enough.

By the time we got downstairs, two of the three other apartments had already gotten the party started. Between the four apartments, there would be nearly forty people here tonight, which made it feel like a real event.

The first floor of the building was the perfect space for a party. Our heels echoed on the concrete floors, and the sound bounced around the open rafters. With the gym equipment dragged off to a storage closet and the bikes leaned up against the building outside for the night, we had plenty of space for food, drinks, high-tops, and a dance floor. The wide garage doors ordinarily made it drafty and cold, but there were enough people packed in for the party that the air was warm and humid.

We all first made a beeline for the bar, clearly sharing the same priorities. Henry and Cal ladled deep red punch into plastic cups, doling them out like we were a group of small children in the lunch line. Henry's fingers brushed against mine as he handed me a cup, and I wished I hadn't noticed.

By the time the night was underway, the party was a banger. Jan took over the speakers, and for once we didn't mind his eclectic taste in house music. We flocked to the dance floor in droves and had to restock the bar before midnight. Raja had said this was one of the best nights of the year, and so far, I had to agree with her.

Liv and I spent so long dancing that every song blurred into the next, and it wasn't until I felt Henry's eyes on me that I became aware of my own body again. He stood on the outskirts of the dance floor, back against the wall, beer in hand. One of our neighbors, an American named Lucas, was standing next to Hen, gesturing wildly in what appeared to be a one-sided conversation. I was dancing with Liv but no longer looking at her.

With Lucas still talking, Henry grabbed his camera from the high-top in front of them and lifted it to his eye. I kept my eyes on him but didn't stop moving for fear of what I might look like at that hour in a still frame. Liv and I danced around each other, twirling and laughing with our heads back and spilling drinks on the concrete, and Henry kept his camera trained on the dance floor all the while.

"I need another drink," Liv said between songs. "I think the entire contents of mine are on the floor. Or on that bloke's shoes." She nodded to a guy standing next to her, who I didn't recognize. "Need one?"

"A top-up would be grand, if you wouldn't mind," I said, handing her my cup.

"You got it. Try not to miss me too much." She danced off the floor, and as I'd hoped, Henry took the opportunity to fill her place.

"Finally escaped the clutches of Lucas and his tales of the Big Apple, have ya?"

Henry took a long swig of his drink, and I watched his Adam's apple bob in his throat as he swallowed. "You know, Bernstein, I try really hard to be a good person." He was slurring just a little, the way I was beginning to recognize he did when he was tipsy. "I try to listen when people talk, try to be a good conversationalist, but bloody hell, is he exhausting."

He pretended to faint onto my shoulder, and I actually had to exert effort to keep him upright.

"I would think someone as drunk as you would be able to tune him out," I teased.

"Oh, you think I'm drunk, do you?"

"I know you are," I said. "Can see it in your eyes."

"You've been looking at my eyes."

"Only now, as we've been talking."

"Well, could I have taken a photo like this if I was so drunk?" He turned his camera's screen to me, and I gasped audibly. It was a shot of me, but it looked like it could have been an advertisement. My arms were above my head, and my hair just masked half my face. I was the one in motion, but everyone else looked like a blur. The deep burgundy of my curls and the emerald green of my top were twice as vibrant as they'd looked in the mirror, and a glimmer of light caught my necklace in a way that turned it into a spotlight.

"Not bad, right?" he asked over my shoulder as I looked at the tiny screen.

"'Not bad' doesn't even begin to cover it," I said, at the risk of sounding vain. "Henry, I—"

"Had no idea how much there was to it?" he finished for me, echoing his sentiment from earlier. "Most people don't. But that doesn't bother me."

I'm not sure whether it was his blinding smile or the way my own words sounded in his mouth, but I had to cross my arms over my chest and bury my hands to keep myself from reaching out and pulling him in.

"Has anyone ever told you you have a way with words?" I asked.

"Yes, actually. But they usually only say it when the words are my own."

Liv returned with my drink, saving me from having to think of another clever response. "Hen, I'm glad you remembered to bring your camera, because I totally forgot to remind you."

"I couldn't have forgotten," he said to her, but he was looking at me. "There are some important things I had to shoot tonight."

"Have you gotten anything good?" Liv asked, oblivious to the building tension.

"Yeah, great," he said. "Gorgeous, really."

"Do share them tomorrow, will you? We have no pictures of us around the apartment, and we've been living in it forever. It's time." She was slurring too, only she had no chance of convincing us she wasn't totally wasted.

"Let me pop inside and upload this lot now, so I don't forget. Luce, give me a hand, will you?"

I laughed. He was unbelievable. "You need me to give you a hand doing something you literally do for a living?"

"It seems something has distracted me, and I fear I've forgotten how."

Liv disappeared into the crowd, leaving the two of us standing there alone in a sea of people. "Fine," I conceded. "But only because that's what friends do."

I followed him from the party back into the apartment, resisting the urge to reach for his hand as we wove through the crowd. It was quiet and dark upstairs, save for the distant thumping of the bass and the glow of the streetlights outside the windows.

Instead of heading to his studio, he stood outside the one I'd used earlier.

"What are you doing?" I crossed my arms again, leaning in the doorway as he had a few hours before.

"Lend me five more minutes of your time, Lucy. I have an idea."

"Tell me the idea before I agree." Being in there alone in the dark felt like a dangerous game. *There's no harm in pushing the boundaries right to the very edge, is there?*

Instead of saying anything, he handed me some leftover winterberry branches and gestured to a spot near the window.

"You want to take pictures of me in this dingy studio with a pile of leftover flowers?"

"Well, when you say it like that, it doesn't sound quite so romantic, but yes. That's exactly what I want."

"'Romantic' is the last word we should be using to describe anything we're doing tonight," I reminded him.

"You trust me, don't you?"

"In terms of photography, absolutely. The jury's still out on everything else."

"Good thing we're just taking photos, then."

Was that flutter in my chest disappointment?

"Right, then." I cleared my throat. "Where do you want me?"

He was sitting on a stool adjusting the settings on his camera, but he stopped at this and looked up at me through his eyelashes. "For the photos," I clarified, trying to wave off the suggestive glint in his eyes.

"Right over here," he said, resting his fingertips on my hips so lightly, I wasn't fully sure they were there as he moved me toward the workbench. "Up here." I hopped up, surprised to see this put us eye to eye. Inches from each other.

"Just like that," he whispered. I wished he would stop saying things like that. Every time he did, the flutter in my stomach dropped lower, and it was getting harder to deny the pull toward him. I crossed and uncrossed my legs, trying to gather myself.

We fell into silence, except for the occasional whispered direction from Hen. He posed me this way and that, using the wilting bundle of flowers as a prop.

"You see," he explained, "it's the juxtaposition of you and the flowers and the industrial studio that makes this work. On their own, the flowers are beautiful but cliché, and on its own, the studio is cold and inhuman. But with you in the shot . . ." He stopped talking, replacing his words with the shutter of the camera.

"So you did plan on teaching me something after all."

"Lucy, I am a man of my word." He dropped the camera around his neck, looking at me straight on now instead of through the viewfinder.

"I wish I could say the same for myself."

He stepped into the space between my legs, testing the waters. I knew this was wrong. I knew I'd had more to drink than usual and this would likely hurt worse than the hangover in the morning. But I also knew I wanted nothing more than Henry in this moment, so I surrendered.

I pulled his camera from around his neck and replaced it with my arms, savoring the way he leaned into my body. He pressed his lips to mine, and I let the flowers fall to the floor. Unlike our first kiss, this one started hungry.

I laced my fingers through the hair at the nape of his neck, and he wrapped a strong arm around my back, pulling me into him. The sound of our breathing overwhelmed the distant thump of the bass, and the party ceased to exist at all. As far as I was concerned, we were the only two people in the warehouse. In fact, we might as well have been the only two people in the city.

"Lu, are you in here?"

Raja. *Bloody hell.* I uncurled my legs from Henry's body, and he braced his hands on either side of me on the bench, turning the veins in his forearms to ropes.

"Yeah, in the studio, just a second, Raj." I scrambled to gather myself and Henry ran a frustrated hand through his hair, which wasn't helping my case. I brought a finger to my lips, fearful he'd blow our cover, but instead of listening he grabbed me by the jaw and kissed me hard where my finger had been.

I stumbled from the studio, dropping the curtain back in the doorway before Henry had a chance to leave behind me.

"What are you doing up here?" Raja asked, looking around the apartment.

"Er, I left my phone in here while I was working earlier. Came up to grab it."

"You're obviously lying, but I'll care about that later. We need to get Liv back upstairs. She's three sheets to the wind, and I think she swung at Finn when he suggested she stop drinking and go to bed. And you know it's bad if Finn is trying to cut someone off."

I laughed at the thought of Liv swinging at anyone, and I thought Henry might have done the same from behind the curtain.

"Well, then, let's go get her."

"Oh, did you see Henry while you were in here? I thought Liv said he came in to upload photos, but that might have been rubbish. But he's a good voice of reason, so might be helpful to have him around."

"Hey, Raj," he said from behind us, with no evidence that he'd been in my studio. "Liv was right, actually. Had to quick purge the memory card. But it sounds like you two could use a hand, so let's crack on, then."

"You two are both liars, and you're lucky our friend is in need, otherwise I'd be asking a ton of questions."

"Quite lucky, indeed." Henry smiled.

"Don't think it isn't coming," Raja threatened, and he raised his hands in surrender. "We just have to deal with this first."

"Roger that." Hen saluted, and we headed back into the party with a very different mission than we'd been working on a few minutes ago. Probably for the best, although it felt like nothing could have been worse.

By the time we'd coerced Liv into bed with a large glass of water and a few Tylenol, a sad glance between me and Henry over Raja's head confirmed what we both already knew: This, like everything else, would have to wait.

AS IF GETTING out of bed the morning after a party wasn't difficult enough, it was raining buckets and freezing cold. If I hadn't promised Liv and Cal I'd help with breakfast, I might have stayed in bed forever.

By the time I got to the kitchen, those two were in full swing. I didn't know Cal could cook, which wasn't surprising, since I didn't know much of anything about Cal in the first place. But with a towel over his shoulder and an apron around his waist, he looked like the real deal.

"How can I help?" I meant to ask at a normal volume, but since those were my first words of the day, they came out as more of a squeak.

"Luce, glad you're here," Liv said. "You're creative and artistic. We need that. Do you mind putting the table together? I want it to feel special."

"I nicked some of the flowers off the tables at the end of the night, so we can reuse those if you want. Save ye some time," Cal said, gesturing to the counter beside the fridge where he'd set the arrangements from the party.

"They're beautiful, and they look like mistletoe," Liv said, which made me laugh. Then it made me depressed, because the last thing I wanted to think about this morning was kissing.

"On it," I said.

The table was long and thin, made of unfinished wood and surrounded by colorful mismatched chairs.

I fished a tartan runner from the depths of a basket in the makeshift pantry and used it to line the table, draping it over the ends. We had no nice dishes, but at least the ones we had were a stark white that looked polished and seasonal against the runner and the flowers. I set out silverware the way my parents used to, careful to arrange it in the appropriate positions, although I knew full well no one in the apartment would give it a second thought.

"Oh, Lucy, I almost forgot," Liv said. "I picked up a little something else while we were on Oxford Street as a surprise for you. Let me grab it. It'll be perfect for the table." She disappeared into her room, returning a moment later with a small gift bag.

"You really shouldn't have—" I started.

"Just open it."

Inside, wrapped in tissue paper, was a little silver menorah and a packet of birthday candles.

"Sorry about the candles," Liv said. "That's all I could find."

I threw my arms around her before she could finish apologizing. This might have been a small gesture for Liv, but it was a big deal for me. Sometimes it felt like London had fewer Jewish people than the Vatican, especially around the holidays, and I was delighted to feel seen.

"Liv, this is the sweetest gift I've ever gotten. The candles are perfect. The menorah is perfect." I squeezed her again. "Thank you."

"It was a selfish gift," she joked. "I've never celebrated Hanukkah before, but I've always wanted to."

"Then we'll have to light a candle together." She squealed and returned to the kitchen, and I took an extra second to admire the menorah on the table. It didn't matter that the holiday didn't start for another week. If the season was about giving, Liv had really nailed it.

"Cal, how'd you get so good at a full English?" I asked, plating what felt like a hundred pieces of toast.

"As soon as I moved in here and this lot learned I could cook, they didn't leave me much of a choice," he laughed. It was a nice laugh. There was something warm and genuine about Cal that reminded me of most British grandfathers. He looked kind of tough on the outside, what with his thick beard and heavy hands, but he was much softer on the inside. His girlfriend was very lucky.

Liv rallied the rest of the apartment as Cal and I brought the food to the table, and everyone emerged in various levels of hangover. How Liv wasn't the most hungover of the lot was a mystery, but I think the holiday spirit was to blame. She must have woken up for this brunch like it was Christmas morning and forgotten all about last night. How I wished I could have done that.

Henry was somehow more of a dish half asleep than he'd been at the party. His hair, which he seemed to have no intention of cutting, was tangled in all the right ways, and his ratty old T-shirt exposed an inch of skin above his joggers that begged to be touched.

"It looks like a proper Christmas morning in here," Finn said, flopping into a chair at the table. "Well done, you three." The rest of the roommates echoed his comments, adding how hungry they were and how much they regretted drinking so much last night.

"How was your first Warehouse Holiday Party, Lu?" Raja asked with twinkling eyes.

"Great, thanks," I said, shooting her a look that said *I'll kill you if you say anything else.* She rubbed her hands together like a cartoon villain but otherwise dropped the conversation. I knew we would have to dish at some point, but I needed to make sense of things myself first.

Once everyone was seated, Liv took the head of the table with a giant bag of gifts on the chair in front of her.

"First of all," she began, "I'd like to thank everyone for getting me into bed safely last night." We gave a light clap and a few cheers, but she quieted us down so she could continue. "And I'd like to thank you for sparing me stories of all the embarrassing things I probably did. Would be brilliant if we could continue keeping those under wraps. But more important, happy holidays." She raised a glass. "I'm glad we could be together today, even if just for a quick breakfast before everyone parts ways. You lot are like family, and I think we're quite lucky to have found each other."

"God, Liv, do you have to be so sappy at this hour?" Margot moaned, but even she couldn't hide her smile.

"She has to be sappy at every hour," Jan said.

"He's right. And before I'm done, I have a little something for everyone." She distributed the gift bags we'd put together the day before, which everyone tore into at once.

"Don't make fun," Liv said. "Socks and dessert are apparently the only things all eight of us have in common."

"They're perfect," Henry said, pulling the socks onto his feet, exposing his lower back in the process. "Thanks, Liv."

"To Liv," Jan said, and we toasted.

"Are we lighting this thing or what?" Finn said, gesturing to the menorah like an eager toddler. "Lucy, this is your job, right?"

"It is," I said. I put one of the birthday candles in the middle and another on the far right end and accepted Jan's proffered lighter to do the honors. I said a quiet prayer in Hebrew, then lit the candles to the sound of applause. I wasn't quite sure I'd ever been applauded for this before, but it felt good nonetheless.

"Thanks, Liv, and everyone, for doing this with me."

"You're family now, too," Raja said. "Which means your traditions are our traditions."

Surely it was due to the emotional roller coaster of last night, on top of the dull hangover this morning, but I felt tears pricking at my eyes. I was embarrassed for having ever been reluctant to live in the warehouse, and now I couldn't imagine leaving.

We passed around heaping plates of eggs, baked beans, black pudding, scones, and whatever else Cal had found in the kitchen and turned into breakfast. Jan poured champagne for mimosas, and Margot kept the kettle bubbling on the stove for tea. We were a well-oiled machine when we weren't bickering, and this was the perfect way to celebrate the holidays as a flat: one wild, drunken party, and one quiet, heartwarming breakfast. If Henry could have photographed the juxtaposition of the past twelve hours, I was sure it would have been beautiful.

"What's the update?" he asked as we leaned back in our chairs, so full we could hardly move. "Anyone have anything?"

"There's a new headmaster at my school, and she totally sucks," Liv said.

"Sorry to hear that," Henry said, and I could tell he meant it.

"There's a new season of *Bake Off* set to come out next week," Raja offered.

"Now *that* is some good news." Henry and I exchanged tired smiles and I kept my mouth shut about any updates on my end, figuring we'd try to stay on a positive note. My updates were all worry, concern, and cliché Christmas marriage proposals.

"What's your update, Hen?" Margot asked. "Find home yet?"

"Not yet, but I've learned quite a bit. I've learned I'll be happy shooting anything, not just musicians, which gives me more options. And I'm glad I'm kind of setting up this career path that will benefit other photographers, so I've also learned I like giving back."

"Aye, so maybe all the soul-searching is paying off after all," Finn said.

"You do seem more yourself than usual," Liv added. "Almost glowing, even, the more I look at ya."

He rubbed the back of his neck in the way I knew he did when he was nervous, and I kept my eyes trained on the table in front of me, heat rising to my cheeks.

"Thanks, Liv. It's felt good to be home this weekend. I'm not sure I look any different, but if I do, that would be why."

"Reckon it could also be because of what you got up to last night?" Raja asked, dropping her fork to the table with a clatter for effect. I was paralyzed, but I wished so badly I could bring my eyes to hers like laser beams.

"Aye, could be." What the hell was he doing? "Got some great shots of the flat. I'll share the folder with you guys when I get the chance. Some of the photos are a right laugh."

Well played, Henry Baker. Raja, far less satisfied at his response than I was, tutted under her breath. He flashed her a winning smile, fully knowing what she was getting at, and I chewed my thumbnail, hoping the whole thing would blow over.

It wasn't so much that I was embarrassed or particularly private about things like this, I just wasn't keen on reliving the disappointment. And I was strangely worried about the judgment I'd receive from Margot, seeing as she'd warned me about this. I wanted to be a stronger woman than one who caved and kissed men she knew not to, so I preferred to keep last night's events under lock and key.

We had hardly finished washing up when Henry announced it was time for him to go.

"Where to now?" Raja asked.

"Well, first my parents', then Switzerland."

"They couldn't send you somewhere warm in the winter?"

"If only," he laughed. "I'm looking forward to Switzerland, actually. It'll be good to spend some time in nature. And I'll be a bit remote so I won't have much access to my phone, which is a blessing and a curse, I suppose. Trying to look at it as a blessing, though."

As far as I was concerned, it was most definitely a curse.

"Well, I can't wait to hear all about it." Raja smiled, and Henry disappeared from the kitchen to gather his things.

I pretended to go to the bathroom but stopped in his bedroom doorway on my way there.

"It's my month next, you know," I said, leaning on the doorjamb.

"As if I wasn't excited enough already."

Silence lingered between us, making space for one of us to say something, anything, about last night.

"Does your month happen to include finishing what we started last night?" he asked eventually, looking up at me from his luggage. I'd been turning this very question over in my mind since the second we heard Raja's voice the night before.

"What fun would it be if I just told you?" I said.

He rolled his eyes, bringing a hand to his chest like my mother did when she was disappointed.

"Patience," I said.

"I'm choosing to remain optimistic, because the answer isn't 'no.'"

"But it should be."

"But it isn't, is it?" He stepped a bit closer, shrinking the gap between us.

"No, I suppose it isn't," I said, my voice hardly above a whisper. Had he been across the room and had I had a blindfold on, I might have been firmer. But alas, he was inches from me, smelling of shampoo and cinnamon, looking down at me through soft, pine-green eyes. I would've had to be a saint to resist, and even then I think I would've risked being shunned.

I was going to have to do some soul-searching of my own in these few weeks if I wanted to make sense of any of this. My head was screaming *no, no, no,* but the rest of me was on strike. It might have even been unionizing. Henry and I had only been in the city at the same time for a total of nine days, and I was already losing my grip.

"You should go," I said, putting distance back between us. "You don't want to be late to your parents'."

"Right, then." He grabbed his luggage, noticeably disappointed the moment was over. "I'll see you for New Year's in a few weeks."

I wanted to tell him how much I wished those weeks would pass in the blink of an eye, but I knew that wouldn't be helpful to either of us. I was going to have to play it cool if I wanted the upper hand, which I needed to keep my feet on solid ground, so I said a casual goodbye and omitted anything about wishing he would stay.

He disappeared into the elevator with nothing more than a light kiss on my cheek and a wave to whatever roommates were left in the kitchen, and I watched the doors as the elevator carried him out of sight.

January

> Hey guys—bad news. Well, good news. But also bad news. Got the last-minute opportunity to shoot a massive holiday festival this weekend in Zurich, but that means I'm going to miss Warehouse Weekend.

I read Henry's text so many times, the words became gibberish. I watched the rest of the conversation roll in, frozen with my phone in my hand, while I waited for the bus.

> **Raja:** you're going to miss New Year's?

> **Liv:** I can't believe you're bailing on a major holiday.

> **Henry:** I'm so sorry. I'll be home for February, promise. X

> **Margot:** Congrats on the opportunity, Hen. Well done.

> **Cal:** Second that. Congrats, mate.

> **Finn:** remember us when you're famous you lucky bastard

I wanted to join in congratulating him, but I couldn't bring myself to do it quite yet. I needed to finish being selfish and wallowing in my own disappointment first. The bus pulled up to the stop, and I contemplated getting on and just riding aimlessly around the city until the sting wore off. One look at the crowd on the bus, however, convinced me otherwise.

I looked at my phone again to see if anyone else had replied in the group message, only to see that Henry had sent a separate text just to me.

> Not sure if you saw my text in the group, but I wanted to apologize. I hope you understand. x

I stared at it for a while before I answered, hovering my fingers over the keyboard and considering my words.

> Congratulations on the opportunity, Hen. Best of luck! Xx

It wasn't much, but it was the best I could do. Any more would have given away my disappointment, and I had no interest in exposing myself.

As soon as I got home from work, Raja called me into the kitchen.

"Want to order in tonight and watch a film or something?" she asked by way of a greeting. "I could go for a beer on the couch."

I'd wanted to be alone tonight, but suddenly a beer on the couch sounded much better. "Count me in."

"Good," she said, looking me over from head to toe. "You look like you could use one."

I ignored her, but I knew we'd be revisiting it later. We both got changed into our coziest sweats, reconvening on the couch with a few beers and the Deliveroo app.

"Chinese?" she asked.

"We did that last week. Curry?"

"That good place is closed for renovations. Pizza?"

I narrowed my eyes. "With what on it?"

"Those hot peppers they always have and extra cheese? From that place across from Zara?"

"Atta girl. You order. I'll Venmo."

We settled into the couch, cracking beer tabs and staring at the blank projector screen.

"Bummer about Henry, huh?" she asked after a while.

I took a long sip, thinking of something to say. "Yeah, bummer indeed" was all I could come up with.

"What's going on there, Lu? I mean, is this becoming something real or what?"

I resisted the urge to groan at the top of my lungs.

"No, definitely not," I said. "But I didn't expect to get so invested. At the beginning I was just intrigued, thought I was having fun, but I think now I might be in over my head."

She nodded, seemingly agreeing. "Try to stay afloat," she said. "I don't like the idea of you losing yourself in someone who isn't totally lost in you, you know?"

"You don't think he's into me?" I asked, surprising myself with how hurt I sounded.

"I didn't say I don't think he's into you. I'm just saying to keep your head about you, that's all. You're different people, and you want different things, and sometimes that's really tricky. But of course I think he's into you, because I think everyone is into you, and if they aren't, I think they should be."

I was glad she ended on a lighter note, because the idea that Henry might not be into me, or that we might be a terrible match, was bringing an unwelcome heat to the back of my eyes.

"Okay, we need to stop talking about this," I said. "It's vaguely depressing, and I need to move on. New Year's is the perfect time to do so."

"Because it's so romantic and you can shag someone else in your studio instead?" She waggled her perfect brows.

"For the millionth time, we did not shag in my studio. And no, I do not plan on chatting anyone up this weekend, or maybe ever again. I just mean the holiday is about new beginnings or whatever. Fresh start."

"Whatever you say," she said, leaning back into the couch and closing her eyes while she sipped. We still hadn't bothered to turn Netflix on, but I didn't mind. Once we stopped talking about Hen, I welcomed the silence.

Raj grabbed the pizza when it arrived and brought it to the couch.

"What are your plans for the new year?" I said, digging in.

"Oh, you know, finish my degree, get a job, the usual."

"How do you do it, Raj?"

"Do what?"

"You're so confident in your future. You never seem stressed about school, you're not worried about getting a job—it all seems so easy for you."

"I know what I'm good at," she said, as if it were that simple. "And I know what I like. And so do you, so there's no reason you can't also be this confident. Except for the fact I am ridiculously good-looking, but you'll be all right, I suppose."

"Raj!"

"I'm kidding, would you relax?"

"You're right, you're right, I do need to relax."

"Starting now," she said, then, a little softer, "It's going to be a great weekend, Lu. We don't need Henry to have a good time. We have each other. And a whole city of attractive people who actually live here all the time."

"But most important, each other," I said.

"I'm just saying." She clinked her beer against mine. "Cheers to you, cheers to me," we toasted in unison, then both took a big swig.

Eventually, we turned on the TV, jumping into a random season of *Derry Girls* and restoring our comfortable silence. Tomorrow wouldn't be ideal, but at least it wasn't totally hopeless.

EARLIER IN THE WEEK, I'd scored last-minute tickets to a swanky après-ski-themed New Year's Eve party at a club in Soho, and it was in full swing when we arrived. Fairy lights, presumably left over from Christmas, hung from the rafters, and electric fireplaces stood along the walls. Skis, snowshoes, and pine branches completed the décor, and nearly every drink appeared to be a mulled version of a regular cocktail.

"Well?" I asked the group before we made our way to the bar. "What do we think?"

"Bang-on," Cal said, and the others agreed.

"Seriously," Liv said. "This is great."

"Liv just wanted an excuse to wear metallic pleather pants," Margot said, and Finn whistled. "But she's right. It is great."

"Well done, Lu," Raja said, and I smiled. I'd been nervous about my first go at planning a Warehouse Weekend, and was glad to hear I hadn't totally screwed it up. "Shall we?" Raja asked, nodding in the direction of the bar, and we followed her lead.

We ordered a handful of imported craft beers and mules

packed with cinnamon sticks, then took a lap to get our bear-
ings. A large digital clock mounted above the bar counted the
minutes to midnight, and I tried to do the opposite.

I had had such different expectations of this night, making
it hard to embrace the festivities. A cloud of disappointment
floated over the bar, turning the faces of every guy I looked at
into Henry's. I had approximately two hours and twenty-one
minutes to pull myself together so the start of the new year
wouldn't be as melancholic as the end of this one, and I'd need
something a lot stronger than a mule to do it.

"Let's do a shot," I said to Liv over the music.

"Can we do it off a ski? I've always wanted to do a shot off
of a ski."

"Come on," I laughed, pulling her by the hand to the bar.
Liv was unapologetically enthusiastic, and I was trying to let
her positivity rub off on me. Finn was standing behind her, and
she grabbed him, and he grabbed Raja, and pretty soon the
whole lot of us was lined up at the bar, poised to drink cheap
tequila out of shot glasses glued to an old ski.

"Ready?" Cal asked, looking at us one by one. We cheered,
then lifted the ski together and brought the shot glasses to our
lips. "Go."

The tequila burned my tongue, my throat, and everything
else it touched on the way to my stomach. I closed my eyes and
let the feeling settle, imagining my disappointment burning
away with it. We laughed, linked arms, and shuffled back into
the party as a family. I was ready to embrace the night.

Naturally, Raja dragged us all onto the dance floor, and everyone at the party fell away. I looked at my roommates' faces
in turn as we danced, watching as they mouthed the words
to a song or teased each other for their terrible dance moves,
and for a while, I didn't miss Henry at all. I had everything I

needed right there, with those six people, and maybe that's what I was to expect in the new year.

We were headed to the bar for another round when I saw him.

"Hi," he said, addressing only me, despite my entourage, and extending his hand. It took me a minute to register what was happening, which probably made me look like an idiot. "Oliver," he said.

"Lucy." I shook his hand, and we both held on for a moment too long.

"I saw you earlier, on the dance floor—where you looked great, by the way, but you also looked like you were having far too much fun for me to interrupt. Is now a better time?"

"Yes, it's a perfect time, really," Raja interrupted, smiling at him over my shoulder.

I snapped my head around to shoot her a look, but she wasn't having any of it. Her look was even more stern, imploring me to entertain this conversation.

"Lucky me, then," he said. He took a sip of what looked like an old-fashioned, and I couldn't help but notice the glossy sheen it left on his full lips.

"Lu, we're just going to be over by this fireplace," Raja said in my ear so as not to interrupt us. No matter how many drinks we'd had or what conversations we were in the middle of, we'd be damned before we lost one another in a crowded bar.

I turned to her and asked with my eyes, *What the hell do I do?*

"Stop thinking about Henry," she whispered through barely parted teeth. "Start thinking about this gorgeous stranger instead." The rest of my friends were at the fireplace, within sight but too wrapped up in each other to notice us. "And Lu, have a little fun, for the love of god."

I shooed her away, nervous Oliver might have heard her. When I turned back in his direction, he was smiling lightly and staring at me with deep, kind brown eyes, and I decided I deserved this. I deserved someone kind, patient, willing to actively pursue me.

I also decided I was well on my way to drunk, but in the good way.

"You have good mates," Oliver mused once Raja had returned to the rest of the lot.

"They're definitely something," I laughed. They were playing some sort of drinking game, and Finn's beer was foaming over the top and forming a puddle at Liv's feet.

"Are you here with friends, or . . . ?" I wasn't exactly sure what I was asking, but I figured it was best to make sure he wasn't trolling the bar for single women alone. Or worse, that he'd come with a date and abandoned her.

"Well, I was, but one's in a fight with his girlfriend and the other was invited to smoke a joint in the alley with a coworker, so . . . They aren't quite as considerate as yours, I have to say." His candor was disarming.

A giggle that I was certain didn't belong to me escaped my lips, but I let it slide in the spirit of new beginnings. I raised my glass to his for a toast. "Pleased to meet you, then, Oliver."

"I'd say the same, but 'pleased' doesn't do it justice," he said, clinking our glasses. "So, Lucy, tell me about yourself."

"I'm a florist," I said, a sense of pride creeping into my chest, followed closely by anxiety that I might not be able to say this with such confidence for much longer. "I work at an independent shop in Islington."

"How romantic," he mused. "That must be hard work, then, isn't it?"

"Yes," I said, perhaps with a bit too much enthusiasm. "Sorry, people usually assume it's really easy, but in fact, it's the opposite. And keeping the job is sometimes as difficult as doing the job, if I'm honest." I didn't mean for that bit to slip out, but something about his face made me want to tell him things.

"Nothing about that seems easy to me. Your clients are all undergoing something emotional, right? It must almost always be either celebration or mourning, if I had to guess. And it must be intense to be surrounded by that."

"Do you happen to also be a florist?" I laughed. "You're bang-on, really."

"I'm in the restaurant industry. A chef, actually. So at work, people come to me with the same range of emotions, but I get to handle them from behind the scenes. Not quite as difficult as being front and center, I imagine."

"Seems plenty difficult in its own right," I said.

"I'll drink to that," he said. "Fancy another?" He nodded to my empty cup, and I realized I hadn't gotten in on the last round with my roommates.

"Please," I said.

I watched him order for us, forcing myself not to remember the times I had watched Henry do the same.

"So, that accent's American, is it?" he asked, handing me my cocktail.

"Embarrassingly so," I said. I'd been living in London long enough that I seldom seemed like an out-of-towner, but the accent was a giveaway.

"It's charming," he said.

"Is that code for something?" I asked, narrowing my eyes.

"If you're asking because you don't think you're charming, Lucy, then we're going to have a problem here." He sipped his drink, keeping his eyes on mine. "And I quite like you, so I'm not keen on having a problem just yet."

"Duly noted," I laughed. Any other response was escaping me, but he didn't seem to mind.

He asked about my background, what had brought me to London, what I liked to do when I wasn't working. I asked about places he'd traveled, what had led him to the kitchen, how else he liked to spend his time. We told bad jokes, ordered shots, touched each other's arms. We whispered about other people at the bar, commented on the music. We watched the clock.

The impending pressure of midnight mingled overhead with the lights strung around the rafters and the scents of beer and cinnamon. People kissed at midnight on New Year's. He knew it and I knew it. And my friends constantly glancing over at me from the fireplace knew it. But his charm might have been the sort of effortless kind men like this use with everyone, regardless of their interest, and my head wasn't clear enough to decide if that was the case with me.

In the forty-five minutes we'd been standing together, we'd all but closed every inch of the gap between us. A deep breath would put my chest against his, and I could feel the heat of his body, warmer than that of the crowded bar.

"You don't want to get back to your friends before midnight?" I asked, nodding to the clock that signaled there were only a few minutes to go.

"Trying to get rid of me?"

"Hardly." *Trying to give you an out in case you want one before I embarrass myself, is more like it.*

"Good," he said, running his fingertips up the length of my arm. "Because I'd much rather ring in the new year with you, if that's all right. Unless, of course, you'd like to get back to *your* friends?"

"Now that I think about it," I teased, turning on my heel and pretending to leave. Before I had even turned all the way around, he caught me by the wrist, pulling me up against him. This time, he was the one who gestured to the clock.

"At this rate," he said, "you'd hardly have time to get back to them anyway." Midnight was less than a minute away. I wasn't leaving, but he was right. "Might just be more logical to stay, don't you think?"

"Pegged me as a woman of logic, did you?" I leaned into him just enough for him to know it wasn't an accident.

"If I'm honest, I hope you're more a woman of spontaneity."

"Then you're in luck."

When the clock above our heads read 00:00, the club erupted. And I was kissing Oliver. Or Oliver was kissing me. I'm not sure how it happened, but I knew that as fireworks exploded above the city, as bells and whistles rattled the bar, and as my friends celebrated a few yards away, Oliver and I were kissing.

He tasted like oranges, and I had just wrapped my arms around his neck when I heard my roommates cheering.

"All right, then, Lucy!"

"Atta girl, Lu!"

"Oh my god!"

Oliver and I pulled away from each other, and I felt light-headed. He just chuckled at the sight of the six of them falling over each other and making kissy faces like a bunch of children, but I was hit with a wave of embarrassment.

What if someone tells Henry? I wasn't sure whether he would even mind, but it would be embarrassing nonetheless. Then again, why would anyone tell him? Kissing someone on New Year's Eve wasn't exactly groundbreaking, and Henry and I weren't exactly anything, so it didn't matter.

Still, that didn't stop his face from flashing across my mind. But fortunately, before it could linger for longer than a second, my roommates came barreling over to where Oliver and

I stood at the bar. Frankly, it seemed like the entire *club* came barreling over to where we at the bar. It was like everyone had been waiting for midnight to get another round, and we were swarmed by other partygoers in flashes of neon and metallic '80s-style ski clothes.

Oliver's hand slipped from mine as Raja pulled me into a hug, and by the time I finished hugging the rest of my room-mates and turned around, he was gone.

"Oliver?" I said, looking past Cal and Margot to where he had been standing, a space that had been swallowed entirely by the crowd.

"Where'd he go?" Raja asked, following my line of sight and stepping away from the rest of our roommates. "Did he leave?"

"He was just here," I said. I turned to face Raja and echoed her question, trying to suppress the oncoming embarrassment. "Did he leave?"

"I'm sure you just got separated by the crowd," she said, confidently enough that I could believe her. "Everyone just flocked to the bar for another drink, or they're all running around hugging and kissing and celebrating. It's a madhouse in here." She looked around for effect and I did the same, taking in the crowd and secretly still scanning for Oliver.

"You're probably right," I said eventually.

"I'm definitely right. Now, come on." She grabbed my elbow and led me back toward the group. As I took a step back in their direction, my phone vibrated in my pocket. Figuring it was a text from my mother, I pulled it out to check.

> Happy New Year's, Lucy. Hope you're having a great night, wherever you lot ended up. Looking forward to seeing what this year will bring. And looking forward to seeing you next month when I get home. Xx

I stared at my phone like an idiot, then shoved it back into my pocket and rejoined my friends. If I was going to answer that, this wasn't the time. I'd made it this far into the night without thinking of him for more than a second at a time, and I wasn't going to start now.

"How is it possible you were the one who got a midnight snog?" Liv teased as soon as I was back in earshot. "You didn't even want one."

"I'll snog ya, Liv, if that's what yer looking for." Finn slung an arm around her shoulders, more brotherly than romantic.

"Ew, Finn," she said, pushing him off.

"Sorry, am I not as fit as Lucy's bloke? We can't all look like a young Idris Elba, can we?"

"All right, all right, enough," I said. "He's not 'Lucy's' anything. We are never going to see him or speak of this again, okay?"

"Oh, now she's shy."

"Bugger off, Jan."

"Right, then. It's already ancient history, Lucy." Cal offered a warm smile, and everyone else settled down and followed his lead.

"Right, sorted," Finn said, pretending to zipper his lips shut.

When the midnight chaos settled into the quiet blank slate that is the start of a new year, we made our way home. The streets were teeming with other drunken partygoers stumbling around arm in arm, shouting resolutions at the top of their lungs.

"Let's do that when we get home," I said before contemplating whether I actually meant it.

"Scream our resolutions to strangers on the street?" Jan asked.

"No, just make them, I mean. Let's all set at least one goal for the new year before we go to sleep tonight, then try to stick to them like proper adults."

"Can we make a frozen pizza or something while we do it? I'm famished," Finn said.

"When has anyone ever said no to frozen pizza?"

"I knew I liked you, Lucy."

We decided to change out of our ski clothes before gathering in the kitchen, which gave me time to grab pens and paper for our final weekend activity. If we were going to do this, we were going to do this right.

"What is this, school?" Finn asked as I distributed the materials.

"Finn, I find it hard to believe you ever touched pen *or* paper in school."

"I take back what I said about liking you, you know."

"Liar."

"Get on with it, then, would ya?" Jan said, spinning his pen like a drumstick.

"Okay, okay. So everyone is going to write their resolution on their slip of paper, then we're going to fold them up and put them in this little box." From behind my back, I produced a box that I'd found in a corner of my studio. "Then someday, once we all accomplish them, we'll have a ceremonial burning of the papers."

"You know if there's fire, I'm in," Jan said.

"And what if we don't accomplish them?" Margot asked.

"Would be quite embarrassing, wouldn't it?" Cal said.

"For you, maybe. Nobody ever really sticks to these things, do they?"

"Margot, would it kill you to just be optimistic? Maybe you never stick to yours because you have that attitude," Raja said, always coming to the rescue.

"And besides," I added, "this is supposed to hold us accountable. Cal's right. It would be embarrassing to be the only one with a paper left in the box."

"Should we loop in Henry? Even though he isn't here, it feels weird leaving him out of something significant." Finn already has his phone out, which made me think it was less of a question and more of an announcement.

"Well, if he wanted to be part of this, he'd be here, wouldn't he?" Six pairs of eyes shot in my direction, and I immediately knew how I sounded. "But yeah, I mean, I guess you're right. Shoot him a text, then," I said, trying to recover. "Now get to work."

The silence in the kitchen meant everyone was taking the assignment seriously, which was likely just the magic of Warehouse Weekend. When we were all together, we just dove into each other's ideas, no matter how ridiculous.

As we finished writing, Finn's phone made a noise. I held my breath, petrified that he'd read Henry's resolution out loud.

"He said he'll fill one out when he's home in February, so his can also be private," Finn announced. I exhaled, feeling silly for being nervous in the first place. Surely his paper would say something about finding a new place to live and making advancements in his career, nothing we didn't already know, so I wasn't quite sure what he needed to be so private about.

We took turns tossing our crumpled papers into the box, which I then closed and stashed above the refrigerator for safekeeping. "Is everyone's initial on the outside so we know whose is whose?" I received six nods of confirmation. "Good. Now it's official. We have a new set of goals for the new year, and we have a system to keep us all accountable."

"This house loves a system," Raja said.

"It's the only way to get eight people to cooperate on anything," Cal said. "Without our systems, we'd be quite a mess."

"We already are quite a mess," Liv slurred.

"But in the best way," I said.

"Here we go, getting sappy around the holidays."

"Margot, we've been over this. Stop pretending you don't love us. Literally no one believes you," Jan said.

"Yeah, yeah."

"I don't know about the rest of you, but I'm knackered," Cal said through a yawn. "Thanks for a great weekend, Lucy. Happy New Year, everyone."

We followed suit, bidding each other a Happy New Year as we passed around a bottle of ibuprofen. Raja and I were the last two lingering in the kitchen.

"What'd you write?" she asked once everyone else had left.

"If I tell you, it won't come true."

"It isn't a birthday wish, you nut. Goals don't work like that."

"Fine. I'll tell you if you tell me. Deal?"

"Duh."

"I wrote that I want to be promoted at the shop. I'm not even sure to what, since the business is so small, but I'd like more responsibility. Renee claims she doesn't want to burden me with the difficult stuff that happens behind the scenes, but I know I can handle it. And that I want to start taking on bigger events, even if it means I'm working on them alone." Raja slung her arm around my shoulders and pulled me in for a hug, and a blush flared across my cheeks. "Oh, stop."

"I'm really proud of you, Lu."

"I haven't even done anything yet."

"But you've set a goal, and that's sometimes the hardest part. And it's good to see you putting yourself out there."

"Perhaps I should've written that, too. It's about time I was a bit more of a chancer, I think."

"You know I'll always support a little risk-taking."

"You're a really good friend, Raj, you know that?"

"Of course I do." She beamed at me, and I couldn't help but laugh at her.

"You're crazy. What'd you write?"

"That I want to graduate in the spring with honors, obviously, then find a job at a Big Four consulting firm. I know I mentioned it last night like it was nothing, but it's really everything."

"I'm proud of you, too, Raj. You make school look so easy sometimes, but I know how hard you work. It's going to pay off in a big way."

"Hope so."

"Know so."

We pulled each other into another side hug, nuzzling our heads together. We'd both been so busy lately, the quiet moments we'd had together this weekend had really been a treat.

"Cheers to you," I whispered.

"Cheers to me."

We said good night and made our way to our rooms, giggling under our breath as we passed Liv's room's open door and empty bed, knowing she'd gone to cuddle Finn.

I was hoping sleep would find me a bit easier, but there was something to be said for staring at the ceiling long after everyone else has gone to sleep, contemplating what might lie ahead with little regard for what might have already happened.

If I was going to stick to my goal, I would have to focus. I would have to take risks. I would have to put myself out there and make it happen. And I would have to avoid wasting my time on Henry in the process. He had his goals, I had mine—they were not compatible, and that didn't matter anymore. It was a new year.

February

"Luce, come see this," Renee said, beckoning me toward where she stood at the front of the shop. She was prone to getting distracted watching the street from beyond the giant windows, and this morning was no different. "Looks like something's finally moving in across the way, doesn't it?"

I followed her gaze, clocking a few men and women in suits in the doorway opposite ours. The space had been up for sale for some time, and we'd been worried about what might end up there and how it would impact our business.

"Huh," I said, trying to catch a glimpse of anything that might give them away. "What do we think it is?"

"Something posh, probably. Everything seems so trendy these days. No one is interested in family businesses or shopping small anymore." It was a gloomy thought for an otherwise nice day, but I couldn't disagree with her, could I? She was onto something, whether we wanted to accept it or not.

"For what might be the first time ever," I said, "I hope you're wrong." We both laughed, but it didn't sound particularly genuine. "Maybe we'll get lucky and it'll help our business instead."

"Girls can dream, can't they?" she said. We shared a sigh, neither having much else to say.

"Are you sure you don't need help?" Renee asked, clapping

her hands together and redirecting our attention back to the studio. We both spun on our heels, turning our backs to the suits.

"For the millionth time, it's sorted," I said, holding my hands out to frame my work like I was the host of a game show. It was a sort of wedding arch, similar to a huppah, underneath which a couple would be married this afternoon. It only needed to be transported down the block to a nearby garden, but I couldn't relax until it had gotten there in one piece.

"It really is remarkable," Renee said, joining me in admiring it. Dusk-colored daphnes crowded the curves, folding over blush quinces and bright white crocuses. I wondered if anyone involved in the wedding knew this combination symbolized new beginnings and immortality, and whether that mattered to them nearly as much as it mattered to me. "I knew you had it in you, Luce," she continued, "but this is really something."

"I told you I could handle it," I said. About a month ago, after a few awkward conversations and some uncharacteristically pushy behavior on my end, Renee had agreed to let me try my hand at a wedding. Reluctant at first, she'd caved only after I presented her with a full plan of how I was going to create the arrangements on my own. The bride and groom were friends of friends of hers, and the wedding would be quite a small affair in the park, needing only the arch, a few centerpieces, and some arrangements to line the aisle.

"I knew you could," she said. "I just wasn't sure if I—or the shop—could." She sank into a chair, her eyes still trained on the arch.

"February has been promising for us, hasn't it? What with Valentine's Day this week, I feel like we've been churning out pieces faster than usual. Or at least I hope we are, with the overtime we've been putting in."

"I'm getting too old to be putting in these kinds of hours, pet." She tried to laugh, but it came out dry and cold. She must have seen the worry in my face, because she continued before I could say anything. "But I'll do what I have to do. We both will, until we don't have to anymore. And you're right. Valentine's Day has been a bit of a blessing, and we should be thankful for that."

"If you'll trust me with more of this stuff, these small weddings and whatever else we can find, I promise I can boost our income. And we haven't raised our prices in years, so we can afford a bit of an uptick. Nothing crazy that would drive our customers away, but just enough to bridge some gaps. Keep up with the bigger retailers." I didn't mean to deliver a full pitch just now in the studio, but since the new year, I'd been determined to be more vocal about my ideas.

"You have quite the vision for this business, don't you?" She lowered her glasses, and I spun my rings on my fingers to avoid eye contact and channel my nervous energy.

"Let's just see how this wedding goes," she said before I had a chance to say anything at all. "Do you need help getting the rest of the pieces there?"

"Nope," I said. "That's sorted, too. Carla is coming to help me load the truck, and the groom's brother is coming to collect the arch." I smiled, trying to look excited instead of triumphant.

"You just have it all figured out, don't you, Miss Bernstein?"

"I try."

"I've taught you well."

"There's no denying that," I agreed. "Now it's my turn to shoo you out of the shop. Didn't you say you had Valentine's Day plans today?"

"Ah, yes. With my grandchildren. My husband and I aren't

celebrating until Tuesday, so we're taking the little ones to-day to give my daughter some time for a little romance of her own."

"Lucky girls. What's on the agenda? Baking cookies? Bundling up and teaching them to tend the garden? Guessing which chocolates are which without looking at the bottom of the box?"

"Am I that predictable?" She laughed, but a real one this time. Her hair tumbled into her eyes, and her bangles clanged against each other as she reached up to re-pin the rogue curls.

"Not quite predictable," I said, searching for the right word. "Reliable. And it sounds like a lovely weekend."

"You're going to get out of here at some point, too, aren't you?"

"Yes, yes, just after I see this off."

"What's on the agenda for Warehouse Weekend?"

"Who knows. It's Margot's weekend, so it really could be anything. All we know is we're supposed to be ready to leave tonight by six thirty, in clothing that gives us 'full range of motion.'"

"Oh my. And Margot is the one who was broken up with last year? Still hasn't recovered?"

"Yep," I confirmed. "That's the one. You'd think we wouldn't be doing anything Valentine's-related, but I have a secret theory that she's a closet romantic. Not quite sure what to expect."

"And Henry will be home this time, hm? What is there to expect from him?"

"Do we have to go there?"

"You know the answer to that."

I moaned, sinking onto a stool beside her. "We've hardly spoken since he bailed on New Year's. I've really only heard from him in the group text, which I guess makes sense, because we haven't had much to say to each other otherwise."

"Are you looking forward to seeing him?"

"I shouldn't be."

"That's not what I asked."

"Must you be so tough?"

"I wouldn't have to be if you'd just be honest," she said, noticeably gentler than before.

"Of course I'm looking forward to seeing him," I conceded after a patient moment of silence. "Which makes me so stupid, I know. I just can't stop thinking about him. Even when I was kissing someone else on New Year's Eve, I was thinking about him. And I don't want to be, because it's complicated, but I can't help it."

"That sounds like the opposite of stupid to me. Go easy on yourself, Luce. It's a tricky situation."

"Easier said than done."

"And don't think you're getting off without talking about that New Year's kiss," she said. "I'm only sparing you now because you're emotional. But we will be revisiting this."

"Don't you have to get going?"

She waved me off like I'd done to her a thousand times, then gathered her things and left to go collect her grandkids. Carla would be at the shop any minute, which meant I would be able to leave soon and head into whatever was happening at home.

I was sure Henry was back already, but I planned to avoid seeing him until we were all together for whatever we were doing tonight. That way, any interaction we had would be around the rest of the roommates, so it would have to be pretty platonic.

It was silly to be frustrated with him for missing New Year's.

I knew that. But knowing it didn't stop me from feeling it anyway. And it definitely didn't stop the lingering guilt I felt for kissing someone in his absence, either.

I waited at the shop until I received word that the arch had arrived in one piece, at which point I unclenched my teeth and released my shoulders from my ears. According to Carla, everything looked wonderful, and both families were pleased. I resisted the temptation to text Renee and gloat, but I was over the moon.

I was one tiny step closer to burning my New Year's resolution, and it was only February. Maybe I was a woman of my word after all.

By the time I got home, I had only a few minutes to change and shove half a sandwich in my mouth before it was time to go. I figured a vintage crewneck sweatshirt from a vacation to Canada gave me enough "range of motion," and it didn't look half bad with a pair of boyfriend jeans and high-top trainers. Not that it mattered, because I had no one to impress.

"All right, Mar. What are the big romantic Valentine's plans for this weekend? We're dying to know," Finn was prying when I got downstairs to join the rest of the lot in the foyer.

"Patience, grasshopper," Margot replied. "Do we have everyone?"

"We do now," Henry said from the stairs, jogging down to join us. He was leaner than he'd been last time I saw him, which made the angles of his jaw so sharp, I was surprised it didn't cut through his skin.

He flopped down right next to me on the couch like this was something we did every day.

"No welcome back?" he whispered.

"Hi," I said, barely glancing in his direction. Fortunately,

Margot started talking again before I was expected to say anything else.

"Right, now that everyone's here, here are the plans: tonight, axe throwing, and tomorrow, charcuterie-making class."

A painful silence settled over us as we collectively tried to make sense of tomorrow's plans. Axe throwing made sense. It was cool and trendy and appropriately violent for a Valentine's weekend planned by the heartbroken. But charcuterie?

"I have a coupon from when Ella and I went there last year and I don't want it to go to waste," she mumbled almost inaudibly, seeming to sense our collective surprise.

"Well, you know I'm all in on that," Cal said.

"Me too," Finn added. "Can't quite say no to meat and cheese. Or throwing giant knives, for that matter."

I knew the boys were being genuine, but there was a sense of pity in their tones that I never thought would be directed at Margot. Her mouth was set in a hard line, but there was a softness in her eyes that I wasn't sure was always there. This must have been a tough weekend for her. We'd have to make the best of it.

"Well done, Mar. This is the perfect way for a bunch of single people to spend Valentine's Day weekend," Liv said. She hated being single, but she was being a good sport.

"Hey, don't lump me in with you lot," Cal said, palms raised.

"Are you even going home to see your bird for Valentine's Day?" Finn asked. "Because from the looks of ya right now, you're pretty single to us."

"I'm going next weekend, if you must know. Not that it's between anyone other than me and Isla, but you're a nosy bunch. Besides, I was just there not that long ago."

"You were?" a handful of us said at the same time.

"How did we not notice?" I asked.

"He's hardly ever home, anyway, and he's so quiet when he is. Makes sense he just slips out and we're none the wiser," Finn said. "Sneaky bastard."

"Wind up Henry for not being home if you wanna get at someone," Cal said. "I'm here plenty."

"I'm here now, aren't I?" Henry said defensively.

"But is it against your will?" Margot asked, squinting her eyes in a challenge.

Henry crossed his heart with his index finger. "Quite the opposite, promise. Two months was a long time away. I missed you lot, you know. Was eager to get home."

"Is Henry Baker getting sentimental about being away? Does he secretly love London after all?" Liv was joking, but I was dying to know the answer.

"Is teasing all we get for trying to say a nice thing in this flat?" Henry asked. "Besides, it isn't about the city at all."

"So it's about us, then," Jan said, waggling his eyebrows. The ring in the right one bobbed up and down, catching the light.

"Just about wanting my own bed for a minute, that's all."

"Boooo," we said together, an unrelenting chorus.

"Are we ready to head out, then?" Margot's voice cut through the cacophony. "Everyone's getting edgy, and it isn't cute. Let's throw axes and relieve some Valentine's-related tension, yeah?" We could always count on Mar to shut it down when we got carried away, but this time, I was disappointed. If it wasn't about London for Henry, what *was* it about? Surely not just sleeping in his own bed, right? It was hardly more than a flimsy mattress on an old pallet.

"More than ready," Henry said, swiping his camera and his wallet from the counter, clearly ready to be done with the conversation. "Let's do this."

The more I felt myself overthinking his return, the more it sounded like throwing axes would do me some good.

The inside of the place was crowded, packed with other anti–Valentine's Day parties not unlike our own, plus a few awkward couples on dates and families who looked a bit lost. Margot settled our reservation, and we grabbed a few pitchers of beer before heading to our stall.

"Let's do an update before we start," Henry said. "I've a feeling once the axes start flying, we're going to forget to catch up." We nodded in agreement, and he poured beer into plastic cups as we gave our updates.

"The manager of the show I've been working on signed me to another contract," Margot said. "I know it doesn't mean much to you all, but it means I'll get to do another period piece, and I'm guaranteed another eighteen months of work on the production."

"It does mean a lot to us, Mar," Henry said. "That's really impressive." The rest of us agreed, and we all raised our glasses. "I like when we start with good news. What else do we have?"

"Winter conferences are done," Liv offered.

"We will definitely drink to that," Raja said. We knew how much stress that had been putting on Liv, so it was nice to hear it was in the rearview.

"I did a wedding," I said. "I mean, a really small wedding. It was nothing, really. But bigger than a bouquet or an arrangement for the lobby of a retirement home."

"Why is everyone downplaying their successes?" Henry asked. "Lucy, that is also amazing. I know that's been important to you, so I'm glad to see it's working out."

"It's not the only thing Lucy's gotten up to." Finn snickered.

"Finn," I said through clenched teeth.

"Oh?" Henry said. "What else is there, then?"

"Nothing, truly," I said. "Not the slightest clue what Finn's on about."

I shot Finn a look, begging him to stop, but he was either too tipsy or too careless to listen. "Come on, Luce. You'd have to be daft to forget a kiss like that."

I wanted nothing more than to bury my head in my hands and stay like that until Henry left again. Why couldn't Finn ever just keep his mouth shut?

"A kiss, huh?" Henry mused, though I'm certain he wasn't enjoying the thought.

"It was midnight on New Year's and he was a stranger and it didn't matter. You can say whatever you want, but it's ancient history."

"A stranger, hm?"

"A really hot one," Liv added.

"Okay, thank you, everyone! That's about enough of that." My face was burning, begging for this to be over. Henry clucked his tongue and leaned back against the wall, mulling it over. I willed the floor to drop out from underneath me, but no luck.

"What about you, Hen?" Raja asked, saving me. "What's your update?"

He rubbed the back of his neck for a moment before he started speaking. "Aye, nothing quite as exciting as Lucy, apparently. Copenhagen breezed right by because I was so busy, but I did enjoy the bits I got to see of the city. The festival in Zurich was really grand, though," he said. "Cool to shoot something that size, and my photos made it into the local papers and magazines, so that was a nice bonus. Then I left directly for Brussels, where I spent the past few weeks. I found the architecture to be the most inspiring there, with the old gothic buildings and the pastel facades and whatever else, so perhaps we're onto something."

"But still, you missed us terribly and wanted to come home," Liv said, resting her chin on her hand.

Henry smiled, but it didn't reach his eyes. "Something like that. But still, I'm off again next week, so don't get used to it."

"Where to next?" Margot asked.

"Amsterdam. And judging by how much I fancied Brussels, I think it'll be promising. My brother has a friend who lives there and swears by it, so we'll see how it goes. If we're lucky, maybe I'll find a home there."

The look in his eyes made him seem keener than ever to do exactly that, and I hoped it wasn't because I'd kissed someone while he was gone. Then I kicked myself immediately for thinking me kissing anyone had any impact on his soul-searching journey.

Then I stopped to wonder if it had any impact on *mine*. If Henry could be so prepared to embrace change, why couldn't I?

"Good for you, mate," Cal said eventually, clapping him on the shoulder. "Keep it up."

"Cheers."

We all raised a cup, then took a few gulps, preparing for the task ahead. Or washing down the horrible taste left by yet another reminder that Henry wasn't staying. Or maybe that was just me.

"So what's the deal here?" Jan asked, nodding toward the target. "Imagine someone we hate and picture their face on the bull's-eye?"

"That's one way to do it," Cal laughed.

"That's the only way to do it, as far as I'm concerned," Margot said.

"Then lead the way." Jan handed her an axe, which looked enormous and heavy in her tiny hands.

She stepped up to the line, heaved the axe behind her head,

and threw it at the target. Before we could even register the throw, we were looking at a bull's-eye. We stood in silence, watching the axe reverberating in the wood, searching for something to say.

"Bloody hell," Henry said eventually.

Margot turned back to us, a grin plastered across her face. "Not bad, huh?" she said.

"Have you done this before?" Jan asked, pretending to back out of her way like she was dangerous.

"Not once. It was all the strategy, really. Pick someone's face, aim, throw."

"I wouldn't want to be that person," Jan said. "And not just because she had to date you."

"How do you know it wasn't *your* face?"

That shut him up and sent the rest of us into a fit of hysterical laughter. It was good to see Margot making light of the weekend, and I supposed it wouldn't kill me to do the same. Who would have ever thought Margot could teach me a thing or two about levity?

"All right, Lucy, you're on," Finn said, handing off the axe.

"This thing weighs a ton," I said, struggling to lift it. "How'd you make it look so easy?"

"The strategy," Margot, Jan, and Finn said at the same time.

"Come on, Lu. You can do it." Raja smiled at me, flicking a quick glance in Henry's direction.

"Think about someone who's really pissed you off lately," Liv said. "Get really mad, then take a deep breath and toss."

I stepped up to the line, feeling the smooth wood of the axe handle in my hands. I knew that how I felt about Henry didn't come close to how Margot felt about Ella, but it fueled the fire all the same.

Perhaps my frustration wasn't even with Henry at all, but

with myself. I was the one who went back on my word and got involved when I had said I wouldn't, and let myself develop feelings for someone I could never be with without it ending in heartache and more disappointment. It made me want to pull my hair out.

On the count of three, I raised the axe over my head and threw it as hard as I could. The throw was terrible, and the axe stuck in the wall a foot from the bull's-eye, but I didn't care. It was more cathartic than I'd expected, and I felt substantially lighter. My roommates whooped and cheered as I turned back to face them, despite the rubbish throw, and I took a small bow, relishing the burst of adrenaline.

"Note to self," Finn said. "If there's ever an intruder in the flat, don't rely on Lucy to defend anyone."

"Hey!" I protested. "I threw it hard, though, didn't I?"

"Yeah, that's true. So I guess if we ever need to hit someone a meter to the left of the intruder, then we can rely on you," Henry said.

"Let's see you do it, then," I said, retrieving the axe and thrusting it into his hand. I wasn't sure yet if our banter was friendly.

"Watch and learn."

With what looked like a gentle flick of his wrist, he launched the axe twice as hard as I had, missing the bull's-eye by an inch.

"Must you be good at everything?" Liv moaned. "It looked like you didn't even try."

"Still not as good as I am," Margot said. "But not half bad."

"You were right about the strategy," he said to Margot, sliding onto a stool beside me.

"Picturing my face, then?" I asked, hoping a joke would conceal my discomfort. Was he mad about the kiss? Did I want him to be?

"Don't tell me you didn't do the same," he said, nudging my knee with his. "You've been cold to me since I got home, haven't ya?"

"I haven't been cold," I lied. "We're good." My smile probably looked as fake as it felt, but it was the best I could do.

"You're a terrible liar."

"I know."

"Talk later, then. Maybe you should get a few more tosses in before we do that, though. I think it'll go better for me if you do."

I tried to glare at him, but it came off as more of a smirk. *Goddamn it.* If I wanted to stand my ground, I'd have to keep reminding myself this would crash and burn. I would repeat it like a mantra if I had to. *Don't get involved. It'll end in heartache. Don't get involved. Don't get involved.*

The more we threw, the better we got, and the lighter we felt. We were hitting the target somewhat consistently, even me and Liv, and we'd lost count of how many times we'd refreshed the beer pitchers. Margot might have been heartbroken, but she planned one hell of a Valentine's weekend.

When we were thoroughly exhausted and our time was up, we finished our drinks and shuffled home via the Underground in the freezing cold, desperate to get back inside.

"Great start, Mar," Raja said through a yawn as we filed out of the elevator. "What time tomorrow?"

"Meet down here at eleven? That'll give us plenty of time to get over there."

"Better get to bed, then, Jan," Henry said. "I know getting up before noon is a challenge for ya."

"Just as much as not being a wanker is a challenge for you, I'm sure." Jan grinned.

"Piss off," Henry said.

"What happened to tuning it out?" I said. "That's how we're supposed to handle the endless banter, isn't it? You should take your own advice, you know."

He faked a gasp. "Using my own words against me, are we? That's cold, Lucy. I didn't expect that from you."

"Maybe you don't know me as well as you think you do," I said.

"Is this a lovers' quarrel?" Raja asked.

"No," Henry and I said at the same time.

"Really believable," Raja said. I cut my eyes to Henry, hoping to read his expression, but it was hard with his thumbnail between his teeth and his gaze set a solid foot higher than my head. "So, on that note, I'm off to bed." The others followed her upstairs, mumbling half-hearted good nights on their way up.

"I should do the same," I said, trying to get out of what I knew was about to happen.

Hen grabbed my arm, then immediately let it go. "Luce, we gotta talk this out."

"I'm not sure there's much to say."

"So you haven't been avoiding being alone with me since I got home? You haven't been shaking off my attempts to chat? I've been reading this all wrong?"

I was backed into a corner, and I couldn't lie my way out.

"You're right," I groaned. Time to be honest. "But can you blame me? I mean, the way we left off in December made me think . . . I don't know. Made me think maybe getting involved wasn't such a mistake. But then it was so easy for you to just bail on our plans and stay on the road over New Year's, so I just felt a bit silly for having thought otherwise."

"It wasn't easy for me to bail, Lucy. I had a great work

opportunity, which I thought you would understand, since you're working for the same thing, but maybe I was wrong. I had to take it, but it wasn't easy."

"Don't patronize me, Hen. I know what was at stake. But that doesn't make it less disappointing that we didn't see you for two months."

"You didn't seem to mind when you were kissing someone else on New Year's, did you?" he said. I knew that was going to come back up, but I hadn't expected it to be thrown in my face like that.

"You weren't here," I said, trying to keep my voice level. "And you and I weren't anything. And he was a meaningless stranger, so I'm not even sure why we're talking about it at all."

"I was just surprised, that's all," he said, backing off a bit. "I didn't expect that."

"I have a life that goes on when you aren't here, you know. Not that kissing strange men is part of it, but there's a lot that goes on in the weeks you're away. Especially when you're away for two months at a time."

"You're right. It's easy to forget sometimes, when I'm wrapped up in my own thing in another country, you know?"

"I can imagine."

"He really meant nothing? You're not going to start dating him or anything, are you?"

"Henry, please." I almost laughed. "It was a midnight kiss for New Year's and nothing else. Just in the spirit of the holiday." Was that true? And if I had wanted to date him, who was Hen to stop me? I pushed the thought from my brain before it slipped out of my mouth. "Besides, had you been here, I might have been kissing someone else at midnight."

He huffed a frustrated sigh, and the sound of it made me wish I could feel his breath against my skin.

"Please," he said. "Don't make me any more jealous than I already am."

"I didn't have you pegged as the jealous type," I said, secretly relishing the confession.

"Of course I am," he said. "You think I want to imagine someone else kissing you? On a major holiday, with fireworks and champagne?" Whatever kind of chat I thought we were going to have had not prepared me for this. "I'm sorry I wasn't there."

"You didn't have a choice," I said. "I get it."

"But I'm here now."

"You keep saying that, but it doesn't mean much of anything when it's only for a day or two," I said. The scale was tipping from flattery to frustration, and I couldn't stop it. "And who knows when you're going to stop coming home at all, right?"

He tousled his hair in the way he did when he was frustrated, and I forced myself not to pay attention to his hands. "Right," he said eventually. "I suppose that is still the plan."

"So where does that leave me?" I asked, though we both knew the answer. "I think I deserve a little more than just waiting around, Henry. I spend so much time waiting for you to come home, but really all I'm doing is waiting for you to leave for good, and I'm not big into either, if I'm honest."

He considered this, and I fought the urge to apologize. I wasn't sorry; I was just feeling uncomfortable in the silence following confrontation. But it was something that needed to be said, and I didn't intend to take it back.

"You're right," he said eventually. "You do deserve more. And I wish I could give it to you, Luce. I wish I could see more of you when I was on the road. Hell, I wish I could see more of the whole lot of you when I was on the road."

"So, you do miss us," I said.

"Some of you more than others." His smile was a bit tired, but it sent a warm current coursing through me. How did he keep pulling me back in like this? Had I no self-control?

We stood in a heavy silence, closer than we needed to be, but I resisted the urge to reach out and touch him.

"If only, though, right?" I said. "There's no way you could come home more than once a month, is there?"

"Sadly, no. Even getting these few days off every month is a stretch."

"Then why do you do it?"

"For my sanity. I need a home base, even if I'm hardly ever here."

"And you still want that home base to be London, even if it has nothing to offer?"

"Old habits die hard, I guess. And like I said, I miss you lot."

If he couldn't come home more and had no plans to stop traveling, there was still nowhere for us to go from here. But the more he said he missed me while he was away, the more I wanted to make this work while he was home.

"We miss you, too," I said, but it came out hardly more than a whisper. I wasn't really speaking for everyone, which I hoped he understood. "Which makes me want to make the most of our time together when you're home."

"But?"

"But I know it'll end with one of us getting hurt. And that one is probably me."

"I wouldn't hurt you, Lucy."

If there was a self-control Olympics, I would take home the gold. He pushed his hair behind his ears and out of his eyes, revealing the deep green they turned in the dark. He really sounded like he meant what he was saying, which was perhaps the hardest part.

"Not on purpose, maybe," I said. "But the circumstances aren't promising, are they?"

"How do we know if we haven't even tried?"

"What is there to try?"

"We could try long distance, Luce. We'll have no idea what we're missing if we don't give it a proper shot. We might not be able to see each other in person, but we do have phones and computers and video calls. It's not such a crazy idea."

I hummed, considering the proposal. If we couldn't stay away from each other, maybe it was time to stop trying.

"At least give us a chance to decide we hate each other," he continued, and I exhaled, relieved to be on lighter ground.

"We think hating each other is going to be the problem, then, do we?" I asked.

"Absolutely. In fact, I think the distance might not be the problem at all. I think it might be your terrible personality."

"Henry!"

"It's so easy to wind you up, I can't resist," he laughed.

"You're cruel."

"Aye, so maybe it's *my* terrible personality that'll be our downfall."

"I suppose there's only one way to find out," I said.

"Is that a yes?"

"Don't make me regret this."

He beamed at me in the dark, and heat spread across my skin. He was right; it wasn't such a crazy idea. And besides, after Renee agreed to let me do the wedding, I owed it to myself to go after what I wanted, even if I couldn't be sure of the outcome.

"WELCOME, CLASS. Please grab an apron, find a seat wherever you're comfortable, and prepare to get started." Our instructor for today, retired chef and cookbook author Hillary Adams, stood at the front of the room and ushered us in. She had a warmth you'd expected more in a yoga teacher than an executive chef.

"Two to a bench, please," she instructed as we shuffled to the back. Of course, before I could even glance in Raja's direction, I was interrupted by Henry, directly in my line of sight.

"Partners?"

I glanced around the room and clocked that Raja was paired with Liv, Cal with Margot, and Finn with Jan. For the sake of Margot and our anti-Valentine's weekend, I didn't want to do anything romantic, but I would've been lying if I said I wasn't happy Henry and I ended up together anyway.

"Partners," I confirmed.

"Off to a good start." He smiled, and led me to our bench with a hand on my lower back. It was a good thing he couldn't see my face, because I was sure my grin looked as goofy as it felt.

I slipped my apron over my head when we arrived, fumbling with the strings.

"Turn around," Henry said. When I did, he pulled the apron strings tight against my back, tying a quick bow with deft hands. I could feel him towering over me, and I savored the feeling of his hands against my body, even if it was only the brush of his knuckles.

"All right, then. Are we ready to get started?" Chef Adams pulled me back to Earth, and we all nodded to confirm our readiness. I shot a glance over at Margot to see how she was holding up. She smiled at something Cal whispered, and it reminded me platonic love was just as important as romantic love.

Chef Adams introduced us to the variety of meats and

cheeses spread across our benches. We sampled hard cheeses, soft, spicy, goat's-milk, nondairy, stinky, crumbly, creamy, and sharp to our heart's content before learning where to place them on our boards.

"Taste this one," Henry said, offering me a cube of something the color of marigolds. I opened my mouth, feeling his fingers against my lips and the salt of the cheese on my tongue.

"That's the spirit," Chef Adams said from behind us, making her rounds. I was so embarrassed, I nearly choked.

"Did you guys not get the memo that we were doing this ironically?" Finn laughed from his station. "For Margot," he whispered. "We all hate Valentine's Day, remember?"

"Of course," I said, scrambling. "We were, uh, just getting in the spirit of the irony."

"Someone teach this woman to tell a lie," Finn laughed. "Raja, she needs help."

"I do not," I protested.

"She needs more help than even I can give her," Raja said.

I scoffed at them both, returning to my bench and pretending to focus. I watched Chef Adams roll salami into roses, listened as she explained the importance of creating a meat "river" through the center of the board, and sipped my wine at a faster pace to soak up my embarrassment.

"My roses look like rocks," Henry whispered, trying to contribute something to the board, which was largely becoming my creation.

"Watch me," I said.

"Yes ma'am." He put his hands behind his back and studied my technique. "Have you considered doing meat floristry for a living instead? I'd pay good money for a bouquet of these roses instead of real ones."

"Good thinking, Hen. Maybe I'll throw my whole career

out the window to roll salami around a teacup for the rest of my life. Then I'd definitely be able to afford to leave the warehouse."

"You're planning on leaving the warehouse?"

I'd meant it as a joke, but his concern told me it had come out otherwise. "I mean, it was only supposed to be temporary. I was hoping to find a way to make more money at the shop or find a flat cheaper than my last one that I could afford alone." Truthfully, I hadn't even thought about leaving the warehouse since I moved in, but that had been the plan once, hadn't it?

"Bummer," he said.

Finn and Jan's fighting interrupted the moment, which was probably for the best.

"I think they look good over there," Finn was saying, gesturing to a pile of almonds in the corner of the board.

"You don't know the first thing about nuts, Finny," Jan said.

"Ew, Jan," Liv said from her bench. "Can't you two just behave like adults?"

"If we wanted to die of boredom, maybe," Jan shot back.

Margot and Cal seemed to be the only two totally focused, and their board was beautiful as a result. Bright slices of oranges cut through the otherwise neutral colors, and sprigs of fresh herbs gave the board quite a professional look. Cal was spooning chutney into a ramekin, and Margot was arranging crackers in a fan around the dish.

"Why don't you two ever do this at home?" Raja asked, also admiring their handiwork. "I'd pay for something that looked that good."

"Would you pay *us*?" Margot asked.

"Well, no, but—"

"Then that's why we don't do it." Margot smiled. "Quite a bit of work to be doing it for free, isn't it?"

"But think about how happy you would make us," I added. "Isn't that worth more than a couple quid, anyway?"

"You've been hanging around Liv too much," Margot said. "You've gone soft on us, Lucy."

"Oh, please. She was soft before she got here," Raja said. I offered just a shrug in response, looking to Liv in solidarity. Being soft wasn't so bad. Sometimes.

"I like that about you," Henry said.

"What?"

"That you're soft. You aren't shy about your feelings. Good or bad. It's refreshing. Most people aren't like that."

I wanted to crawl under the table. I'd never been good at hiding how I felt, about anything, really, which had made for a lot of big, public, embarrassing feelings in my childhood.

"Refreshing, is it?" I said. "All the other girls you've dated have been, what? Too cold? Emotionally stunted? Unavailable?"

He laughed, which made me relieved. We've never addressed our dating histories, so I felt a bit bold going there.

"Nonexistent," he said. "Not much of a relationship guy, what with traveling always on the horizon. Haven't even been in a proper one, really. And my own emotional range hasn't always been, er, developed." It was his turn to stare at his shoes, which surprised me.

"You mean to tell me you haven't always been so straight-forward?"

"Far from it," he said. "Still not even close, really. I might seem bold at the beginning, but if I'm honest, I have a habit of speaking before I'm finished thinking, which might also be the reason I haven't dated much." He occupied his hands arranging a pile of grapes between two wedges of cheese, so I did the same. If, for once, he didn't want to be making extremely intense eye contact, I could allow him that. "Not to say I haven't been on dates," he added, "because of course I have. Just nothing serious."

"Never?" I asked. I couldn't believe someone like Henry had never been in a serious relationship.

"Nope," he said. "Bit embarrassing, now that I say it out loud."

"Nothing to be embarrassed about. Relationships aren't always all they're cracked up to be."

"You've a long line of ex-lads, then?"

It was my turn to laugh. "Hardly. A couple of insignificant relationships over the years, nothing worth remembering. No one who put in the proper effort, really."

"Wankers, then," he said. "The whole lot of them." I might have also been embarrassed by my confession, but his smile changed my mind. "More wine?"

I swallowed what was left in my glass and held it out to him. "Please."

By the time the class was finished, we'd all eaten way more than we'd gotten onto the boards. The few couples in front of us took turns whispering to each other and turning around to give us dirty looks, but we were having too much fun to care. We took our boards to high-top tables in a room across the hall to eat, mingle, and keep drinking. While everyone else was looking lovingly into each other's eyes, clinking champagne flutes, and holding hands across their tables, we were throwing grapes into each other's mouths, putting on fake posh accents, and reminiscing loudly on Valentine's past.

"Remember that bloke Jan brought home last year?" Raja said. "The one who burned a hole in the couch with a cigarette?"

"Better than the one you brought home the year before, who left to go see his ex in the middle of the night," Jan said.

"We've really brought home some winners, huh?" Raja laughed. How she laughed these things off instead of getting upset about them, I would never understand.

"Cal, what'd you get Isla for Valentine's Day?" Liv asked. "Anything good?"

Cal sighed, then looked around and leaned in to speak. "I can't believe I'm telling you this," he said, "especially because I know none of you can keep a secret, but here goes." He pulled out his phone and scrolled through his photos, then turned the screen to us. We stared in silence at a picture of a glittering diamond ring in a suede box.

"Oh my god," I whispered.

"Bloody hell," Henry said from behind me.

"You're proposing?" Liv said, suppressing a squeal.

"Our Callum is becoming a man, is he?" Jan said.

"All right, all right, settle down." Cal put his phone back in his pocket. "But yes, I am proposing. We've been together since school, and I can't imagine my future with anyone else, so it's time." It was the most I'd ever heard Cal say about Isla, and it might have just been the wine, but my eyes felt a bit misty.

"Does that mean you're leaving us, too?" Liv asked, and Cal laughed, a warm, hoarse laugh.

"It's about bloody time I leave you lot. Isla and I have been doing long distance for too long, so we've started looking at properties near her parents' farm in Scotland. It's looking like we're going to sign by the end of the summer, then I'm on my way out."

Liv threw her arms around him first, then the rest of us piled on. He was arguably the least affectionate person in the house, second only to Margot, but he let us have our moment.

"I can't believe everyone's leaving," Liv said.

"Let's relax," Finn said, gesturing to himself. "Not everyone."

"Let me rephrase. I can't believe all the good blokes are leaving," she said.

Finn opened his mouth to argue, then decided against it. "They are good blokes," he said. "Better than the two of us, anyway." He looked to Jan, who nodded in agreement. "Can't argue with that."

"Are you leaving before Henry, then?" Margot asked Cal.

"Depends on when Henry leaves," Cal said, raising a thick brow.

Henry waved him off, taking a large sip of wine. Too large, as far as I was concerned. "Must we talk about leaving?" he said. "Can't we just enjoy the time we have as flatmates without always worrying about when we'll no longer be flatmates?" He appeared to be addressing the group, but a small part of me worried that this was directed at me. He smiled and raised a glass, which softened the edge in his voice. "To Margot, for another great Warehouse Weekend," he said.

"Yeah, this was a great idea, Mar," Jan said, downing the last of his wine. "Thanks for this."

"That's how you know Jan's three sheets to the wind," Raja laughed. "He's actually complimenting Margot."

"Is it so hard to believe that sometimes I can be nice?" he asked.

"Yes," we all said at once.

"You're all arseholes."

"Learned from the best," Liv said, flashing him a smile.

"How romantic," Finn said, pretending to swoon. Liv stuck a finger down her throat, and Jan flipped his middle one up at Liv.

"We should be getting out of here," Henry laughed. "We're running the risk of making a scene."

"But that means Warehouse Weekend is over," Raja whined.

"There will always be another," he said, pulling her in for a quick hug. "At least for now. And isn't next month your turn?"

"Damn right, it is. And we're all in for a treat. As soon as I figure out the plan, that is."

"Well, I'll be counting the minutes," he said.

"Can't stay away from us, can ya?"

"Bugger off," he said, and she sighed.

"I love these weekends."

"Amen to that," Finn added from behind us as we filed out.

Henry threw a quick smile in my direction, then looked back at Finn. "Almost makes you wish we had more of them, doesn't it?"

What a tease.

March

I'd been at work since what felt like the crack of dawn and the bell above the door had sung its song into the silence fewer than a handful of times. I was running out of scraps to fidget with, and the collection of posies I'd been mindlessly arranging all morning was no closer to being purchased than it was when I started. With spring on the horizon and Mother's Day less than a week away, we'd doubled our order of silky pastel hyacinths, and I'd watched as they wilted little by little, confined by the Lotus's walls.

"Why don't you take off?" Renee said, ambling into the studio and clocking me sweeping dead leaves from the workbench into my hands.

"What?" I almost never left the shop early, especially this time of the year.

"Let's not kid ourselves, pet," she said. "You've not had much to do all day, and it doesn't seem like that's to change before we close." We both looked around the empty shop, and I could have sworn I heard crickets chirping in the distance.

"What's—"

"It just must be those bigger retailers, that's all," Renee said before I could finish asking what was going on. We both knew nothing good would come of asking, but I couldn't help myself. "Now get going," she said. "You don't want to be late."

I called Henry on my walk to the station, hoping for some comfort before I settled into the weekend. My watch told me he should still be home getting ready before heading to a gig, so I wasn't surprised when he picked up.

"Hey, you," he said, and the sound of his voice washed over me like a warm tide. "Are you out early or calling from the studio?" We were getting to know each other's schedules, given how frequently we worked around them for phone calls and FaceTimes, but I was still sort of embarrassed to tell him the truth.

"Out early," I mumbled, "but not for good reason. We had, like, no business today. Or all this week, really."

"Even though Mother's Day is coming up?" he asked. I knew his ask was genuine, but it felt like salt in a wound.

"Yep," I confirmed. "I'm really worried about the shop, Hen."

"Do you think Renee would tell you if you had something to worry about? Maybe it's just a slow month. All shops must have a lull sometimes, don't they?" He made good points, and I tried to believe them.

"I don't know if she would," I said. "She might be too proud."

"Sounds like someone else I know," he said. Silence passed between us, and I was sure he could hear my smile over the phone. "I miss you, Luce."

"I miss you, too." I sighed. I was getting so used to his voice over the phone that I was beginning to worry I'd forgotten what it sounded like in person.

"I love the traveling," he continued, "but for our sake, I wish it didn't always have to be like this. I would love to assuage your worries with a cheese toastie and a Pimm's right about now," he said, and if it weren't for the levity in his voice, I might have cried outside the tube station like an idiot.

"That sounds like heaven," I said. "I'm counting the minutes until we can do just that."

"I'll be back in London before we know it," he said.

We hung up just before I ducked into the station. I turned our conversation over and over in my mind, picturing him alone in his apartment, sitting in the window he usually called from, the one he kept telling me I would love. I mulled over his words, his tone, the aching space between us.

What if we didn't have to wait until he was back in London after all?

"YOU'RE DOING WHAT?" Raja picked her head up from her pile of homework and stared at me like I'd just announced I was joining the circus.

"Going to Amsterdam," I said. "To surprise Henry." Raja pretended to clear her ears of imaginary water, and I tried to remain calm. "Stop it," I said. "You're making it weird. It's not a big deal. We were on the phone before, saying we missed each other, and then I saw an ad for discounted Ryanair flights, which felt like fate, so here we are."

"Are you sure the ad was fate and not just data mining?" she laughed. "Besides, it's a huge deal. You're surprising him in a foreign country! That's intense, Lu."

"It is not," I said, but I wasn't sure I meant it. "It's not, right? Please tell me this isn't a huge mistake. It sounded more casual in my head when I bought the ticket, but now saying it out loud to you, I sound insane, and I just—"

"Sit down," she said, halting my spiral. I obeyed, kicking my shoes off and jumping onto her bed. "Breathe. I didn't mean it in a bad way. And I don't think you're insane. I was just surprised you guys are already at this point in the relationship, that's all."

"I know, I know, it's early. Things have just been going so well with long distance. We've really been clicking, Raj. And it's hard just over the phone." I knew I was rambling, but I couldn't stop myself. I wanted her to be on my side. "And didn't you notice last month that he'd been missing home?" I continued. "He even said to me he wished he could see us more when he was on the road. So I'm doing him a favor, really," I said. That was one way to justify it.

"I'm really glad things have been going so well," she said. "I can't even remember the last time you were this happy because of a man."

"But?"

She sighed. "Has anything changed about the future? I don't mean to ruin your plans, Lu, but you still don't want the same things, right? You have no plans to leave London or the shop, and he has no plans to stay, so what's next?"

"Well, if the shop closes, maybe I will leave London after all," I said. "Not that he's asked me to, or that we've even been on a proper date in real life, so I know I'm getting ahead of myself, but I'm just saying."

"Quit being so morbid. The shop isn't closing."

"What if it does? And what if I spend all this time clinging to a job in London that might not even exist this time next year?"

"Do you really think that's what's going to happen? Or are you being dramatic because you're nervous?"

"Both?" I said. "I don't know, Raj. Renee seems more stressed than ever, especially since we didn't get the boost we'd been expecting from Mother's Day."

"Have you talked to her about it?"

"I don't want to hurt her feelings, and I don't want to worry her, either. Every time I bring it up, she seems to take personal offense. But that isn't even the point right now," I said, too stressed about my impending trip to also be stressed about work. "Either way, what I'm saying is, there might be hope for me and Henry. He might change his mind about being chained to the road, and I might not have a choice but to find a new job, which could be anywhere."

Henry and I had spent the past few weeks on video calls, sometimes late into the night, telling stories from our childhoods and laughing and staring at each other and sharing experiences from our jobs and moaning about the weather and asking more questions like *What's your favorite color?* and *What are you most afraid of?*

"If I was a flower, what kind of flower would I be?" he'd asked one night over the phone, long after we should have been asleep.

"Hollyhock," I'd said after a minute, wondering if that was the right choice. "They represent ambition, so I think they suit you." He'd hummed, considering my response, but said nothing right away. "Or maybe tiger lily," I'd continued. "It represents confidence and pride, which also suits you."

"Do you think those qualities are going to be my downfall?" he'd asked, catching me off guard. His voice had been quiet, and I didn't think that was because he was tired.

"Do you?" I'd asked, trying to proceed with caution.

"Sometimes," he'd said, even softer this time. "For us, anyway."

Us. The word had floated between Amsterdam and London like a heavy cloud. It wasn't the first time we'd addressed ourselves as an item, but the word still brought warmth and chills to my spine in equal measure.

"I think they'll only be your downfall if you let them," I'd said, hoping that was adequate. I hadn't been sure whether he was saying he anticipated our downfall or whether he was self-aware enough to prevent it, and I'd been too afraid to ask.

"Then I'll try my hardest not to," he'd said, and I had just barely heard a smile return to his voice. I'd wondered if he could hear mine, too.

"What kind of flower would I be?" I'd asked. He'd laughed, and I'd thought it was because he knew nothing about flowers, making it a silly question.

"Lucy," he'd said eventually, "you're the whole bloody bouquet."

The memory raised the hair on my arms the same way it had that night. I wasn't insane, was I? I hadn't dreamed these moments. They'd happened, and they meant something. Or they represented a very promising connection, at the very least.

"Just . . . be open-minded," Raja said, ripping me from my reverie and bringing me back to the moment, which wasn't entirely pleasant. "If you have no idea how things are to work out, it's important to consider all the possibilities, you know?"

"You don't think it's going to work, do you?"

"You're always putting words in my mouth. I didn't say that."

"But you implied it."

"I just, I think you should be careful," she said, her tone a dangerous mingling of concern and pity. "Sometimes we're too close to our own stuff to see how it's going to play out, and it might help to get some perspective. And from mine, I just want to make sure you aren't putting too much pressure on a new relationship, that's all."

"I get it," I said. "And thank you. I know I can be stubborn, but I appreciate that you're always looking out for me."

"That's what best friends are for."

"I feel good about this one, Raj. I know it seems like we're moving fast, but honestly, I kind of feel like it's been the opposite. It's been so much back-and-forth and talking around and around, but we haven't really spent quality time together, and I think we need to at this stage, to see if this is going to work. And maybe he'll think I'm fun and spontaneous, surprising him in a foreign country."

Raja laughed. "You've really thought this through, haven't you?"

"Of course I have. I'm not *that* spontaneous."

"How do you know where he's staying?"

"I had to mail him that memory card for his camera he left at home, remember? He sent me the address for the Airbnb then."

"Sneaky girl," Raja said, clucking her tongue. "And how do you know he's going to be home when you get there?"

"Because we have a FaceTime date scheduled for then, duh." I smiled at her, proud of myself for actually being able to pull this off, even if she thought it was crazy.

"I'm impressed." She leaned back in her chair, crossing her arms. "So, what are you bringing to wear?"

We spent the next half hour combing through our wardrobes, trying to put together outfits that were equal parts hot and casual, which was harder than we'd anticipated. By the time my luggage was packed, it was nearly time for me to head to the airport.

"Wish me luck," I said from Raja's doorway.

"Bonne chance." She blew me a kiss, which I pretended to catch and plant on my cheek. "It's going to be great," she said. "I can't wait to hear all about it. And talk to Renee when you get home, will you? While you're busy sorting things?"

"One thing at a time," I said. "But yes, yes, I will."

"Cheers to you," she called after me as I left her room.

"Cheers to me," I called back from down the stairs.

The flight was hardly longer than an hour, so I passed the time by pretending to read and listening to a playlist Henry had made me on Spotify. Most of the songs were flower-themed, save for a few from bands he'd shot that he thought I would like, and all of the songs made me think of him.

Beads of sweat gathered on the back of my neck like dew, but I knew if I pulled my curls into a bun, there would be no getting them back down when I landed, and the last thing I wanted was to get off the plane looking like a sewer rat.

The longer I stared longingly out the plane window, however, the more I realized looking like a sewer rat was the least of my problems. This could be totally insane. He could be someone who hates surprises. I wondered if there were any flights directly back to London at the exact time I was getting off this one. I could disappear from Amsterdam and he would be none the wiser.

Then I thought back to Renee, and her endless encouragement to "be generous" with my heart. She was fearless in her passions, and she'd be so disappointed if she knew I was constantly second-guessing myself. She would have thought she taught me nothing, and that couldn't be further from the truth.

And I thought about Raja. Even though she might not have fully approved of the execution of this plan, she'd been pushing me to be more of a chancer since college, so I owed it to us both to at least try it on for size.

And I thought again about Henry. The wistful way he'd talked about wishing to see us more when he was on the road, how I'd hoped when he said "you lot," he wasn't really talking about the *whole* lot, how he sent me pictures of things from his travels that reminded him of me.

What I didn't think of was how much he was loving Amsterdam and how quickly it was becoming a contender for his new home.

At the sound of the landing gear, I swiped my face with a wet wipe and added another flick of mascara for good measure. Plus, a little extra deodorant. It might have been cold outside, but stress made me sweat.

I dislodged my backpack from the overhead compartment and took a deep breath, imagining myself as the main character of a film. I shrugged my shoulders for effect, then headed off to find a ride to his apartment.

I texted him from the back of a cab.

Looking forward to our FaceTime. Still on for 7:30, right? xx

He texted back almost immediately.

Yeah

That's it? Just "yeah"? He wasn't usually a one-word texter, which meant I wasn't off to a hot start. I struggled to remind myself to breathe. Maybe he was just busy and only had a second to be on his phone. Maybe he meant to type more but sent the text too soon. Or maybe he just had nothing else to say, which was also a perfectly viable option. I needed to calm down.

I dropped my phone in my lap and leaned my head against the cab window, watching Amsterdam flit by. The tall, narrow buildings nestled against each other like an antique Christmas village, and the golden light of the sunset bounced off hundreds of windows. Tulip season was just beginning, and I admired the tenacity of the few colorful buds I saw dotting window boxes and small gardens along the sidewalk. They were still tightly closed, but preparing to bloom—just waiting for their time.

For the tulips, that was easy. It was the only way they knew how to survive. And I knew it was silly to envy a flower, but sometimes it was impossible not to envy a thing that knew itself so well: how to grow, how to turn its face to the sun, how to become the best version of itself, over and over again. And when they were fickle, those times we didn't give them enough water or sun or love, we couldn't blame the flowers. We just gave them grace and care and promised to treat them better next time.

Flowers were universally valued and accepted as emblems of love, comfort, celebration. They were beautiful even when they withered and died. We pressed their petals between the pages of old books, soaked them in glossy resin and hung them around our necks, buried them in wax and burned those candles late into the night. Sometimes, on long days in the shop, I dreamed about what it would be like if we gave the same grace and love to each other.

The cab wound through the last few narrow, cobbled streets to Henry's Airbnb, then deposited me on the sidewalk outside. I thanked the driver, paid the fare, and stood facing the door like a statue.

"Is this the right address?" the driver asked through the open window.

"Yes, er, just not ready to go inside yet." That was more information than he needed, but my nerves had returned and turned me into an idiot.

"Very well. Have a good night."

"You too."

I decided to take a walk around the block before the big

surprise. I needed a minute to gather myself, and I was a bit carsick from the ride over. The cool, damp air was making my hair frizzier by the minute, but it was too refreshing for me to care. I let it settle on my face, breathing deeply and counting my steps as I walked.

I'd timed it almost perfectly—we were set to FaceTime in five minutes. It was now or never. I texted him with jittery hands, circling back toward the house.

Hey, check the front door before we jump on FaceTime. I had something delivered. X

Thankfully, he returned my text right away.

You what?

Was he in a mood? I pulled my coat tighter around my body, feeling more insecure the longer I stood there. Had Raja been right?

Before I could even text back, the heavy door flung open. And there he was.

His lips parted just slightly, surprise sitting in the open space. It was probably only a split second before he registered me on the doorstep, but it felt like hours.

"Luce," he said with so little enthusiasm, my name practically disappeared on the gentle breeze.

"Surprise," I said. "Is this a bad time, or . . ." I gestured to his raggedy house clothes and his tousled hair, which was long enough now to need to be brushed, though from the look of it, I wasn't sure he knew that.

"No, no, I'm just shocked, that's all. Come in. What are

you doing here?" He smiled the breathless kind of smile that seemed to take a few minutes to settle in.

"Last time you were home, you were saying you wished you could see more of me while you were on the road, so I figured I'd bring me to you." We were still standing in the entryway, blinking at each other with the door open.

"Wow," he said, rubbing the back of his neck. "What a surprise."

"Is everything okay?" I asked. This was crazy. I knew that now. Standing there in the foyer of his temporary Dutch home, both of us with our arms by our sides, I had a feeling I'd made a huge mistake.

"Yes, absolutely fine," he said. "It's great to see you." He pulled me into a hug so brief I hardly had a chance to lift my arms to hug him back. He closed the door behind us, gesturing up the stairs to another heavy wooden door.

"I'm flat three here," he said, fumbling with a key. "Feels like a bit of a step up from two at home, doesn't it?" He swung the door open and I stared into his apartment, letting my eyes adjust to his new place. Three large windows lined the far wall, a single pillow sat on the sofa, and a small collection of takeaway containers cluttered the kitchen counter.

"Sorry, er, I wasn't expecting company." He swept the containers into the trash and pushed his hair behind his ears. "Can I get you anything? I don't have much to offer, just, er, a few beers, and I can pull together beans on toast? I don't have a toaster, but I can do it fine in a pan."

"A beer and beans on toast sounds perfect," I said, partially because he seemed stressed and I was trying to be agreeable since, and partially because I had been so nervous, I hadn't eaten all day, and I was starving.

"Roger that." He got to work in the kitchen with his back to me, hardly saying a word. What the hell was going on? If I were back in London, we'd be FaceTiming right now, probably laughing and flirting and having a ton of things to say. Now, radio silence.

Maybe we were both just out of practice seeing each other in person. That was probably it. We'd spent the past few weeks getting comfortable behind our phone screens, so now it was hard to readjust to being together in real life.

"It's a nice place," I said, if only to fill the silence.

"Thanks. You still had the address from when you mailed me the memory card, I'm assuming?"

"Yes," I admitted. "I hope that was okay, but if it isn't, I can just—"

"No, no," he said, interrupting my rambling. "I'm glad you're here." He handed me a beer and returned to the stove without another word. *Liar.*

I must have adjusted my position on the sofa a thousand times, trying to find a way to feel less out of place.

"All right?" he asked.

"Fine, thanks." Was this how the weekend was going to go? We were just going to say "all right?" back and forth until I left? I decided to make a move, fearful of what would happen if I didn't.

I took a large swig for a little liquid courage, then joined him at the stove. I resisted the temptation to put my hand in his back pocket, since this wasn't a teen movie and I was an adult woman in the real world, so I rested my hand on his back instead, pretending to examine the toast in the pan.

"Looks good," I said.

He became stiff as a board, relaxing only when I removed my fingertips from his spine.

"Good," he said. "How long did you plan on staying?"

Before I got here? The whole weekend. But now, since you're acting like I'm an alien, just long enough to book a flight home, I wanted to say.

"Just a day or two," I said instead, shooting for casual. "Look, Hen, if I'm imposing, I can find a place to stay instead." I put my beer down and took a step or two in the direction of the door, hoping he'd stop me before I got there.

"No, you just got here," he said, as if the only reason for me to stay was so I didn't have to get back on a plane right away. I raised an eyebrow, urging him to continue. "Why don't we go out for a drink?" He slid the food onto my plate and leaned on the counter, watching me. "Eat first, take your time, then we'll go."

Okay, we were going to get a drink. That was promising. We were warming up. I wasn't yet ready to move my suitcase from the doorway, but maybe by the time we got home from the pub, I could at least unpack a toothbrush.

We walked just around the corner from his apartment, down the tree-lined sidewalk, under streetlights just beginning to cast their glow. If the air between us weren't so dense, it might have been a beautiful March evening.

An emerald vinyl awning with faded gold lettering hung above the door, which Henry held open as he ushered me in. The bar was a bit more upscale than the pubs we frequented at home, and I looked down at my sneakers, feeling a bit out of place.

He signaled the bartender as soon as we sat down, hardly giving me a second to flip through the cocktail menu.

"Uh, a gin and tonic, please," I said, sensing the bartender's impatience.

"Two, please," Henry said. I spun my stool to face him, but

he kept his eyes trained on the bartender. Maybe this wasn't as promising as I'd thought.

"Can we also have the tab, please?" Henry said when the bartender delivered the drinks.

"Got a hot date?" I asked.

"I do, thanks for asking." His chuckle when I snapped my head in his direction loosened the knot in my chest, if only for a minute. I rolled my eyes, trying something that resembled normalcy.

He settled the tab, then drank half his drink in one sip, eyes closed. I opened my mouth to ask what was really going on, but he beat me to the punch.

"Listen, Luce," he started, meeting my eyes for what might have been the first time since I arrived.

"Oh god. I never should have come. That's what you're going to say, right? That this was a mistake?" I wanted to get it out before he did. If there was any chance to save face, at least I would be the one to call this what it was.

"It wasn't a mistake," he said. He looked up to the ceiling like the proper way to reject someone was scrawled across the beams. "It's just . . ." He spun his watch around on his wrist, and I wanted to shake him.

Spit it out, Henry. At this rate, I might die of embarrassment before you say anything at all.

"I'm just really surprised, that's all," he said eventually. "I didn't expect this, and I'm sometimes overwhelmed by surprises. Especially when I'm on the road, because I'm always alone. Which is sometimes lonely, but other times, like when I'm really getting into a groove somewhere, it's easier to work uninterrupted." He rubbed his hand along the back of his neck before dropping it into his lap and twisting it with the other.

"'Uninterrupted'?" I said. "Had I known all I'd be was an

interruption, I could definitely have saved a couple quid on the plane tickets. I'm sorry I invaded your space, Hen. I just thought since you had a month of space at a time, you might welcome a day or two of company, but clearly I was wrong."

"I didn't mean it like that."

"That phrase is familiar to you, isn't it?" I asked. "I take it you also 'didn't mean it' when you said you missed me when you were traveling and you wished you could see me more?"

"It's not that I didn't mean it, Lucy. I sometimes just speak before I'm finished thinking. I don't always consider the implications of what I'm saying when I say things in the moment. It's a bad trait, I know."

"Which is why you haven't had many relationships," I said, remembering our conversation from Valentine's Day. "Did you need more time? Should I have given you more space to think?"

"It's nothing you did, Lucy. None of this is your fault. I just, I didn't handle the surprise well. I don't have a lot of relationship experience. I'm not perfect."

"Of course you aren't, Hen. Nobody is, and I never expected that from you. I just keep thinking I know you better than I actually do, and then something like this totally throws me for a loop and I feel like such an idiot." There wasn't enough gin in the world to save me now, but I was really wishing he hadn't settled the tab.

"You aren't an idiot, Lucy. Far from it."

"Then how do you explain this mistake?"

"It wasn't a mistake. It was just, er, a miscommunication. Or rather a lack of communication? I just wish you'd told me, Luce. I'm not exactly keen on surprises, and we could have just talked about it beforehand."

Now I wished he'd never spoken at all. If he'd turned me away at the door and I'd gotten right back into a cab to the airport, it would have been less painful. I released a dry, joyless laugh.

"You're right," I conceded. "And so was Raja. She was worried this was too soon, and I tried to convince her it wasn't. But had I waited, I might have learned that you didn't like surprises and wouldn't be here now, totally embarrassing myself." The string of words tumbled out all at once, and I hated how it sounded.

"No need to be embarrassed," he said.

"Amsterdam is home for you, then?" I asked before he could say anything else that resembled pity.

"What?"

"Earlier, you said you were really finding your groove, before I interrupted. Do you plan on moving here?" His plans had seemed so distant before, when he couldn't see himself in any of the places he'd traveled, but now they seemed as real as the tears burning behind my eyes.

"Aye," he said. "I haven't made any plans yet, but it's the place I've felt most myself since I started this journey. My head is clearer here, and I've been able to do a lot of thinking. Mostly about home, what that means, what I want from it, that sort of thing. The answers I've been looking for might not be as clear as I thought they were, which is why I wanted to do this alone."

I nodded, but I wasn't really hearing anything beyond that he was moving and that he didn't want me here.

"So now what?" I asked, though I wasn't sure I could stomach the answer.

"Well, I'm to finish out the year as planned, so I'll still be traveling on schedule until July."

His failure to mention us told me all I needed to know. This was over before it had even started.

"Right, then," I said. "Well, I should be getting back to London."

"It's late, Luce. Why don't you at least stay the night?"

"I can get a hotel near the airport if I can't find a late flight. If you could just let me up to the flat to get my things, I'll be gone like I was never here."

"Lucy," he said, reaching for my hand.

"It's fine, really. I'd just like to get my things and go." The tears I'd been battling since this conversation began were threatening to come crashing from my eyes, and I wanted to be far away from him when they did.

"That's it, then?"

"It's pretty clear that's it, don't you think?" He said nothing, only stared at me with bloodshot eyes that made his irises look like emeralds nestled in clay. "I just feel like we're never quite on the same page," I continued, "and it's a bit daft to keep trying. Besides, now I've made a fool of myself, and I'd like to walk away with at least a shred of dignity."

"I'm sorry, I didn't mean to—"

"Please don't," I said. The last thing I needed was pity, and I was certain I'd burst into tears if he was nice to me right now.

We got my luggage and called a cab in silence, though I was sure my heartbeat was loud enough that all of Amsterdam could hear it. By some miracle, the last flight out of Amsterdam to London was at eleven, and there were still a few open seats. I booked it from the cab, then said a silent thank-you to a higher power I wasn't even sure I believed in.

Coming home tonight, I texted Raja. **Not keen on talking about it yet, but I'll be home some time after midnight. Don't wait up. Just thought I'd let you know.**

A pair of tears finally broke free as I waited for her response, imagining what I would tell her whenever I *was* keen on talking about it. A few more tears followed, then a few more, until I was fully crying in the back of a cab in a foreign country.

Are you safe? she asked.

Yes, yes. In a cab on the way to the airport. Gutted, but unharmed otherwise.

I'll wait up, she said. And I know I don't have to, so don't bother arguing. And we don't have to talk right away. But I'll be here. Safe flight, Lu. xx

That made me cry even harder. I couldn't wait to get home to her and out of Amsterdam and far away from Henry. I was never good at being rejected, but it hurt even more after coming all this way. After I'd misread every sign. After I'd learned he was right when he told me he sometimes has a habit of saying things he doesn't mean. After I'd taken a chance, put myself out there, convinced myself taking a risk was a good idea. After I'd tried to be more generous with my heart.

It was a good thing I hadn't written anything about putting myself out there on my New Year's resolution, because at this rate, I was never going to do it again, ever.

"OH, GOOD. YOU'RE HERE," Renee said before she was even fully through the door.

"I'm always here."

"Right, I wanted to talk to you about something." She dropped her purse onto the counter, followed by her coat, then motioned for me to have a seat.

"What's going on? You're making me nervous."

"No, no, nothing like that." She waved her hand like she was brushing away my concern, then readjusted her glasses so she could see me better. "The Renaissance asked us to do the window displays for their opening." I searched for something to say, but she continued before I had a chance. "And I think we should do it."

"The Renaissance?" I asked, making sure I'd heard her correctly.

Shortly after the morning Renee and I saw the suits and clipboards and handshakes across the street, it had been announced that the Renaissance, a posh new restaurant, would be taking over the space. Their chef was some hypercreative thirtysomething who was causing quite a stir in the restaurant industry, and the restaurant's facade was already making a bit of noise on our otherwise quiet street. In a line of unimposing beige storefronts with the occasional faded awning, its ruby-red entryway made it impossible to ignore.

"That's the one," Renee confirmed. "Apparently we were recommended to one of their designers, and since we're local, they want us to do the arrangements."

"Who would have recommended us?"

"Your guess is as good as mine, but I'm not quite sure that matters, does it? This is a huge opportunity, Lucy. And I've been thinking more about what you've been saying, and I think you're right. If we want to stay afloat, we have no choice but to do something like this."

"Don't say things you don't mean," I said, squinting at her. "Are we really doing this?"

"Well, you more so than me, I'd hoped. I mean, of course I'll be around to help, but I was hoping you'd take point on this one. I'm getting to be a bit of an old bag, so I'm not sure I'd accept this without you." She'd been making jokes lately about her age (which was usually my job), but since they seemed to be coming from a place of insecurity on her end, I tried to let them be. Surely she still had a few more years of floristry in her, right? She wasn't *that* old. "After the wedding," she continued, "I just figured—"

"Of course," I interrupted. "It'll be my honor."

"There's just a minor issue."

I raised an eyebrow, too nervous to ask.

"It's during this month's Warehouse Weekend," she said. "And I hate to ask you to work on the only weekend of the month you take off, and I know it's last minute, but I thought you'd want the opportunity."

"Oh, er, I—"

"I know you probably want to be home to see Henry, to maybe patch things up, but you've been wanting a chance like this, haven't you? I'd hate for you to throw it away for a boy, no matter how dreamy he might be."

I laughed aloud, though it quickly turned into a defeated sigh. "It's not that at all, actually. It's Raja's weekend, so I don't want to disappoint her. But as soon as she hears about the opportunity, I'm sure she'll be chuffed. And frankly, there's no patching anything up with Henry, and since I'm not sure I can face him just yet, this might be the perfect thing to let me avoid that. For this month, anyway."

Renee exhaled a sigh even more dramatic than my own. "Thank god," she laughed. "Because I already said yes and I don't think I could pull this off without you."

"Renee!" I said, joining in her laughter. "I guess it's a good thing you won't have to."

"Atta girl. Best get started planning, then. Not a ton of time on this one, I'm afraid."

"Consider it sorted."

"Well, that's good, since their designer is coming by this morning to discuss the plans."

I faked a gasp. "How'd you know I'd say yes?"

"A bit of wishful thinking and a bit more blind confidence. If you turned this down for a man, you wouldn't be the employee or the woman I thought you were."

She smoothed my hair and disappeared into the office, leaving me alone in the studio. I hadn't given her the full story of what had happened in Amsterdam in the hope of preserving some dignity, so she was still holding out hope that Henry and I might work things out. And for once, she was alone on that one.

I'd break the news that I'd be missing the weekend to the rest of my roommates when I got home, and I'd let someone else break the news to Henry. Not that he would mind. In fact, he'd probably be delighted not to see me. Not that it mattered.

Renee's words swirled around the back of my mind, and heat crept into my chest at the thought that I might have passed this up if Henry and I had been on good terms. Had he reduced me to the kind of woman who would let a man interfere with her career?

Certainly I wasn't using this opportunity just to avoid him. I couldn't have been that woman. I was prioritizing my career, which I had been hoping to advance for quite some time. This was good. Grand, even. Avoidance was merely a bonus.

I busied myself with an anniversary arrangement while I waited for the designer. The pinks and purples of fresh hyacinths signaled the oncoming spring, which seemed a lovely time for an anniversary. The client was an older gentleman, and I imagined the couple renewing their love every year along with the season. It was a beautiful, painful thought.

Floristry was difficult for a million reasons, but one of the worst parts was celebrating someone else's love life when your own was in the gutter. I would have to create this bouquet like

I hadn't just been mortified, hurt, and turned off from romance completely. I'd have to remind myself that sometimes it does work out, and that that is worth celebrating. Though I wasn't sure I believed it at all.

The cylindrical blooms sat high on firm stems, so I cut the canvas paper wrapping low enough for the flowers to be seen from all angles. Some bouquets needed to be snuggled in, protected from prying eyes and harsh elements, but this one demanded to be on display. These were some of the first vibrant colors of the season, and just because I didn't want to focus on a celebration of love didn't mean nobody else did.

The bell above the door interrupted my pity party, and I tied the last of the ribbons around the arrangement to refocus myself. Renee emerged from the office to greet the customer, and I wiped my hands on my apron and followed suit.

"Ah, here she is," Renee said when she saw me. "Lucy, this is Eve. The designer from the Renaissance." Eve was tall and slender, clad in a tweed blazer and a pair of slim trousers. She had cropped white-blond hair, which emphasized the perfect heart shape of her face. My curls looked even more unruly in comparison, and my apron hardly disguised my oversize cargo pants or my unintentionally distressed jumper.

"Pleased to meet you," I said, offering my hand.

"You as well."

"Come in, please." I gestured into the studio, which we both scanned for a clear place for her to sit. "Er, sorry, we don't usually do much consulting back here." I cleared a stool, and she pulled her blazer tighter around herself before sitting down.

"You come highly recommended, so I trust you have the experience for this project," she said.

"Certainly," I assured her, hoping she couldn't tell I was lying through my teeth. Maybe not the experience, but I did have the talent, and wasn't that what mattered? Besides, there were more pressing things at hand. "May I ask who recommended us, if you don't mind? We don't typically have clients in your industry, so I'm keen to know who made the suggestion."

"Oliver Burton, of course," she said. "The chef. He said he was an old friend of yours?"

It took a minute to sink in, but then it hit me like a punch to the gut. Bloody hell. It was Oliver. Oliver from New Year's. Oliver, whom I'd kissed in front of an entire party, including all my roommates, because I had assumed I would never see him again.

"Ah yes," I said once I'd gathered myself. "Of course."

How had he remembered this was where I worked? And surely he'd never seen any of my work, so how could he recommend me for his restaurant?

"Please, tell me your vision. I'll do everything in my power to bring it to life," I said.

"We're looking for something bright. Something eye-catching. Something brilliant. But familiar. We want people to feel at home with us, if their homes were a bit more posh and had an elite team of chefs and servers on at all times. We want colors that complement the red awning, maybe yellows or oranges, like a sunset. And nothing too big that it couldn't still be delicate. Can you do that?"

It was not surprising that she had such a list of demands. The opening was supposed to be rather extravagant, and she seemed like someone who was used to having her every need met. But that was quite a difficult balance to strike.

"Absolutely," I said, the wheels already beginning to turn.

"We want surprising, but consistent. Creative, but conventional."

"I'm thinking narcissus."

"Excuse me?"

"The flower," I said. "Narcissus. The daffodil. The contrast of the yellow against the red facade will give you that pop you're looking for, and since the flower is quite common, it'll give you a sense of familiarity, which makes it inspired for a restaurant window display."

She rested her manicured thumbnail between her teeth, staring at me. I was just about to tell her I took back everything I'd said when she clapped her hands together and stood up.

"I love it. Oliver was right about you."

"And what did he say, exactly?"

"That your passion drove your work, which is what made it brilliant. I've worked with quite a number of florists, but none who've understood our vision so quickly." I wasn't sure if my blush was the result of Oliver's compliment or hers, but I couldn't stop it either way. "I look forward to seeing how your plans come together. You'll send me an email of a finalized design, will you? And then I'll be back around a few days before the installment next weekend to see the progress."

This woman did not mess around. She was all business, and I needed to be the same. Which meant no thinking about Henry, or Oliver, really.

"Sounds brilliant," I said. "Thank you, Eve, for this opportunity. I'm very much looking forward to it."

"Thank Oliver," she said. "He insisted."

We shook hands and exchanged polite smiles on her way out, but it wasn't until she was out of sight that I could really exhale and let my smile take over my face. None of it made any sense. How could Oliver know I wasn't a terrible florist? Was he just trying to give me business since I had overshared about my job-security concerns at the bar? It couldn't be that he'd done all this to see me again, could it?

I physically shook the thoughts from my brain like they were a bug caught in my hair. None of it mattered. I had to focus. This had the potential to be a big break for the Lotus, and I had just established I wouldn't muck it up for a bloke. Oliver could join Henry offstage. No blokes. Only flowers.

The rest of my workday floated by on a daffodil-shaped cloud, and by the time I was ready to leave, I had come up with almost an entire plan for the opening. This was a chance to prove myself, and I was going to do it for me. And for Renee and Eve, who were intimidating and inspiring in equal measure. And for Oliver, but only because he'd given us the opportunity.

When I got home, I found Raja studying in the living room. She looked focused, but I couldn't resist interrupting.

"I have good news and bad news," I said. "Which do you want first?"

"The bad news, obviously."

"I'm not going to be around for this Warehouse Weekend, and I know it's yours, and I'm so, so sorry," I said, hoping I could roll right into the good news.

"Wow, Lu. You're not avoiding Henry, are you?"

"Okay, ouch," I said. "No, it's not because of that. He hasn't done anything to me. Except all the embarrassment and the rejection a few weeks ago, but I'm not quite keen on reliving that. I'm skipping because I got a massive work opportunity, and you'll never guess who recommended me for it."

"I'm listening," she said, closing her textbook and resting her chin on her hands.

"Oliver," I said. "From the party on New Year's, remember? He's the chef at that new restaurant that's going in across from the Lotus, and he requested I do the window displays for the opening."

"Bloody hell," she said. "Why didn't you say that from the beginning? I mean, I still don't love that you're missing my weekend, but this is big enough that I'll allow it." I rolled my eyes, and she continued. "So you're going to see him again."

"That's not the point," I said, though I got butterflies at the thought that she was probably right. "The point is, this is a huge break for the Lotus, and a huge opportunity for me to prove myself."

"Yeah, yeah, we already know you're brilliant and talented," she teased. "It's no surprise anyone would choose you, whether or not they've seen your work. But surely you'll run into each other if you're working together, right? And now that we're totally over Henry, maybe we can take Oliver seriously?"

"Slow down," I said. "Just because I'm over someone—which I'm not even sure I am, if I'm honest—doesn't mean I need to immediately pursue someone else. It was just a nice compliment that he recommended me, that's all."

"If you say so," she said. "But this better be the best opportunity of your career so far, if you're blowing us off for it."

"Why didn't you give Henry such a hard time when he skipped for work?"

"He's not my best friend, duh."

She had a point. "Thanks for understanding, Raj."

"Have you told Henry you're skipping?"

"Do I need to?" I asked. "Based on the way things ended a few weeks ago, I'm not sure it matters whether I'm around for the weekend. Now that we're over and he's just another flatmate, he'll find out with everyone else when I send a text to the group."

"But you'll still be around when you aren't working, right? Like, you might run into each other in the flat, yeah?"

"Yeah, I suppose so. I'll be gone all day that Saturday for the opening and I'm working most of Sunday, and I think I'm going to have dinner with my parents on Friday, so I suppose Saturday night is our only real risk. And if I play my cards right, I can make sure I'm home and in bed before you lot, and that way we won't run into each other at all."

"You've really thought this through, haven't you?"

"Just want to save face where I can. No need for us to see each other quite yet, so might as well avoid it altogether."

"Right, then. Well, I'm excited for you," she said. "I'll miss you while we're out and about tearing up the city, but I'm really proud of you for how hard you work. The Renaissance is very lucky."

"You're gonna make me cry," I said, wiping fake tears from my eyes.

"Oh, go scratch," she laughed. "I mean it."

"I know, and I love you for that. Thank you."

"Now go send that group text so I don't have to be the one who breaks the news when you don't show up. And do let me know when you see Oliver, will you?"

"Whatever you say," I said, leaving her to study.

Hours after everyone else responded to the group text with pleasantries and congratulations and we'll-miss-yous, Henry sent a text just to me.

> Quite bummed you're bailing—was hoping we could find time to have a chat while I was home.

I almost laughed out loud. What was there to chat about?

Not bailing, just seizing a work opportunity. I'm sure you can understand, I texted back.

Right, then. Well, best of luck. And congratulations on the opportunity, Lucy. I'm sure you're going to smash it. Hopefully we can find time for that chat soon.

I tossed my phone onto my bed, unwilling to continue the conversation. I had no interest in a chat. If he was just planning to reject me again, in our home country this time instead of a foreign one, I was even less interested in hearing it. And if by some stroke of madness he was trying to convince me he'd changed his mind, well, I had no interest in hearing that, either. I was moving on, and I was sure he was doing the same.

"Lucy, it's miraculous." Eve stared at the window display with her fingertips pressed to her lips. "How did you make a common flower so . . . so avant-garde? So New Age?"

The way she talked about flowers made me laugh, but I held it in so as not to offend. "Just a bit of creativity, that's all. I'm glad it suits your vision. Really, I had an easy canvas. The restaurant is beautiful."

"Only because you've made it so." A male voice floated over my shoulder, and I recognized it before I even turned around.

"Oliver," I said, laying eyes on him for the first time since our kiss.

"Lucy," he said. He leaned in and pressed his lips gently to my cheek, and it was not lost on me that the last time those lips touched my body, they had been pressed against my own. "After we got separated in the crowd after midnight and I hadn't gotten your number, I was worried I'd never see you again. I'm quite pleased you accepted the job." Raja had been right after all.

"How'd you know? To request me, I mean," I said, lowering my voice, even though Eve had stepped out of earshot, tend-ing to other business in the last hours before the opening. "I could have been a rubbish florist, and this would have been a massive mistake."

"Nothing about you could be rubbish," he said at full volume. "And besides, the way your face lit up when you talked about floristry would have made it impossible for you to be rubbish."

"And it had nothing to do with the fact that I mentioned I was worried the Lotus might be going under?"

"What's wrong with giving a little business to local vendors?"

"Everything, if it comes from a place of pity," I said, to which he chuckled.

"I can assure you, I haven't felt an ounce of pity. You're too strong a woman for me to pity."

"You hardly know me."

"I'd like to change that," he said. "What are you doing tonight, after the opening?"

"Oh, er, that's soon. Won't it be quite late by the time you're out of here?"

"I sometimes forget not everyone keeps chef's hours," he laughed. "What about tomorrow?"

"I have to work." Did I even want to be going on a date with Oliver? Was he even asking me on a date?

"Ah, another time, then."

He must have sensed I wasn't sold on a date just yet, and I had to applaud him for his intuition. "But soon," I said, fearful of losing the opportunity, in case I decided I did want it.

"You say the word. And thank you, Lucy. For this display. Eve is right, you know. It really is miraculous. Though I'm worried my food won't quite hold up to the promise this is making to our customers. But I suppose I should thank you again for motivating me to try."

"You are too kind," I said, fighting a blush. I was so pale, I wasn't sure I ever won that fight, but I owed it to my dignity to try. "Your food is the real reason they'll come. As the head chef, you're really the main attraction here. These are just flowers."

"We both know that isn't true."

He was right. To me, they weren't "just" anything. They were everything. And these particular flowers were going to help me unlock a future in commercial design, if the reporters sent to the restaurant for the opening took notice of them. And given the sheer size and abundance of the arrangements, it would be impossible not to.

"Why don't you join us for dinner?" he said. "It'll be a bit of a packed house, but we can certainly seat you at the bar."

I checked my watch, thinking about where my roommates might be right now. Raja was hoping I'd be able to meet them out somewhere, but I'd told her it wasn't likely. If they were on schedule, they'd be heading into a disco yoga class somewhere in Camden, which I wasn't booked for, so I figured dinner at the Renaissance wouldn't hurt.

"That sounds lovely," I said, then immediately glanced down at my dirt-stained apron. "I have to, er, go home and change."

"Take your time. We'll be waiting for you." He disappeared inside, and I could finally relax, knowing I probably wouldn't see him again for the rest of the night. He would be busy in the kitchen, and I would have a quiet dinner, then slip back into the apartment undetected.

Before I left to change, I stood for another moment and admired my creation. The yellow flowers were even brighter than they'd been in past years, and they looked electric climbing the facade and clinging to the overhang. Behind the windows, they tumbled over stacks of crooked plates, exploded from empty wine bottles, and filled the spaces in antique frames. It really was a work of art, if I did say so myself. All I needed was for a reporter to think so as well, and to print it with the review. No pressure.

By the time I returned, opening night was in full swing. The host was working double time to seat everyone crowding the doorway, and the kitchen staff was slinging plates at the speed of light. It was a perfectly choreographed dance, and I was thrilled to witness it.

I settled in at the bar, perusing the menu. It was the perfect balance of gourmet and familiar, validating the requests Eve had made for the display. There was no denying Oliver's creativity, and though I had yet to taste his food, I could understand why he was becoming such a sensation.

I ordered a Korean-inspired vegetarian stew and all but licked the bowl clean. Unfamiliar spices danced on the back of my tongue, but the stew still had all the warmth of my parents' home cooking. Oliver, too, was miraculous.

"Can I leave a note for the chef?" I asked the bartender. "Will you get it to him?"

"Ah, compliments?"

"Something like that." Before I lost this burst of confidence, I scrawled a note on a napkin:

Oliver,

Thank you for dinner—it was the loveliest meal I've had in a long time. Perhaps next time we share a meal, we can sit across the table from each other.

Xx Lucy

I scribbled my phone number on the bottom, then folded the napkin and passed it to the bartender, hoping he couldn't see the message.

"I'll pass it along as soon as I can," he said.

"Cheers."

I slipped from the stool and out of the restaurant, already tempted to check my phone for a text. If I was looking for something to occupy my mind and give me a glimpse of hope, this was already doing the trick.

April

"C al's gonna be down any minute," Raja said from the doorway of my studio. "Are you almost ready?"

"Just about," I said, putting the finishing touches on a practice arrangement I'd been working on. It was inspired by something a celebrity florist I followed on Instagram had posted, but Renee would've killed me if I tried it in the studio. She didn't seem to understand that being inspired by other artists didn't infringe on our creative integrity, so I had taken to experimenting at home instead.

"Are you actually invested in this project, or have you just been avoiding someone all morning?" Raja asked as she perched on a stool opposite my workbench.

"Raja, look at this thing," I said. "Does this look like I'm not invested?" We both admired the crescent-shaped arrangement of cerulean forget-me-nots and bright white anemones, secured to the frame with twinkling golden wires.

"Okay, fine," she conceded. "I can't argue with that. You're getting really good, you know. Have you tried bringing some of this stuff into the shop? Since you've had a bit of a surge in business since the opening, might it be a good time to get Renee on board for trying something new?"

"If I'm honest, Raj, I'm not sure I have time," I said. "The surge has been great for business, but Renee isn't working as fast as she used to, so I'm pulling a lot of extra weight. Which is great, because it's my job, and we're thrilled to have the business."

"Good thing those projects are increasing, then," Raja said. "You're too creative to keep doing what you've been doing all this time. Really, you need your own shop, Lu. So you can do your own thing."

A defensive knot crept up my throat. "I can do my own thing," I said. "Sometimes. And Renee's taught me nearly everything I know, so I can't go totally rogue. Besides, I did that wedding, remember? And the opening last month was huge."

"That's exactly what I'm saying, though. Look how much you thrive when you're on your own. I'd just love to see you be able to do more of that, which is why I think you should think about your own shop someday, that's all."

"And with what money am I supposed to do that, hm? The Lotus is hardly holding up financially and it's been around for nearly thirty years. I can't even afford my own flat, let alone my own shop. And besides, after everything Renee has done for me, I couldn't leave her like that." That didn't mean I hadn't dreamed about what it would be like to have my own place, but I left all that in a journal under my mattress. No sense in bringing it to light.

"I understand," Raja said, raising her hands in surrender. "I just hope you recognize your talent, that's all. I don't want you to ever waste a second of it because you're trying to please someone else."

For Raja, this was as easily said as done. She wouldn't hesitate to walk away from something if it wasn't suiting her. I, on the other hand, had a hard time even thinking about it.

"I reckon it's about time to go, then, isn't it?" I said, hoping to end the conversation.

"What about Henry?" Raja whispered, grabbing my arm. "I mean, is this going to be so weird? Last time he was home and you missed the weekend, didn't he want to, like, have a chat or whatever?"

"I've been so preoccupied I nearly forgot all about the chat," I said, surprising myself. "But I'm sure it was just to try to make amends, if only to absolve himself of the guilt of hurting me in Amsterdam. It's been well over a month now, though, and things between us were practically over before they started. We've both moved on." I sounded cooler than I felt, but maybe I could fake it till I made it.

"*You've* moved on." She snickered. "I'm not sure he can say the same."

"Let's not get ahead of ourselves. I've been on, like, five dates." Five incredible, swoon-worthy dates.

Oliver had texted immediately after the opening, and almost every day after that. We'd been out to a couple nice dinners and a swanky cocktail bar, and gone for a few lingering walks in the park. He was as clever as he was kind, and he did things like pull out my chair and pick up the tab and laugh at my jokes even when they were bad. It felt quite good to spend time with someone who actually made time for me.

"You're being more casual about this than I thought you'd be, you know. I thought you'd be a right mess seeing Henry, but you seem really good. I'm glad you're out the other side."

"I'm not sure whether that's a compliment," I said. "But I'm definitely on my way there." I was, wasn't I? And if I wasn't, I was going to have to find a way to be, and fast, if I didn't want this whole weekend to go to shit.

"Ah, my little Lu. Growing up right before my eyes."

"Piss off," I laughed. "You're no better at getting over crushes than I am. It's all a facade, as far as I'm concerned."

"That, my dear, is terribly offensive. And it's also the truth."

Almost as if he knew to save us from ourselves, Cal called us into the foyer. I braced myself for seeing Henry, then immediately tried to remind myself I didn't need bracing. Oliver's purpose wasn't to distract me from what had happened with Hen, but it was a welcome side effect. If I could stay ahead, keep the upper hand, I might make it through this weekend just fine.

Then I saw him. A familiar lump returned to my throat, and I had to swallow a few times to dislodge it. I had managed to avoid him last month, having gotten home and into bed before the rest of the lot the Saturday of the opening, but this weekend I was going to have to face him head-on. And the way a flush had returned to his skin with the spring and his bare forearms in a short-sleeve shirt threatened to make that quite difficult.

Our eyes met briefly and we exchanged a polite nod, and I stood behind him in the group so it wouldn't happen again. With all eight of us there, it was possible I could avoid him and participate in Cal's activity at the same time. It wasn't perfect, but it was a plan. Establish civil borders, and do not cross them. No matter how good his hair looked now that it had reached his shoulders or how tall I'd forgotten he was.

"Okay, Cal," Margot said once we were all together. "Lay it on us. What are we to do this weekend?"

"Right, then. I figured I would do you all a service by making dinner, and perhaps even a charcuterie, since it seemed to be such a hit on Valentine's Day—"

We cut him off, whooping and cheering before he could finish. Cal rarely cooked for the whole lot of us, but it was a real treat when he did.

"I'm sensing a 'but,'" Liv said, eyes narrowed.

"We're all doing the shopping. Kind of like a London market scavenger hunt. Since it's finally springtime and the markets are full again, I figured we'd divide and conquer. Split into teams, search the markets for specific ingredients, make it sort of a competition. Then reconvene back here later for a big dinner and maybe some cocktails on the roof?"

"Cal, darling, this is exactly how you do a Warehouse Weekend. After the last time it was your turn and we spent the afternoon at the cinema and then in a brewery down the block, I wasn't sure you had it in ya," Liv said.

"I loved that brewery," Jan said. "I think you did well by us, mate. Don't listen to her."

Cal laughed. "I figured since this was my last turn at this, I'd give it a good go."

Unsurprisingly, Isla had accepted his proposal, and they were set to marry this time next year. He would be out of the apartment by summer, as soon as they closed on their house in Scotland, but we had yet to even consider finding a replacement.

"Well, then, let's make it a good one," Henry said. "Cal's last hurrah as leader of the Warehouse Weekend. He deserves to go out with a bang, don't you think?" He looked around at us for confirmation, and I kept my eyes locked on the concrete floor.

"To Cal!" Raja shouted, like she was proposing a toast. We echoed, laughing, then settled down so he could continue explaining.

"An honor, really," he said. "Okay, so here's how we'll do this. We'll pick pairs out of a hat or a bowl or a hollowed-out grapefruit rind or whatever we can find in this place, then the teams will get their lists and set off to find everything on it. First team back to the warehouse wins."

"Wins what?" Finn asked. "What's at stake here, Callum?"

"Bragging rights, of course," he said. "But also . . . booze. What else is ever at stake in this place?"

"The man has a point," Jan said, and we all agreed. "Let's get to it, then."

I felt like a kid at school when the teacher assigned a group project. I wanted to whine, *But Cal, can we please choose our partners? There are some people in this class I just can't be partners with. You understand, don't you?*

I held my breath as he and Margot scribbled our names onto slips of paper and shuffled them in an empty popcorn bowl we found on the table.

"Pair number one," he said, pausing for effect. "Raja and Finn."

Raja put Finn in a headlock like one might a little brother, tousling his orange hair with her long nails. "All right, Finny. We better win this thing," she said.

"Do I ever lose?"

"Yes," she said. "Literally all the time." Most of us laughed, but I couldn't do anything but stare at the bowl and wait for Cal to pull the next pair.

"Me and Jan," he said, nodding to Jan.

"Let's rock," Jan said, shooting finger guns at him.

"All right, and next we have . . ." He fumbled two pieces in his hands, struggling to unfold them both while also holding the bowl. "Lucy and Henry."

I let a curt laugh escape at the sound of our names paired together before trying to disguise it by clearing my throat. "Grand," I said, mostly to myself.

"Couldn't have planned this better, could ya, Cal?" Jan said, crooked smile growing wider by the minute. Cal turned his palms toward us, pleading innocence.

"Don't blame me, mate. It was all up to chance."

"Maybe we should play the lottery today," Finn said. "Reckon with these odds, we might win something."

"All right, all right, that's enough," Henry said. "You're all just nervous you're going to lose, aren't ya?"

"To you two?" Jan asked. All eight of us shared a knowing glance that made me want to melt into the floor.

I wasn't sure how everyone knew about what happened, but in a tight-knit friends-turned-family situation, it wasn't really a surprise that they did. Not that that made it any less embarrassing.

"Jan, I said that's enough, mate," Henry said, a bit firmer this time.

"Well, then," Cal said. "That only leaves Liv and Margot." Both seemed excited to be paired up, since they were the most likely to become dangerously competitive.

Cal distributed our lists, a mix of ingredients for charcuterie and a proper roast dinner, even though it was a Saturday.

"And we can do booze after we get home, once we have a winner. Are we ready, then?"

"How do we know you and Jan don't have the easiest list?" Finn asked.

"Because I assigned them blind, you wanker. And unlike everyone else in here, I'm not a cheater."

"Ah yes—Callum, our moral compass," Raja said.

"You lot are relentless. Are we doing this thing or not?"

"We are, we are, let's go," Margot said, pulling Liv by the hand.

I turned our list over in my hands before following them out. We were all being sent to some combination of markets fairly distanced from the apartment; Hen and I had Borough Market and Old Spitalfields. It appeared we were supposed to get most of the cheese for the charcuterie from Borough, and a few candles and some incense from Spitalfields to replace what we'd burned through at home.

"Lucy, we don't have to do this if—"

"No, it's fine," I said. "It's all water under the bridge, anyway, isn't it?"

"Hardly," he said, looking around to make sure we were out of earshot of the rest of our roommates. They were all but out the door, so he continued. "Listen, Luce, I know I really hurt you. And I just—"

"Hen, please," I said. "It's over. Just a bruised ego, that's all. I was fine then, and I'm fine now." The lie tasted like copper on my tongue. "The only thing I'm not fine with is losing this competition because we're standing around having a chat instead of getting our asses on the Tube."

Frustration clouded his eyes, but I could tell he had nothing else to say. And even if he did, I wasn't going to let him. I was finally healing, and the last thing I needed was to rehash what had happened in Amsterdam. Even if he was on the brink of delivering a well-deserved apology.

The tube ride was mostly silent, both of us careful to keep our fingers from touching on the pole. We caught each other's gaze more than once, quickly averting our eyes to our shoes, other passengers, the maps we knew by heart. The more crowded it became, the closer we were pressed together, and the more difficult it was to hate it.

"Right, then," Henry said, holding the list between us as we approached the entrance to the market. We put our heads just a bit too close, and his scent floated into my nose: heady and familiar, warm spices and soap. "Cal really is sending us on a ride, isn't he? D'you recognize the names of any of these cheeses?"

I grabbed the list from his hand, giving it a closer look. "I do, actually. But that's probably because I don't live on takeaway curry and frozen pizza." It was hard not to slip back into our usual banter.

"Ouch," he said, bringing his hand to his chest. "Lead the way, then, lady."

"Don't mind if I do."

The market was bustling, and we bobbed through lively throngs of people in search of the right stalls. Winning might have been the only thing we could agree on, but it was the only thing that mattered for now, so that was enough.

Intoxicating smells of fresh-baked bread, ripe citrus, and foreign spices swirled around us in a potent cloud. I looked back at the list to focus.

"Okay, so we need to find a Durham blue, a Red Leicester, and a Camembert. Easy enough," I said, scanning an opening in the crowd for a dairy vendor.

"Up ahead," he said, nodding in the direction of a stall he could see but I couldn't. "Two o'clock."

He stepped ahead of me, and I resisted the familiar urge to reach for his hand. We wound around slow-moving tourists and bustling Londoners, and he checked behind him once or twice to make sure I was still following. I contemplated reaching out to touch his elbow, just to stay together through the crowds, of course, then all but swatted my own hand away. I couldn't let Jan be right that this was to be a mistake.

"Good find," I said as we approached the stall.

"Maybe I'm not useless after all," he whispered to me, then ordered the Durham blue from the seller. She didn't have the other two cheeses, so we ducked back into the throngs, on the hunt again.

"Lucy, look," he said, nodding to a stall with dozens of small plastic cups nestled in an ice bath at the front. "The Borough Market Pimm's Cup is back."

He must have remembered me raving about it on one of our FaceTime dates, and the recall sent a flutter through my chest.

"My favorite," I said, contemplating it. "But we're in a race, Hen. We gotta find these cheeses and get the hell out."

"Oh, come on, Luce. It's one drink," he said, already halfway to the stall. "We can drink on the road."

"Just one," I said, following him. I couldn't resist. The Pimm's Cup, that is.

He paid for two drinks, one for each of us, and we paused our cheese hunt to bask in the glory of the first sip.

"Well?" I asked. "Is it as good as I said it was?"

"Of course it is. Your word is good as gold, you know."

I filled my mouth with another sweet, gingery sip, partially for the head rush, partially to avoid having to respond right away. The cup was packed with cucumbers, citrus, and loads of fresh mint. The flavors reminded me of springtime, the season of new beginnings, which made me think maybe I too should let go and start again. Hen and I could be proper friends at least, couldn't we? We were roommates, after all.

"Any time I see flowers like this, I think of you," he said, gesturing to a stall dripping in fresh blooms. It was almost like he knew I was just beginning to reconcile a platonic friendship and decided to thwart those plans. "And I stayed in Amsterdam for most of April, too, so I've been seeing quite a lot of them," he continued. When I didn't say anything right away, he turned to face me. "Honestly, Luce, it isn't just the flowers. I haven't been able to stop thinking about you at all since the moment you left. You've been on my mind every single day, and I'm terrible at fighting it." It would have been better if he'd just ripped the thorns from those stems and pressed them directly into my chest.

"Hen . . . ," I started.

"I know, I know, I lost my opportunity to say things like that a while ago. I just thought you should know."

We stared at each other in silence just long enough for it to hurt before I took out our list and refocused our attention to the safety of the task at hand.

"Right, well, thank you. For letting me know, I guess," I said without looking at him. I felt myself slipping right back to that familiar place, and I knew I couldn't. And besides, I had Oliver now, so this was meaningless. "I think back over there, near that Italian butcher, I saw a vendor with a ton of cheeses. He must have both of these other ones, then we can head over to Spitalfields. Shall we?" He nodded, seemingly disappointed to be back to business.

After securing what we needed at the last vendor, we took another silent tube ride to Old Spitalfields, staring at our phones despite the fact that we didn't have an ounce of service.

Like Borough Market, Old Spitalfields was teeming with people. We confirmed our readiness with a silent nod, then headed into the masses. This time, we were engulfed in smells of fresh paint, authentic leather, and patchouli oil.

A young woman playing a guitar crooned from the entrance, and Henry stopped to throw a few quid in an upturned hat she had on the ground.

"Just the candles here, then we should be good to head home," I said. "Any idea where the others are?"

"If I had to guess, Mar and Liv are home already, Cal and Jan are somewhere in line with us, and Raja and Finn have murdered each other and one of their bodies is floating in the Thames."

"Dark," I said, trying not to laugh. "But probably true."

"But on the off chance Margot and Liv aren't getting along today, we owe it to ourselves to leg it."

"I hate it when you're right." We flashed a smile at each other, finally, then took off in the direction of the candles.

"We have to find something good," I said. "I hated the ones Jan brought home last time."

Henry laughed, surely remembering their smell, reminiscent of burning tobacco and gasoline. "Here," he said. "Close your eyes."

I did, feeling particularly vulnerable standing there without being able to see, waiting for his next move. He floated a candle underneath my nose.

"Guess the scent," he said.

"Eucalyptus," I said immediately, then sniffed again. "With a hint of lemon?"

"Bloody hell," he said, turning the candle over to reveal the scent: Eucalyptus Lemon Balm. "How on earth?"

"I'm a florist, Hen. I'm buried in these smells every day of my life."

"Oh," he said, rubbing the back of his neck. "Duh."

I laughed, and instructed him to close his eyes. "Your turn." I pulled one that was called Cinnamon Sin and reached up to hold it under his nose. I studied his face as he inhaled, clocking the way his dark lashes spread across his freckled cheeks, the way his bones took sharp turns, the symmetry of those angles.

"It smells like Christmas," he said, without opening his eyes.

"You're close," I said.

"Has to be pine."

"Pine?" I laughed, and he opened his eyes at the sound.

"What? What's wrong with pine?"

"It's cinnamon, you sod. It smells nothing like pine."

"You said I was close when I guessed Christmas!"

"Yeah, because I was thinking about mulled wine and biscuits, not trees. Besides, I thought that would be an easy one. It smells just like you." That last bit slipped out before I had a chance to stop it, and it danced between us like a flame.

"You know what I smell like?"

I blushed, stumbling over my words as I tried to change the subject.

"Luce—"

"Do we like either of these? The eucalyptus or the cinnamon? You said it yourself—if we want to beat the girls, we have to leg it."

"Both are fine," he said.

Why did I have to make it weird? Or why did he have to make it weird? Why couldn't we both keep our big mouths shut and get what we needed without having to let Jan be right?

We wordlessly chose a few more candles, paid, and caught the Tube home. The time we'd spent on the Underground was adding up, and I was beginning to feel claustrophobic.

When we finally got back to the apartment, we were met with silence.

"Mar?" I called. "Liv?" Nothing.

"Holy shit," Henry said, laughing to himself. "Have we done it?" We peered around the apartment, checking in studios and open bedroom doors, but found nothing.

We turned to each other, arms out, ready to embrace in celebration, then both pulled back at the same time. The last thing we needed was that much physical contact, and I was thankful we were at least on the same page about that.

"Well done, Luce."

"Cheers," I said. We unpacked our findings, dancing around each other like live wires. Just moments later, Margot and Liv came crashing through the door, and I could have kissed them both. I could breathe again now that Hen and I weren't the only two people in the apartment, and we could gloat a bit about our victory.

"Bloody hell," Liv said, dropping her bags to the floor. "Are you having a laugh? How long have you been here?"

"Just a few minutes," I said, helping her with the bags. "But that's all it takes to win, isn't it?"

"We were so sure we had it," Margot said. "Maybe if one of us didn't have to pet every dog we passed on the way, we would have been faster."

"It wasn't quite the dogs so much as the pretty barista at Leadenhall, wasn't it?"

"I should have left you in the tube station."

"Losing is tearing you apart, innit?" Henry laughed. They both shoved him out of the room, reunited over a common enemy. We settled into the kitchen, guzzling water and picking at a sleeve of stale crackers while we waited for the others.

They came home in exactly the order Henry had predicted they would: Cal and Jan shortly after Mar and Liv, then Raja and Finn quite a bit later, tattered and arguing.

"We were starting to get a bit worried you two wouldn't make it home," Cal said when they arrived. "The sun set, like, half an hour ago."

"We know that, Callum," Raja said, still glaring at Finn. "We're not ready to joke about it yet."

"Speak for yourself," Finn said, kicking off his sneakers and sitting on the kitchen table. "It was good craic. You lot should have been there."

"If we'd been there, we wouldn't have gotten here first, would we?" Henry asked.

"You jammy bastards," Finn laughed. "How did you pull it off?"

"Team chemistry," Henry said, glancing in my direction. I could feel his gaze, but I wasn't yet ready to meet it. I'd fully lost control of my initial plan to keep my distance, and I needed to regain my footing if I wanted to keep the upper hand. Not that I needed an advantage, because we were just friends, but it felt good to have it anyway.

"So, what are we drinking tonight?" Cal asked. "Jan and I can run across the street to grab the booze if everyone just wants to Venmo, except Hen and Lucy, of course."

"Pimm's Cup," Henry said, and I looked straight at him this time.

"Really?"

"You're the reason we won, aren't you? I hardly did a bloody thing other than point out a cheese vendor. It should be your drink tonight."

"You two are so gross," Finn said, pretending to gag himself with his finger.

"Eat it, Finn," I said. "Pimm's Cup it is, Cal."

Cal and Jan nipped across the street to our favorite liquor store, and the rest of us laid out the dinner ingredients alongside the other items we'd grabbed on the hunt today while we waited for them to return.

"Lu, would you mind just giving me a hand with something in my room?" Raja asked. I looked at her like, *What the hell?* but she just clenched her jaw and nodded in the direction of the mezzanine.

"Okay, then," I said, following her up the stairs. She pulled me into her room, closing the door behind us. "What's going on?" I asked. The conspiratorial look on her face did not bode well for me.

"You tell me," she said. "I thought we were over Henry?"

"We are," I said. "What are you on about?"

"Oh, so all the flirting is, what—how normal friends treat each other? Should I be flirting with you more, then?"

"There's no flirting," I said. "Would you relax?"

"Would you stop lying to me?"

"I'm serious, Raja. Today was mostly really awkward. A little banter, sure, but mostly harsh reminders about everything that's happened."

"Are you sure you're not backsliding?"

Raja could be so annoying sometimes. If I told her as much, she would say it was because she was always telling the truth, even if I didn't want to hear it. As far as I was concerned, she was just driving me mad.

"No, no one is backsliding. Stop asking. I'm interested in Oliver now, Henry and I are moving forward as friends, or just mere acquaintances, and it isn't helping that you aren't letting me do that in peace."

"You should invite him tonight, then."

"Who?" I asked. "Oliver?"

"No, Prince Harry," she said, and I rolled my eyes. "I'm serious," she continued. "If you're over Henry and you two really are just 'acquaintances,' I think it wouldn't do any harm for him to see you with someone else. And you know how much I'm dying to get to know Oliver. Seems like the perfect time, doesn't it?"

"Is this a challenge?" I asked. "Like I somehow have to prove that I'm over Henry by inviting Oliver here?"

"Would you stop being so dramatic? I'm just saying, if it really is what you say it is, then you don't have to be worried about Oliver coming by. It's a casual night, anyway, so it'll be a low-pressure way to introduce him to everyone."

I squinted at her. "Are you sure you're not just trying to prove a point?"

"Not everyone is plotting against you, Lu."

"He's been dying to meet you, too," I said after a moment. "Properly, I mean." A smile crept onto my face, and I hated that she might have actually had a good idea.

"See?" she said. "Text him right now. See if he'll come for post-dinner roof cocktails."

I had to admit, the thought of having him here for drinks made my stomach turn in all the best ways. He was not only kind, but also hot and outwardly interested in me. After the humiliation in Amsterdam, it would do me some good to show everyone I'd moved on. And, admittedly, that I'd done quite well for myself.

Before Raja and I made our way back downstairs, I shot Oliver a text inviting him for drinks, which he answered almost immediately.

> I'm having dinner with my sister, but it's an early res so I can be by around half nine. Does that work? Looking forward to meeting everyone.

"He's so proper," Raja said, reading his text over my shoulder. "Does he know we're a bit of a mess?"

"He saw you all on New Year's, remember? Not much to hide after that, I'm afraid."

"You're right," she laughed. "And he's still interested in you after that? Well done, Lu."

"Oh, shut up," I said. "Let's get back downstairs before anyone gets suspicious."

When we got back to the kitchen, the boys had returned with the booze, and Cal and Margot were getting started on the charcuterie.

"You're just in time for the updates," Margot said, arranging triangles of cheese in a fan around a pot of chutney.

"For once, I actually have something," Raja said, thrusting her arm into the air. She usually told me the second anything remotely significant happened to her, so I hadn't the foggiest idea what her update could be. Made me a bit nervous, to be honest. "I just got an email on the way home, which, Lu, is why you didn't know first." I nodded, accepting her explanation and urging her to continue. "I was offered a job with H.M. Whitaker."

Silence blanketed the kitchen, save for the sound of Cal's chopping on the wooden board.

"And that is . . . ," Finn prompted, the only one brave enough to admit he had no idea what she was talking about.

"Bloody hell, do you all live under a rock? It's one of the Big Four consulting firms in the city. It's the dream job for a ton of MBA grads, which I basically am, since my program ends at the end of the month, and they're infamous for their difficult hiring process. I was feeling pretty confident after the first few rounds of interviews, but I didn't want to jinx it by saying anything, you know? But they want me to come in next week to formally accept and discuss next steps." She was almost out of breath by the time she finished, and I was swelling with so much pride, I was nervous I'd float out of the skylight.

I let out a shriek at a pitch I hadn't hit since I was a little girl, then threw my arms around her neck. "Oh my god, Raj," I said, probably too loud for how close I was to her ear. "Congratulations."

The rest of the lot echoed those sentiments, joining us in a group hug. Despite having only learned what H.M. Whitaker was a few minutes ago, we showered her with compliments, expressed our pride, and told her how lucky they were that she'd be working for them.

Eventually she brushed us off, telling us we could all buy

her bottles of champagne if we really wanted to extend our congratulations.

"And you?" Henry said, looking at me once Raja's moment had died down. "Any update?"

"None quite so exciting," I said.

"Oh, but are you sure you have nothing to say?" Raja prompted with raised brows, which made me want to kill her.

"Oh, er, Oliver's coming tonight," I said, hoping it sounded like a casual afterthought. The collective blank stare from the crowd warmed my cheeks like the flame under a teakettle, making me think I hadn't even come close to casual.

"Who?" Jan said.

"The guy from New Year's, you wanker," Liv said. "Lucy's been dating him for like a month. Don't you ever pay attention?" She flicked him in the ear, and he nearly pushed her out of the room.

"Ah, the guy from the kiss, then, is he?" Henry said, slow to look up from the pile of grapes he was picking from their stems.

"Er, yeah. He's just coming by for rooftop drinks after dinner. I hope that's okay with everyone. And if it's not, we have Raja to blame. It was her idea."

Raja shrugged, a wry smile on her face. "Not sorry."

"You shouldn't be," Henry said. "Chuffed to meet him."

I tried to meet his eyes to read some shadow of emotion on his face, but he was staring back at his hands before I had a chance.

"Me too," said Liv. "I mean, we've kind of already met him, but you know what I mean."

"He's a good guy, then, this Oliver?" Cal asked.

"Very," I assured them. "I think you'll like him."

"We know you definitely do," Finn said, nudging Jan to get him in on the joke.

"Please don't be this weird when he gets here," I said. "I'm begging you. Behave normal, for once."

"Not quite sure they're capable," Henry said.

"I'm going to regret this, aren't I?" I tried to joke, but I got nothing in response. I supposed that was my answer. I had a feeling this was about to go balls-up, but I tried to squash it. We were all adults here, more or less. And things were over between me and Henry, so surely we could handle something as easy as a few drinks on the roof.

"Should we get this dinner on the road, then?" he asked, changing the subject at the first available opportunity.

"Yes sir," Cal said, chuckling a little to himself at the new-found sense of urgency. "One Saturday roast, coming right up."

Cal was going to miss us, and we knew it because he let us pile into the kitchen while he was working and pick bits and bobs from cutting boards and pans, and he didn't say a word about it.

We cracked open beer after beer, passing the time while we waited for the meat and veg to roast. Henry spun a record from a band he'd shot when he was in Iceland, and their music filled the apartment with gentle strumming and gravelly voices.

I imagined what we looked like from the outside, how someone might see us if they were looking through our windows like a snow globe. All eight of us crowded in the kitchen, passing cutlery and setting the table, singing made-up words to songs we didn't know, dancing barefoot on the concrete floors.

Eventually, two roast chickens sat proudly in the center of the table, surrounded by sky-high piles of Yorkshire pudding, buttery vegetables, and golden, crispy potatoes. We passed dishes around, shoveling food onto each other's plates and gushing over how well Cal had done.

The imaginary onlooker would have seen eight friends who had become a family, telling stories and bickering like siblings under the warm glow of the oversize lamp hanging overhead. They would have seen us dissolving into laughter as we reminisced about past Warehouse Weekends, bad dates, and wild nights, argued over the best takeaway pizza, and asked prying questions about one another's futures.

"I never thought I'd say this," Cal said, leaning back in his chair and linking his fingers behind his head, "but I'm actually going to miss this."

"I knew it," Liv said. "You've loved us all along."

"Let's not get ahead of ourselves, here."

She threw a crumpled napkin in his direction, which he caught with one hand and threw into the trash behind him.

"We have become a bit of a family in here, haven't we? Feels like we're really losing one of our own," Jan said, wiping a fake tear from his eye.

"Not for another few months, you know," Cal said, but we waved him off.

"Before you know it, everyone's going to move out and we're going to be left here to rot. Or to fill the rooms with strangers so we can still afford the rent," Raja said, dropping her head to Jan's shoulder.

Henry stood up from the table, wordlessly stacking plates and cups in his arms to bring to the kitchen.

"Got somewhere to be?" Finn asked, cocking his head. "What's the rush, mate? We'll help you do the washing up when we're not too full to move, you know."

"Just figured I'd get a jump on it," Henry answered, his back to us.

We exchanged concerned glances around the table as he dropped the plates into the sink.

"What's his problem?" Margot asked at a volume Henry could definitely hear.

"Maybe he's pissed because Lucy's new guy is coming over tonight," Liv whispered.

"Liv, come on," I said, and she hung her head for a second, regretting the joke.

"Maybe he's pissed because he's just cornered himself into doing the washing up," Jan said.

"Or maybe he's just trying to keep this place clean," Henry called from the kitchen.

"Living alone is changing you, mate," Jan said. "I thought our mess didn't bother ya?"

"That was before I lived alone," Henry said from the other room, his tone unreadable.

When he was away, it seemed like he never wanted to come home. And when he was home, it sometimes seemed like he didn't want to be away. I was sure I'd lost the privilege of asking the kind of personal questions required to sort this out, but I wished someone else would. Mostly because I knew Liv was wrong, and this had nothing to do with Oliver and everything to do with whatever Henry was going through and not telling us.

"Now, would one of you get in here and help me do this washing so we can start really drinking?" he asked.

"Aye, he's back," Jan said. "Now we're talking."

We gathered the rest of the dishes from the table, forming an assembly line in the kitchen. We scraped bits into the trash, squeezed leftovers into Tupperware, and fought over who would wash and who would dry. Henry's shoulders came down from his ears as soon as we changed the subject, and I immediately hated myself for noticing his shoulders at all.

A text from Oliver brought me back to the moment.

> On the way. Can I bring anything?

An open mind, I replied. If you remember from New Year's, it's kind of a crazy crowd. Lol.

> I remember fondly. See you soon.

I put my phone away and refocused on the group, trying to control my nervous energy.

"Was that Oliver?" Raja asked, nodding to my phone.

"Yeah, he's on the way."

"Okay, everyone, be cool," Finn said. "It's important we don't embarrass Lucy. She does enough of that on her own, so we shouldn't add fuel to the fire." This got a laugh from everyone except me and Henry, and I forced down the lump rising in my throat.

When I agreed to inviting Oliver, I had been caught up in the moment. I wanted Raja to know I was serious about him and over Hen, but I wasn't sure I'd really thought it through. And now it was happening regardless, so I had to prepare myself.

I slipped off to the bathroom to run my fingers through my hair, wipe away the mascara smeared under my eyes from laughing, and take a few deep, steadying breaths. Away from my roommates' constant teasing, it was much easier to be excited about Oliver's arrival. This was good. Necessary.

By the time he arrived, we were already well into our first Pimm's Cups on the roof. It was a chilly night, but it had been so long since we'd been able to tolerate being up there at night that we just bundled up and embraced it.

When I left to let him in, I thought I heard Finn whisper *showtime* behind me, which turned my stomach to knots. Thankfully, the minute the elevator doors opened and I set eyes on Oliver's warm face, the knots untangled themselves and turned back into butterflies.

"The cold does wonders for your cheeks," he said, kissing them both. "Flushed is a good look for you." My peachy face must have turned crimson at the compliment, but he seemed to like that, too.

"Are you ready?" I asked before I opened the door to the roof.

"As I'll ever be." The corners of his eyes crinkled when he smiled, and for a second I imagined tracing those lines with my fingertips.

"I'm really glad you're here," I said, and I meant it.

"Me too. Now let's do this thing." He swung the door open, and we headed out onto the roof with the rest of them.

"Aye, the man of the hour," Finn said, already a little drunk. "Welcome to our humble abode."

"He's always this weird," Liv said, brushing him off. "Just ignore him. That's what the rest of us do."

"Oh, is that what you do, Liv?" Finn said. "Because if we look back at, I don't know, any time we've gotten home from a party—"

"Can we get you a drink?" Liv said to Oliver, interrupting Finn and shooting daggers in his direction.

"That would be grand, thanks."

Liv got to work on a cocktail, and I introduced Oliver to everyone else, most of whom he remembered vaguely from New Year's.

"You must be the one who travels," he said, shaking Henry's hand. Either he knew because he didn't recognize Henry from the party, or because my descriptions of Henry were more thorough than those of anyone else, but I was too distracted by Henry's expression to care. His lips were tight, the curve of a smile nearly nonexistent.

"So Lucy's told you about him, has she?" Finn asked. Oliver adjusted his coat, looking at me, trying to make sense of Finn.

"Right, then, Finn. I've told him about everyone, haven't I?" I said. "Introducing anyone to you lot requires quite a bit of preparation." I tried to laugh to keep things light, but I had a feeling Oliver was too perceptive for Finn's comment to slide under the radar. "Now, let's stop treating him like a museum exhibit, shall we? And go back to having a normal night?"

"Not quite sure anything around here is ever normal, but I second at least the first part," Raja said. "Come sit. We were just about to play a drinking game."

"We were?" I asked.

"I mean, I hadn't proposed it yet, but is anyone opposed?" She looked around, and no one disagreed. "Right, then. I'm thinking King's Cup?"

"A classic," Jan said. "I'll go grab a cup and the cards."

"Grab a handful of beers while you're at it," Henry called after him. "We're gonna need them."

"For the game, or for whatever record you're trying to set tonight?" Liv said. "You drank quite a few at dinner, too, didn't ya?"

"Since when are you my keeper?" he snapped.

Her eyes went wide. "Jeez, Hen. I was just joking."

"Right, sorry."

Eight pairs of eyes darted around, looking for something to make this less awkward. I hadn't noticed he'd been drinking a lot during dinner, but now that I looked at him, his eyes were a bit glassy. Usually when he was drunk, he was just a bit of a lush, but I had a feeling that wouldn't be the case tonight.

When Jan returned, he studied our faces in the silence. "Did someone die?"

"Henry's sense of humor, maybe," Finn said. Bold of him to crack another joke.

"Yeah, yeah," Henry said, a lopsided smile returning to his face. "Everyone's just taking the piss, aren't they?"

All nine of us seemed to exhale at the same time, turning our attention back to the game. If we were lucky, he'd stay in good spirits.

Jan placed an empty cup in the center of the plastic table and fanned the cards in a circle around it. "Oliver, you know the rules?"

"I've been to university," he laughed. "So, yes. Pick a card, follow the rule, pour a bit of your drink in the cup if you draw a king, chug the cup if you draw the last king and lose the game?"

"He's a natural. Good find, Luce," Jan said.

I stared at Oliver's profile, silently agreeing with Jan. He *was* a good find, wasn't he? He fielded their ridiculousness with deft hands, and now he was planning to play a drinking game he probably hadn't played in years, on account of him being a proper adult, and he was going to do it with enthusiasm.

"Ready?" Jan asked, hand poised over the first card. We nodded, and he turned it over. "Six—chicks," he announced, waggling his eyebrows at the four of us. Raja, Liv, Margot, and I raised our glasses to each other, rolling our eyes at Jan. Margot tapped her glass ceremoniously on the table before she brought it to her lips, and Raja chugged way more than a sip. The boys whooped as we drank, and the game was underway.

In a way, it was symbolic. A little piece of each of us carefully poured into the centerpiece until it became an amalgamation of all the characters in the house. I always felt the King's Cup held strange secrets, and if it were ever to be knocked over, they would come pouring out, right onto the floor. We would bathe in each other's dark pasts, most embarrassing desires, and deepest skeletons.

We drew card after card, drinking if we were the last to point to the floor, the first to repeat a rhyme, the one who laughed instead of responding to a question with a question. Most important, each time we drew a king, we poured a little of our drink into the King's Cup at the center of the table.

Henry drew next, pulling a jack—"Never Have I Ever." We all raised three fingers in preparation.

"Last jack of the game, Hen," Raja said when he turned the card over. "Better make it a good one."

"Never have I ever . . ." He trailed off, biting his lip while he tried to think of something he hadn't done. "Never have I ever used someone to get over someone else."

I froze, three fingers poised in the air. He wasn't really doing this, was he?

"Aye, a bit dark there, mate," Cal laughed, but Henry only shrugged. He *was* doing this.

"Jan, you better put a finger down, you sod," Finn said. "Remember that poor guy who came around after Sebastian? The one with the face tattoo?"

"I did not use him. And he has a name," Jan said.

"Oh yeah? What is it, then?"

We burst into laughter at Jan's silence, and he dutifully put a finger down. Henry stared in my direction, and I tried to look anywhere else but back in his.

"Anyone else?" he said before we moved on. All the air in my lungs turned to ash, and taking a deep breath seemed nearly impossible. Oliver hadn't a clue about my history with Henry, and this wasn't exactly how I wanted him to find out. Besides, Henry had rejected me. How could he be mad at me for moving on?

"Nope," I said, finding the courage to meet his gaze. "Well done, us. Who's next?"

He laughed a humorless laugh under his breath, one I wasn't sure anyone else noticed but that made my blood feel like lava. He cracked another beer despite the graveyard of empty bottles beside him, and I counted the cards left on the table, trying to determine how much longer this would go on.

"All right, I'm next," Liv said. "Never have I ever smoked a cigarette." She flicked her hair off her shoulders, smiling at each of us as we all put a finger down and took a swig.

"You should try it sometime," Jan said. "Might loosen you up a little."

"I don't need to be loose, thank you."

"Suit yourself," he said, snickering with Finn. "All right, Luce, you're up."

"This should be good," Henry slurred to no one in particular.

"Never have I ever rejected someone, then regretted it," I said, the words tumbling from my mouth before they even registered in my brain. My instinct was to cover my mouth with my hand, but it wouldn't have made any difference. The words were already out. Bloody hell. If Henry was doing this, apparently so was I.

I watched his jaw clench and unclench, but he said nothing. Did nothing. A laugh Finn must have been holding in exploded in the silence, and he raised a glass to Henry. "Drink up, mate," he said.

Henry shot Finn a look that could have burned a hole in his boyish face, at which Finn recoiled wordlessly into himself. "You done, there, Finn?" Henry said, hardly parting his lips to speak.

"Yes sir."

"We've all been there, haven't we?" Raja said, putting a finger down and taking a sip. I was sure she was trying to soften the blow, to help me save face, but I might have been past the point of no return. The longer the tension hung above the roof, the more I let it seep into my bones. This was his doing. He didn't get to be the one who was mad.

"Anyone else?" I echoed Henry, raising my eyebrows in his direction. The bloodshot whites of his eyes turned his irises to emeralds, which made it hard to look away, whether or not I wanted to.

He drained the rest of his beer in one go, then let the bottle clatter to the floor beside him.

"And that's three," Raja said, making a fist to show she'd put all her fingers down. "It's always me, isn't it? Who's next? Someone pick a card."

We scrambled to get the game back on track, but Henry and I were moving in slow motion. There was an undeniable burning in my chest, and I wasn't sure if I was angrier at him for winding me up or at myself for retaliating. Either way, the burning was becoming nearly unbearable.

Oliver was still smiling next to me, hand on my knee, getting back to the banter with everyone else, but I had a feeling I'd have to answer for this later. And so help us all if Henry got his way and drove a wedge between us. If that was, in fact, what he wanted to do.

I spent the rest of the game in a daze, trying to make sense of Henry's behavior and hating myself for wasting another second on him at all. From time to time he ran his hands through his hair, eyes closed, his frustration seemingly melting into sadness. Embarrassment, even.

"Bloody hell, Oliver's done it!" Jan's excitement ripped me back to the game just as Oliver turned over the last king.

Oliver buried his head in his hands, groaning at the prospect of having to drink the King's Cup. "How did it get so full?"

"I think we've all been pouring a bit in it the whole time, if I'm honest," Margot said. "We always say we're going to play by the proper rules, but we never do."

Oliver picked up the cup, swirling the liquid around.

"It's not a fine wine," Cal laughed. "Just close your eyes and chug it."

"You lot are having a laugh," Oliver said, staring closely at the drink. "I think there's even a dead bug in there."

"A little extra protein never hurt anyone," I said.

"That is disgusting, Luce."

"Too posh for the King's Cup, are you?"

He took a deep breath, eyeing me from the side. "You're lucky I like you." With that, he brought the cup to his lips and chugged. We cheered him on, laughing as he squeezed his eyes shut and slammed the cup on the table when he finished.

"Well done," Margot said, clapping like she was on a golf course. "He isn't too posh after all."

I admired how well he was getting on with my roommates, proud that he'd fit right into my world. This was a tough lot to crack, but he'd done it in no time at all. I wanted to wrap my arms around his neck and pull him in for a kiss and thank him for being so kind. So easy. So uncomplicated.

"Right, then," Henry said, clambering to his feet. "Oliver's quite brilliant, isn't he? Perhaps he should come to every Warehouse Weekend. Maybe he can even replace Cal. Or me, once I'm gone. Would make sense, that, wouldn't it?"

"And you, my friend, are cut off," Jan said, joining Henry on his feet and slinging an arm around his shoulders. "Off to bed, then, are we?"

Henry shrugged Jan off, then stumbled toward the stairs, bidding us a slurred good night on the way down, Jan close behind. I watched through wide eyes, my dry, speechless lips parted in disbelief.

"I can't believe he listened to Jan," Finn said once they were out of sight. "I thought we might have a riot on our hands."

"He's usually the one to cut everyone else off," Liv said. "He must have known he was out of line. What the hell is going on with him?"

Oliver put his beer on the coffee table, then wiped his hands on his thighs and started to stand. "I'm not quite sure what's just happened, but I can go if—"

"No," I said, reaching for his hand. "You stay. He's just got, er, some other shit going on."

"Are you sure? I feel I might've done something to offend, which of course wasn't my intention."

"He's been on edge with everyone lately," Raja jumped in, always quick to save me. "It's like all he wants to do is leave London, but then any time we bring up that he's leaving London, he gets upset. He was in a bit of a mood before you got here, so I wouldn't worry too much."

"Well, I don't want to step on anyone's toes. I'm not here to disturb the peace, just to get to know you lot."

"You aren't disturbing any peace," I said. "Ignore him. Please." My head was reeling, trying to balance wanting to sit here and reassure Oliver that none of this was personal and wanting to storm inside and wring Henry's neck because all of this *was* personal. "Why don't we clean up and go inside?" I said.

My remaining roommates agreed, collecting armfuls of beer bottles, emptying ashtrays, and packing playing cards back into the box. I lingered on the roof a moment with Oliver after they'd all gone down, realizing there was something else we'd yet to discuss about the night.

"So," I said, looking at my watch. "It's getting late, and I'm not quite sure you'll be able to find a tube . . ." I hoped he would finish the thought.

"I could call an Uber," he said. "Or I could stay over? I know we haven't done that yet, so if you're uncomfortable, just say the word and I'm in a cab on my way home."

"It's silly to go all the way home at this hour," I said, resting my hands on the collar of his jacket, trying to erase the tension of the past few minutes. He put his hands over mine, then gently returned them to my sides.

"If I'm going to wake up in this flat tomorrow, Luce, be honest with me for a minute. What was that about, just now? With Henry?"

"It was nothing," I said in a high-pitched voice that didn't belong to me. He said nothing, just waited patiently for me to tell the truth. "Okay," I started. "So we have a bit of history. Nothing serious. Almost nothing at all, really. Over before it started. It was never going to work, anyway, so it wasn't even worth a try."

He stared into the darkness, processing these fragments. "You're sure it was nothing serious? I mean, there must have been some kind of falling out, right? He seemed quite cheesed off about my being here."

"Yes, I'm sure. I mean, yes, it wasn't serious, and yes, there was a falling out. He rejected me, it was pretty embarrassing, but it's all in the past now. And I like the present much better." I reached for his hand, and while he didn't pull away, he didn't grab mine back, either.

"Me too," he said, not quite matching my level of conviction. "I just hope the past is really in the past."

"I can assure you it is. For me, anyway. Which is what matters. And I'm sorry about his behavior tonight, Oliver. I've really never seen him like that. I think the girls are right—it's mostly because he's going through something else, I guess, but it wasn't personal. I don't want him to scare you off."

"Lucky for you, I don't scare easy. But I do trust easy, and I don't want to be fooled, Luce. If there's still something there, please say so."

"There isn't," I said, crossing my heart. "Promise."

He tipped my chin up to kiss me, but for a second, it wasn't his face I saw.

"Good," he said. "Now let's make a cuppa and get into bed. I'm knackered and also maybe a bit drunk."

When we got back inside, the apartment was mostly quiet. Everyone else had found their way to bed. I wasn't sure what Cal had planned for tomorrow, if anything at all, but I supposed it was best to be prepared for the day either way.

"I'm just going to wash my face," I said when we were back in my room. "Back in a minute."

I was almost in the bathroom when I heard a whisper from down the hall. Henry's whisper. Calling my name. I squinted in the darkness, trying to make out his figure.

"Luce," he said again. "Can we talk?" He came into the sliver of light in the corridor, chest bare, joggers hanging low on his hips, and I could make out rosy rings around his eyes and disheveled hair pushed behind his ears. I wished he'd stayed in the dark.

"I have nothing to say to you," I said, trying to keep my voice low so Oliver wouldn't hear. "Except that you are a miserable sod when you drink too much, and that was an embarrassing display of, well, whatever that was. I thought we were headed in the right direction, you know. After today. But I should have known better."

"I'm sorry," he said at full volume, missing my cues to keep his voice down. I looked around, careful to check that no one else was around to see us, then ushered him into his room. If we were going to do this, we definitely weren't doing it in the corridor. "I know that was out of line," he continued. "But so was bringing him here, don't you think? I mean it's been, what, just over a month since Amsterdam?"

"Since we ended things, you mean? Because really, I could have moved on the next day and been sure it wouldn't matter to you."

"Of course it mattered to me," he said.

I laughed in his face, feeling my voice rising. "Is that just another one of those things you feel the need to say in the moment? Even though we both know you don't mean it?"

"It's not like that," he said.

"Then why don't you tell me what it's like, Hen? Hm?"

He rubbed his eyes with the heels of his hands, as if his answer would appear in the galaxy behind his eyelids.

"I've been trying to keep my cool this weekend," he said eventually. "I know I messed up, and we both know now I've been regretting that, but I've been trying to give you some space. But then seeing you with him, he's just so—"

"So what?"

"So not you. I mean, is that really what you want? Someone so posh? So put-together?"

"Maybe it is! Why is it so hard to believe I'd want someone who's mature?"

"At this stage of your life?" Henry asked. "The stage that's supposed to be a mess? Just because someone is mature doesn't mean they're right for you, Lucy."

"And you don't think Oliver's right for me," I said, more a statement than a question.

"No, I don't. And I don't think you do, either."

We stared at each other, chests heaving with deep breaths, the room silent save for the constant creaking of the warehouse.

"I'm not doing this," I said eventually, willing my heart rate to return to normal. "You lost your right to have an opinion. Especially on a night like tonight, when we've been drinking and tensions are high, and I am just exhausted from going around and around with you." I surprised myself with how rational I sounded, given how badly I wanted to cry.

He raised his hands in surrender, hanging his head just enough to mask his eyes. "I'm sorry," he said again, sounding more like a boy than a man this time. "I let the night get the best of me, Luce. And I really shouldn't have." He lifted his head to meet my eyes, and he looked exactly how I felt. Tired, sad, frustrated. Lost.

"I know," I said, slipping out of his room and heading back to mine before either of us could say anything else. Washing my face would have to wait until the morning.

When I pushed open my door, Oliver was pulling on his coat.

"Going somewhere?" I asked, feeling my heart rate rising again. I tried to sound casual, but it came out more panicked than I'd hoped. He stopped moving, squaring his body to face me.

"I'm not an idiot, Lucy."

"What?" I felt the color drain from my face, fearing the worst.

"I wish you would have just told me the truth, you know?" He rubbed his chin with his hand, looking everywhere but my eyes. "Especially because I gave you so many chances to do exactly that."

"You heard," I said, mortified. He offered little more than a tight-lipped nod, and I exhaled hard enough to blow out a candle. "God, Oliver, I'm so—"

"When he pulled that jack earlier, was his never-have-I-ever meant for you? Was he suggesting you were using someone to get over someone else?" Before I could even respond, he shook his head and continued. "He was suggesting you were using me to get over someone, wasn't he? To get over him?" Silence. "Was he right, Lucy?"

"Of course not," I said eventually. "I'm not using you, Oliver. I would never." I was scrambling, I knew, but the upper hand was so far out of my reach, scrambling was the best I could do.

"But you aren't over him at all, are you?" The question hung over our heads like a storm cloud, saturated and heavy and ominous.

"I am. I don't know how much you heard, but whatever was between us was just complicated, that's all. But it really is over. I meant that when I said it before, and I mean it now. That's what I was telling him."

"I want to believe you," he said, his deep voice rumbling in the quiet. "I'm just not sure it's true."

"Why does everyone think they can tell me how I feel tonight?" Frustrated tears pooled in the corners of my eyes.

"I didn't mean to be telling you how you feel, Lucy, and I'm sorry that I was. I just think that that passion between you two, which you might think is anger, is a spark. And life is simply too short to ignore the sparks."

"Don't you and I have a spark?" I asked, though deep down, I knew the answer. "What about that?"

"More of an ember by comparison, maybe," he said, smiling a gentle, sad smile. How was he smiling right now? "I like you, you know. And these past few weeks have been grand. But I don't quite think we're looking for the same things. So perhaps it's best we just call it before anyone gets hurt."

"It doesn't have to be like this," I said, blinking back tears.

"No, it doesn't. But it should be. And that's okay." He

dropped his phone and his wallet into his coat pockets, then brushed my tangled curls from my eyes. He was still so tender, even after all I'd put him through, and it made me like him even more. Made me hate myself even more for mucking it up. And made me want to strangle Henry, most of all.

"I'm sorry about tonight," I said. "This wasn't how any of it was supposed to go."

"You did warn me that you lot were a bit of a mess," he said. "Seems par for the course after all." That was a fine thing for me to say, but hearing it from an outsider made me defensive in a way I didn't have time to entertain. One more feeling would have put me over the edge, so it was best to let it go.

"Let me at least walk you out," I said, mostly because I had nothing else to say. There was no salvaging this, and I was as much to blame as Henry.

"Ah, I know the way. Be well, Lucy. I'm sure I'll see you around." He kissed me on the cheek, then tiptoed down the stairs and into the elevator, disappearing from the apartment entirely.

I was hardly face down in my bed before I heard a knock on my door. I still hadn't even taken off my shoes.

"I'm sleeping," I said.

"Just a minute, Lucy, that's all I'm asking."

Henry.

"Why, so you can gloat?" I asked, swinging open the door. "Congratulations, Hen. You got what you wanted."

"You think this is what I wanted?"

"You spent the whole night being a right wanker to Oliver, and now he's gone, so what else am I to think?"

"Please," he said, reaching out to touch me, then pulling his hand back as if he'd realized he was reaching for fire. "The last thing I wanted was for you to be unhappy."

"And yet here we are," I said. "I really can't do this again. First you, then Oliver, now you again. Something's got to give. I can't go back and forth all night, Henry. I'm tired, and I have nothing left to say, and if everyone seems to know how I feel already, then why can't we all just get on with it?"

He grabbed the edge of the door before I had a chance to slam it, his body blocking all the light from the corridor.

"I have no idea how you feel," he whispered. Quite frankly, neither did I.

"Look, Hen," I started, just to buy myself time. "I really don't want to talk anymore tonight, and I'm—"

"Then just listen, please." A single tear carved a path from my eye to my chin, but I said nothing. Just waited for him to continue. He didn't deserve it, but I was too tired to fight. "I didn't mean to reject you when you came to Amsterdam. I was surprised, and I was also having a weird day, and I handled it terribly. Which is why I wish we just could have talked first. I was scared, and I know that's a cop-out, and I won't use it as an excuse for being an arsehole, but it's the truth. I wasn't ready for things to be moving so fast because I was feeling so strongly about you and also about Amsterdam and I knew I was in over my head. You'd been saying the whole time that we were bound to crash and burn, that whatever we were had an expiry date, and I let it get to me. But I don't want that to be true, Lucy. I've never had something like this. Something I was afraid of losing."

"Why did you wait until now to say it, then?" I asked. "Talk about communication, Hen. Why didn't you tell me any of this then? Or in the long weeks since?"

"I was trying to respect your space," he said, opening and closing his hands like he might reach out for me. "I don't know where the line is between fighting for you and disrespecting your choice, and I'm afraid I'm always on the wrong side."

I let this wash over me, studying his face as I did. Had he reached out, come after me, tried to bridge the gap, would I have thought he was disrespecting me? Disregarding my choice to leave? I hadn't considered that before, and it was a lot to consider right now.

"What's the plan, then?" I said eventually. I needed something concrete to bring this conversation to a close so I could get into bed, alone, and let this whole night burn away.

"The plan?"

"Yeah, Hen. The plan. Because so far nothing we've tried has worked. We're never on the same page, and I never know which version of you to expect or what your intentions are, and I need clarity to move forward. I need a plan."

"I just need time," he said, almost as if he knew that wasn't enough. "I need to figure this out. This has been a crazy year, and I still have a few more months of being on the road, and I need to sort things for myself. But I like you. I really do. And I know I have a lot of work to do to regain your trust, but I'm prepared to do it, Luce. I don't think we should write this off before giving it a proper try."

"Didn't we give it a proper try?" I said. "Or is that not what we were doing before I came to Amsterdam? Please, Hen, tell me what a proper try looks like for you, because I can't risk embarrassing myself again."

"Can we just, I don't know, take things slow? Go back to our FaceTime dates when I'm on the road, spend some time together just the two of us when I'm home, tell each other before surprising each other in foreign countries?" It sounded so absurd, I actually laughed. "I don't know how to manage this, but I know I want to try."

"That means you have to talk to me," I said. "I mean *really* communicate. I'm not a mind reader, you know."

"Would be easier if you were, though, wouldn't it?" He flashed a shadow of a grin, which made me have to fight back my own.

"I'm serious, Henry."

"You're right. I'm sorry. I'm serious, too. And if communication is what it's going to take, then I'm going to work at it."

"I'm not asking for perfection. I'm just asking for effort."

"I can do effort." His voice had edges that Oliver's didn't, and I hadn't realized how much I'd missed it. He always sounded like he'd just woken up, the kind of rasp that made my hairs stand on end.

"It's been a long night," I said, trying to keep my eyes from drifting to his naked torso. "And I also need time."

"Right. Please, take all the time you need. And when you're ready, you know where I live."

I swiped a tear from my face with the back of my hand, settling on nothing more than a nod in response.

"Sleep well, Luce." He kissed the same cheek Oliver had moments before, then wandered down the corridor and into his room. I watched his back, studying his broad shoulders as he went, the rhythm of his walk, his long limbs, his milk chocolate–colored hair. The way he could bend in the wind like a daisy, stretching endlessly toward the light.

Only, if Henry were a daisy, I would be able to predict exactly what he wanted. And he would never change his mind—he would want the same things, day in and day out, and they would be as clear to me as the summer sky.

But he wasn't a daisy. He was equal parts enticing and infuriating, and by this time of the night, the only thing stronger

than the pull I felt toward him was the one I felt toward my
own bed and drunken, dreamless sleep.

I woke some time midmorning to the sound of a text. Henry's name appeared on the screen, and I opened the text before
I could stop myself.

> When you're up and moving, come to the roof. If you're
> keen, that is. (I know we said we needed time, but I'm hoping
> a few hours of sleep was enough.)

I didn't answer right away, as I was still blinking through a
developing hangover and needed time to process. Another—
much more alluring—text came a minute later.

> Kidding. About that last part, anyway. And in case you need
> convincing, there is coffee. Strong coffee. But again, only if
> you're keen.

I wished I was more difficult to please, but alas. The promise of strong coffee was too tempting to ignore, so I threw on
slides and a hoodie and stared at myself in the mirror. My hair
was one giant knot, and the bags under my eyes were so dark,
I looked like I'd been in a fistfight.

By the time I'd wrestled my hair into a braid, swiped some
concealer under my eyes, and centered myself, I was prepared
for whatever I was walking into. I felt strangely relaxed as I
made my way up to the roof, possibly since I was sure things
couldn't get any worse.

I held my breath as I pushed open the door, trying to steel
myself against whatever awaited me. That same breath hitched
in my throat when I saw Henry beside the table, which was

laden with a collection of golden pastries, dewy fresh fruit, and takeaway coffee from my favorite place down the block.

"You're up," he said, seeming surprised to see me. His smile stretched wider by the second, so bright it was hard to imagine he'd been so drunk the night before.

"I got a text," I said, forming a slow smile of my own.

"I didn't mean to wake you," he said. "Kind of the opposite, actually. I'm so sorry for keeping you up last night with my behavior, which was proper shit, I know, so I wanted you to at least wake up nicely. To start this day way better than last night ended, you know?"

"Is this what I think it is?" I asked, picking up a coffee and narrowing my eyes.

"If what you think it is is a hazelnut latte with oat milk, then yes," he said. "It's also a peace offering, but the caffeine is more important."

I took a long, slow sip, letting the coffee warm me from the inside out. I couldn't be bought, but this was a good attempt. "A peace offering, is it?" I asked, settling onto the couch with a croissant the size of my head. A buttery pastry could convince me to do just about anything, including hearing Hen out, even when he was infuriating. I wasn't proud of that, but it was the truth. I let the layers melt on my tongue, watching him gear up for what looked like a prepared speech.

"The first of many, I imagine," he said. "Look, Luce, I know effort goes far beyond a few pastries and a latte. I just want you to know I'm prepared to try. I may not be as good as you are at communication, but that just means I have to put the work in. Which I'm more than willing to do, obviously. Well, I guess it isn't obvious, or at least it wasn't, but I hope it is now."

I contemplated his words, thankful my mouth was full so I didn't have to respond right away.

"And don't feel like you need to say or do anything right now," he said, reading my mind. "Or ever, really. I know I've lost the privilege to expect that. Just know that whatever you decide, I'll be here."

"With lattes?" I asked, fighting a smile.

"All the lattes in the world, if that's what it takes."

"I'm holding you to that," I said.

"Which means you aren't writing me off, then?"

I hated how easy it was for him to walk me right into what he wanted. We shared a soft smile, knowing he was right and I'd given myself away before I was willing to admit it.

"I suppose not," I said, "but only because I get breakfast out of it."

"Whatever you have to tell yourself," he said, his laughter returning to me like the tide. I nudged him with my shoulder, and he ripped off a piece of my croissant for himself.

"Watch it," I said. "I can change my mind at any time, you know."

"I really, really hope you don't," he said, any trace of a joke gone from his tone. "Would it help to take some time this month to focus on ourselves?" he asked after a minute of silence. "If we're less of a mess, then maybe whatever's going on between us will be less of a mess, too, won't it?"

"I like that idea," I said, basking in its simplicity. "I like that a lot."

"Just try not to forget about me, will you?"

"I couldn't if I wanted to."

We would both have to tread lightly, but dipping our toes in felt like the perfect place to start.

May

sn't it time for you to get going?" Renee asked, all but shoving me out the door. "I can manage here without you, you know." Lately, I wasn't so sure about that. Not that I'd ever say that aloud.

"I know, I know," I lied. "But I feel so bad for taking the whole weekend off when we have projects to do. Let me just finish this before I go." I nodded to the pile of spiky cornflower and delicate lily of the valley on the table, which I was determined to turn into a giveaway for a small bridal shower before I left for the weekend.

"I can manage," Renee said. "It's a bridal shower, Lucy."

I wasn't worried about the quality of her work so much as her well-being. Lately, trying to hide the way the shears trembled in her hands seemed exhausting for her. Her office chair had far more back support than the stools in the studio, and she'd been rolling it out lately to sit in when she was working on arrangements. When I first started at the Lotus, she could stand for hours at the workbench and never so much as stop for coffee. Now a cup of tea was a permanent fixture in her hand, and she did more admiring of my work than creating her own.

"Why are you looking at me like that?" she asked. I hadn't realized I'd been staring, and I scrambled for a response.

"Like what?" I tried to play dumb, but I should have known better.

"Lucy, I said I'm fine. I have my daughter giving me that look often enough. I'm not sure I need it from you, too."

"I didn't even say anything."

"Those big brown eyes of yours say enough. And you've been hovering for weeks, pet. Every time I lift a box larger than a biscuit, you stop what you're doing to watch me like I might crumble to bits on the spot." She was right, and I was a fool to think she wouldn't notice. Jewish pseudo-granddaughters were just as anxious as Jewish pseudo-grandmothers.

"Sorry," I said. There was no point in denying it. "I can't help it."

"I know you can't, and I love you for that. But do please try, will you? You'll give yourself a migraine with all that worrying."

"*Now* who's doing the worrying?"

"The old lady, as it should be." She shot me a wink, flashing an eyelid nearly as blue as the cornflowers. "Now finish this up. I don't want you to be late."

"Sorted," I said, getting back to work.

I didn't want to be late, either. This wasn't really a Warehouse Weekend I could be late for. We'd known what we were doing for this one in advance, given the level of planning and preparation it involved compared to other Warehouse Weekends.

Finn's parents were opening a bed-and-breakfast in Cork, and we were all spending the weekend there so the staff could get in a practice run before the real guests started to arrive. And since we could hardly get ourselves to happy hour down the street in one piece, it was proving to be a hell of a project getting the whole lot to Ireland.

As I finished the piece for the bridal shower, tying off the bouquet with a glittering gold ribbon, I tried to ignore the short list of other projects on the bench beside me. It was just one weekend, and it wasn't a ton of work. Renee could handle the rest. She'd said so herself, hadn't she?

"Are you sure you have the rest of these?" I asked, gesturing to the list. I couldn't resist double-checking, even if I was being a nuisance.

"I've been doing this for nearly sixty years," she laughed. "I can handle this weekend."

"You're right," I said, hoping it was conviction I detected in her voice, not tension.

"What about you?" she asked. "Can you handle this weekend?"

I hadn't seen Henry since he left the Sunday after our last Warehouse Weekend, and since he was in Glasgow for the month, he was just meeting us in Ireland instead of coming home first. We'd been back to routine texts, takeaways over FaceTime, trying to line up Netflix so we'd be watching the same film at the exact same time, constantly missing each other's calls, and dancing on the fine line between something casual and something real.

We'd been strategically avoiding the "what are we" conversation that plagues every new relationship, but since we had agreed to take it slow, I tried not to push it. I had a feeling, however, that Ireland would force our hands.

"What choice do I have?" I said to Renee. "But I'm sure it'll be grand. I've been dying to see Henry, and I think things are actually going well for us." I knocked on the wooden worktop, just in case I'd jinxed it. "Then again, usually as soon as things start going well, they immediately go to shit, so who's to say what this weekend has in store, really?"

"Glad to see your attitude has changed," she said. "Having

hope is part of being generous with your heart, you know. Allowing yourself to see the best instead of expecting the worst."

"Any other parting wisdom, fairy godmother?" I asked.

"Watch yourself," she said, opening and closing the pair of shears in her hand. "I'll cut that tongue right off." I pretended to zip my mouth closed with my fingers, and she nodded her approval. "Go have fun, pet," she said. "Try to enjoy the weekend. Don't get so caught up in what is supposed to be or what might be or what was. Try to just focus on what *is*."

"Easier said than done," I said. "But for you, I will try."

"You should try for yourself, you know."

For reasons I was grappling to find, heat pricked the back of my eyes. Did I try anything for myself, or was doing things for other people my default? Didn't I deserve to enjoy this weekend just for me? Would I have even had that thought if Renee hadn't said it?

"You're right," I said.

"I always am." She offered a soft smile, her head cocked and her kelly-green glasses perched on the end of her nose.

"Right, then. I guess I should be going."

"It's about time."

"Call me if you need anything. We've done some stuff for Vivienne before so she shouldn't give you any trouble, but let me know if she does."

"For the last time, I'll be fine."

I took a deep breath when I got out onto the sidewalk, trying to exhale the stress of my job so I could focus on the weekend ahead. Because we were going to Ireland, I was certain we would see all four seasons in a day, but the warmth of the spring sun in London was enough to restore my excitement and make the weekend seem a bit more promising. I could shed my nerves with the cool breeze and turn my face to the sun for once.

Since we were all running on different schedules as we closed out the workweek, we had decided it'd be better to meet at the airport instead of trying to convene at the warehouse first. I'd brought my luggage with me to work so I could leave without stopping at home.

I was thankful for the time alone on my ride to the airport, but by the time I arrived, I was ready for my noisy roommates to interrupt my endless overthinking. We had just enough time for a pint at a crowded bar before we had to board, and my body welcomed the alcohol to steady my nerves.

"Are you excited to see Hen?" Raja whispered to me on the plane as we squeezed down the narrow aisle looking for our seats.

"I'm nervous," I said. "What if it's, I don't know, what if it's different in person?"

"Judging by how it usually seems in person, I think you're going to be just fine," Liv said, joining the conversation. The three of us found our seats, just across the aisle from Margot and Cal and in front of Jan and Finn.

"I hope you're right," I said to Liv.

"And I hope you and Henry aren't going to christen my parents' brand-new bed-and-breakfast," Finn said from his seat behind me. Apparently, I needed to be talking at a pitch only dogs could hear if I didn't want everyone weighing in on the conversation.

"No one's having a shag anywhere," I said, though a minuscule part of me hoped that wasn't true.

We settled in for the flight, each of us occupying ourselves with a book, music, a nap, more alcohol, or idle, mindless chatter. I let a playlist called Cruising Altitude lull me to sleep, hoping my nervous energy would disappear into a REM cycle.

Henry had texted while we were in the air to say he was

only about thirty minutes behind us. My stomach turned itself over the way one might flip an omelet, which was quite distracting, given the silence of the Irish countryside.

The only sound that rippled through the expanse of land was that of our luggage rumbling along the unpaved paths. Finn had warned us that an Uber couldn't pull directly up to the B and B, but could "get right close." We quickly learned that Finn's definition of "right close" was at least a 20-minute trek across neighboring farms on muddy, overgrown paths. I wondered how this would affect business but refrained from voicing my concerns aloud. Liv was doing enough whining for all of us, and the last thing we needed was more negativity.

When the B and B came into view, I had goose bumps for reasons that had nothing to do with Henry. It was even more brilliant than it looked in pictures. A traditional rectangular structure, the building boasted high brick walls smothered in wild ivy. Hidden lights illuminated the B and B as the sun set, casting the entire property in a warm glow. The garden stretched out of sight in all directions, and the air smelled of sweet primroses and freshly cut grass. Each window of the B and B held a small candle, like a storybook, and a wildflower wreath covered most of the front door. It was magical.

"Deadly, innit?" Finn said from the porch, watching us all admire the estate in silence.

"It's like a property fairy tale," Liv said, leaving her bad mood behind on the path.

"Told ya," Finn said. "Let's get inside and meet Mum and Da, then I can show you to your rooms and give you a proper tour."

The inside of the building was even more gorgeous than the outside. It was quaint in the way we had imagined it would be, with all the charm of the country we missed so badly sometimes in the city. An oak staircase with an ornate banister dominated the center of the small foyer, and the kitchen and living rooms sat humbly on either side.

An antique chandelier cast a warm glow from the center of the ceiling, blanketing the foyer in golden light. The other lights in the house were dim, save for the glow of a roaring fire, which was surrounded by leather armchairs and crooked stacks of books.

Finn's parents came bustling out of the kitchen, interrupting our collective trance. Rory, Finn's dad, was as tall and skinny as Finn, with a scruffy gray beard and the same twinkling boyish eyes. Aoife, Finn's mum, was much smaller, her petite frame wrapped in an apron and her rosy cheeks glowing under big doe eyes.

"Oi! Welcome! Please, please, come in." Aoife unraveled her apron from her waist and tossed it onto a chair beside a massive grandfather clock. "Oh, it's so good to meet everyone." She beamed, making her rounds and kissing us all on both cheeks. She smelled like sugar and gardenias.

"Pleasure," echoed Rory, firmly shaking our hands and patting our backs, wide smile matching those of his wife and son. "Why don't you get settled, then pop down for a nightcap?"

"Oh, Rory," Aoife said. "They must be knackered."

"Never too knackered for a nightcap," Jan said, speaking for all of us.

"Isn't there supposed to be one more of ye?" Rory asked, looking around as if the eighth of us was hiding somewhere.

"He's just behind," I said, perhaps a bit too quickly. "Be here in no time."

"Grand. Perhaps he'll also be keen to join us for a drink. We'll let you get settled, then. Finny, lead the way."

Finn led us up the staircase and down the narrow corridor,

flinging open guest room doors along the way. "So, unfortunately, not every room is ready yet," he said, holding his arms out by his sides. "But the girls said they would share, so there's definitely room for everybody."

Raja and Liv scoped out the largest room, noting it held a double bed and a single, as well as plenty of wardrobe space.

"You think you'll be joining us, Lu, or might you end up in bed with someone else tonight?" Raja said without opening her lips, but still not nearly as quietly as I'd have liked.

"I absolutely think I'll be joining you, you cow," I said, shoving her into the room and dragging Liv in behind us.

"Margot, wanna join?" Liv called into the hallway. "Ireland bed-and-breakfast sleepover?"

"Do I have to?" Margot said, gesturing to a vacant room next door. She must have been trying to sound as dry as usual, but I could detect a laugh somewhere in her tone.

"Suit yourself," Liv said.

Everyone else filed into the surrounding rooms, claiming their own and leaving one open for Henry. The one directly across from ours, not that it mattered.

After we were properly showered and free of the grime of our muddy walk, we started to make our way to the kitchen for a nightcap. I had just finished raking the last bit of product through my hair in hopes of combating the frizz when a text from Henry in the group chat announced his arrival. I changed from a hoodie into a sweater and back again, hoping for effortless while feeling the opposite, then headed out of my room.

"Hey, you."

I nearly smacked right into him, startling all the breath from my lungs. I'd expected to see him in the kitchen, for our reunion to be at the same time as his reunion with the rest of our roommates, not alone in this dim corridor, only a centimeter from each other.

"Oh god, you scared me," I said, forcing a laugh. "I didn't expect to see you right here."

"Well, are you happy to? Or should I leave and try again?"

"Of course I'm happy to," I said, relishing the familiarity of his voice. It was deeper in person than it was over the phone, but the gravel I'd grown so used to was the same.

He pulled me into a hug, and I rested my head against his chest, listening to his heartbeat. He wore an open maroon flannel over an off-white T-shirt, both of which made his green eyes look like shamrocks, and his windswept hair was begging to be untangled. I imagined my fingers combing through it with his head in my lap, looking down at his eyelashes as he told me stories of Scotland, or maybe how he'd missed me while he was away.

"Henry, get dressed and get down here, will you?" Finn called up the stairs. Hen and I laughed at the interruption, reluctantly disentangling ourselves. I pulled back, nodding to his room.

"They saved that one for you."

"Right across from you? On purpose?" He raised a thick eyebrow, and I shook my head.

"Who knows with this lot. I'll see you downstairs?"

"I'll only be a minute," he said, dropping his luggage, then turning around to look at me again. "It's really good to see you, Luce."

"You too," I said, biting the inside of my lip to stop myself from smiling like a lunatic.

The kitchen itself was small and crowded, but it wasn't hard to imagine a slew of Irish chefs dodging each other to prepare a Sunday roast. The ceiling on the right side curved into an upside-down U shape, and just beyond was a surprisingly large dining room. The same warm lights from the entryway studded either side of a dark wooden mantel laden with sunset-colored geraniums and a collection of mostly melted candles. I inhaled slowly before I joined everyone at the table, basking in the swirling scents of nostalgia.

"Lucy, so glad you could join us. Please," Aoife said, dragging a chair away from the table and gesturing for me to sit down. Everyone else, aside from Henry, was already seated, mugs in hand.

"Whiskey or tea?" Rory offered both with a wave of his hand. At my hesitation, he spoke again. "Perhaps both?"

"A hot toddy," I said, smiling. "That sounds lovely. Thank you, Mr. Kennedy."

"Please, call me Rory. Mr. Kennedy is my father," he joked.

"Who has been dead for fifteen years," Aoife said.

"And a blessing that is!" Rory cheered, raising his glass. "Right bastard he was," he added, clinking his glass against Jan's. We laughed hard, and I couldn't help but feel a wave of appreciation at how willing the Kennedys were to welcome strangers with open arms. They were the perfect B-and-B hosts.

"What'd I miss?" Henry said, flopping into the chair next to mine. His wet hair smelled like shampoo and was already starting to curl along the back of his neck.

"Rory's just lost the plot, is all." Aoife swatted her husband's arm and offered a tray of cold corned beef sandwiches to Henry, who accepted with a grateful smile.

He was wearing a battered green Henley that stretched across his chest, and I had to avert my eyes from the two undone buttons at the base of his neck. Despite being roommates for a couple of days every month, and despite the dozens of video calls, this was the most perfectly disheveled I'd ever seen him. I had never before seen his dark eyelashes slick with droplets of water or his bare feet without dirt on the inside curve from kicking a soccer ball. He looked like a painting.

Rory's voice interrupted my daydream, which was for the best, really, seeing as heat that I knew wasn't from the fire was starting to crawl over my body .

"You're the photographer, are ye?" Rory asked, nodding to Henry.

"I am, yes. I was actually hoping you wouldn't mind if I took some photos of the place this weekend. It really is quite beautiful, and since I shoot musicians and venues for a living, I figured I might be able to get some cool shots of the property. If that's all right with you, of course."

"All right?" Aoife laughed. "It would be an honor, dear. Rory, can you believe we're to have professional photos of our place? Oh, Henry, do please send them to us, will you?"

"Of course," Henry said, returning her warm smile.

"And if you need a musician to shoot while you're here, we have one in-house," Rory said, looking at our faces and relishing our confusion. "Finn, play us something, would ye?" He gestured to the looming piano on the far side of the room.

"Da, please," Finn said, more boyish than usual. "Now?"

"Aye, don't be shy! I'm sure yer friends would love to hear ye. Wouldn't they?" We nodded like children, practically begging Finn to play.

"Didn't know you played," Henry mused. "Let me get my camera. Then please, do play us something." We all wore matching Cheshire Cat smiles, equally amused by the fact that Finn played the piano at all and that we were going to see it live.

"Where have you been hiding this, then?" Liv asked, resting her fingers on her pink lips.

"Change your mind about me, does it?" Finn took a seat at the piano, waggling his eyebrows at Liv.

"Depends how well you play," she teased.

"Oh, shut up, you."

"Finn, don't talk like that to a lady," Aoife scolded. We all shared a laugh at how much Finn had reverted back to a lad in Cork, but he just waved us off as he settled onto the bench and rested his hands over the keys. Henry returned with his camera, and we all looked on in silence, waiting.

All at once, Finn's bony fingers began dancing from octave to octave, filling the silence with a classical piece I didn't recognize. Minor chords unfurled into the night, and Finn's eyes fluttered closed as the piece picked up.

The room seemed to assume a collective heartbeat, a tandem rise-and-fall of our chests as we breathed in the music. Finn rocked back and forth as he played, the old wooden bench creaking beneath him, drawing the charm of the bed-and-breakfast into the symphony.

Rory cleared his throat in a way that was hardly audible, and when I looked in his direction I caught him wiping a tear from the corner of his eye. Despite having only known him an hour or so, I could see how generous he was with his heart, and for a moment, I envied him.

Applause broke out in the dining room as Finn played the final notes of the song, and all but one of us was smiling in his direction. I felt Henry's eyes on the side of my head, but I tried to keep my own eyes trained on Finn at the piano.

"I could watch you listen to music all night," Henry whispered over the cacophony of voices showering Finn with compliments.

My teeth found that familiar spot on the inside of my lip,

stopping me from losing it altogether. "You can't say things like that to me in front of everyone," I said, feeling suddenly shy.

"Who's going to stop me?" he said. "Besides, you look cute when you blush."

I bit my tongue before I ruined the moment by saying something I would regret. If I was going to let go of the past and really be here with him, I had to accept the compliment without opening old wounds. I had asked for honesty, and I would have to trust he was giving it to me.

After another half hour of pleasantries and friendly jeering, we were well and truly knackered. "This has been a pleasure," Rory said, standing up. "I'm looking forward to the rest of the weekend. You'll need a good night's rest to put up with us for two more days, so off you pop." He herded us like sheep out of the dining room, despite our offers to help tidy up.

We called a series of "good nights" over the banister as we dragged ourselves into our rooms, tipsy from the whiskey and full to the brim with biscuits and corned beef.

Liv and Raj were fortunately too tired for more than a few minutes of chatting before bed. We covered how gorgeous the place was, how quirky and generous Finn's parents were, and how different it felt to be together away from our usual place of togetherness. After agreeing on the value of a sound night's sleep before our first official day in Cork, we slipped into our respective headphones or eye masks and knocked out the lights.

As always when I was spending the night in a new place, restlessness kept me awake. I tossed and turned until the creaking of the mattress became too much, then admitted defeat and rolled onto my back. I wasn't sure how long I was lying there, staring at the ceiling, but eventually the vibration of my phone ripped me from the purgatory between awake and asleep. *Damn it.*

I felt for my phone on the night table. The light of the screen was blinding when I brought it to my face, and I had to squint to be able to read anything.

Henry Baker
Message

I rubbed my eyes like I was a cartoon and checked it again, mind reeling at the possibilities of what the text might say.

You up?

If I wasn't before, I definitely was now. I sat bolt upright, if only to stop my stomach from flipping, and took a deep breath to compose myself. Was this what I thought it was? I had expected him to say something more casual, like, *Is there any heat in this place*, or *Can you also hear Jan snoring from across the hall?*

Henry Baker, is this a booty call?

My eyes were now fully adjusted to the light, and I stared impatiently at my phone like a teenager while I waited for his response.

Do you want it to be?

Did I? Surely not here in this bed-and-breakfast, right? We had agreed to try not to make things weird for our roommates, and I did promise Finn no one would be having a shag tonight, so the answer had to be no. Besides, we hadn't crossed that line just yet, and I wasn't sure I wanted to cross it on a midnight booty call.

I'm just winding you up. He texted again before I could answer. Every creak in this place is keeping me awake—fancy venturing to the kitchen for a cup of tea?

I exhaled at the prospect of tea. That was much safer ground, and I could've really used a cup.

Meet you in the kitchen in five.

I stifled a chuckle and felt around in the dark for a hoodie and slippers. I was sure I looked shite at that hour, so I skipped a glance in the mirror and tiptoed downstairs.

When I crept around the corner and into the kitchen, Henry was already working on the kettle. His presence dominated the stillness of the room. He stood unmoving, hands braced on either side of the stove, the muscles in his back just barely visible under his shirt. His head was bent low, and I studied the notches of his spine at the base of his neck.

A creak from the floorboards gave me away before I could speak, and he spun to face me.

"Ah yes," he said. "Another creature of the night."

"Only because a certain creature woke me up and convinced me to get out of bed," I said.

"Oh, please. You were awake already, and you hardly took any convincing." He dropped tea bags into two mugs and took the kettle off the stove. As he slowly poured the water into the mugs, I could see the flex in his forearm through his shirt-sleeve, and I made no effort to look away this time.

"You don't think Rory and Aoife will hear us, do you?" I whispered. Somehow the silence of night made even tea feel scandalous.

"Well," he said, moving to the side of the island where I stood, "we aren't doing anything we shouldn't be, are we?"

"Nope, just tea." I smiled, taking a sip for effect and ignoring the increasing beat of my heart. He placed his full mug on the island, then took mine out of my hands and did the same.

"It doesn't have to be 'just tea,'" he said, his voice barely audible. I opened my mouth to protest at the same moment his hands found my hips and lightly pushed me against the counter.

"Henry," I whispered. "Are you joking? We're in the kitchen, and surely the Kennedys are still up."

He put a finger to my lips. "Listen," he said, turning an ear toward the rest of the house. Silence, save for the quiet hiss of the old radiator and the wind whistling outside. "Doesn't sound like anyone's awake to me, does it?"

"What's gotten into you?"

"I've missed you, Lucy," he said, his smile twisting into something more serious. "I just want to make the most of the time we have together." He pushed my hoodie up from my hips just enough so his hands were against my bare skin, and I nearly lost all semblance of rational thought.

"You're right," I moaned, leaning into the warmth of his hands as he bent down to kiss my forehead. "Two days is not enough."

"Maybe it won't always be like this," he said. I pulled back, looking at him with raised brows. He laughed gently, pulling me back to him. "I don't know, Luce. It's impossible to know what the future holds, isn't it? You think you want one thing, but then when it's right at your fingertips, you want something else entirely. D'you know what I mean?"

"What are you saying? Are you saying you don't want to move?" I was trying to tread lightly, but my chest was burning at the possibility that this might be true.

He released me for a moment, pinching the bridge of his

nose with his calloused fingers. "Maybe," he said, flicking his eyes to the ceiling and choosing his words carefully. "Maybe it isn't what I thought it'd be, leaving London. I thought it had nothing left to offer me, but I might have been wrong."

I looked up at him, at the softness in his eyes as they returned to mine and the curl of hair that had fallen into the center of his forehead.

"London would be lucky if you stayed," I said. "She wouldn't want you to sacrifice your dream or anything, but if you did decide she was the place you wanted to call home, she would be lucky."

"Oh, would she, now?" he said, smoothing my hair and bringing his forehead closer to mine. I tried to keep my nerves steady, to avoid getting my hopes up, but was he really saying what I thought he was saying?

"If she got to spend more than two days with you at a time, I'm sure she would be thrilled."

"As would I," he said. "And I mean it, Luce."

I ran my fingertips up the length of his arms and laced them through the curls at the back of his neck. In one swift motion, he sat me on the island like he had in my studio the night of the holiday party and brought his lips to mine. He tasted like mint toothpaste and whiskey. Every creak in the old house told me to pull away, but every hair standing up on my arms told me otherwise.

From my perch on the island, we were nearly eye to eye, which made it all the more intense when we did pull away. He leaned his forehead on mine, and I listened to the way his shallow breaths matched my own.

"We should—"

"Get out of the kitchen?" I finished for him, hoping that was where his sentence was going.

"You read my mind," he said, laughing lightly against my lips. He ran his fingertips along my jaw, lifting my face so our noses were touching. "Come to my room, Luce."

A new heat ripped through me, catching in my chest and sending my heart rate into overdrive. We both knew where this was headed. I weighed potential future heartbreak against the way he was looking at me now, the way his chest felt against the palms of my hands, and made the easiest decision I'd made about Henry in a long time.

"Lead the way," I said, taking his outstretched hand.

Our slow climb up the stairs was punctuated by groans from the old wood beneath our feet and our uneven breaths, and the silence otherwise only amplified the tension between us.

At the end of the corridor, we slipped into his room, closing the door behind us as quietly as possible. Neither of us reached for the light switch.

He leaned over me, my back up against the door, and kissed me again. Soft at first, like he was testing the waters. I slid my hands under his shirt, feeling the warmth of his bare torso. His hands were already above his head, braced on the door on either side of me, so I lifted his shirt off, signaling my consent.

Hen and I looked at each other in the dark through half-closed eyes, and that second of recognition was all we needed. We might not have known what the future held for us, but we knew we both wanted nothing more than this right now.

Before long, his shirt was at the bottom of a heap of clothes, carelessly discarded.

In another world, this moment might have come and gone in the blink of an eye. At home in London, we might have torn our own clothes off without a second thought and been staring breathless at the ceiling only minutes later. But we weren't at home. We were here, in this bed-and-breakfast, under the spell of an old Irish village where nothing was urgent and everything was sacred.

We took our time, savoring the feel of each other's skin, the heat of each other's breath, the sound of each other's moans. Dense clouds obscured the dull moon outside the window, but our senses were only heightened by the darkness. The feeling of his teeth on my bottom lip sent pins and needles through my body, and his wandering hands electrified me entirely.

I felt the ripple of his naked back under my hands and thought of how many times I'd admired the way his shirts stretched across that very space. I thought of that tantalizing inch of skin left exposed between the old T-shirts and joggers he wore around the apartment, and let myself explore it. So much of Henry was familiar, but feeling his body in the dark was quite the opposite.

Being in the same physical space only two or three days a month meant Henry was continually revealing himself to me. I was getting to know parts of him slowly, intentionally, and every layer exposed something that drew me to him even more.

And now, every low growl, every swear whispered in my ear, every kiss on my neck painted Hen in colors I'd never seen. The way he said my name had an entirely new sound, and I would never be able to unhear it. I didn't want to.

We lay there together, limbs entangled, fingers still laced in each other's hair, skin against skin, as we steadied our breathing and readjusted to the darkness with open eyes.

"Would you say this qualifies as 'making the most of it'?" I whispered.

"That doesn't even begin to cover it," he whispered back, the deep notes of his voice rumbling through my body.

I nestled my face into his shoulder to stop myself from speaking and ruining the moment. Maybe it was true, after all, that we wouldn't always be battling distance. That we could actually call the same place home.

We never returned to our heap of clothes on the floor, spending the rest of the night intertwined under the tartan sheets, watching the night crawl toward the morning. He told me stories about his family, I compared his eyes to every green flower I could think of, he took photos of my mahogany hair spread over the pillowcase in the dark. We laughed at embarrassing memories, traced each other's spines with our fingertips, whispered secrets to be carried away with the moonlight.

For once, I wasn't concerned with the future. All that seemed to matter was the gentle rise and fall of Henry's chest under my head and the way the first streaks of sunlight carried in all the promise of new beginnings.

SLEEP NEVER SEEMED to find me, but I wasn't bothered. I was content listening to the rest of our roommates getting ready and padding downstairs for breakfast to the tune of Henry's deep breathing and a few timid birds outside the window. I didn't quite care if I ever moved again, to be honest.

Cork had a stillness about it that let you come into the day on your own time. In London, the city set the pace. It woke up every morning and swallowed you whole. Cork was the opposite. It stretched out green fingers in every direction, inviting you to lose yourself in it. Or maybe find yourself in it. Either way, the choice didn't belong to Ireland.

When Henry finally stirred awake, I watched a lazy smile spread across his face, the dimple deepening in his right cheek.

"I could get used to this," he said, smoothing my hair back from my face.

"Me too."

"Do I smell bacon?" He sat up, leaning back on his elbows. I admired his shirtless chest, the valley of his sternum, the way his pecs turned into his shoulders.

I picked up my phone to check the time and saw I had a text from Raja. I'd almost totally forgotten I was supposed to be sharing a room with her and Liv, and that of course she would've noticed I never returned to it, so I opened the text to make sure she hadn't exposed us to the whole lot just yet.

You don't waste any time, do you? she'd written, complete with a winking emoji.

I groaned and flopped onto my back beside Hen.

"What's wrong?"

"Raja is already winding me up about not coming back to the room last night," I said, half laughing, half mortified. "You don't think they heard us, do you?" I was suddenly concerned, given that we could hear Jan's snoring all night and the sink running every time Liv got up to use the toilet.

"I doubt they heard me," he said, rolling over and throwing an arm around my waist. "But you, on the other hand . . ."

"Henry!" I buried my head in my hands, stifling my laughter. He stood up from the bed, tossing me my sweats from last night and a flannel of his.

"Well, we're going to have to face them eventually, and I'm starving, so. No time like the present." He flashed me a cheeky grin and pulled a white T-shirt over his head, then stepped into a pair of sweatpants and ran a hand through his hair. "I'll meet you downstairs, yeah?" he asked, and I nodded.

He closed the door behind him, and I finally emerged from the sheets to get dressed. I slipped his flannel on, just to see what it would feel like to be in his clothes, then immediately shrugged it off and left it on the bed. If we were going to play it off like we hadn't christened the B and B last night, showing up to breakfast in his clothes was not the way to go about it.

When I got downstairs, everyone was already crowding around the breakfast table, chatting over plates piled high with all the makings of a proper full Irish: bubble and squeak, black pudding, toasted Irish soda bread, beans, tomatoes, mushrooms, heaps of fatty bacon. The smells were intoxicating, and I wasn't surprised to find myself ravenously hungry.

"Did ya sleep well, dear?" Aoife asked, pouring me a mug of tea the size of my head.

"Did ya sleep at all?" Raja asked before I had a chance to respond, shooting me a knowing look.

"Just fine, thanks," I said to Aoife, then glared at Raja. "And thanks for breakfast. This looks incredible."

"Worked up an appetite, did you?" Finn asked just as I took a sip, and a mouthful of tea nearly shot from my nose. When we made eye contact, he stuck his tongue out of his open mouth and raised his barely there eyebrows.

"Right, then," Henry interrupted, holding in what I thought was a laugh. "What's the plan for today?"

Part of me wanted to crawl under the table and die of embarrassment, and the other part of me wanted to climb into his lap at this breakfast table without a care in the world. It was complicated, and I needed caffeine to process. I wasn't usually the type to kiss and tell, so I had no idea what to do with these newfound urges.

"Eager to just move right on, are we?" Jan joined the teasing, a piece of bacon between his teeth like a cigarette.

"I've not a clue what you're on about," Henry said, sipping his tea. "Just looking forward to spending the day in Cork, that's all."

"Oh, so you've nothing to do with Lucy not coming back to our room, then?" Liv asked.

"What Lucy does is her business," Hen said. "Who knows what she gets up to? Quite a mystery, that one."

I held my lip between my teeth to control the idiotic grin trying to force itself onto my face. My cheeks surely matched the roast tomatoes on the table, but I could hardly fight that, either. At that point, I wasn't even sure I wanted to fight anything anymore.

"And does this mystery have anything to share with the crowd?" Liv asked, smiling at me and holding out an invisible microphone.

"If I did, how would I remain a mystery?"

I was met with a collective *boo*, but I was too hung up on catching Henry's smile out of the corner of my eye to care. Regardless of what they thought they knew, Henry and I had something to share between just the two of us, and that was all that mattered to me in that moment. That, and the steaming buffet of food calling my name.

"Anyway, I thought we would just spend the day in town," Finn said, refocusing the lot of us and giving Henry and me a moment of reprieve. "It isn't much, but there's some shopping and one single pub I think you'll fancy."

"Right, well, I'm going to need a nap first," said Jan, leaning back in his chair and throwing his napkin on the table.

"You literally just woke up," Liv said.

"Yes, Liv, and then I ate more than your body weight in sausage, and now I need to be sleeping again," he said, as if he were talking to a child.

"Gross," she laughed. "Well, I just need to put my face on, then I'm ready to do whatever it is we're doing."

"Aye, of course. What would a day in the Irish countryside be without a full face of makeup?" Henry teased.

"Excuse you," she snapped. "You won't be teasing when I look fit and you look, well, however it is you look," she said, then shuffled out of the kitchen in her plush slippers. Margot and Jan offered applause, and Henry dropped his head into his folded arms on the table.

"She's got teeth, that one," Margot said, standing and pushing her chair in. "Jan, get dressed, you big baby. We'll get you some coffee and you'll be good as new." He groaned and rose to join her, and they both disappeared upstairs.

The rest of us followed suit, taking our time under hot showers, finding the right layers for Ireland's unpredictable spring weather. There was still a damp chill in the air, so I settled on a light puffer coat and a pair of black patent boots that doubled as wellies.

Finn rallied us in the room with the fireplace like a college tour guide before we headed out. "Everyone have yer shit together?" he asked. "Town isn't exactly close, and you lot aren't keen on leaving a pub early, so we won't be back for quite a while."

"Cheers, mate," Henry said on behalf of the group.

"Follow me, then." Finn led us through a door we hadn't been through before.

"Finn," I started. "If town isn't close, how are we getting—"

"Voilà!" Finn flicked on the light, and a garage stretched out before us. He framed a 1999 Renault Grand Scénic minivan with his arms like he was on a game show, and we stood in silence. The jade-green paint was chipping off to reveal rust and bare metal, and one side mirror was missing entirely.

"Finn, are you having a laugh, mate?" Cal asked. "Were you even born when this thing was made?"

"Aye, Cal. Nice of you to get a sense of humor for the weekend," Finn said, but Cal only laughed. "All right, get in, arseholes. Unless somebody's got a better idea?" He had us there. We piled in and Finn yanked the van into gear, driving us down unpaved roads, past farms and swamps, and, eventually, into town.

The town center was as quaint and charming as anything else we'd seen so far, perhaps with a bit more emphasis on quaint. A variety of faded colorful shops and boutiques ran down two roads that intersected at a statue of a saint on a horse. Finn had no idea which saint it was and seemed to think it ridiculous that we'd ask.

We first entered an antique jewelry store, which was so small it was a miracle all eight of us fit inside. The walls glittered with gems in every color: emerald, ruby, sapphire. Odds and ends in the process of being restored littered the countertops, and an old woman wearing a headlamp stood behind the cash register, barely able to see over the top. She was draped in velvet of the same tones as the jewels, and her accessories clanged around in a discordant symphony as she worked. Jan whispered to me that she was as much of an antique as her wares, and I had to stifle my laughter.

"Well, I think this is where I'll be spending the rest of the day," Margot said, running her fingertips along a mannequin adorned in a silk robe and walnut-size fake diamonds.

"We should have known," Finn laughed. "Take good care of her, Helene." He pointed at the old woman behind the counter, who did nothing more than nod in agreement.

"Is this one of those towns where everyone knows everyone's name and everyone's family and everyone's business?" I asked Finn when we stepped onto the sidewalk.

"Aye, you mean a small town in Ireland?" Finn joked. "It's

a nice community. They don't have much else to do other than watch the sky turn from rain to sun and back again, so minding each other's business passes the time."

"Doesn't that drive everyone crazy?" I couldn't fathom the whole town knowing what I was up to without having told them myself. How did people exist in a place with no privacy?

"Nah," he said. "It's not so bad. Nothing wrong with people caring about ye or being interested in yer business. We're all family here." He wasn't looking at me as he spoke. "And that's why I love the warehouse so much," he continued. "It's kind of like a small town. We know each other's business whether we want to or not. We're family there, too."

I looked to Hen, expecting to share a laugh at this explanation for why everyone knew what had happened last night, but he was staring straight ahead. Something in the way his eyes wrinkled at the corners looked sad. Forlorn, even.

"We are, aren't we?" he said, without looking at Finn.

"Well, we were until you blokes had to go and make plans to leave," Finn joked, looking at Henry, then Cal, and back at Henry.

"Aye, no one's gone yet," Henry said, a bit too quickly.

"And we'll still be a family even if we aren't in the flat," Cal added.

"Thank god," Liv said. "We'd be right lost without you two."

Cal laughed in his warm, quiet way. "You'd be just fine."

"We're hardly going anywhere," Hen said. "Metaphorically, I mean."

I shot my eyes in his direction, but the second they met his, he returned his gaze to the sidewalk. I swallowed the bubble of hope blocking my airway, trying not to say anything else, but I couldn't help but notice he'd fumbled. And he rarely fumbled.

And yet the more we talked about his move, the more he seemed to be changing his mind.

Puffy cartoon clouds floated away from the sun as we walked, exposing a periwinkle sky. We turned our faces to the warmth, basking in the day, and for me, the possibility of the future.

Finn led us down each path like a tour guide, and as much as he messed around in the apartment, he was serious about his hometown. The history of shops and their owners flowed from him like water from a fountain, and for once we were all actually listening. He spun stories of shop owners having affairs with the shop owners next door, shops made up of only nicked goods, shops that have been around longer than the city itself; the tales floated from a bottomless well.

Each facade was faded on the side most often whipped by the wind, and the hues matched those of the pennants waving proudly above the storefronts. It looked like a postcard. Not a postcard just taken off the rack, either, but one that had been sent halfway around the world and read over and over again, cherished until it faded.

The effect of coral pinks after sage greens after dandelion yellows was hypnotic, and by the time I snapped back to reality, Jan had left us for the pub and Liv was spending her entire paycheck on a bag no bigger than a sausage roll. We were nothing if not consistent.

"I suppose we can split up if we want, enjoy the day," Finn said as we came to the end of our makeshift tour. "We've already lost a few, so might as well pop into the shops we enjoy. Find each other at the pub later, yeah? There's more to this little square than meets the eye, I promise."

"You don't have to convince us of that," Cal said. "Reminds me a bit of home. Thanks for the tour, Finn."

"It really is charming," Raja said, eyeing a housewares boutique. "Someone shoot a text when we're ready to find each other at the pub? I'm sure Jan will be smashed by then, but what else is new?" We laughed, confirmed that we'd text, and parted ways, each in the direction of something that had caught our eye. Except for Finn, who went to go find Liv, I thought. Which I supposed was the same thing.

In a mindless scan of the street, just taking in the moment, my eyes caught on some sort of hybrid shop selling candles and used books. The window display was nothing more than a few candles dripping wax onto stacks of old Irish titles, but I couldn't resist.

A brass bell above the door announced my arrival to no one other than the shopkeeper and his mangy cat. The owner was around middle age, sporting a thick flannel shirt, dark corduroy trousers, and a scruffy beard to match his feline counterpart. If I had had any secret hopes of finding solace or answers in the wise old shopkeeper, they were dashed the moment he did no more than grunt at my presence.

The intoxicating scents of leather and lavender coated the air, masking the musk of dusty pages. It seemed dangerous for the scattered candle flames to be dancing atop stacks of books, but I was too enchanted to mind. Poetry volumes lay atop one another like lovers under a bath of candlelight, and anthologies of stories by local Irish authors stood proudly on display. I didn't believe in heaven, but if I had, it would be this shop. Sans its other occupants.

I was so engrossed in a poem about a gardener that I didn't hear the bell announce another customer. It was titled "Forget Me, Forget Me Nots," and the page was dog-eared on the left side.

"Let me buy that for you," Henry whispered, despite the

fact that we weren't in a library. I jumped, surprised to hear his voice in the silence, and he laughed. "Sorry, didn't mean to startle you." He plucked the book from my hands, tucking it under his arm.

"I was reading that, you know."

He leaned in so that his lips grazed my ear. "And you looked beautiful doing it."

I cocked my head back, meeting his eyes. "You say that about everything."

"And I mean it every time." He kissed me quickly on the cheek, then returned to a normal volume. "Find some other books you like. Let me treat you."

"What for?"

"I can't just do something nice for you because I want to?"

I narrowed my eyes at him, but he only widened his playfully in return. "You're flirtier this time around, you know," I said, starting to browse the stacks a bit more intentionally.

"I'm feeling good lately." He trailed his fingertips down my shoulder as he spoke, sending a chill up my spine right to the base of my skull. I thought of his hand in that place last night, the gentle tug of my hair that brought my lips to his. I resisted turning around, forcing myself to remember we were in public. "I feel, I don't know, clearer," he continued. "Getting off the road isn't as disappointing as it used to be. Quite the opposite, if I'm honest."

"Ah, every girl's dream," I joked. "Not to be a disappointment."

"Who said I was talking about you?" I turned around this time, batting him lightly on the arm with the book in my hand. He snatched it from me, his laughter drowning the sound of my gasp. "You know I'm just winding you up."

"What else is new?"

"It's how you know I like you." His dimple deepened as he smiled, and he closed the space between us.

"Is that what your parents told you when someone teased you on the playground in primary school? That it certainly meant they had a crush on you?"

"Yep. And that's probably why I proposed to my grade-two girlfriend after she threw sand in my eyes."

"You really are damaged, aren't you?" I said, fighting a laugh.

"Part of my charm, isn't it?" The candlelight danced in his eyes, and I couldn't chat for another minute without wanting to take his clothes off right there in that shop. I had a feeling Flannel and his cat wouldn't have approved. "Now, I'm serious," he continued. "Find some other books you love so I can have the pleasure of watching you read them."

"In all the time you spend at home?"

"Watch it, Bernstein," he said through a smile, pointing a long finger at my face. "With all that attitude, I'm starting to believe you don't want me home after all."

"We both know that's the opposite of what I want," I whispered, holding his gaze. The wrinkles in his forehead softened as he looked at me, and for a minute it felt like there had never been any distance between us at all.

He bought me a small stack of books, trying and failing to charm Flannel and the cat as he paid. We ambled back onto the street, ducking in and out of shops, idly conversing with shopkeepers, musing at the sky as heavy silver clouds obscured the pale blue of early spring.

As we wandered past a small produce market boasting an impressive selection of local blooms, I couldn't stop my mind from floating to work. The shower would have been that morning, and I needed confirmation that Renee had gotten on okay.

I slid my phone from my pocket, figuring one text wouldn't hurt, and then I could go back to enjoying the weekend in peace.

> Hi Vivienne. Just checking everything went okay this morning? Congrats again on your day.

Henry and I had only carried on a few more steps before she responded. I slowed my pace to read the message, stopping altogether before I reached the end.

> Lucy, hi dear. Glad you texted. This morning wasn't quite up to your usual standard at the Lotus, if I'm honest. The original delivery was missing two bouquets, and some of the centerpieces were coming loose by midday. I know you're on holiday so I don't want to be a bother, but I thought I'd let you know. And as always, thank you for your work.

"All right?" Henry asked, watching me staring at the text.

"Renee screwed up this morning a bit," I said, still staring. "The client said it 'wasn't up to our usual standard.' Some pieces were missing, and others were falling apart, it seems." I collected my hair in my hands, holding it off the back of my neck to cool myself down.

"Oh, man. I'm sorry, Luce."

"I leave for one weekend, you know?" I said, letting my frustration get the best of me. "And Renee assured me things would be fine for the shower today. She's been doing this job her entire life, Hen. And if she can't do it without me any-more, why can't I have a raise?" I was suddenly on the verge of throwing a tantrum, and I needed to reel it in before I made a scene on the sidewalk. "I know, I know, she would if she could," I said before Henry even responded. "But I feel like lately I'm doing all the work for half the pay."

"Maybe it's time you talk to her about it. For real, I mean, not just in passing. If it's going in this direction now, I don't see it turning around. Do you?"

"If I said yes, would you know I was lying?"

"Everyone always knows when you're lying."

I moaned audibly and rested my forehead against his chest, hoping his heartbeat would steady my own. He ran a large hand up and down my back, and I tried to let my frustration melt away with its warmth.

"I suppose since Vivienne knows I'm on holiday I don't have to answer right away," I mumbled against his sweater. "And Renee doesn't even know I texted to her, so I don't have to talk to Renee yet, either."

"Right you are," Henry said, resting his chin on the top of my head. "And since you're on holiday, there's only one thing to do."

"Drink?"

"Drink."

The rain returned just in time to accompany us to the pub, where Jan had saved us a booth in the back of the room next to a growling fire. We squeezed past the bar, which was beginning to amass a bit of a crowd, and joined the rest of the lot in the booth. As we took turns sharing our findings and hearing how everyone had spent the afternoon, my feet found their way back to solid ground. There was nothing I could do about my job from here, so I might as well pretend it didn't exist at all. Good practice, too, if someday soon I would no longer be pretending.

The pub was as quintessentially Irish as Finn himself. I savored a moment picturing him here as a child with his parents, and later as a teen, sneaking pints with his friends, trying to take home college girls. None of the rest of us had grown up in small towns like this: I grew up in Syosset, Jan in Rotterdam, Margot in Bristol, Henry in Liverpool, Cal in Edinburgh, Raja in Dubai, and Liv in Essex.

We had been to homely pubs before, but never one like this. The bartenders knew the names of every patron, people traveled from table to table catching up on their kids and their farms, teenagers in school uniforms giggled together in the back under the watchful eyes of their parents in the front. There was plenty of room in the booth but we snuggled closer anyway, caught in the open arms of Finn's little village.

"Safe to assume we're hungry, then, are we?" Finn asked, looking from face to face.

"Starving," Jan said, and the rest of us agreed.

"I'll go put in an order with the bartender for the table, if that's all right with you lot? I know all the best bits here, and you've never been the picky type."

"Finn, you are really going above and beyond, mate," Henry said. "Five-star service."

"I aim to please," he said, shooting Henry a wink, at which Hen rolled his eyes. "Back in a min."

Cal and Henry took drink orders, following Finn to the bar. Before long, the table was covered in hearty bowls of Irish stew and family-style plates of shepherd's pie, corned beef, and boiled cabbage. We'd all worked up quite an appetite from wandering around town and spending money we didn't have in little shops all day, and the warmth of the food brought comfort in the cool rain. I relished every salty bite, washing them down with a Guinness.

Somewhere under the cover of the laughter, the banter, and the storytelling, Henry slipped a hand under the table and squeezed my knee. I felt the warmth of his palm through my jeans, and traced the knobs of his knuckles, memorizing the feel of his hands. Though this weekend was making me feel like I might not have to memorize it at all. He might be available for me to study, to admire, to embrace whenever I wanted. It was becoming increasingly difficult to avoid getting my hopes up, but with every sip of every pint and every glance at his wide smile, I was powerless to stop myself.

As we finished dinner and got ready for another round, a folk band began setting up across what I hadn't realized was a dance floor. Made up of six large men who dwarfed their tiny string instruments, the band settled into an old routine on the makeshift stage, bows in one hand, beers in the other.

As soon as the band started to play, Finn and Raja ushered us out of the booth, demanding that we dance.

"Raj, I don't think any of us know the first thing about Irish dancing," I laughed.

"What better time to learn?" She took a parting swig of her drink and grabbed me by the hand, dragging me from the safety of the booth. I managed to scoop my pint from the table and chug the last bit before we hit the dance floor. Everyone else stopped at the bar on the way, bringing us pints when they'd made their way back to us.

"My lady," Henry said in an accent far posher than usual, handing me the beer. I knew he was joking, but the thought of being "his" anything warmed me in a way a strong pint never could.

"Everyone can do this one," Finn shouted over the music as it began to pick up. "Just grab each other's hands and feel the music." At our confused faces, he added, "Just jump around a lot!" He was already bouncing around the dance floor, linking elbows with various partners, twirling old ladies, swinging other dancers around by the hands. The rest of us shrugged at each other and jumped in, each doing our own version of a little "feeling the music" and a lot of "jumping around a lot," sloshing beer all over the floor all the while.

The crowd of dancers heaved together like one pulsing body, and the band sped up, feeding it. We were open-mouth laughing as we bobbed around strangers, dipped in the arms of old Irish men, lost our drinks as soon as we put them down, and slugged pints that weren't ours. Despite the wet chill outside, sweat dripped down our backs and forced our hair into sloppy buns.

Time stopped in this pub. It smelled of warm bodies and pine needles. There was no personal space. No boundaries. Everything the Irish may have lacked in communication, they made up for on the dance floor. The combination of the music, the drinks, and the movement made the room spin, and it was only when Henry swooped me into his arms that everything slammed to a halt.

The band sounded like they were playing underwater, and the bodies around me warped into nothing more than a blur of dull spring hues. Henry's hand on my lower back was becoming an increasingly familiar sensation, only this time, the heat of his gaze outweighed that of his hand. With our eyes locked on one another, we spun in circles with the crowd, somehow managing to stay on our feet. His lips were parted just enough to take panting breaths, and the heady energy between us sent a welcome chill through my veins. I shook my hair loose from its perch on top of my head and let it fall all the way down my back.

In the midst of the chaos on the dance floor, things between us were easy. It didn't matter where we lived, what would happen with our jobs, where we'd find ourselves in the future. It didn't matter if this was going to work. What mattered was that it *was* working, right now, under the spell of this Irish pub. We were pressed up against each other, drunk and uninhibited, spinning wildly under the dim golden lights, falling through space and time.

Every song thereafter sounded like a record spun too slow, warm and full and just a bit lopsided. One by one we stumbled back to the booth, out of breath and knackered from the dancing.

"I told you you could do it," Finn said when the eight of us had collapsed into our seats. "Good craic, that, isn't it?"

"Who knew the Irish countryside could be so fun?" Liv sighed.

"Me," Finn said, deadpan. "I've literally been saying that to you lot since I moved into the flat."

"Oh, Finny," Liv said, ruffling his hair. He shoved her off, then immediately pulled her back in when he saw her pouting.

"Are we ready to get out of here, then?" Henry asked, nodding in the direction of the road. We exchanged a few tired groans, agreeing that it was time to be getting back.

"Finn, give me the keys, mate," Cal said, hand outstretched.

"Yer just as hammered as the rest of us," Finn said, squinting one eye to see Cal clearly. "We'll call a taxi."

Cal snatched the keys from Finn, laughing at the sight of us. "Unlike the rest of you, I can stop myself after one drink and live to tell the tale. Let's get you lot home, shall we?"

We followed Cal's directions, and once more piled into the Grand Scénic, rumbling down the unpaved back roads that had gotten us there, this time to a soundtrack of drunken snoring inside the van and howling wind outside its open windows.

Upon our return, we spent a few minutes in the kitchen pouring massive glasses of water and shoving a few cookies in our mouths to soak up the alcohol, then most of us found our way to bed. We had an early flight, so no one was particularly interested in oversleeping.

Hen and I lingered the extra minute, pretending to tidy up but really stalling while we inwardly debated which bed I'd be sleeping in. He broke the silence first.

"Well?" he said, running a dish towel around the rim of a drinking glass. "Are you coming to bed, then?"

"Depends," I said, taking the glass from him and returning it to the cupboard. "Are you going to keep me up all night again with your snoring?"

He gasped, swatting at me with the dish towel. "I do not snore, I'll have you know." I rolled my eyes, surprised when he pulled me closer to him by my belt loop. "But I might keep you up all night with something else." He brought his chest to mine, the gentle pressure soothing my racing heartbeat.

"We both have early flights," I whispered.

"Then it's a good thing we don't plan on sleeping," he said, lips grazing my ear as he spoke. "We'll be sure not to miss them." I leaned up to kiss him, and he held me by the jaw, stopping me just before our lips touched. "Come on."

For the second night in a row, I took his hand and followed him upstairs, trying to keep my breathing steady. As we rounded the corner at the top of the stairs, we ran smack into Rory in the corridor, and the breath I was holding came out all at once.

"Mr. Kennedy, er, Rory, hi, we were just—"

Rory held up his hand, stopping my fumbling for everyone's sake. "I was just checking a wonky radiator," he said, using his hand to obscure his face. "You didn't see me. Please, enjoy your evening."

The three of us tried to stifle a collective giggle, which

turned into full-blown laughter once Henry and I were in the safety of his room.

"Bloody awkward, that, wasn't it?" Henry said, flopping onto his back on the bed.

"Could have been worse, I suppose. Could have been Finn," I said, imagining the scene he would have made if he saw us holding hands and whispering on our way to bed. We both shuddered at the thought. "At least let's set an alarm while the moment's temporarily ruined," I said. "Just in case."

I felt for my phone, but when I came up empty-handed, I figured I must have left it in my bag downstairs. "Mine's on the nightstand," Henry said, recognizing my dilemma. He was stretched out on top of the covers, arms over his head, making no indication of moving.

I reached for his phone to set the alarm, and that was when I saw the email.

No more than a few lines, a preview, lit up on the screen from hours ago. From the Amsterdam Housing Association. I was reading before I could tell myself to stop.

> Henry, thanks for getting back to me earlier this week. I'm thrilled you're still interested in the flat in Amsterdam Noord, and I . . .

"Do you need my passcode?" Henry asked, probably because I'd been holding his phone for a beat too long to just be setting an alarm. His voice was distant, like it was being carried by the wind from the shore. "Luce?"

"You're moving to Amsterdam?" I fought to keep my voice measured, dragging my eyes from his phone to his face.

He propped himself up on his elbows, looking at me from under his furrowed brow. "What?"

I tossed him his phone, watching him as he studied the email. His expression was unreadable, so I waited for him to say something, anything, that would make this make sense.

"Oh god, Lucy," he said eventually, sitting fully upright and rubbing the back of his neck. "I haven't signed a lease or anything, I just—"

"Reached out to an agency this week about an apartment?"

"Right, yeah. The venue offered me something more permanent, so I reached back out to the agency. But I'm not sure that's quite the same as moving, is it?" He reached for me, but I pulled away, putting as much distance between us as possible in the tiny bedroom. What was previously cozy became claustrophobic, the walls pressing closer with each shaky breath. "Oh, come on, Luce," he said as I recoiled.

"'Come on, Luce'? Don't give me that, Hen, I'm not the one who is out of line here." My voice came out clipped and cold, but there was no sense in trying to fight it.

"Out of line? I've hardly done more than send an email."

"You can be so dense sometimes," I said. "It wasn't just an email. It was a job offer and an email about moving to a new city, and you sent it just a few days before you were seeing me? And told me about neither? Timing was shit, don't you think?"

He fumbled for something to say, but we both knew he wasn't getting off easy. I'd heard enough excuses, and I needed honesty. He owed me that.

"You're right," he said eventually, dipping his head toward his chest. "Timing was shit. Timing of this whole year has been shit, hasn't it? What am I supposed to do?" He brought his eyes back to mine and I had to take a deep breath to find some resolve.

"You're supposed to just be honest," I said. "You said this was only temporary. You told me you'd be chuffed if we could spend more than two days together at a time. That London might actually have something to offer you, and that you thought you wanted to move but then when it was at your fingertips, you realized it might not be what you wanted after all. What's the truth, Hen?"

He gathered his hair in his hands, pulled it a little, then dropped it again and pushed it out of his eyes. "Right, I know. I'm not sure this counts as a lie, though, does it? I just, I didn't think you'd take that to mean I wasn't still considering leaving."

"Classic," I said, waving a hand in the air.

"And what d'you mean by that?"

"This is what you do, Henry. You speak and you act sometimes without any regard for how it might affect me. It's like you don't even see me sometimes. We keep going around and around because you give me hope that things might change. And maybe I'm to blame since I keep believing that might be true."

"You've known this was the plan all along," he said, his frustration emphasizing the gravel in his voice. "Yes, the timing of the email wasn't brilliant, I get that. But I'm still on the fence, which you know, and I need to keep my options open."

"In case something better comes along," I said. "Right, then."

"You know it's not like that."

"What's it like, then? Surely it's not that you're keeping me on the back burner as a plan B, right? That you're keeping me around to have a little fun with when you get home, but never had any intentions of being serious about me at all?"

"I'm hardly keeping you on the back burner, Lucy. All I do is think of you. I take photos, I muddle through gigs, and I think of you. I can't figure out where the hell I'm supposed to live because I'm so busy thinking of you. My focus has gone out the window, and I have no idea where this year is headed, because of how much time I spend thinking of you."

"Thinking about me is one thing, Hen," I said, trying to stay collected despite the goose bumps crawling up my spine. "But is it enough to make this work?"

"I could ask you the same thing," he said. "Don't you think we both have a lot to consider? You've been taking on more and more at the shop, which is sure to continue becoming even more of a massive commitment." I said nothing. "I'm just saying, I think we both have to consider the timing, that's all. We're both going through some pretty significant changes in our lives, and it's hard to figure out how we factor into each other's."

"So the wanting isn't enough," I said as it settled in. It didn't matter how much we thought about each other, how much we wished things were different, how much we wanted to try. It wasn't going to work.

I watched his jaw clenching and unclenching as he searched for something to say. Eventually, when the lines softened around his eyes, my heart did the same. It was like melting, standing there having that conversation, and I had no idea how I'd make it out in one piece. And by the look on his face, I wasn't sure he would, either.

"It's just not as easy as you're making it sound," he continued, dropping his voice so low it was almost hard to hear him. "I'm serious about you, Lucy. I'm just also serious about my job and my place in the world, and I still have to figure that out. I have to stick out the year, at least. It's just so bloody hard to figure out how to handle both. Us and the job, I mean. Both of our jobs."

"We could have figured it out together," I said, wishing we'd tried harder.

"Could we have? I mean, I wish that was true, but at the end of the day, if I leave and you stay, isn't that kind of the end of the road?"

"If you were serious about it, it might not have had to be." We stared at each other in a glassy-eyed standoff, searching the silence for something worth saying. "You should have told me," I said eventually.

"Nothing was certain yet."

"It doesn't matter. That's what you're missing. When you're invested in someone, this is what you do to make it work. You tell them things. Especially if those things are plans to move to another country, even if nothing was certain yet." I pulled my hair off my face just to have something to do with my hands.

"I was going to tell you."

"When, after you slept with me?" I knew it was a low blow, but it came out before I could stop it.

"You know it isn't like that." He reached for me, but I didn't move. "I don't know how to do this."

"At some point, you have to try to learn," I said. "I didn't know how to put myself out there, but I managed to do it over and over again for you. Even knowing it could end like this."

"So this is the end, then," he said, less like a question and more like a heart-wrenching confirmation of fact. One we might have known was coming all along.

"Seems to be what you wanted," I said, all the edge draining from my voice.

"I'm sorry, Lucy," he said. "I wish it didn't have to be like this. But we both have our careers to prioritize at this stage, don't we? And besides, you've said it yourself—we both know you don't deserve to be waiting around, and I'm sorry I ever expected that of you. It isn't fair."

"Right, then," I said, wishing against all logic that he could just be the one to give me what I deserved. I opened the door, but he grabbed the edge before I could pass through.

"I really am sorry." His voice shook, and I had to get out of there before mine shattered altogether.

"Yeah," I said, a single hot tear leaking from the corner of my eye. "Me too."

The gentle closing of his door was a final, conclusive sound. A sound that coaxed the rest of my tears from my eyes in two salty rivers, cutting paths down my burning cheeks.

I pressed my ear to the door of my room, trying to determine whether Liv and Raja were still up and about inside. There was only silence, and I slipped through the door and into bed, unnoticed.

I tossed and turned, letting stray tears stream over the bridge of my nose, feeling them pool on the flannel pillow beneath my head. I should have seen this coming. I should have listened to my gut when it told me not to get my hopes up. I should have walked away the first time he said something he didn't mean. The first time he led me on.

But I hadn't. And I couldn't go back in time and change it. And I couldn't change Henry, either. If he couldn't see me, couldn't see what this could have been, there was nothing more I could've done. It really had been over before it started.

The realization bloomed in my chest and flowed through me like white water, and I could no longer distinguish anger from sadness from betrayal from heartbreak. The minutes turned into hours. The cracks in the exposed ceiling beams slipped in and out of focus. The box-breathing method I had learned from my therapist in college worked to steady my breathing but not my mind, and I let the thoughts race like cars on a track, crashing into each other, spinning out of control, catching fire. Eventually, sometime deep into the night, exhaustion won, and I fell asleep.

When I awoke, the sun had reached its feeble fingers through the flimsy window shades. I wasn't sure how long I'd slept, but I knew it hadn't been long enough. I blinked myself awake, trying to adjust to the light. Liv and Raj were still asleep, so I had a few blissful moments of silence to gather myself before our alarms ripped us awake and we would be forced to leave the Irish countryside and make our way back home.

I was lying on my side, staring at the room through only my right eye, which was swollen half shut, thinking of my elementary school art teacher. She would let us hang upside down on the monkey bars for "perspective," then ask us to draw the world from that angle. I wondered what she would think of me now. And I wondered about the world from this angle. Seeing as I wasn't drawing what I saw and I was lying in this position not for perspective but because I didn't yet have the will to sit upright, I figured she would be disappointed.

Henry was heading back to Scotland, so the only time we'd be forced to spend together this morning was the ride to the airport. Then we could part ways, fly to our separate destinations, and avoid each other forever. Or at least until he left the apartment to move to Amsterdam.

Raja and Liv were pretty hungover, so I played at the same, thankful we were mostly getting ready to leave in silence. I wasn't interested in having to relive last night just yet, so it was all I could do to pray everyone was too hungover to ask any questions.

When we all finally made it downstairs, Rory and Aoife were poised to send us off with breakfast and snacks for the journey, despite the fact that it was no more than a couple of hours back to London.

"Seriously, we cannot thank you enough for this weekend. Everything was brilliant," Henry said on behalf of all of us. His voice was level and energetic, but the bags under his eyes told me he hadn't slept much, either.

"The pleasure was all ours," Aoife said, beaming so wide, we knew she meant it. "It's the least we could do for you lot, for taking such good care of our Finn in the city." She reached up to ruffle his hair, and he let her.

"All right, Ma, that's enough." He rolled his eyes, then kissed her on the top of the head. Their love for each other was almost enough to warm my cold heart, and it made me wish we could have stayed in Ireland forever. Perhaps I would come back here when I needed to hide from my life in London.

We said our final goodbyes and collected our things, heading out the front door. I turned around to take one last look at the place, only to find Henry looking at me. He opened his mouth like he might say something, but I reverted my gaze back to the path before he had the chance.

Nothing he could say would make the events of this weekend hurt any less. Nothing he could say would change the truth about our careers, our circumstances, our feelings for each other, our failed attempts at balancing them.

There was nothing he could say about us, because there was no longer any "us" at all.

June

Clutching my phone was making my hand clammy, and Renee's text was starting to blur the longer I stared at it. The words *There's something we need to talk about* were branding themselves on my eyes, but I couldn't look away.

This was it. The North London Lotus was closing. Last month had been the final nail in the coffin. I had known it was always just a matter of time, but I suppose I'd never imagined it actually happening. It was wishful thinking that we would be able to keep up with bigger businesses, especially if we weren't at the top of our game. The rogue small wedding and restaurant opening just weren't going to cut it, and it was time I accepted that. Besides, with the way Renee had been working (or not working) of late, I doubted she could keep this up even if we were on par with those bigger shops.

"I'm off to lose my job," I said to Raja from her doorway on my way out.

"Excuse me?" She pushed her blue-light glasses to the top of her head, rubbing her eyes. "You're what?"

"Going to lose my job. Renee texted me that we need to talk as soon as I get in today, which can only mean one thing."

"Ah yes. Of course. Every time anyone's boss ever needed to have a conversation, it was because the business was closing and all the employees were being laid off."

"I'm serious, Raj," I moaned. "The shop's been struggling for the better part of this year, so we should have seen this coming."

"But what about all the stuff you've been doing to try to save it? Surely that's bringing you business, isn't it?"

"Not enough. Which seems to be a theme for me lately."

"I'm going to pretend you didn't just say that. Let's not worry until we have to worry. We have no idea what she's going to say, and jumping to conclusions isn't going to get you anywhere. You're just going to give yourself heartburn."

"Joke's on you, I had heartburn when I woke up anyway."

"Because you live in a constant state of anxiety. Take some deep breaths, Lu. Might do you some good."

"I'll breathe after I'm fired," I said. "At least then I'll know what the future holds. No job, no men, just me and my flowers, living in this warehouse forever."

"You're so dramatic, you're starting to sound like me," she said. "Besides, there are worse things than not dating and not working and living in this warehouse forever, you know."

"Raja Ali, ever the optimist."

"Don't you have somewhere to be?" she asked, nodding toward the door. I rolled my eyes and let out a sigh before realizing she was right. I had to get going. "It's going to be fine," she said more softly as I started to leave. "Whatever it is, it's going to be fine."

"I hope you're right."

"I usually am."

With that, I set out for the Lotus, trying to control my breathing. Raja was right. She had to be right. Whatever happened had to be fine. Because in the past few weeks, nothing else had seemed to be fine, and I wasn't quite sure I could handle another falling out.

"Is that you, pet?" Renee asked as soon as I opened the door.

"It is," I said, the crack in my voice embarrassingly noticeable. "What's going on?"

"Come in, come in." She waved me into the office, shuffling a stack of papers on the desk. The trailing vines from the plants perched on the file cabinets tumbled to the ground, and I wondered whether that was intentional. Come to think of it, everything in the office was a bit overgrown. White jasmine petals were browning at the edges, piles of open envelopes spilled onto the floor, and Renee's gray curls had escaped the clip at the back of her head. She inhaled to speak, and I braced myself for the end.

"It's no secret things have been changing around here," she began. The knot in my throat grew to the size of my fist, but I let her continue. "And as much as I try to fight it, it's no secret I'm getting older, either. Which means I can't run the Lotus forever."

"So we're closing," I said on an exhale, more of a statement than a question. "I guess I knew it was coming, I just didn't want to accept it. I thought that—"

"Closing?" she said, stifling a laugh. "Is that what you think?"

"Is it not?"

"Lucy, look around!" she said, gesturing vaguely around the shop. Piles of new order forms cluttered the desk and the worktops were hardly discernible under the mountains of blooms. "We've been thriving, dear. And I have only you to thank for that."

"Renee," I started, "that isn't—"

"I'm serious," she said. "We both know I can't work the way I used to anymore. We've only accomplished all we have in the last few months because of your talent and ambition." I blushed at the compliment, resisting the urge to disagree for her sake. "The Lotus is headed for big things, you know."

"Like what?"

She reached across the desk and grabbed my hands. "That, my dear, is up to you." We stared at each other long enough for her to register my confusion, so she continued. "The shop is yours, pet. If you want it."

I opened and closed my mouth, searching for something to say. "It's mine?" I asked, dumbfounded.

"Only if you want it," she said again. "For quite some time now I've been thinking it might be time to retire, but I couldn't imagine handing it over to anyone other than you, so I just wanted to make sure you were ready."

"This has all been a big test, then, has it?" I asked, finding some levity amid the shock.

"If it was, you passed with flying colors, dear. I wanted to make sure you had two feet firmly on the ground first. That you could handle the kind of projects the Lotus needs in order to thrive. And you've exceeded my expectations time and time again. You're going to have to work hard, Lucy. You know it isn't all rainbows around here. But you're a real talent, and it would be an honor to hand you the reins."

Teared pooled in the corners of my eyes as the news set in. "Renee, I don't know what to say."

"Say you'll take it," she said. "And say you'll still let this old hag come in from time to time." Her smile stretched across her face, bringing color to her cheeks.

"Of course I'll take it," I whispered, for fear of what my voice might sound like at full volume.

"And say you'll put your heart in it."

"Someone very wise once told me to be more generous with my heart, so I'm not sure I could do it any other way."

"Sounds like she taught you well."

"She taught me everything I know."

A delicate silence blanketed the office, punctuated only by a sniffle or two as we tried to compose ourselves. Eventually, we dissolved into laughter.

"Look at us," she said, wiping her eyes. "Crying in here like two nutters."

"I expected to cry today, but not for this reason," I said, feeling quite silly now. "I can't believe I thought we were closing."

"Pleasant surprise, innit?"

"To say the least. I suppose we have some logistics to cover, don't we?" I asked, looking around the cluttered office and imagining the amount of work ahead of us in turning over the business.

"Do the Anderson pickup, then enjoy the weekend with your flatmates. We can start talking through logistics on Monday."

"Are you sure? I mean, we must have loads to do."

"Celebrate with your mates first, pet. Legalities and paperwork can wait."

As soon as I imagined announcing the news to the apartment, Henry's face flashed in my mind. I'd been savoring the distance between us over the past few weeks, and imagining what the apartment would be like if he never came home at all.

Fortunately, taking over the shop was just exciting enough to distract me from my heartbreak. I was floating on a cloud that not even Henry Baker could pull me down from, and I was determined to keep it that way.

Once the Anderson delivery was safely refrigerated and prepped for Sunday, I raced home to tell Raja the news. It was way too big to text, and I'd been counting the minutes until I could get back to the apartment to make the announcement.

I stepped off the elevator expecting to dash up to her room, but instead I was met by most of my roommates chatting around the kitchen table with drinks. No sign of Henry or Cal, but it looked to be about everyone else.

"Oh, Luce, you're home!" Liv said, reaching for a beer to throw my way. "Sorry we started without you, but you haven't missed much of anything yet. We're just—"

"Renee is giving me the shop," I said before I could stop myself. Their collective chatter turned to silence as they waited for me to continue. "Sorry, er, I didn't mean to just blurt it out like that. I'm still kind of in shock."

"She's just handing it over?" Margot asked.

"Yeah, I mean, she's retiring, so. She wants to work part-time still, and we have a lot of legalities to cover, but yes. It's going to be mine." My giddy smile felt a bit silly, but I was too excited to care. Saying it out loud to my mates made it feel real, and my chest pounded at the sound.

"Bloody hell," Finn said, getting to his feet and slamming his beer on the table.

A second later, everyone else exploded in celebration. There was hugging and cheering and chugging of beers, and I was smiling so hard my cheeks started to hurt.

"So, no getting fired after all, huh?" Raja teased, nudging my shoulder.

"Quite the opposite."

"I'm really, really proud of you, Lu. I know how hard you've been working to keep the shop afloat, and it's no surprise all that work paid off. I can't think of anyone more deserving."

I threw my arms around her, savoring the rare moment she was serious. "Thank you," I whispered into the hug.

"Cheers to you," she whispered back.

"Cheers to me."

"Well then, it looks like celebrations are in order, doesn't it?" Jan said, gathering a few more drinks and bringing them to the table.

"Where are the other two?" Liv asked, and my heart thudded against my ribs as I listened for a response.

"Cal's finalizing some stuff for the house, so he won't be home until tomorrow," Margot explained, "and Henry should be home in a bit, I think. But who's to say with him, really? Haven't heard more than a word since we left Ireland, so I guess we'll just see him when he shows up."

"Who needs them?" Raja said, reading my mind. Nothing against Cal, obviously, but I could do without Henry—I was trying to maintain my good mood. "Everyone has five minutes to text me what they want from Nando's if you want me to place the order. Starting now."

We claimed spots around the table, texting Raja our orders and opening fresh beers, settling in for the night. It was the kind of night where we spent a couple of hours sitting in the same seats, sharing food and collecting empty cans, too lazy to move or change the playlist or talk about anything other than who was watching what and when the rain looked like it was going to clear up.

"Oh my god," Raja said after a while, nearly knocking over her chair as she scrambled to her feet. "Lu, we have to burn your resolution. You wrote on the paper that you wanted to be promoted, right? That was the goal?"

"Oh my god," I echoed. "You're right." The rest of the lot cheered lightly, encouraging me to go collect the box.

When I returned, I was met with expectant gazes and anticipatory silence. The lid of the box creaked open, our resolutions nestled among each other inside, save for Raja's, which we had burned the night she signed her contract with H.M. Whitaker. My hands trembled only slightly as I fished mine out, holding it up to the crowd.

"Wow," I said, more to myself than to my roommates, turning the paper over in my hands. If the reality hadn't set in before, it certainly had now. I took a deep breath to maintain my composure as a familiar tingling began at the back of my eyes. Only this time, they were happy tears that threatened to fall.

"Burn, baby, burn," Finn chanted, pounding his fists on the table. Jan handed me a lighter, and I watched the flame dance around the edge of the paper before setting it ablaze.

I watched it consume my resolution, a cursive declaration in black ink, a shout into the universe for a promotion. What I had gotten was far more than that, and for a second I was embarrassed that I might not have dreamed big enough. I'd gotten a whole shop. Which was now my shop. A shop that belonged to me.

Maybe I could afford to start dreaming a little bigger after all.

My little dream turned to ashes in the tray on the table, and the cheering came in waves all around me. I had done it. I set a goal, and I hadn't just reached it—I surpassed it.

I had my own shop.

If I could have bottled that feeling, the confidence, the pride, the unadulterated joy, I would have sipped it every day for the rest of my life.

Once the cheering subsided and the ashes were swept onto the floor, we settled back into a natural rhythm around the table. The idle conversation was comforting as I picked the damp corner of the label on my beer, contemplating my future as a shop owner.

It was the first time in weeks I could lower my shoulders from my ears, unclench my jaw, and release some of the tension in my chest. I wasn't bogged down by a breakup or the stress of losing my job. I was coming out on the other side of the fog, turning toward the sun.

Or so I thought. When Henry's voice floated into the kitchen as I was finishing washing up, that familiar tightness returned to my shoulders. The rest of the lot had gone up and I'd thought I was alone. I tried not to startle at the sound.

"Congratulations," he said, voice barely audible over the running water in the sink. "Finn told me the news."

"Thank you." I hadn't yet found the resolve to turn around, so I kept my back to him while I cleaned my glass.

"You deserve it, Luce," he continued. "You're going to be incredible at running the shop."

I spun to face him, glass and sponge still in hand. He was disheveled from his travels in a way that used to make me want to make him a cup of tea and smooth the wrinkles in his clothes, only now he looked far more tired than charming.

"Thanks, Hen," I said again, at a loss for anything else.

"I also have some news," he said, closing the gap between us ever so slightly. "I mean, not to make this moment about me or anything, because you're the one who's made the huge accomplishment and all I've done is make a decision really, but this might be a good time to share, if that's—"

"Spit it out," I said, secretly relishing his nervous rambling.

"I'm not moving to Amsterdam."

That was not what I expected.

Time stopped just long enough for me to remember who

I was talking to. "Is that true? Because sometimes you say things and they aren't necessarily true, and I don't want this to be one of those times."

I returned the sponge and glass to the sink, crossing my arms over my chest to stop myself from fidgeting.

"I'm serious, Lucy," he said, stepping closer now. "I'm not moving anywhere else, either. I'm staying in London. And I'm not just saying that for the sake of the moment, or implying it, or hinting at it. I'm saying it because it's true."

"What about your job?" I asked. "Your future apartment? The great big dream that was so important to chase?"

"I'm being promoted," he said, in a voice far more measured than my own. "I was just piloting the program before, but now the company is turning it into a concrete position for newer photographers, so they need someone to oversee it from head-quarters here."

"So that's all it took, huh?" The creases in the corners of his eyes deepened as I spoke, and I could sense perhaps I was being a bit harsh. Still, I couldn't help it. I felt the sting of my position on his list of priorities all over again, and it would have been unbearable to relive.

"I told you, Luce, sometimes you think you know what you want until something better is right in front of you." He stepped closer, and I backed away until I was up against the sink. I sensed he wasn't talking about the job anymore, and I was terrified to venture into that territory.

"Right, well, congratulations," I said, hoping our conversation could end there. "Thrilled it worked out for you."

"I was hoping it might not be the only thing that worked out . . ." He let his voice melt away, waiting on me to fill the silence.

"Well, we don't always get the things we hope for, do we?"

"We can't even talk about it?"

"There is nothing left to say, Henry. I'm glad things worked out for you. Really, that's grand. But it has nothing to do with me anymore. You can't see me only when it's convenient for you, and I need more from someone than just living in the same city."

"Right, then."

It took more resolve than I was proud of to keep the distance between us, but I was determined to do what I thought was right. Even if it hurt like hell. I offered no more than a curt smile before brushing past him to leave the kitchen, careful for our shoulders not to touch.

I slipped into Raja's room instead of my own, needing to unpack Henry's news if I was to function as a normal person this weekend. Or ever again.

"I was sleeping, you know," she said as I climbed into her bed.

"Henry's staying in London," I said.

"He's what?"

I gave her the same spiel he gave me, at which she sat up and turned on the light. "So, does this mean he's, like, going to be in the flat all the time? Starting when?"

"I don't know," I said, flopping onto the pillows. "I didn't ask any questions. I was so bloody bothered that he thought that was enough to fix things, and I didn't want to think about having to see him every day, and I just wanted the conversation to be over."

"Wow," she said, laying back on the pillows with me. We stared at the ceiling in silence, contemplating the news. "And what does this mean for the two of you?"

"Nothing," I said, but I couldn't even muster enough conviction to sound like that was what I wanted. "I can't do it again, Raj. It's too complicated. Especially now that I'm taking over the Lotus. I'm not sure I can afford the distraction."

She turned out the light again and snuggled up to me. "It's okay to still have feelings for him, you know. You can be excited about your new gig and sad about Henry at the same time. Last time I checked, conflicting emotions were allowed as part of the human experience."

I was glad she had turned out the light before she said that, because it made my bottom lip start to quiver. Fighting emotions was most often harder than feeling them, and I regretted spending the past few weeks trying to pretend I felt fine. At the end of the day, lying to myself felt worse than lying to anyone else.

At some point, I would have to decide where to live, I would have to address that Henry would be back in the apartment full-time, and I would have to properly distance myself if I wanted to avoid further heartbreak. But it was late, and I was tired, and I didn't have to do any of those things until at least the morning.

So, I focused on Raja's breathing, letting mine match her pace until I dozed off beside her.

"DO YOU GUYS have any idea what we're doing today?" Liv asked, turning on Raja's light.

"Sleeping," Raja moaned, pulling the covers over us both. "You should be doing the same."

"It's nearly ten," Liv said. "And Hen won't tell us what we're doing until everyone is up and moving, so. It's time to get up and moving."

Raja and I groaned in unison, Raja at the prospect of moving, and me at the sound of Henry's name. A few hours of sleep had given me nothing by way of clarity, and I still hadn't the foggiest what I was to do about him staying in the city. Which would make for quite an interesting day, wherever we ended up.

"First, we need coffee," Raja announced, throwing on a sweater and heading for the kitchen.

"Just going to pop into my room first to change, but I'll meet you down there," I said, hoping I could buy a few minutes to collect myself.

"Roger that," Raja said, then disappeared down the stairs. I shuffled into my room, rubbing sleep from my eyes and reaching for the light switch. When the dull fluorescent bulb cast its glow around my room, I couldn't quite process what I was seeing.

An envelope with my name scrawled across the front sat in the center of my bed, and I made my way over to it in what felt like slow motion. I reached for the envelope with unsteady hands, breath held in my chest.

I slid my index finger under the flap, revealing a note on ivory cardstock and a dozen glossy photos. Of me. I tried to keep my eyes from wandering to the pictures until I knew what any of this meant, so I steadied myself as I read.

Lucy,

I will never be able to apologize enough for making you feel like I didn't see you. I want you to know my greatest privilege was, in fact, getting to see you, especially in these stolen moments. In the fairy lights around the holidays, at work in your studio, making magic, the way you laugh, eyes closed, curls down your back. I saw you, Lucy. And it would be an honor to keep seeing you.

Hen x

I let the note flutter to the bed, bringing a hand to my lips. The words alone were overwhelming, and when I turned my attention to the photos, I ran the risk of unraveling entirely. Each was matted in white like framed stock photos in the shops, and they were stacked in a way that told the story of our time together.

I picked them up one by one, studying them as I went. It was only then that I connected nearly every Warehouse Weekend with the steady click of his camera, like a distant metronome. Had I heard it, had we both let it keep steady time, maybe we wouldn't have been in this mess at all.

There were photos from the Jack the Ripper tour, my fingertips pressed up against old windows, my head on Raja's shoulder as we shared a flask and huddled together for warmth. There were photos from the Christmas party, Liv and I on the dance floor, my hair masking my eyes, my body a blur under the twinkling lights. In my studio, where I was hardly more than a silhouette, backlit by the moon, the shadow of a bouquet in my hand. The axe-throwing anti–Valentine's Day weekend, my knuckles white against the wooden handle and our smiling roommates in the background.

There were even photos from the market search back in April, ones of my face as I studied cheeses and chatted with vendors. My cheeks were glowing from the warm spring weather, and my eyes were almost golden in the sun.

And there were ones from Ireland. My profile as I watched Finn play the piano, Raja and me with our arms around each other in the center of town, beaming against the sharp Irish wind. My hair splayed across Henry's pillow, my irises buried under my lashes, looking up at him.

I felt like he had just reached his long fingers into my chest and wrapped them around my pounding heart. If we had learned anything about time and distance, it was that we couldn't go back and do things differently. We could only move forward, and try to change the future instead.

And he had taken the first step into that uncertain future. We couldn't undo what had been done, but did that mean we had to carry it forever? Was there a way to use it as a stepping stone, the kind of wobbly, slippery one that still managed to get you to the other side of the stream?

I returned the letter to the envelope and flipped through the pictures once more before piling them neatly on my desk. Liv was shouting downstairs, trying to rally everyone in the kitchen so we could get the day started, which meant I didn't have time to try to work through any of this just yet. The most I could do was count a four-second inhale followed by an eight-second exhale, accompanied by a silent prayer to the universe that I might get through this day unscathed. That I might get some kind of sign telling me where to go from here. What to make of any of this. How to get out of my own way.

By the time I arrived in the kitchen, almost everybody was crowded together, standing over the stove as Cal made breakfast sandwiches. The smell transported me right back to that first morning in Cork, and I had to physically shake my head free of the image of Henry's naked body under the sheets.

"Well?" Finn prompted Henry as soon as I arrived. "That makes eight. What's the craic, then?"

Henry cut his eyes to me before he answered Finn, undoubtedly searching my face for some hint that I'd seen the envelope. I watched his eyes travel to my fingers, resting on the hollow of my throat where I'd been fidgeting with my necklace, both of us now frozen in a hopeful sort of standoff. The corners of my lips crept into something that resembled a soft smile before

I could control them, which he returned with a glisten in his forest eyes.

I couldn't yet manage more than a breath of acknowledgment, but fortunately, that seemed to be all he was searching for.

"Right, then," he said, clapping his hands together and clearing his throat. "It's the Sundance Gardens season opener and Lantern Festival for us today."

The sound of these words sent rivers of sparks through my body. It had always been a dream of mine to see the Lantern Festival at Sundance Gardens, but getting tickets was nearly impossible, not to mention quite pricey.

"Are you having a laugh?" Jan asked, interrupting my reverie and nearly spitting a mouthful of coffee back into his mug. "A garden? Weren't you telling me a month ago we were supposed to be at a gig or something?"

"Change of heart," Henry said to Jan, though he was looking directly at me, his single dimple deepening in his right cheek.

He wasn't having a laugh at all. We were really going. And not because Henry was interested in flowers or lanterns, but because I was. He'd done this for me.

His intentions swirled around my brain like the creamer in my coffee, sweet, gentle, and decadent.

"How?" I asked before I could stop myself, feeling this was all too good to be true.

"I know a guy," he answered, clucking his tongue at my expression, which must have been one of unfiltered awe and intense appreciation. "And said guy happens to be married to the director of marketing for the festival, so they were able to pull some strings and get us in."

Words eluded me, and I was left standing there like a fool, hands clasped at my chest, saying nothing.

"Well, it's clear what this is all about," Raja said, nodding in my direction.

"Not quite sure what happened there in Ireland," Finn said, "but you made a right mess of things, didn't ya, Hen?"

I unclasped my hands only to bury my face in them, not sure if I was going to laugh or cry.

"Maybe I'm just really into gardens now," he said.

"Oh sure," Margot said. "You're really into something, all right."

"Okay, enough," Henry said, waving them off. "Be ready to leave by half three. And leave your gossiping and prying at home, would you?"

"Never," Raja answered for the group. "You did this to yourself, darling." Henry's eyes searched mine for support, and for the first time in a long time, I felt like we were on the same team.

Sundance Gardens swallowed us whole the minute we stepped through the gates, transporting us from the grimy city center into what felt like a painting of the countryside. The overlapping scents of the peonies and hydrangeas was intoxicating, lulling us all into a trance as we wound along narrow paths, reaching out to graze our fingers over the endless blooms.

Gentle fountains bubbled in each clearing, surrounded by stone birdbaths and the occasional statue of a goddess. I fielded a handful of questions from my roommates as we perused the flowers, their interest in my greatest passion warming me through to my core. I took out my phone to snap a few photos to send to Renee when I got home, though I knew Henry's would be the ones I'd end up framing.

I noticed his camera now, clicking in time with the distant calls of birds and lovers, the whispers of wind through the trees. I studied his set jaw as he trained the viewfinder on a tunnel of sweet peas, remembering how it had felt that night in Ireland, under my fingertips, digging into my collarbone, nestled against the top of my head.

"Get Jan in there for some juxtaposition," I whispered to Henry as he set up a shot against a wall of zinnias. He barked a short laugh into the quiet of the gardens, and our six roommates whipped around to look at us.

I put my hand up in apology, as if to say *nothing to see here,* and Henry nudged me in the ribs. The spark from just the touch of his elbow traveled straight into my chest, thrumming along with my heartbeat.

"So you did learn something after all," he said, lowering his camera and slowing his long strides. A mental film reel unraveled in the back of my mind, flashing moments of the things he'd taught me that night in the studio, but also of the things he'd taught me on the street in Amsterdam, and again while his phone had wobbled in my shaky hand in Ireland.

"Oh, I've learned quite a bit from you, Hen," I said. "And not all of it has been clever, I might add." I tried to soften the expression in my eyes when I looked at him so he'd know I was more introspective than angry, especially after this morning, but I wasn't sure I succeeded.

The smile dropped from his face, and he reached for my elbow as we slowed to a stop, our roommates continuing toward a champagne tent ahead of us.

"Lucy," he started, looking around as if the rest of his sentence might appear somewhere in the gardens. "I'm so, so sorry. I meant everything I said in that note. Though I think the pictures might have done me one better. But I need you to know how sorry I am."

"I like you better when you're direct," I said, fighting a sigh. "And thank you, Henry. For the photos, and for the apology."

"It was long overdue," he said. "I know I got us into this mess." His usually too-loud voice was reduced to a soft rumble that I could feel deep in my chest.

"It wasn't just you," I said. "I wasn't exactly always rational, which only further complicated things for us. So I'm sorry, too, Henry, for my half of the mess."

"Thanks, Luce." His gentle smile washed over me like a wave. "And just so you know, I'm determined to get us out of this mess. If you'll let me, that is."

"The photos and the note were a good start," I said, a tentative tone reaching the edges of my words. "And the gardens were a good follow-up."

"So is that a yes?" The gold flecks in his eyes glittered in the setting sun, making it nearly impossible to look away. Though I did have to laugh at how he could go so quickly from adult man to eager, hopeful lad.

The flowers surrounding us were a constant reminder of all I'd learned at the Lotus over the years, and Renee would kill me if she knew I had tried to ignore it. While I was internalizing the constant heartache that walked in and out of our doors, the mourning, the apology flowers, and the canceled orders, I had also internalized the hope. The celebrations, the proposals, the thinking-of-yous and happy-nothing-days. The fact that the apology bouquets were not always groveling, but more often trying to fix things. Trying to use the beauty of flowers to mend. To heal. To reunite.

Which was exactly what Henry was doing today.

"It's a start," I conceded eventually, offering a slow smile. He seemed to exhale with his entire body, releasing the tension in his broad shoulders, closing his eyes for a beat longer than a blink. "A slow one," I added when a greediness returned to his gaze.

He raised his hands in surrender, releasing a light laugh into the breeze. "Whatever you want," he said. "And I mean that, Luce. Anything."

"You know what I really want?" I said, leaning in, watching anticipation dance in his eyes. He inhaled slowly through parted lips, so close we were nearly touching, so I decided to put him out of his misery. "A hot dog."

"A hot dog," he repeated, laughing from his chest this time and tilting his sharp jaw toward the sky. "She wants a hot dog. I bare my soul to her and all she wants from me is a hot dog."

"You said *anything*," I said, laughing along myself. "Come on." I tugged him gently by the forearm in the direction of our roommates, trying to ignore the excited chills dancing down my spine at the way his toned arm felt beneath my fingertips. "I need sustenance in the form of hot dogs and champagne if I'm to do any soul-baring myself."

"Then how could I possibly say no?"

I had missed that cheeky grin. The single dimple. The mischief that turned his cheeks pink under his freckles. Slow was going to be harder than I thought.

As we rejoined our roommates, Raja was laying out a picnic blanket. All eight of us were armed with a drink and something to eat, prepared to spend the rest of the evening wasting away in the garden until it was time for the lanterns. Sundance Gardens didn't always allow a picnic, but they made exceptions for their opening night. Food and drink vendors dotted the paths, a live band played covers somewhere under a canopy, and the entire garden came to life.

We laid our heads in each other's laps, intertwined our limbs, watched the clouds pale against the darkening sky. As the sun escaped the city, fairy lights flicked on above the garden, lining the paths and the greenhouses and casting the flowers in a delicate glow. It didn't matter that we couldn't see stars. It was like we had them all floating right above our heads, winking down on us, illuminating warm smiles and telling eyes and stolen glances.

It didn't take long for the entire garden to be blanketed in darkness and for the Lantern Festival to begin. Employees of the garden floated along the paths, distributing a few paper lanterns to each group along the way.

A voice sounded from hidden speakers, welcoming us to the festival and detailing its history. I tried hard to focus on the opening remarks instead of counting the number of lanterns we were given, though I already knew it was four. And we were eight. Which meant we'd be sending them up in pairs.

"Now, this works best if we spread out a bit," the voice instructed over the speakers. "Give yourselves some space, find somewhere nice and quiet, perhaps a bit private if you so choose, make yourselves comfortable."

"I'm comfortable right here," Jan said, stretching out on the ground with his arms behind his head and closing his eyes.

"God, Jan, would it kill you to get involved just once?" Liv said, glaring in his direction. "Get up. We're going to find a nice place and we're going to write something nice to burn in this lantern because that is how you do a Warehouse Weekend." She stood over him with her hands outstretched, ready to drag him from his place in the grass.

He moaned, accepting her hand and following her in the direction of a bubbling fountain. I kept my eyes locked on them, trying to quell my pounding heart.

"Fancy finding a spot of our own?" Henry whispered from

behind me, confirming what I had already known. When I turned to face him, I was caught off guard by the hopeful wrinkle between his eyebrows. For someone who usually looked terribly confident, he now looked more like a nervous child.

As I was looking around for a spot that was private enough per the instructions but not too secluded that I'd be tempted to do something I shouldn't, he got to his feet, extending his hand in a much gentler way than Liv had to Jan a moment ago. "Come on," he said. "I know just the place."

"Bold claim for someone who's never been here before," I said, accepting his hand and letting him pull me to my feet.

"I did my research." A broad smile stretched across his face, setting off a flurry in my stomach. We were still clasping each other's hands, warm in the heavy summer air.

"Have fun, you two," Raja said, tongue resting against the back of her teeth. "Don't do anything I wouldn't do."

"Raj, I'm not sure there *is* anything you wouldn't do," Henry laughed.

"Bodes well for you two, then, doesn't it?"

"We're leaving now," I said, shooting her a look before she could say anything else. She stifled her giggle with a swig of champagne and waved us off.

"Lead the way, then," I said to Henry, letting him pull me by the hand away from our mates and down a path I hadn't seen before. My nerves were twisting and turning alongside the vines, and I was sure Hen could feel my heartbeat through my fingers.

I trailed behind him, wondering how it was possible he knew the route. He held the lantern in the hand that wasn't holding mine, and I studied the way his long fingers flexed around the wire structure.

"Hen, where are we—" Just then, the view answered my

question, choking the words in my throat. We had emerged in a clearing beside a running stream, delicate lily pads and assorted pastel petals traveling along on the gentle current, uplit flower beds dotting its banks. It looked like we had stepped into a Monet. "How did you—"

"Research," he said again. "I went to the website, looked at a map, that kind of thing. I even read a blog." I faked a gasp. "I wanted this to be perfect," he said. The seriousness in his face matched that in his tone, and I stopped laughing altogether. He gestured to a spot right alongside the stream, and we sank into the soft grass beside each other.

On cue, the voice sounded over the speakers once more. I hadn't the foggiest how the sound was reaching every corner of the gardens, but I figured it was easiest to attribute it to the magic of the festival.

"Hopefully by now everyone has found a comfortable space, for it is time to begin." We exchanged a glance, and I relished the second it gave me to admire the way his eyes reflected the fairy lights. The way they resembled the river and the gardens, the soft green of a watercolor painting.

"Attached to your lanterns are matches, a slip of paper, and a pen. Use that paper and pen to share your hopes, dreams, fears, accomplishments, missteps, desires, secrets—whatever it is that lights you on fire. It will look different for everyone, and this, my friends, is the beauty of the festival. Then, when you're ready, ignite the paper and use it to send your lantern into the sky."

In any other circumstances, I might have thought this was cheesy. I might have laughed with the rest of our mates at the whole ordeal, participated in whatever teasing they were up to about each other's secrets.

But with Henry so close to me, without another soul around,

with the very possibility of our future unfurling between us, the opportunity to turn the past and the heartache to flames and ashes, I thought it was enchanting.

"Take your time," the voice said, noticeably quieter. "Send your lanterns up only when you're ready, and together we'll watch them take your secrets to the stars."

Once the voice disappeared, the only sounds were the babbling of the stream and a distant orchestra. It was like we had walked away from the rest of the lot and into a fairy tale, and I tried hard to shake the feeling that it was too good to be true.

"Well," I said, hardly above a whisper, taking the pen and paper in my hands. "What should we write, then?" I held my breath while I waited for his response, trying not to agonize over the possibilities.

"I had another idea," he said, reaching into his pocket and producing a slip of paper of his own. It was folded neatly, and as he turned it over in his hands I spotted a single "H" on the outside.

I opened my mouth to speak but closed it again before I could say anything that would interrupt the beauty of the silence. Instead of reading the paper aloud, he handed it to me. "It's the resolution I wrote when I came home in February," he explained. "And as per your rules, I believe we're supposed to burn them once we've accomplished them."

I unfolded the paper and read, clocking the heat of his gaze all the while. It was a short resolution, only five words in his sharp, angular handwriting:

find what feels like home

I read it over a few times, stalling, before looking up to meet his eyes. "London feels like home now, does it?" I said eventually, searching in vain for something more meaningful. My heartbeat in my ears blocked any semblance of rational thought.

He laughed softly at my question, reaching for the matches. "No, Luce. *You* feel like home."

My sharp intake of breath was audible, deafening, even, as we stared at each other under the warm glow of the garden. The lines that had spent the past two days writing concern all over his face had softened, and I could just barely detect the beginnings of a tentative smile.

"And I'm sorry it took me so long to see it," he continued. "The more time I spent on the road, the more I realized that feeling I've been chasing for so long isn't in any foreign country, or behind any stage, or in any airport. It's right here, with you. Home isn't on the road, and it isn't in London, either, Luce. It is simply where you are."

Tears pooled in the corners of my eyes, and I had no choice but to let them gather as he continued.

"I have spent the last year learning from an incredible woman that I need to think before I speak if I want to keep her around. And since I cannot imagine another second without her, it's time I heed that advice."

"She sounds lovely." I smiled, a single tear rolling down my flushed cheek. In another world, I might have been embarrassed, but the way he was looking at me convinced me otherwise.

"She's everything."

Lanterns started to float into the sky around us, dotting the midnight blue like shooting stars. "So," he said, gesturing to the lantern on the grass between us. "What do you say, Luce?"

A year's worth of memories danced in his eyes alongside the reflection of the twinkling lights, giving me a glimpse into our future. A future where we didn't spend all of our time apart. A future where I didn't have to guess how he felt about me. Where our dates didn't have to be virtual, where I could kiss him whenever I wanted, wear his clothes, watch him work. Collect new memories like photos. Where we didn't have to rely on games of chance to make us partners. Where we could choose each other, over and over again.

"Give me a match," I said eventually. "Let's burn this thing."

The second the words left my mouth, his lips were on mine, like he'd been waiting a year for this moment. I could feel his smile through the kiss, and we were both nearly giddy by the time we pulled away. We savored the moment, forehead to forehead, our collective heartbeat drowning the hum of the garden.

"Please," he said eventually, handing me the matches, "you do the honors."

With that, I struck one against the side of the box and held the flame to Henry's resolution. He slipped it into the lantern, and we sat together in silence as we watched our future, our past, our mistakes, our secrets, our promises, and our love float toward the stars.

July

S ince this is Cal's last weekend in the flat, I think we should
finally do something to memorialize this family," Jan announced to the rest of us. We were gathered in the living room,
arguing over which episode of *Bake Off* to watch.

"Jan, for the last time, we aren't getting a flat tattoo," Liv
said. "Even if we are all going to the convention tomorrow, it's
not happening."

"Bug off, Liv. For once, I have something else in mind." He
got up, and we followed him with our eyes as he disappeared
into his room, then reappeared with a paint-splattered duffel
and headed toward the stairs to the roof. "Well?" he implored
when we didn't get up right away.

We scrambled to our feet and followed him in a slow proces-
sion up to the roof. The night was warm, and a gentle breeze
ruffled the plants I'd been desperately trying to keep alive up
there.

"Is this where you murder us and stuff our chopped-up bodies into that duffel?" Margot teased. "If so, I'd quite like another beer for that."

"Everyone's a comedian," Jan said, unzipping the duffel to
reveal a rainbow of spray paints, everything from neon greens
to metallic golds to matte blacks. He gestured to the wall behind him, entirely empty save for the door to the apartment.

"Jan, we don't own the place," Liv scolded. "We can't just be painting it wherever we want. What if we get in trouble?"

"Come on, Liv," Hen said, taking Jan's side. "It's a warehouse. We haven't heard from the landlord since sometime last year, and if I'm honest, I think he's got bigger problems than a little art on the roof. I say let's do it."

Liv searched our faces for reinforcements in vain. Normally I was also a fan of the rules, but lately none of them seemed to matter. It was a lot more fun to pretend they didn't exist at all.

"Seven to one, lady. Majority rules." Finn clucked his tongue in her direction, and she rolled her eyes. Jan tossed everyone a can from the bag and we stood at his back, waiting for him to make the first move.

The only sounds were the metal marbles rattling around inside the cans and the dull roar of the city below. Jan shook a can of bloodred paint back and forth until he deemed it adequately mixed, then pointed it at the wall and pressed the nozzle.

The steady stream of paint whistled into the night, and we watched with bated breath as Jan scrawled *2B* in the center of the space, then surrounded it with a cloud. The font bubbled over itself, all round sides and bulging shapes. He switched to a can of glittering silver and highlighted the curves to make it pop off the wall, and we stood in awe of his talent.

"I'm not the only one having proper fun, am I?" he asked, turning to face us. With that, we joined in.

We doodled shapes around the cloud, trading colors, stretching over one another to reach the edges of our designs, admiring and mocking each other's work in equal measure. I painted a lotus on the perimeter of the chaos, a personal nod to my own new adventure. The deed of the shop was officially in my name now, and Henry and I were due to have a proper celebration next week. I was still afraid to say it aloud, but things really seemed to be falling into place.

I was admiring our work when Henry braced himself over my body, both of us facing the wall, and pressed a gentle kiss to my temple before scribbling an *H* and an *L* in a deep, shiny green. I leaned back against his shoulder to take it all in.

It had only been a few weeks since he'd been back at the flat full-time and we'd gotten back together, but it felt like we'd made up for the lost time tenfold. Everything was as exciting and new as it was comfortable and familiar, and I'd long since stopped keeping track of the last time I'd slept in my own bed. Sharing a space even in the monotony of the day-to-day was more intimate than any virtual date could have been, and I sometimes had to pinch myself as a reminder that this was real.

Our initials sat proudly between a lightning bolt and a Union Jack on the edge of Jan's initial creation, and the indelible nature of the graffiti made me hopeful for what was to come. As if somehow, if our initials were always plastered there on the wall at the site of our first kiss, regardless of what the London weather threw their way, we too could withstand even the harshest rains.

I ran my fingers over the cold paint as it dried, imagining our untouchable future. The chatter of my roommates was merely background noise until an explosion of laughter interrupted my trance.

"Raja, don't you dare come over here," Margot said, holding up her hands and trying to turn a smile into a frown.

"Surely a little paint never hurt anybody," Raja teased, neon-pink palms pointed toward the sky. "What's wrong, Mar? Scared a little color might actually do you some good?"

Before any of us could process what was happening, Margot

grabbed a can of paint from Cal and smashed the nozzle, slamming Raja square in the chest with a sunburst that matched the deep gold of her eyes.

There was no moment of silence before we laughed. We simply couldn't have held it in. All eight of us roared in hysterics, thrilled that Margot had put Raja in her place. Everything after descended into madness.

We laughed ourselves to death, tagging each other's clothes until we looked like a Jackson Pollock. Moans about perfectly straightened hair and new sneakers were drowned out by our collective cackling and teasing. When we were out of breath and nearly out of paint, we stood back and looked at our creation.

"It needs a finishing touch," declared Jan, motioning for us to turn our palms up. We followed his unspoken order, and he covered eight hands in royal blue. We knew what to do.

At once, we pressed our palms to the wall. It would have taken hardly more than a second for the paint to stick, but we stood for a minute or two, looking at one another down the line. Eight cheeky smiles framed eight handprints beside the doorway in a way that made my heart ache.

Henry was right. As long as we were together, we were home.

Acknowledgments

From the moment I started writing this book, I've been thinking about the acknowledgments. I've been thinking about how I could possibly thank everyone who has been a part of this process, everyone who has inspired me or brainstormed with me or listened to me talk endlessly about this story and its journey or championed this book in any way—and the list has only continued to grow. And not a second goes by that I am not overwhelmed with gratitude for the people and the experiences that have made *Weekends with You* what it is.

(It is worth noting that I didn't want my acknowledgments to be too long. Really, I didn't. But as a writer, this is the best way I can express my thanks, so none of us should be surprised that I couldn't help myself.)

I owe a debt of gratitude to my agent, Hannah Todd, who's been screaming with me on Zoom calls since the beginning and never laughs when I cry a little every time she gives me good news. Hannah, I cannot thank you enough for seeing the potential in this story and offering your insight, expertise, and encouragement to get it to where it is now. I'll cherish our first little Pret date in the office forever.

And to my editor, Ariana Sinclair, for seeing the heart of these characters, believing they should be out in the world, and doing whatever it took to get them there. Thank you for answering my millions of questions, editing with such intention to detail and still such kindness, and supporting me and my work on every step of this journey.

I owe the same gratitude to every member of the teams at Madeleine Milburn, Avon, and HarperCollins, who worked together to get *Weekends with You* from a Google Doc to the shelves. I am endlessly amazed at your talent and dedication, and none of this would have been possible without you.

And to the kind warehouse-dwellers willing to share their stories with me via FaceTime, the strangers and friends who served as inspiration for this quirky cast of characters, the experiences of my early twenties that informed some of the peaks and valleys in this story, and the city of London for its bottomless well of magic.

And to my biggest supporters, my guiding lights, my beta readers, my confidants, my cheering squad, and my ego-checkers: my family.

To my mother, Hillary, who taught me how to read before kindergarten and has encouraged me to read everything I could get my hands on ever since. Because of you, Mom, I have developed my confidence as a writer (even if you let me read embarrassing poetry in the elementary school talent show), and I am eternally grateful for your encouragement, love, and line edits.

To my brothers, Dan and Jake, for cheering me on and making a ton of noise in the group chat every time I have an update. I'll be visiting soon to celebrate, and I'm looking forward to you picking up the tab.

To my dad, Michael, and stepmom, Kristen, for manifesting and brainstorming over greasy diner breakfasts, sorting my finances, and celebrating this journey from start to finish to future.

To Adam, for showing me that if you have the kind of unavoidable, undeniable chemistry Lucy and Henry have, the only thing to do is give in and enjoy it. And there is *nothing* more enjoyable.

And to you, reader, for taking a chance on me and this story, and inviting these characters into your world. My gratitude is endless.

About the Author

Alexandra Paige is a writer and educator. She is enthusiastic about all things romance, and her work often serves as a love letter to European travel and the chaos of being twenty-something. She currently writes in an apartment she shares with her boyfriend above a downtown pizzeria, though her stories are always taking her elsewhere. She has an MFA from Lindenwood University and lives in New Jersey. *Weekends with You* is her first novel.